Number One Chinese Restaurant

Lillian Li

ONE

AN IMPRINT OF PUSHKIN PRESS

Pushkin Press
71–75 Shelton Street
London WC2H 9JQ

Number One Chinese Restaurant was first published by Henry Holt, 2018

First published by ONE, an imprint of Pushkin Press in 2019

3 5 7 9 8 6 4

Hardback ISBN 13: 978-1-91159-007-1
Export Trade Paperback ISBN 13: 978-1-91159-016-3

Typeset by Tetragon, London
Printed and bound by CPI Group (UK) Ltd, Croydon CR0 4YY

www.pushkinpress.com

To family

1

The waiters were singing "Happy Birthday" in Chinese. All fifteen of them had crowded around the party table, clapping their hands. Not a single one could find the tune. A neighboring table turned in their chairs to look. Their carver kept his eyes on the duck. The song petered out. The customer blew out the candle on her complimentary cheesecake, and, still applauding, the waiters scattered back to their tables, speaking the restaurant's English again.

"We need great leader," one waiter said to no one in particular. "Song not even song if no him."

Sitting silently in a booth nearby, Jimmy Han fingered his duck-patterned tie. The waiter had clearly meant for him to overhear. No one called him "great leader." Jimmy *did* have a strong and supple singing voice—a surprise, especially to those who knew him—but the staff's real nickname they used behind his back: "the little boss." Disrespectful, but what could he do? Most of the waiters had been around long enough to remember him as a boy. Some of them for thirty years. Who else outside his family had known him for that long? The waiters picked their way through the restaurant. Jimmy's chest began to ache, and he pressed his hand against the bulging fabric of his jacket pocket. The thick envelope resting inside seemed to seize, like a second heart.

On the other side of the booth, Uncle Pang betrayed nothing. He didn't look like a man about to walk away ten grand richer. He looked like a man who'd just finished his potstickers. Shallow pools of oil spotted his saucer. His thumbnail ran lazily over a blot of black vinegar on the tablecloth. Uncle Pang was always picking something apart.

"Will you be serving duck at your new restaurant?" he said suddenly. He'd been looking around the dining room, but his attention fell back onto Jimmy.

Jimmy let a familiar tingle of lightning shoot through him. He considered what had once been an impossible question.

"We'll see." He wet his finger in his glass of seltzer and cleaned a smudge off one of the framed headshots on the wall. "I have a lot of decisions to make." The envelope seized again; the lightning disappeared. "What can I even afford?"

Uncle Pang didn't react. He merely shifted in his seat. His right hand began to tap an impatient, cascading beat against the tablecloth, the rhythm skipping on the ring finger's turn. Forty years and Jimmy was still not used to the missing finger. The stub had just enough flesh to bend at the knuckle.

"A fool could tell you." Uncle Pang looked around once again for Ah-Jack, their waiter, before scratching at an unseen speck on his crystal watch face. "Duck is simply a chicken that takes longer to make."

Jimmy used his fists to push himself out of the corner he'd sunk into. "I'll go see what's keeping your duck." He bumped his ass down the squeaky vinyl seat, his long legs tangling beneath him.

"I was very happy to hear that Jack had come out of retirement," Uncle Pang said. "But he might no longer be Duck House material, don't you think?"

"It was Johnny's idea to hire him back," Jimmy said as he stood up. His older brother, in Hong Kong for another month, had a nasty habit of making decisions for the restaurant over Jimmy's head. This one he'd made right before jetting off in January. "Loyalty counts for too much with him."

"Yes." Uncle Pang inspected the blade of his knife and rubbed at a water stain. "A good thing loyalty means less to you."

Uncle Pang's English, always fluent, had grown more dramatic over the years, to great effect. A cold tail of sweat curled down Jimmy's lower back.

"I'll be quick." He bumped his hip lightly against the table.

"Take your time," Uncle Pang said. "I'll find someone to keep me company."

A quick scan of the crowded central dining room did not reveal Ah-Jack. Jimmy shifted his feet impatiently, before making his way through the restaurant. The main room's long, rectangular shape made it too narrow for the number of tables they'd managed to squeeze inside. The gaudy, overstuffed décor didn't help. A deep, matte red colored everything, from the upholstered chairs to the floral carpet to the Chinese knots hanging off the lantern lighting, their tassels low enough to graze the heads of taller customers. Framed photos of famous clientele protruded from the walls. His father's idea of class. The man had decorated the secondary dining room in the same fashion, except for a thick maroon curtain at the very back. What a pain in the ass to keep clean. Jimmy paused his search to beat the dust off the velvet drapes, pretending to inspect the air-conditioning vents above. He made sure the fabric still hid the blank wall behind. People preferred to believe in windows they couldn't see.

From the hostess stand, his niece, Annie, asked, "Have you tried the private party room," pointing to the doorway across from her. They could both clearly see that Ah-Jack was not in the private party room. She really was her father's daughter. Who else would wear heels to a job that had her on her feet for hours, heels that made her stand almost as tall as him? Jimmy snapped at her to stop leaning against her podium.

"It's your own fault your feet hurt," he said. "Stomping around like a damn ostrich . . ."

He trailed off, the rest of his sentence forgotten.

Uncle Pang had found company after all. William, the newest busboy, was standing next to his booth. Uncle Pang said something, and the busboy lowered into a crouch. Jimmy drifted closer, until he was leaning against the bar. A section of the wall blocked the men from view, muffling their conversation.

"Amigo," he thought he could hear Uncle Pang saying, using the restaurant's nickname for Latino staff. "I heard you had a baby girl recently." The man wouldn't, of course, say where he'd heard this news; his sources were numerous, like worms beneath the soil. Jimmy stuck his head as far past the wall partition as he dared.

William was visible again, as he got up from his crouch. The busboy's hand was now in his pocket. Uncle Pang must have slipped a trinket into his fingers. Perhaps a pair of gold earrings, 24 karat and soft enough to eat. A few seconds later, William walked past the bar on his way to the kitchen. His head still respectfully dropped, he didn't see Jimmy trying to wave him over. Jimmy stopped himself from calling after the busboy. He was being paranoid. Uncle Pang had never been more than friendly with the restaurant staff. But Jimmy had underestimated the man before. He probed the false tooth embedded where his right canine should be.

Part of the Han family not by blood or marriage but by circumstance, Uncle Pang had known Bobby Han since Jimmy's father first arrived in America. Uncle Pang was, or had been, Bobby's longtime adviser and best friend, a man who'd darkened certain family photos like a finger on the lens. Although Uncle Pang was now in his late sixties, Jimmy had trouble seeing him as an older man. His physical movements might have slowed, but he continued to glide through the world as oiled as the remaining strands of his jet-black hair.

It was effortless, the way Uncle Pang granted wishes you didn't know you had, gluing you to him while you were busy fawning over a pair of baby's earrings. It pained Jimmy to realize he might be no better than the busboy, though at least *he* had been trapped by something larger than metal in a pretty shape. At least he had actually used Uncle Pang's connections. Without them, the Georgetown owner of that tapas chain would have never accepted his bid to buy out her lease on the waterfront. She hadn't even returned his calls before Uncle Pang stepped in. Of course, now Jimmy had to find the money he'd so generously offered. Uncle Pang had promised to take care of that as well.

Jimmy felt for the envelope, then turned on his heel before Uncle Pang could catch him spying. Blood pounded in his ears. He slipped into the cramped hallway that led into the kitchen. Where the hell was Ah-Jack?

At the mouth of the hallway, a current of Duck House staff buffeted Jimmy along. The Chinese and Spanish he'd banned from the dining room filled this narrow space, echoing off the walls. Waiters blocked traffic to grab beer from the lower fridge. Those stuck behind them pushed and scolded. On the opposite wall, busboys huddled against the main waiter station, pouring leftovers into paper cartons with hasty precision. At the end of the hallway, Jimmy nearly fell against the busing cart. An impatient Ah-Michael had shoved him while trying to grab an extra zodiac placemat from the shelf.

"So sorry, so sorry." The waiter pressed himself tight against the wall and slipped away. His tray dipped and rose above the heads of other rushing waiters and busboys. His tureen of duck bone soup barely rippled.

Already flushed from his search for Ah-Jack, Jimmy felt more heat rising up his tight collar, first at the nerve of Ah-Michael, with his poached-egg face, and then from the uncomfortably high temperature of the kitchen. Behind the stainless-steel divider, flames whooshed up to embrace giant woks, each cook casually stir-frying as fire sprang, volcanic, from the deep, blackened burners. How awestruck Jimmy had been by these sparking flares when he was a kid. Stuck at the restaurant on the weekends and through every summer, he used to sneak into the kitchen to stare at the sweaty cooks maneuvering the gas dials with their knees. He was transfixed by the fire roaring under their control. Inevitably, his father would drag him back out to pour water for the customers. But in those brief moments, Jimmy could forget his own misery.

"Where is Jack?" Jimmy grabbed one of the duck carvers, who had just hoisted her tray over her shoulder. "Where is the duck for table eight?"

"They go." She gestured her head toward the kitchen's side exit. Her large, braided bun tapped against the duck on her tray. Jimmy wanted to yank the mass of hair out.

"Forget your hairnet again and I'll shave you bald."

He pushed her away and took the side exit from the kitchen, which put him back at the front of the restaurant. There he saw, to his anger and relief, the top of a shaggy-haired head. Ah-Jack was bent over, wrapping Uncle Pang's duck pancake.

Nan, his manager, hovered nearby. Hunched at the mouth of the private party room, she looked like an agitated collie, with her thin, feathered hair and bright eyes. Her stomach pooched over the gaudy belt she'd decided was management material. In all the years he'd known her, Jimmy had never seen the woman more than a few yards away from Ah-Jack. He suspected she was the one who'd gotten the old waiter's job back. Her love for Ah-Jack was one of many open secrets at the Duck House.

From the way Nan fiddled with her manager's headset, Jimmy could tell that she had read the dark expression on his face. When she saw him set off for Uncle Pang's booth, she sprang into action too. Jimmy was quicker. Agile only in this restaurant, he dipped under passing trays, squeezed through chairs pushed up against each other, and dodged a small posse of bored children, all without the slightest stumble. Before Nan could warn Ah-Jack, Jimmy was at his side, planting a heavy hand against the waiter's thin back. It was like palming a hollowed-out melon.

"I hope you've already apologized for the wait," Jimmy said.

"The kitchen give me bad duck first," Ah-Jack said to Uncle Pang. "I say, I not give bad duck for VIP! They take long time."

"We are so sorry." Jimmy pressed his hand into Ah-Jack's back.

"So sorry," Ah-Jack echoed, buckling into a bow.

Uncle Pang had already picked up his duck pancake.

"Not a problem," he said. "You're here now." He cleared his throat. "But we can't blame the kitchen for every mistake we make. If you'll humor me, I'd like to lay out how I want the rest of dinner to go."

The situation defused, Jimmy and Ah-Jack settled in for the lecture. But for some reason, Nan continued to approach the booth. What the hell did she think she was doing?

"I hope you remember that I like to eat my duck *with* my entrée, and not before," Uncle Pang was saying. "If you haven't already put in the order for the Szechuan lamb chops, you're going to have to rush it."

"Jack very busy." Nan broke into the huddle. Jimmy grabbed her wrist, but she ignored his fingernails. "May can taking your table. She very quick."

Uncle Pang recoiled as if Nan had rapped him on the forehead.

"I don't think I'll let Jack off so easily." He attempted a smile. "I just wanted to ask him to check on the progress of the lamb. Not a big request."

"You're not asking for too much at all." Jimmy fluttered his hands in front of his chest. "The lamb will be ready, Uncle. Jack probably remembered that you like to dine at a more leisurely pace."

"There is leisure," Uncle Pang said, his finger stabbing into the tablecloth, "and then there is just plain slow."

"We're very sorry." Jimmy tried to keep the sincerity in his voice from going flat. "I won't let this happen again. Let me send you a slice of cheesecake. And your bill is, as always, on the house."

The "as always" slipped out of his mouth so innocently that another person wouldn't have noticed. Uncle Pang, however, didn't believe in such accidents. Indiscretion was equal to insult.

"Jack, go check on my lamb," Uncle Pang said. "Nan, bring me an unopened bottle of this place's finest scotch. And two glasses."

"Just one glass," Jimmy said, but Uncle Pang waved his request away.

"Don't make a man ask twice for a drinking partner." Uncle Pang gestured to the seat across from him. He was acting playful, which meant he was a hair away from losing his temper. Jimmy's remaining nerve bowed in like a decaying floor.

With two sharp jabs, he sent Ah-Jack to the kitchen and Nan in the opposite direction. He settled gingerly into the booth. Nan hurried back with an amber bottle and two glasses. Uncle Pang patted her hand in thanks. He slid one of the glasses over to Jimmy and tipped in a heavy glug of scotch.

"You're too generous," Jimmy said, and felt instantly the quiver of another trap he'd seen too late: Uncle Pang was never generous without cause.

"I want to make a toast." Uncle Pang held up his glass. "Let's drink to the Beijing Glory. Our pride and joy."

Jimmy clinked his glass lightly against Uncle Pang's. He thought about taking a fortifying gulp but held his drink tightly against the table instead, as if trying to cut a circle out of the cloth.

"How's the progress?" he asked.

"We're almost there," Uncle Pang said. "You're doing well. Better under pressure than you used to be. Or maybe you've finally grown up. Another week or so, and I'll deliver what's been promised."

"You found investors?" Jimmy steeled himself against the lilt of hope in his chest.

Uncle Pang put his drink down mid-sip. "I never said anything about investors."

Jimmy pinched the cartilage piercing in his left ear and took a short sip of his seltzer. "You did," he said. "You said you were going to take the Duck House off my hands."

"I am going to take the Duck House off your hands."

The meaning of those words bubbled up so quickly inside Jimmy that he felt flooded. How could he have been so stupid? If Uncle Pang had found investors, he would have said "investors." If he had found buyers, he would have said "buyers." There was only one recourse that required such vague, precious phrasing. One recourse that would wedge Jimmy as far underneath the man's thumb as his father had been. Jimmy shook his head sharply. He wanted out. But Uncle Pang misunderstood.

"You were always a dense boy," he said. "Tell me, what did you think I meant?"

"I don't know." Jimmy wormed his finger into a hole in the vinyl booth. "Something with investors. For the Duck House. So I'd have enough to pay off the Glory."

"And that lump in your chest." Uncle Pang reached over the table to tap against Jimmy's jacket pocket. "What's that for?"

"For your troubles," Jimmy managed to force out.

"You should know better by now." Uncle Pang shook out the napkin on his lap. "Especially with your family history."

Jimmy turned to see Ah-Jack arriving. The waiter held a large serving plate of Szechuan lamb chops, elegantly piled under a hearty mound of onions and red peppers. The meat glistened with black pepper sauce, flecks of spice filling the air with a rich, roasted smell. Uncle Pang greeted him with a clap of his hands, the sound ringing with false delight. Jimmy was suddenly overwhelmed by the noise of everything happening around him. His body was too heavy to move. Something had gotten on top of him, was smothering him with its weight. He'd been having these attacks recently, but always in bed, in the middle of the night. Never in public. He dug the tip of his tongue into the canker sore on his bottom gum. The sharp, acid sting made the panic lift, just enough for him to wriggle out from underneath.

He was probing the sore again when a jangling sound jerked his head up. The gold chains around Ah-Jack's wrists were trembling against the china platter. The plate dipped up and down. The old waiter could barely hold on to the heavy lamb chops with both hands. Who the hell let him leave the kitchen like this?

Jimmy was starting to stand when a resigned, almost amused look passed over Ah-Jack's face. Like he was tired of waiting for disaster to strike. Before Jimmy could stop him, Ah-Jack took one of his hands away from the plate to grab the two serving spoons. His left wrist did not even make an attempt to hold the weight of the plate on its own. Jimmy's outstretched hand caught air.

Heavy with sauce, the lamb chops plopped onto their table. Some landed on the tablecloth, while others bounced off and onto Uncle Pang's lap. The platter hit the side of the table with a muffled sound before ricocheting under the booth. Sauce splattered everywhere, leaving greasy inkblots on their clothes. Someone in the next booth gasped. For a few calm moments, the three of them looked on curiously at the tremendous mess. Then, Uncle Pang was up and roaring. Ah-Jack was left to tremble, cradling his left hand like an injured bird. He looked around wildly, for an exit, or, perhaps, for Nan. Jimmy dove under the table without knowing why. He started picking up the fallen chops, his hands leaving tacky prints on the dirty carpet. Above his head, Uncle Pang was threatening to tear down the restaurant. With a *thunk,* the scotch bottle fell off and rolled under the table, hitting Jimmy in the knee. The smell of cigarette smoke drifted down, as well as Nan's timid voice, asking Uncle Pang to put out his light.

"I'm not going to burn this place down with one fucking cigarette!" Uncle Pang shouted. He stalked away from the booth, toward the front door. Nan's thick ankles quickly followed, with Ah-Jack's jerky shuffle bringing up the rear.

From his temporary sanctuary, Jimmy twisted the cap off the scotch bottle and, for the first time in a year, took a deep, searing drink. The sore in his mouth sang out, then quieted into a buzz.

Outside, the early-August air was balmy and windless. The evening traffic roared by, kicking up litter and dust. At the intersection, a thin white man held a cardboard sign. Jimmy and Uncle Pang stood perched on the restaurant's curb. Every crook and pit on Jimmy's body was slick with sweat. Illuminated by the two faux-Chinese lanterns affixed to the storefront, his face must have looked as shiny as the Peking ducks inside.

"Why are you calling off the plan?" Uncle Pang demanded.

"You should have told me what it was," Jimmy said.

"Stop playing dumb. You've been doing that since you were a boy."

"You overestimated me," Jimmy said. "I would never do that to my father's restaurant."

"Oh, *now* it's your father's restaurant." Uncle Pang wiped at the brown spot on his pants, attacking the stain with unnecessary violence.

"We'll pay for the dry cleaning," Jimmy said. "Jack will be punished."

"That won't change anything." Uncle Pang shoved his handkerchief back into his pocket.

"The stains look bad, but they come out very easily." Jimmy pointed to a spray of dark soy sauce on his knee. "I get stains on my pants all the time."

"Don't be an idiot," Uncle Pang said. "You're trying to cut me out of my fair share." He waved sharply at a car idling in the middle of the parking lot. "After you begged for my help. After you shook my hand."

Jimmy blinked, his eyes dry and dulled from the nips he'd taken of the scotch. What had he been so scared of? Uncle Pang was a childhood boogeyman. Granted, he had once knocked a tooth out of Jimmy's mouth, after Jimmy had snorted most of the coke he'd been tasked to sell. But that was decades ago. He'd been a dumb kid. Now he was forty, with an ex-wife and mortgage payments, and Uncle Pang was pushing seventy. Almost the same age Jimmy's father had been when he died.

"If you say so," Jimmy said. "But I'm saying that we're both businessmen. We know the difference between good business and bad business and personal business, and I hope you understand which one my decision is."

Uncle Pang laughed by clearing his throat.

"You little cunt." He took a step toward Jimmy. "You think you're going to push me out of the Glory? You think you're the first desperate loser to ask for my help, then back out?"

"Don't take this the wrong way." Jimmy held up his hands. "I'll always be grateful to you for finding me the new place. I'll still give you the ten thousand you asked for earlier." He pulled out the heavy envelope he'd been lugging around all evening. The disappearance of its weight felt like a liberation. "For your trouble."

"Money is going to make me forget this?" Uncle Pang's car pulled up to the curb and he wrenched open the passenger door, but not before snatching the envelope. "I'll tell you exactly what I told your father. I've got a long memory and I will ruin you for this."

He spat on the ground, clipping Jimmy's shoe, and dropped his smoldering cigarette into the mess. "Might as well say good-bye to your new restaurant now."

He slipped into the black BMW, disappearing behind tinted windows. Jimmy expected the car to peel off, tires squealing, but instead it continued its vibrating hum. It slid through the parking lot, the purring engine matching the decibel of all the other night sounds, and these little noises collected like smoke, drifting over his head, until he could hear nothing else.

2

As soon as Jimmy followed Uncle Pang out the Duck House door, Nan and Ah-Jack clustered together by the bar. Nan went behind to mix a complimentary pitcher of their Peking punch for customers who'd been startled by the commotion. Ah-Jack rested his elbows on the counter, shifting his weight off his bad foot.

"Who told you to try and handle the lamb chops on your own?" Nan said, speaking Chinese now that Jimmy wasn't around to police them. "You silly old man. When are you going to learn to think before you act?" She scanned the dining floor.

"Take over section four," she shouted over to Ah-May, who was heading back into the kitchen with an empty tray. "Ah-Jack hurt his hand."

"I have enough to do!" Ah-May seemed ready to plant herself in front of the kitchen in protest. Her wide stance added to the sturdiness of her body and she pulled her long braid over her chest like a sash. "*You* take over the section."

Nan knew what Ah-May was getting at, but she kept her face blank. Waitressing wasn't Nan's job anymore.

"You're blocking the path," she said.

"Fuck you too," Ah-May said, but she got moving. Her head swiveled as she stalked away, catching up each passing waiter with the latest gossip. Yet another strike against Nan. Her old colleagues didn't need more evidence of her bias toward Ah-Jack. Did they suspect that he was the reason she'd asked for her promotion last year?

She turned back to Ah-Jack, who had closed his eyes. If she didn't know him better, she would have thought he was meditating. His face was calm and wise. But then he opened one eye and suddenly his entire countenance changed into that of a mischievous boy. It was the first time he'd looked like himself all day.

"Ah-May's on the warpath," he said.

"She's not happy unless she's complaining," Nan said. "Acting like a child. When her own child's already in braces."

Ah-Jack's eyes closed again. "We're on a dying planet," he said. "The little boss is already forty. No fresh blood. Just us clots of dust."

"Pat's only seventeen."

"You want your son to keep working for the Duck House?" Ah-Jack nudged the large pitcher she was filling. "Are you crazy, woman?"

As if on cue, Pat sauntered out of the kitchen's side entrance and into the front hallway. The top of his apron was undone, falling to reveal a chest that was at once too broad and too thin. He headed straight for the hostess stand, where Annie, Johnny's daughter, was drawing on the seating chart. Nan had watched them flirt since Pat started working as a dishwasher a month ago, but at some point, the tide had changed, and their interactions had gone from playful to furtive. Nan had tried to ask her son about his new girlfriend, but he gave her few chances at work to corner him. She thought having him at the Duck House would help her keep an eye on him. At least she'd do better than his high school, which had noticed him only long enough to expel him. But her son was a sneaky boy. When he reached over the hostess stand to fiddle with the keyhole cutout in Annie's qipao, no amount of distraction or disgruntled waiters could stop Nan's heart from clutching.

"Where else can I keep him?" she said to Ah-Jack, who had also noticed the two teenagers. "In a cage?"

"He'll be okay," Ah-Jack said. "You're like a babysitter and a guardian angel, all wrapped up in one." He waggled his eyebrows, which were thick and black and looked out of place underneath his mop of gray hair. Nan laughed.

"You two are looking cozy." Ah-Bing slid behind the bar to make a round of Shirley Temples. Ah-Bing was the same age as Ah-May, and they liked to team up on their tables and tips. It was a familiar sight to see the two of them, crowing back and forth, while they settled platters of pan-fried noodles and stewed fish onto neighboring lazy Susans. Ah-May must have intercepted him in the kitchen. Sure enough, the waitress stepped into the bar after him.

"Good night for you two?" Ah-Jack patted his breast pocket.

Ah-Bing's Sprite nozzle spurted unexpectedly and a bloom of sticky water grew on his shirt front. "What do you think?" he snapped, rubbing the end of his nose, where his glasses were perched. The glasses gave thin, stringy Ah-Bing an impatient squint.

"Nan already gives you all the easy, big-spending customers, and now you're not even working," Ah-May said to Ah-Jack. She stabbed paper umbrellas into the red-drizzled drinks.

"Do you have to be such a clown, everywhere you go?" Ah-Bing added.

Nan handed him a napkin. "You weren't so harsh last week when you were the one who needed saving. During your smoke break. And you." She grabbed the remaining umbrellas out of Ah-May's hand before Ah-May broke them in her grip. "Remember when Jimmy almost caught you pinching an entire duck?"

"What did it cost him to tell Jimmy a few little lies?" Ah-Bing glared down at her, no longer interested in Ah-Jack. "Did it lose him his tips? Did it land him five extra tables to watch while someone else took home the money?"

"You've changed," Ah-May said to Nan. "You're just as bad as the little boss."

Her words had summoned him; the front door opened and Jimmy came back into the restaurant. The timing felt deliberately cruel. Nan came around to the front of the bar, to make their huddle look less suspicious. She wished the little boss hadn't emptied so much of the bottle clenched in his right hand. Even drunk, Jimmy moved effortlessly through the dining room, like a big cat, too fast for them to scatter. His eyes darted from Ah-Jack to Nan to Ah-May and Ah-Bing.

"Why aren't you at your tables?" he asked. Despite his rounded cheeks and large, childlike forehead, Jimmy's face looked sharp and hard. "Do you four need a vacation?"

"Them leaving now." Nan jumped in before she could stop herself. "Ah-Jack taking small break. His diabetes make him need sugar. And make left foot hurt."

"*We* do our jobs," Ah-May said.

"Then go do them." Jimmy had the unnerving ability to make his eyes glow in their sockets when he was angry. He looked lit up from the inside. Ah-May left the bar in a huff. Ah-Bing hefted his drink tray onto his shoulder and followed.

Jimmy turned his attention back to Ah-Jack. "I shouldn't be looking at your face after what you just did," he said. "You should have fired yourself. Save me the trouble."

"We need Ah-Jack." Nan was trying to keep the urgency out of her voice. Johnny could be swayed by feelings, but Jimmy needed hard facts. "Ah-Ling go hospital for test. Ah-Gang needing hip fixed. Too little people if Ah-Jack go. The big party will come next week. They will renting a private room all night."

Ah-Jack added nothing, only stared at the bobbing lime slices in the pitcher of punch. Nan's body buzzed from the inside, as if she'd swallowed an electric charge. Why wasn't he begging like she was? He would go bankrupt without this job, lose the townhouse, and how would he pay for Michelle's chemo then?

A gurgling belch escaped from Jimmy's lips, and a flash of what looked like nausea passed over his face.

"It doesn't matter," he said, almost to himself. "Finish your shift. Give me the tips you've made tonight."

Ah-Jack reached into his blazer pocket and pulled out a neat wad of bills. Jimmy grabbed the bundle and lightly brushed his thumb over the fringe.

"I'll be checking the receipts against this amount," he said. "No more breaks. What're you waiting for?"

"No break," Ah-Jack agreed. He pushed away from the counter and gingerly settled his weight back into his feet. Nan tried not to look at his left foot, entombed in his leather shoe. She stayed where she was. Jimmy hadn't dismissed her for a reason.

"You've got some nerve," he began, jaw popping from tension. "You don't think I've noticed what's been going on in my own restaurant?"

"I am sorry," she said.

"You're sorry!" He laughed and sloshed the liquid around in his scotch bottle. He leaned in. "I *hate* listening to the waiters gossip. Their chattering, like a bunch of dumb chickens. But do you know what I've had to listen to since Johnny made you manager?"

"I am sorry," she said again. She hadn't known the waiters were talking.

"'Nan is giving Ah-Jack all the best tables,'" Jimmy mimicked. "'Nan lets Ah-Jack skip lunch service,' 'Nan told the hostess not to seat any children at Ah-Jack's section.' Get this straight. There's nothing you can do to keep me from firing him."

"I am fair," she said, without conviction. "They like complaining."

"Complaining is one thing," he said. He banged the heavy butt of his bottle against the bar. "But when they bother me, you've gone too far. I don't care what Johnny promised you. Don't get too comfortable. Usually when you have something for thirty years, you throw it away."

"I will be better."

With a noncommittal grunt, Jimmy left Nan at the bar and disappeared into his office at the other end of the dining room. Nan felt her heart start to slow. The flush on her face no longer prickled. The waiters eavesdropping around her went back to their tables.

"Karma," Ah-May muttered as she bustled past.

Nan darted out her hand and pinched the waitress's butt. Ah-May cried out in mock outrage and pinched her right back in the wrist. They were still friends, after all. They were all friends, if one defined friendship as the natural occurrence between people who, after colliding for decades, have finally eroded enough to fit together. That was all Ah-Jack was as well, an old friend.

Their joking and flirting had been the mainstay of their friendship since they'd started working side by side thirty years ago. They watched out for each other, a buddy system that followed them outside of work. He'd changed multiple spare tires for her on the sides of busy roads. Her couch was always open if he drank too much or bet too high at the races. How could Jimmy and the others expect her to change the way she spoke to Ah-Jack, the way she felt, just because she was managing him now?

The irony was that she was probably the best manager the Duck House had ever seen. She had a way of coddling the most belligerent customers, never resorting to throwing half-off coupons on the problem—Johnny's favorite move—or indiscriminately punishing the waitstaff with a week of forced unpaid leave, as Jimmy liked to do. She used her nose for conflict to head off complaints, steering easily chilled matrons away from the air-conditioning vents; handing toddlers balls of dough to play with and gum on; and offering discounted drinks at the bar when reservations were overbooked, as they were every single weekend. When, inevitably, a customer lashed out, she was prepared to take the full force of their anger with a soothing tone. She had a personality that did not inspire people to be better but persuaded them to be comfortable at their worst. Passing out free punch to the dining room, she knew the restaurant would receive no negative reviews for Uncle Pang's outburst earlier.

When her ladle hit the bottom of the pitcher, she checked the room for signs of tension. Not the customers this time, but the waiters. It was impossible to tell—they were professionals on the floor, their faces rubbed smooth of emotion. Though Ah-Bing's back was to her, Nan knew he looked entirely different than before. He would have pushed his glasses up to pinch the top of his nose, which turned his squint feline and friendly. With this simple push, Ah-Bing morphed into the happy, playful waiter she saw out on the floor. He even sounded different, his English boyish and simple, lacking the sharp slyness that textured his Chinese. The transformation was stark and immediate, and pure fantasy. Yet Nan still believed that this motion of shifting his glasses up his nose was what reminded Ah-Bing of who he was allowed to be, and when. Every waiter had a trick. The quartet of little girls at one of his tables cheered as he approached, and he cheered right back.

Ah-May's words came back to her. Had she really been babying Ah-Jack for months? Even if she had, Ah-Jack was so popular and well loved—by both the amigos and his comrades-in-arms—that she'd expected everyone to look the other way. But while Ah-Jack got the easy retired couples, business lunches, and service-phobic Korean families, the other sections got the unsupervised teenagers tossing seven credit cards into the bill holder. They got the first-generation Chinese who pretended not to understand how to tip, and the single-ladies clubs in which every single lady happened to be celebrating her birthday that night. The waiters were tired of trying to keep eight candles on eight separate pieces of complimentary cheesecake lit. They were tired of wrangling booster seats and of chopping up hot duck carcasses for Filipino grandmothers to chomp on. They were tired of nearly getting an elbow to the neck every time they delivered a check to a table of strong-willed matriarchs, each preferring death to letting someone else's credit card be swiped. Could she blame the other waiters for reporting her to Jimmy?

Always, Nan was the failure. In her desperation, she'd turned everyone against her and, worst, against Ah-Jack. No wonder he'd dropped those lamb chops—she hadn't let him carry anything heavier than fried rice in weeks. Ah-Jack was only eighteen years older than she was, and far from the oldest waiter in the restaurant. So why was he the only one who looked truly old?

What she was learning, as she watched her comrades at the Duck House age to the point of retirement, then beyond, was that some men worked to push away the grave. Men like Ah-Sam, Ah-Gang, Ah-Chi, whose skulls looked shrunken on top of their stooped shoulders, could still lift heavy trays with one hand and nap on their feet. Others could not, but had to, and pulled the grave closer with every shift.

Nan went behind the bar again and lifted one foot out of her heels. When her arch pressed against the rubber mat, she couldn't help letting out a grunt. She slowly curled her toes, then released them, allowing the little knuckles to stretch and pop.

Once, for Mother's Day, her son, Pat, had massaged her feet. His small fingers had been too weak to make much of a difference, but the look of concentration on his face had provided a different kind of relief. He'd poured hot water into a bucket so that she could soak her feet afterward. She'd fallen asleep with her feet submerged, waking long after the bubbles from the dish soap had dispersed and the water had cooled. Would he remember if she brought up that act of sweetness now? Or would he pretend not to understand her mixed-up English? Nan wanted to believe that at Pat's core, all his gentle childhood selves were curled up, waiting to be awoken.

"How about a shot of Jack for Ah-Jack?" Ah-Jack walked past the bar on his way to deliver a check. He'd pinched a few shreds of crispy pepper beef from someone's tray and he offered one to her. The beef fat sizzled on her tongue. "What slow tables. Bad luck follows me."

"You never know," Nan said when he returned to the cashier's window at the end of the bar to swipe one party's four separate credit cards. "They might be big tippers."

"Indian man at table twenty found a strand of black hair on his table," Ah-Jack said. "Not even in his food, just near the dish. He pulls the hair out in front of me, and it's long and rough and curly. Looks like the hair on his wife's head." Ah-Jack grasped a handful of his hair, which was gray and soft enough to fall back flat on his head when he let go. "But I can't tell the man it's his wife who has the shedding problem. With my luck, he'll be calling the little boss first thing tomorrow morning."

"Jimmy won't be taking any calls tomorrow morning," Nan said.

Ah-Jack hooted. "If I'd leaned in more while he was talking, you wouldn't need to sneak me whiskey now."

"Stop fooling around, old man." Nan ripped the receipt from the machine and swiped the next card for him. She handed him the shot she'd poured. "Get moving so I can get out of here."

They'd been carpooling since they started at the Duck House. Ah-Jack knew better than to try to get her to leave early.

He knocked back the shot and wiped his mouth.

"Easy, there," Nan said.

Ah-Jack burped delicately in response.

"You'd better have another one waiting for me." He hobbled off, cutting a comic figure as he swung his left leg in front of his right. He could still fool the customers into thinking his lurching walk and shaky hands were part of his character, a Chinese Charlie Chaplin who might look as if he'd spill the tray but never did.

Nan poured him half a shot and added a spritz of water. She waited for him to come back around.

Nan met Ah-Jack waiting tables at the Mayflower. She'd answered the newspaper ad only a few months after she'd left Macau, and Ah-Jack became the first friend she made in America.

The owner hired her to replace three of his waiters, who had fled for busier waters. On her first day, the restaurant's parking lot was so empty that she'd thought it was closed. Ah-Jack—he'd been forty then—had been teetering outside on a ladder, hanging up a banner that advertised the new, desperately attained liquor license. She'd reached out to steady the ladder and noticed the well-shined polish on his shoes.

"You want a Mai Tai?" were his first words to her. She looked up to find a man too slim for American sizes. A layer of air billowed between his skin and the fabric of his uniform.

"A Mai what?"

"Mai Tai." He finished the knot he'd been tying. "You'll need to know how to make all the new cocktails the boss put on the menu. Might as well have a taste."

He jumped to the ground and unrolled his shirtsleeves. Hefting the ladder over his head, he gestured for Nan to follow.

"The poor guy who owns this place won't be in until right before dinner." Ah-Jack was already developing the hunch that would later bend his chin down to his shoulders. "You'll want to look over the menu before he gets in."

The inside of the Mayflower was dark and stuffy. An elderly foursome ate in the corner booth. They didn't look up from their plates when Nan and Ah-Jack walked by.

"Our food is perfect for their teeth," he explained. "When you try to make a Chinese restaurant vegetarian, you end up with a lot of mush."

"Vegetarian?" Nan grabbed a paper menu from the stack by the empty hostess stand. "Isn't life hard enough?"

"I've worked in every kind of Chinese restaurant," Ah-Jack said. "This is the first vegetarian one. But restaurants fail every day for all kinds of reasons."

He fixed Nan her first Mai Tai and recited the litany of jobs he'd held, from dishwasher, to manager, to owner—a small Szechuan restaurant that he'd had to sell when his wife was diagnosed with breast cancer. The prognosis was optimistic, which was the good news.

"What's the bad news?" Nan asked.

"No lawsuit money."

The drink was sweet and orangey, and the alcohol ungreased Nan's mouth enough to tell Ah-Jack that she had also waited tables since she could remember. Originally from Hunan, her parents had fled to Macau when she was two. They would have made the swim to Hong Kong if Nan had been older, and so Hong Kong became the dream. She dreamed while she took orders. While she cleared tables, and plucked chickens, and scrubbed floors. She'd pictured herself one day at the best hotel in Hong Kong, standing behind the reception desk and meeting people from all over the world. But her family's hopes of immigrating had been repeatedly shattered by riots. Then her mother had died. An aunt, hearing the news, had started sending the family money from Maryland. Packages arrived too, filled with chocolate, slices of vibrantly orange American cheese, squares of crackling gum that shot freshness straight up her nose, as well as pictures of the house the aunt's family lived in, a house surrounded by other, near-identical houses, all white and brick and mossy. Nan had fingered the pictures until the colors bled, and slowly, her dreams began to change. When Nan's father passed a few years later, the aunt offered to sponsor Nan's move to the United States. She had jumped at the chance.

By the end of her story, Nan had torn the paper menu in her hands into scraps. Without her noticing, Ah-Jack had gathered the strips into a small pile. When she looked down at it, confused, he gave her a sly smile. Then he blew the bits onto her lap. She laughed until she shook.

Under the pretense of learning how to mix the cocktail, Nan made them both another round. The syrupy citrus masked the rum, and by the time the owner came in, Nan was cooling her reddened cheeks against the cheap laminate of the bar counter. She claimed she was getting over a slight fever, and Ah-Jack, rock solid after two cocktails and a glass of whiskey, assured the owner that he'd been training her all afternoon.

Love came slowly, as weaknesses in the body often do. At first, she merely looked forward to coming to work for a chance to chat with a good-humored man. Not many patronized the Mayflower, leaving the two to talk and graze on the wonton chips meant for the soups.

She started making note of what brought him pleasure—a fresh apple pie from McDonald's, candied cherries from behind the bar, the sound of a wine cork popping. The list grew. What did Ah-Jack yearn for? A winning horse, new work shoes, less rain so that the fallen magnolia petals along his driveway might not rot so soon. Nan's memory became overstretched. Driving home one night, she nearly cried from frustration because she couldn't remember what Ah-Jack had named as his favorite childhood candy. Finally, she pressed against the tender place she'd been ignoring and stood back, aghast but not surprised, to witness the crumbling edge of her reason. Her imagination began and ended with Ah-Jack.

He was a good man but not strong. He liked drinking and

candy and gambling. In a single plastic sleeve in his wallet, he kept a picture of his wife and a jumble of lucky-number slips. Only a pair of faded eyes peeped out through the confetti. In her wallet, Nan carried just twenty dollars, which would last her the entire week. She hated waste, napping, and overeating. At home, she reused the same bowl and utensils for every meal, washing the set once, right before bed. So to fall in love with a man who threw away watermelon with pink meat still clinging to the rind—it was incomprehensible.

She could no longer ignore the heat and breeze of his passing body at work. The space between them when they stood side by side turned electric, raising the small hairs on her skin. One day, he pushed his hands against the crown and base of her spine, to correct her posture, and she went to stand in the walk-in freezer, plunging her trembling hands into the bucket of frozen dumplings until her entire body shivered.

For four months, before the owner's children replaced the entire staff for the summer, Nan lived in a feverish state of alertness. She imagined living like this forever and felt no fear. On their last day of work, she moved sluggishly, unable to picture herself leaving the restaurant, and Ah-Jack, for good. Her aunt had found her a job as an assistant to a loan officer, which paid less but could, her aunt claimed, lead to a real career, or at least a chance to sit down at work. On that last Mayflower night, as Nan and Ah-Jack walked toward the exit at the end of dinner service, Nan asked him to join her for a drink.

"The Earl?" he said. "Just a few shops down?"

She hadn't had a bar in mind.

"Yes," she said. "That's the one."

She spent the ten dollars and sixty cents in her wallet on bright-blue cocktails that stained her tongue and made her legs sweat over the wooden booth. She was barely twenty-two, old enough to understand that a gambling man with a sweet tooth could love a sick wife and cheat on her also.

Soft as he was, Ah-Jack wasn't a nervous man. He never fiddled, as Nan did, and he would tease her about the trail of shredded paper napkins that followed her around the restaurant. At the bar, he passed her each of his emptied beer bottles so that she could tear the wet labels off the brown glass.

"You're unlike anyone I've ever met," Nan said, after draining her last cocktail. She stared at the label she was stripping.

"You probably haven't met enough people." Ah-Jack laughed. "I'm ordinary."

"Maybe to others," she said. "But not to me."

Ah-Jack circled his thumb around the mouth of his bottle.

"I suppose that's all that matters," he said. He flagged down their waitress and asked for the check. But before Nan could panic, he asked, "You find a new job yet?"

"No," she lied. "But there are Chinese restaurants everywhere."

"There's a new one opening in Rockville. The rumor is that tips will be high from the start. If you can hold off working for a few weeks, they're hiring in July."

"Is that what you'll be doing?"

Before Ah-Jack answered, Nan felt a familiar blooming sensation in her chest, followed by a cold sweat on the bottoms of her feet. This ugly, jittery thing had trailed her her entire life, pushing her to dream, pushing her to come to this foreign place. She had fought so hard to do away with this feeling. But when Ah-Jack said he would be first in line to interview at the Beijing Duck House in July, she couldn't stop herself. She allowed hope back into her life.

"We might carpool," he said. "If you decide to work there, Ah-Nan."

She had a job lined up, a chance at life outside a restaurant, with weekends and vacations. Why follow someone blindly? And not a man of caliber or character, not a man she might ever possess, but Ah-Jack! A man with "Ah" preceding his person, like an opaque veil drawn across his body. And she was Ah-Nan to him.

She nodded right as their bill came.

"Call me Nan," she said. She counted out the bills to pay her part of the check. She didn't dare look at him. "At least until we're comrades-in-arms again."

"Nan," he said, drawing out her name.

She met his eyes through the messy wisps of hair that fell short of her bun. A bridge materialized between them, transporting secret packages that would never reach their destinations. Too soon, she looked down again.

3

The first thing Jimmy did once he'd barricaded himself in his tiny office was pour a glass of scotch. The second thing he did was call Uncle Pang's real estate agent, Janine.

While he waited for the connection to go through, he stared at the photograph of his father hanging alongside the office door. The picture had been taken on the Duck House's opening day; his father had been only a few years older than Jimmy was now. It was the same photo they'd sent to the *Washington Post* to accompany the obituary. The actual newspaper clipping was shoved somewhere in his desk drawer—Jimmy had refused to let Johnny frame that too, but the lie it told was so familiar that Jimmy had practically memorized it.

> Bobby Hong Cheng Han, a prominent Maryland restaurateur and founder of the Beijing Duck House, passed peacefully on Independence Day, July 4, 2010, surrounded by his family and friends. Mr. Han was born on February 2, 1940, in Beijing, China, and started his life in restaurants as a dishwasher at the age of twelve. Mr. Han married Feng Fei, his next-door neighbor and the love of his life, and immigrated to America on his own in 1975 to give his family a better life. Separated

from his adored wife and children, Mr. Han worked his way through the restaurant ranks in Virginia, Maryland, and Washington, D.C., to buy their ticket to America. The Beijing Duck House, Mr. Han's crowning glory, opened its doors in 1985, the product of over a decade of hard work and determination. Mr. Han combined the strong flavors and rich seasonings of Northern Chinese cuisine to make the Duck House a hot spot for famous actors, politicians, and even presidents, all of whom credited the signature Peking duck as the best they'd ever tasted. Mr. Han leaves a legacy of two children, John and Jim, and the first of many grandchildren, Annie.

Every time Jimmy looked at his father's young, grinning face, he would be reminded of this strange memorial, which proved that half-truths made for the blandest fiction. A lie that was newspaper sanctioned: What could be a more fitting tribute to his father? And why argue when the lie of his father's life was no different, really, from the eulogy his mother had told at his father's funeral, before she'd vanished inside the mansion he'd left to her. No different from the speeches that Johnny made at charity events and thousand-dollars-a-plate fundraisers. No different from the story Jimmy himself used to pick up women before last call.

Tonight, however, Jimmy was the only one telling the story and the only one listening.

Bobby Han died, stomach bloated with cancer, with only his wife at his side. His two sons stayed behind at the restaurant, as instructed, to take advantage of the holiday crowd.

Han was unlikely to have been born anywhere near China's capital city, since his mother, during her one visit to America, spoke with an accent so incomprehensible that Han's wife had called it "dirt," her word for "country."

Said wife, Feng Fei, was ten years younger than her husband, who, if their screaming matches could be believed, tried to abandon his family as soon as his feet touched American soil.

It was not Han but rather his best friend, "Uncle Pang," who secured visas and later green cards for Feng Fei and the children, incurring a debt they would never fully repay.

Before the Beijing Duck House could open its doors, a fortunate lightning storm had to strike Han's first restaurant, King China, and burn the shithole to the ground, allowing him to flip the insurance into a down payment for an abandoned building right off the highway.

Han was hardly reinventing the wheel with his menu. Northern Chinese cuisine could be summed up in three words: meat, onions, and garlic. And hot spot for the famous? Jimmy had had five years to laugh at the foolishness of that particular line.

So fuck his father's legacy. Fuck his mother's too. Jimmy's new restaurant would not have such cheap illusions. Or clumsy, broken booths. Or incompetent waiters. His new restaurant would be as polished as the silver chopsticks he'd already bulk-ordered. The décor would be tasteful but luxurious. His menu would actually change—every week a new special, a catch of the day. None of the waiters would speak with an accent. His customers would be afraid of displeasing *him*.

"Hello?" Jimmy stopped revising his father's life story at the sound of Janine's soft voice. He straightened in his chair.

"Jimmy, is that you?" She sounded surprised to hear from him. He'd never called her this late before.

"Janine!" Jimmy practically shouted. "We need to talk about the restaurant. This a good time?"

"I just put my son in bed," she said. "So not the best time, but not the worst."

"I wouldn't bother you this late," Jimmy said, "but I just had to get your thoughts on a new project." He crossed his legs and his knee hit the desk. He leaned back in his chair and knocked his head against the wall. He was the only person in his family too big to fit in this office.

"You always bother me this late," Janine said. He pictured the curve of her smile and remembered the conversation they'd had last week. He took a deep breath. She would fix everything for him.

"I fired Pang, like you said to." He kept his stomach clenched tight. Despite the circumstances, a part of him still hoped Janine would be impressed.

"You did what?" Janine's voice amplified. "I never told you to do that."

Jimmy switched the hot phone to his other ear. He had not expected this reaction.

"You told me he was a middleman." He ground his knuckles into the desk. The echo of Uncle Pang's threat bounced back into his head, and his throat grew thick and choked. "Why did you say all that shit last week if you didn't mean it? Don't be a fucking tease."

"I'm going to hang up." Her voice flattened out. "You're drunk. I knew you were drunk when I picked up, but now I'm going to point it out."

The worst thing Janine could sound was bored. Jimmy tried to put the steel back in his voice.

"What I am is offering you a huge opportunity." He hoped this tack would work. He needed her on his side. "Without Pang. I know you want to work with me instead. Or were you lying to my face?"

Janine took her time before answering. She probably knew he was bluffing. But she was also a curious woman. He was giving her a chance to shake things up. He could practically see her weighing her options.

"You sound stressed," she finally said. "That's natural after a big sale. Why don't you come over? We can talk about this opportunity of yours."

"Okay," he said, barely able to believe the offer. They'd always met at her office before. "Okay. That's all I wanted."

She gave him her address and directions for the quickest route. His hand jumped as he wrote it all down, smearing the ink.

"Listen, you took a big risk," she said right before she hung up. "But what's the other option? Keep your heart in a cage like your father did? Buying the Glory was the best idea you've ever had."

He straightened his spine against his chair. "I love you, you madwoman," he said with surprising fierceness.

She said, "You hired the best."

Jimmy left his office with an hour of service still to go. Three busboys were sorting out the dirty linens from the visibly dirty linens in the kitchen hallway. He had never given this nightly ritual a second look before. Each busboy had tied a tablecloth around his neck; the spotted cotton flowed behind like a cape. They shook out each bundle to inspect the damage. Crumpled zodiac placemats and chopstick wrappers fell out of the hamper, like wilted flowers.

"Don't forget to sweep that up before you finish," Jimmy said, when they looked over questioningly. "Run a wet cloth over the floor too—it's filthy." He pointed at the trash on the ground. The three men nodded; none of the busboys knew much English. On a different night, Jimmy would have gone to get the wet cloth, would have demonstrated exactly what he expected. This night, he lifted his hand in a brisk wave and turned to go, banging his briefcase into his leg.

Nan and Ah-Jack were standing at the bar. Looking at the two of them, bumping shoulders, made Jimmy want to break them apart.

"You're looking well rested," he said. Ah-Jack was leaning into the counter, practically lifting his feet off the ground. "Why don't you take all the overtime tables? Let Ah-Sam and Ah-Jin know they can go home."

Jimmy waited for Nan to start arguing with him. But equal parts smart and spineless, she looked down at her hands.

"Work hard enough, and maybe keep your job," he said, in case Ah-Jack was thinking he might slack off once the boss was gone. The old waiter was out for good, but why not squeeze a few more working hours out of him?

Leaving the restaurant to his most senior employees, Jimmy got into his car and drove to Janine's house. To think that only a few hours ago, those two were the greatest problems in his life.

Jimmy had long ago accepted that his older brother negotiated the world on an entirely different plane of principles, a romantic and useless system that endeared him to everyone outside of his family. But Johnny had gone too far. You didn't promote your best waitress for the same reason you didn't rehire a diabetic waiter with a sick wife at home. Johnny had no idea what it actually took to run a restaurant.

His brother's insistence on the restaurant's *dignity* had always interfered with Jimmy's own designs for the Duck House. Especially since Johnny had been working at the restaurant for only seven years—compared to Jimmy's twenty—and without ever straining his back as a waiter before their father made him a manager. As long as Johnny thought of himself as co-owner of the Duck House, he would keep on swanning around the dining halls, over-sympathizing with the waiters and kitchen staff. The bastard even had the nerve to wait until right before he left the country to break the news. On the way to the fucking airport.

Jimmy could have defied his brother's wishes. He could have funneled his frustration directly onto Nan and Ah-Jack until they broke under the weight of his focused fury. But for once Johnny's interfering wouldn't change a thing. This thought alone inflated Jimmy with a generosity that almost passed as mercy.

Why else had he hired Nan's boy a month ago, after he was kicked out of school?

That was before, when he had a guarantee from Uncle Pang that the Beijing Glory would be financed. He'd written a blank check for a man his father had told him never to trust and then crossed his fingers, hoping that the sum would not be too big.

"Your uncle Pang is a dangerous man," his father had once told him. His whispered Chinese had been barely audible over the din of the restaurant kitchen. "He sees everything, and he knows everyone. Remember this when you take over. We pay him to be part of the family, but he's not family."

"That makes no sense," Jimmy had shot back in English, dodging his father's hand. He'd been nineteen, a college dropout who thought he'd be waiting tables at the Duck House for a year, tops. But what had he known? He should have listened to his father. Panic crawled back on top of his chest. He took a drink.

He drove with one hand, rolling the open bottle of liquor in his other. He hadn't had a drink since he'd decided to open his own restaurant a year ago. But drunk driving was like riding a bicycle. The body remembered, and his body especially remembered the rails of damage he'd done to it in his thirties, when he was first taking over the Duck House. A fun few years, he couldn't deny that, but were they worth the begging and fighting and alimony? Pleasure was always followed tenfold by waves of discontent.

He got off the highway as soon as he could. He favored side, suburban streets, which, while covered with speed bumps and stop signs, were also empty of other cars and fixed lanes. His GPS scolded him repeatedly as he took a circuitous route to Janine's place in Takoma Park. Driving on drink alone was a woozier affair than he'd expected. He'd forgotten all the grit he used to put up his nose, its bracing effect; he'd had to give up after the court-mandated stay in rehab. A slap on the wrist, thanks to Uncle Pang. The street he was on was poorly maintained, with streetlights that had burned down to an orangey glow. He swerved to avoid a large pothole and his right front tire popped up on a curb.

It was time for a small break. He pulled into a stranger's driveway, the house completely dark inside.

In his idling car, which had taken on the stale, pressurized chill of an airplane cabin, he wondered if Janine might ever say yes to him. She had put her hand on the bulge of his biceps last week, but what if, rather than an invitation, her touch was meant to keep him at arm's length forever? What if she was lying when she said there was nothing more attractive than a man with his kind of potential? But why else would a woman invite a man into her home, especially one she knew was in love with her?

Certainly she knew he was in love. He'd never said so seriously or soberly, had never even touched her beyond a handshake, but Janine was not someone who missed people's desires, nor a woman who would play dumb when those desires targeted her.

And hadn't she encouraged his behavior, flirting back until he turned bashful? Playfully batting his jealous moods away? He'd accused her of manipulating him countless times, bringing up her working relationship with Uncle Pang, bringing up the size of the commission she was making off him. She'd reacted with teasing disdain.

"You see what you want to see," she liked to say, and then she would be back to texting on two phones simultaneously, looking up only after he'd calmed down.

Jimmy's dashboard clock read 10:00. Janine's son was in bed, and Janine herself freshly showered, perhaps sipping a glass of red wine. Jimmy felt terrifically unstable at the thought of her scrubbed-bare face.

He'd never thought he could get so worked up over another person, but Janine had shaken his understanding of his own desire. He had believed he wanted someone fun and ditzy, a girl as transparent and colorful as stained glass. But Janine was like the ceiling of the Sistine Chapel, a masterpiece that loomed above him, forcing him to crane his neck until it nearly snapped taking in the expanse of her.

Early in their talks about finding a new restaurant, Uncle Pang had slipped Jimmy a single newspaper page, taken from one of the free Chinese dailies Jimmy's father had kept in the Duck House lobby. Janine's ad had caught Jimmy's eye largely because her picture had taken up nearly a quarter of the page. NUMBER ONE REAL ESTATE AGENT! TOP SELLER IN MARYLAND, D.C., AND VIRGINIA. Her face was blurred soft, round with small features, and her hair was teased out big enough to touch the borders of the shot. Beneath her makeup and the pixelated ink of the newspaper, she looked to be in her mid-thirties. Jimmy wasn't sure how proficient this fluffy-looking woman could be at her job, but he was obliged to hire her. He had promised Uncle Pang.

"I'm looking to expand the family business," he'd said over the phone. He hadn't yet admitted to himself that he was actually leaving the family business, and the half-truth fell comfortably out of his mouth. "My father's passed away, and my mother, she's not what she used to be. I just want them both to be proud of their legacy."

"What a good son," the voice on the other end of the line had said. "I bet you were the kind of kid that other parents compared their children to. 'Why can't you be more like Jimmy!'" Her voice was feminine but full-bodied and loud, like a young boy's. Similar to his, her English was lightly accented, confident yet halting, with a cadence that refused to smooth out. She teased him as if they'd known each other for years. He stammered through the rest of the call.

When she arrived to pick him up from the Duck House the next afternoon, he'd been looking out through the glass doors for half an hour. She drove a white Mercedes, large sunglasses covering a third of her face. Her hair was voluminous but nowhere the size of the hairdo she'd sported in the advertisement. She danced across the parking lot in tall shoes. He almost forgot to back away from the doors.

With a hand wrapped around each duck's golden head, she pulled open both doors and shouted, "Jimmy!" as if she were truly happy to see him. How had she known the man fidgeting at the end of the hallway was him?

"You look even cuter in person than you did in that magazine." She clasped his hand.

"I didn't realize people read that article," he said. "I told Johnny to say no, but he thought the exposure would be good."

" 'Best Kept Secret of the D.C. Metro Area,' " she quoted. "Oh, you framed the piece!" She pointed behind his shoulder at the article, which had come out the previous month. Johnny and Jimmy posed with a roast duck. The idiot reporter had harassed them into pinning paper carver's hats to their heads. Jimmy was pleased to see that Johnny looked positively miniature next to his six-foot frame. Though his brother's jawline remained the sharper of the two.

"Johnny's idea. Again."

"What are your ideas, then?" She pushed her sunglasses into her hair.

"Getting the new restaurant." Her face was so expressive that Jimmy grew flustered. Not because she was beautiful, but because her features were so liquid that he couldn't be sure she was not. He wanted to get her outside as quickly as possible, so she wouldn't think he was as tasteless as his restaurant.

"I guarantee we'll find just what you're looking for," she said.

She drove him to five buildings in the Northwest section of D.C. They chatted about nothing in particular, but for some reason, he could not stop calling her Jenny. Each time, she would gently correct him, and in his eagerness his tongue would slip again. Finally, embarrassed beyond what he thought an almost-forty-year-old man was capable of, Jimmy had offered her a large, sheepish shrug. Janine's entire mouth had opened up and she'd let out an enormous laugh. The laugh had been as violent as the sneezes that had once exploded out of his father, a man who believed he was shooing evil spirits from his body. Shocked, Jimmy had expected the small woman to apologize for making so much noise, but Janine had continued as if nothing had happened. How could he ever pull himself away?

In the car, in the dark, in a stranger's suburban driveway, the idea hit Jimmy out of nowhere. He shoved his scotch bottle into the glove compartment and clapped his hands to his cheeks to wake himself up. A light went on in the house next door. Here he'd been, trying to scrabble together a course of action—a confession, a move, anything—but now he saw that he wasn't meant to have a plan. Any plan he made, Janine would have a counter, and a counter-counter. Jimmy steered his car back onto the street. The plan was to make sure nothing went as planned. Janine was going to get a rude surprise when she saw the man she'd invited in. Tonight, change was in the air.

4

Ah-May, her long braid whipping, came into the bar without warning. Nan had been chewing pebbled ice from the cooler. Seeing the waitress's heavy face screwed up in anger, Nan swallowed the ice. Her throat contracted painfully. The waitress couldn't still be mad at her over Ah-Jack's tables. But Ah-May spat out one word: "Pat."

"What?" Nan didn't want to hear about Pat. In the month her son had been working at the Duck House, she'd flinched every time someone said his name.

"We caught him giving it to the boss's daughter in the storage closet." Ah-May brightened at the opportunity to share gossip. "Right over the hoisin barrels."

"Oh my God," Nan said, realizing that she wasn't wearing her shoes. She quickly slipped them back on, and the extra two inches she gained over Ah-May gave her some comfort. "Are you sure?"

"Of course I'm sure. I saw him with his pants around his ankles."

"Oh my God," Nan said again. "Where is he?"

"Out on the loading dock," Ah-May said. "That little cunt told me to fuck off when he saw me, as if I were the dirty one!"

"Don't call my son a cunt." Nan was heading into the kitchen. The waiters gave her a wide berth, their eyes on the floor. Some of them had known Pat since he was a baby, yet the corners of their mouths struggled to stay flat.

"You don't tell me what to say!" Ah-May yelled, though from the sound of it, she'd stayed behind at the bar. "It's not my fault you're his mother!"

Nan nearly slipped when she stepped into the kitchen. She kept forgetting that her shoes were no longer nonskid, and her arms wheeled for a second before a passing prep cook set her right.

"Okay, Mami?" he said, grinning up at her. She flushed with shame. This tiny man with the gold front tooth had no doubt seen her son hunched over the hoisin barrels.

She kept her head low on her way through the kitchen, which was in the middle of cleanup. A pair of dishwashers swept past her with their push brooms. She ignored the warnings from the amigos sitting with their feet propped up on stools. A wave of warm, dirty water washed over her shoes, drenching the hems of her pants. The smell of bleach rose up through the air, but by then she was shoving past the thick plastic curtain, out onto the loading dock. The August night was muggy, reminiscent of the swamps that had once rested over the town. The wet, weighted air was the opposite of what Nan wanted to feel on her skin as she faced her son, smoking with two other busboys. From the grease of the Duck House to yet more oil outside. A strong odor of garbage drifted from the overflowing dumpster nearby.

The busboys—the youngest ones, William and Filipe—flicked their cigarettes when they saw her and went back indoors, jostling each other with their elbows. Pat also dropped his cigarette, but instead of grinding the butt beneath his foot, he watched the ember glint and smoke. He was avoiding her eyes. He was at least a little ashamed. She was humiliated by her relief.

"What am I going to do?" she said in Chinese, which was the better language to scold in. "Every time I think you can't embarrass me more, you prove me wrong."

Pat's face, so quick and bright as a child, had recently turned putty-like and awkward. His features were struggling to grow into his widening skull. He was still handsome, but his brow was heavier, making him look mean. His mouth sometimes had trouble staying closed. Outside stimuli seemed to enter his head at a slower pace, and he often took a few extra seconds to respond to questions. Sometimes, he never answered at all, blinking into the middle distance, his eyelids erasing her words.

"I was bored," he finally said. His eyes went over her head, as if he were trying to watch a TV show and she was in the way.

"You're a disgrace! Even your excuses are disgraceful. And what's worse, you've dragged Annie down with you. After her uncle was so generous, giving you this job. No one is ever going to want to help you again."

"Fine." Pat balled up his fists and stuck them in his pockets. He was wearing his rip-away track pants, and Nan saw that he had clasped the buttons wrong in his rush to get dressed. She was nauseated by how easily she could read him, how the smallest details could tell her his mood, his preferences, his misdeeds. Yet she hadn't been able to stop him from unraveling his life.

"Oh, fine," she said, nearly laughing. "It's fine if you humiliate your family. It's fine if you get fired. Then you can do what you want. You can drink and smoke and sleep with girls and set garbage cans on fire! You can waste your life and get yourself killed."

"Yeah, you'd like that," he said.

Nan's mouth went sour. Pat liked to egg her on to get her to drop the argument and leave him alone. But tonight she was more than tired. Her pants were stuck to her ankles, her feet swollen and sore. Everything she usually did, every attempt to help and protect, had backfired.

"I know you think I wish you were never born," she said. "But you're wrong. I wish you were never born *to me*. Then maybe you'd have a mother who didn't have to work six days a week to keep you fed."

"Wow." Pat's laugh was a sharp, sarcastic sound. "That's awesome. Go ahead, then. Find me my new family."

He walked toward the kitchen; she blocked his path. His head loomed over hers. She tried not to be afraid and forced her face up to meet his eyes.

"I thought we could start over," she said, her voice shy. "You could work in the restaurant with me, and it would be like spending time together, the only way I can. You're my son, and I never want to hurt you or make you feel unwanted, but I have a job."

"I hate this place," he said, but he was running out of steam. "It's yours."

Nan wanted to reach up and smooth the furrows on Pat's forehead, to delight in how her son's tallness forced her to stretch her arm, but she couldn't remember the last time she'd touched him. She'd lost the ability, the right, to comfort him. To remind him that he was hers with a stroke of her hand.

"You're the only thing that's mine," she said, her voice straining from tenderness.

Pat took two steps back.

"I don't want you," he said. Without a drop of venom in his voice to make his statement untrue. He sounded surprised that he had to remind her of this reality. Nan reached up and slapped his left cheek. Under her hand, his skin was baby-soft, edged with hard stubble.

"Nan!" someone called out, as her hand returned to her side.

She jerked her head. Behind her, Ah-Jack's face poked out from the plastic curtain. His expression reminded her fingers of the violence they'd done.

Nan's heart seized so painfully that she thought she might choke. She wished she were strong enough to look back at Pat, to take in whatever hatred or disgust or hurt flashed through that thick, mudlike skin. But she could not bear to.

With her eyes fixed on the floor, she watched Pat's feet, narrow and long, walk away with surprising lightness. Beneath her, the metal dock shifted and popped. The most sensitive spot inside her, vulnerable and open only to her touch, began to pulse. She pressed against it now. She was no good; she was no good.

5

———

Eager to get out of the restaurant, but without a ride until eleven-thirty, Pat ended up standing by the entrance. He could see into the lobby, its brightness making him feel emptier inside. Smoking a new cigarette, he grabbed the door out of exiting customers' hands.

"Have a good night," he said each time, bowing sarcastically. Sweat trickled into his eyes when he strained to look up from his bent position. The summer heat was oppressive even at ten at night, like an oven that had only recently been turned off. He gripped the metal duck head welded to the door handle until his hand grew slippery. He wished he could break its golden neck.

He wasn't angry that his mother had hit him. He knew he'd pushed her too far, and besides, she'd barely grazed him. No, he was angry because his uncle Jack had stuck his nose into their family's business again. Jack was always intruding, interrupting, disturbing, and never apologizing. He burst from one private conversation to another, like a bull stampeding through a house of locked rooms. It was strange because up until Pat had gotten expelled and had to work this shitty job, he'd loved Uncle Jack. He was fun and loud, and he could joke around with Pat in a way that reminded him of his father but nicer.

Back when Jack was gambling, he sometimes let Pat pick his horses, and if they won, he'd peel a few twenties off his bundle of tips, slip them into Pat's hand, and call it a "finder's fee, don't tell your ma." When Jack came into their house, which was always dark because Pat didn't think to turn on the lights and his mother was too tired to, he flipped on every switch he passed, until they were all blinking like bats, happy simply because Jack had arrived.

Then, last month, Pat had been forced into this dishwasher gig, and suddenly, even though nothing had changed, not his mother's behavior, and certainly not Uncle Jack's, Pat found himself getting angry every time he saw the two of them together. He felt as if he weren't allowed to join them in their huddles, that he was the intruder during their commute to work. He couldn't count the number of times his mother had been talking to him about tedious but private matters and Jack had inserted himself into the discussion, taking it deliberately off the rails until Pat grew so frustrated that he had to leave, the sound of his mother's laughter trailing him. He started to wish that his mother found Jack a nuisance too and not, as she did, a welcome distraction.

Pat knew, even as he stewed by the front door, that there was little chance he and his mother would have done anything but stand in painful silence if Jack hadn't interrupted; still, he blamed Jack for showing up and ending whatever else might have happened. Pat raged at the older man in his head, calling him pathetic, desperate, lonely, sad, and tried to ignore what he was truly upset about, which wasn't the interruption exactly but the moment of interruption. If only Jack had been a second later. Stepping through the plastic curtains right when he had, Jack had inadvertently glimpsed the jolt of mortification on Pat's face, a sensation too physical to hide. And even if Jack hadn't recognized it, he was still a witness. Pat couldn't stomach this. Why else had his own mother looked away? Why had May known to shield her eyes as soon as she opened the door to the closet and found him with Annie? Even May understood the violation of staring straight at a person exposed.

Pat had thought it was embarrassing when May had caught him and Annie, but after all the chaos and shouting, when May finally slammed the door shut and left the two of them alone, they had stared at each other for a second before collapsing into silent laughter. In the closet, the embarrassment had been fleeting, a stopgap, holding a place open in his body for the exhilaration, hilarity, and pride that flooded in seconds later. What he felt now was not so easily displaced. With every door Pat opened, with every group of customers bidden goodbye, his humiliation grew pricklier, until it had its own kind of heat.

He wished his mother hadn't taken his phone away, or his Zippo. He had nothing to play with until it was time for him to meet up with Annie. A group of kids were sharing a joint in front of the convenience store. He could smell the skunky smoke from across the street.

He began to fidget more. He was pretty sure that he liked Annie too much. They'd only been hanging out for a few weeks. How much did he even know about her? Just that she never said what she was thinking, because what she was thinking was usually too mean. The kind of mean that made him laugh. Inappropriate, exaggerated. Unapologetic. The first time he'd thought of her as more than just a shimmering mirage was the morning she'd walked in wearing an awesomely short skirt, and May had made a loud comment about the length of it.

"It's ninety degrees out," Annie had said, and then, when she thought no one was listening, "Saggy-pussy bitch."

Pat's laugh was so surprised it came out of his nose, a painful snort that made Annie look over. Seeing she'd been caught, she tucked her hair behind her ear and smiled.

Annie was the first person he'd met who understood what it was like to be in a restaurant family. He wasn't sure at first, because she wasn't a waiter's kid. But she'd said something one day that stopped his heart faster than the first time they'd kissed. He'd been loitering by her stand on his break. They were complaining about the restaurant, making fun of Jimmy and his tight Italian suits, when Annie cracked a joke about how every day at a Chinese restaurant was bring-your-kid-to-work day.

"It's so fucked up," Pat said.

"Like the seven dwarfs." Annie laughed. "Hi ho, hi ho."

"My mom is so happy I'm here. She only knows how to talk about work." The last comment fell clumsily out of his mouth. He couldn't believe how girlish he sounded. He was about to slink back to the kitchen when Annie murmured in agreement.

"My dad's the same," she said. "They're so different in the restaurant, aren't they? They're not your parents anymore."

"I hate the way she sounds." Pat didn't know what he was trying to say. He couldn't find the words and he started to flush. "In the car with Jack, she's normal, but then we get to work and she's . . . weird."

"The waiters aren't real people on the floor," Annie said. "More like cartoons."

Then she poked him in the arm. "You have your mom driving you to work? That's kind of embarrassing. I can drive you. I need the gas money."

He'd tried to pretend it was the endless possibilities of those daily car rides that had taken his breath away.

"That'd be cool," he'd managed to say.

Too embarrassed to keep thinking about Annie, Pat had only the heavy glass door to occupy him. Fewer people left the restaurant; to pass the time, he swung the door open and closed, at varying forces and speeds. The dingy strip mall down the road dimmed and emptied. The convenience-store kids got onto their bikes, shouting and swerving into one another until they were out of sight.

At eleven, dinner service officially ended. When a black BMW drove up, Pat peered into the restaurant's hallway to find its owner. Instead, the passenger door clicked open and a familiar-looking guy peeled out. The careful way he held his body reminded Pat of the old dudes who did tai chi in the park, but this guy looked younger than Uncle Jack and even, in the dim light, Pat's mother. The guy's hair was black but thinning, the sparse strands gelled together to keep his scalp covered. His teeth were big and yellowed. Up close, he smelled exactly the way Pat thought he should smell, of hair ointment, stale tobacco, and shoe leather. The familiarity encasing this guy was spooky.

"The restaurant's closed," Pat said. "But can I help you?"

"Has Jimmy gone?" the guy said, his English a pleasant surprise.

"Yep," Pat said. "Come back tomorrow."

The guy shook his sleeve back and studied his watch, which glinted in the lamplight.

"In that case, I'd like to bum a cigarette," he said. When he reached out to take a Marlboro out of Pat's pack, Pat noticed the missing ring finger and the answer flipped open in his head.

"Sure, Mr. Pang," he said. The waiters had been clucking over the man's arrival all evening. Pat had heard, in the silences gapping the waiters' conversations, the power this "VIP" held over the restaurant. Even his mother had seemed cowed by Pang's name.

"Call me Uncle Pang," he said. "How are you tonight, Pat?"

"Fine."

"You're the new dishwasher, aren't you?" Pang leaned in for Pat to light his cigarette. "I've heard you're a handful for your mother, but from what I can see, you're just a little bored. That's never good for a young kid like you. For anyone, really."

"It sucks," Pat said, eager to commiserate. "This town too."

"So why don't you get out now? You're done with school, aren't you?"

"School's done with me." Pat laughed at his own joke. Pang waited for him to finish.

"That's right." Pang exhaled smoke out of his nostrils. "You're the one who set the garbage-can fire."

Pat ashed his cigarette a little too hard, nearly spinning it out of his fingers.

"Your mother told everyone you were kicked out for skipping too many classes." Pang watched Pat scrape the spindly leaves off a weed with the toe of his shoe. "I can't believe the waiters bought that story. They didn't stop talking for weeks."

"All those waiters do is talk shit. Complain and bitch."

"A caged animal forgets how to be an animal," Pang agreed.

"Yeah, whatever," Pat said. "They talk about money most. Depressing."

"You wouldn't be tempted by easy money?" Pang's crinkled eyes lighted across Pat's face, scrutinizing him. "You would say no to a thousand dollars in one night?"

Pat glanced back inside the restaurant. "They're not making a thousand. More like three hundred."

"I'm not talking about them."

"A thousand?" Pat sucked on his cigarette. "No way. That's not enough."

"So you're not a slave to money. Just a slave to *some* money."

"Shit, I don't know."

Pang peered at him through eyes half closed with humor. "Put your hackles down. You'll die young if you can't laugh at an old man teasing you." He coughed and looked at the lit end of his cigarette. He flicked away the hot ash and drew out a small case from his jacket. "Stop smoking that crap. Try one of mine."

Pat took one of the proffered cigarettes, which were wrapped in mahogany-colored paper with golden characters stenciled on the side. The tobacco smelled sweet. Inhaling as Pang lit the end, Pat tasted cherries in the smooth cloud of smoke that coursed into his mouth.

"There's a better version of everything," Pang said. "If you can afford it. Here, have the rest." He tossed not just the cigarettes but also the case that held them. Pat nearly fumbled the catch. At the intersection, a car pulled up, tripping the motion sensor on the stoplight. The light blinked green, yellow, red.

"Thanks." Pat fiddled with the latch on the antique cigarette case. It looked like real silver. He slipped it into his pocket in case Pang changed his mind.

"You look like you appreciate nice things," Pang said. "How much do you make a night? Seventy? Eighty?"

"Fifty." Most of which went to his mom for safekeeping. He barely had enough to take Annie out to the movies.

"Slave labor," Pang said. "Sounds like you need a better job."

"Can't quit." The suggestion in Pang's voice made Pat edgy.

"Can't?" Pang tugged on his earlobe, as if he hadn't heard correctly. "You got a family to feed?"

The back of Pat's neck flushed. "Community service," he said.

A part of him was relieved to have an excuse to close the door on whatever Pang had in mind. The guy seemed slimy. Not that dishwashing was his dream gig. Pat scratched at the collar of his shirt. He could feel the soap scum on his hands. The smell of bleach and sweat hovered around him.

"*I* worked that out with the judge," Pang said. "And I can work out something new for you too." He caught the expression on Pat's face. "It was my job to keep this place safe. To watch out for the people who work here."

Pat dragged in more of that heavy, cherry smoke. He glanced again at what Pang was wearing. He couldn't tell if the suit was expensive, if the watch was designer. Not even if the dude's shiny shoes were actual alligator skin. These cigarettes—they were the real deal. But everything else?

Pat scratched under his armpit. He was suddenly tired of smoking this fruity thing. He tried to come up with a reason to go inside the restaurant. "So you're basically the godfather," he said.

Pang flicked his cigarette expertly at Pat's chest, singeing his shirt.

"What the hell!" Pat sprang away and brushed at his chest. His shout sounded like a yelp in the empty night. No one was in the lobby anymore. He saw Pang's hand go into his jacket, and the first thought that jumped into Pat's head was that he was going to pull out a gun. Instead, his hand came back pinching the corner of a bulging envelope.

"What do you know," Pang said. "I guess I am."

"I thought you were looking for Jimmy." Pat dropped his cigarette and edged toward the door.

"Jimmy's not here." Pang pulled the envelope out further. "I'm not going to waste a trip. I have other tasks to complete that have nothing to do with him."

Pat looked around. The parking lot was nearly empty; only the convenience store across the street was still open. He glanced back at the envelope.

"Ten thousand dollars." Pang flicked the flap open. The yellow lamplight caught the green ridges.

This was more money than Pat could make in a year. Much more than his mother made in two months. His heart rebounded against his chest with the anticipation of the cash. With ten thousand, he could move out of her house. He could get Annie something nice, like an emerald necklace. He could buy the vintage Nikes he'd been eyeing on eBay, and a Kawasaki moto-cross bike.

Pang tucked the envelope into its hiding place.

"You should see the look on your face." His teasing had a jagged edge to it. "I didn't realize I was dealing with a kid."

No one had treated Pat like a little boy in years. He flexed his back muscles. It would take nothing to push this old guy down. But Pang had the upper hand.

"Let me see the envelope," Pat said.

"Aren't you interested in what you'll be doing?" Pang asked.

"I figured you'd tell me sooner or later."

A laugh rumbled through Pang's throat like a warning. "Get in the car. We'll take a ride around the block. Iron out the specifics." He opened the backseat door of the BMW.

With the money no longer in sight, doubt crept into Pat's head again.

"I have to get back to work," he said. "Thanks for the cigarettes."

"I'll give you a thousand extra, to keep now, if you get in," Pang said, reaching across the front seat toward his driver. A thick roll of bills appeared in his grasp.

"Just around the block?" Pat said.

"You're scared." Pang looked over Pat's head, at the restaurant, a bored expression flattening his face. He dug a thumbnail between his bottom front teeth. "I've got no time for that. Go inside. Find Filipe or William. Tell them Uncle Pang has an offer." He handed Pat the small bundle of money and squeezed his shoulder gently. "Here's a small tip for you. For keeping me company."

Pat shoved the cash into his pants pocket and ducked his head. He climbed into the car, the air-conditioning a shock to his skin. He'd meant to push past the old guy. But Pang had already stepped aside.

The car moved like it was floating above the pavement. Light jazz filtered from speakers in the rear. There was no partition between the driver's section and the backseats, but the driver might as well have been blinkered from the rigid way he stared ahead.

"Good friend of yours?" Pat joked. His throat clogged halfway through the sentence and his voice dipped into the inaudible.

"Anyone can be my good friend," Pang said. "What I want are old friends. Friends who stick around. I like to do favors for these friends."

"Oh yeah? Like what? Can you break someone out of jail?"

"If everyone wins and no one gets hurt, why not bend the rules a little?" This guy never said anything straight. It drove Pat crazy.

"Sure." Pat leaned into the fragrant leather seat. He didn't know why he'd buckled his seatbelt. The fabric chafed against his neck.

"I knew you'd understand me." Pang cleared his throat and his driver passed back a heavy black backpack. "Your boss, Jimmy, needs a favor. I want to help, but I'm too old for the job, and besides, it's not quite my style. It's brainless, really, but it takes a little extra muscle, a little spirit. If you help me here, you'll get the money, as well as my friendship. Jimmy's too."

A puff of laughter escaped from Pat's mouth. Pang shifted forward in his seat.

"Friendship is simply what happens when there's too much debt to be repaid."

"That's blackmail."

Pang pinched the inside of his nostrils, hanging on to the end like a heavy piercing. "You need to loosen up."

"Okay, whatever." Pat sank further into his seat. The car crept out of the lot and onto the block of apartments where William and Filipe lived. Which room in those tall buildings was theirs?

"No need to get impatient." Pang unzipped the backpack and pushed it onto Pat's lap. Something hard poked his legs through the fabric. "Take a look."

Probing through the contents of the pack, Pat recognized everything in there, but what did they have to do with one another?

Pang answered his look. "All you need to know is that everything in that backpack needs to be in—" The big green dumpster behind the restaurant's loading dock came into view, its heavy lid thrown open to fit all the bags inside.

"Set garbage on fire?" Pat wanted to laugh in the old guy's face, the deadly serious expression on it absurd now that he understood. "You're joking."

"Easy ten thousand dollars," Pang said, some irony in his voice. "But you'd be surprised how many boys your age would say no. Men older than you too. They'll steal, they'll cheat, they'll beat a man's face in, but they won't go near a small fire. Why do you think that is?"

"They don't think they can control it." The words were out of Pat's mouth before they'd even crossed his mind.

"Exactly," Pang said. "But you're not afraid, are you?"

Pat re-zipped the backpack. His thoughts were jamming against one another. A loud voice muscled through. He could crawl back to the restaurant—*to his mommy*—with a thousand dollars in his pocket, or he could take the eleven thousand and run.

"We're all friends now?" Pat said.

"No." Pang reached over and covered Pat's hand with his. "But afterward? Jimmy and I will be your best friends. And there's no favor I won't do for a best friend."

"There's a lot of garbage." Pat eked his hand out from under Pang's fingers. "The fire's going to get too big."

"I'll get you a burner so you can call 911 before that happens," Pang reassured him. "I trust you won't make the same mistake twice."

"For eleven thousand dollars." Pat touched the roll of bills he'd shoved into his pocket.

"I'll give it all to you now," Pang said, pulling the fat envelope out, all the way this time. He tossed it over to Pat, who didn't expect the load to make such a heavy noise as it landed between them. "You see? We're becoming friends already."

At the Duck House's front door ten minutes later, Pat climbed out of Uncle Pang's BMW, holding on to the backpack, the heavy envelope, and a prepaid flip phone.

"One last thing," Uncle Pang called. "You got a ride? You'll need a car."

Pat nodded. He had somebody in mind. "You'll text me when the restaurant's all clear?" He had his hand on the top edge of the car door.

"Keep your phone on you." Uncle Pang raised his hand briefly, before pivoting his wrist a quarter turn. The man was as clear in his gestures as he was confusing in his speech, and the meaning of his small, queer movement broke over Pat's head like an egg. Finally on the same page, Pat shut the door as he'd been asked.

6

Every Monday night was a victory for Ah-Jack. Especially now that his battered body threatened to give out before Sunday. He had a special ritual, satisfying in how ordinary it was, to usher in his one day off a week. Nan would drop him home, just as the racetracks were closing, and he would count himself lucky for having worked through another race day. He would sneak a cigarette by the garage, beyond where his wife could see from her bedroom window. Letting himself into the house, he would switch off all the lights she'd left on for him. She herself would have gone to bed hours ago.

This Monday, his forced overtime meant that he and Nan did not get to his place until nearly midnight. A security sensor clicked on when they drove past, washing the row of town-homes in wasteful light. A sunken basketball had been wedged between the grates of his storm drain. Nan, always reluctant to acknowledge what was bothering her, had been silent for much of the ride, and Ah-Jack, exhausted by the extra hours, had not tried to charm her out of her funk.

He should have been panicking. Jimmy had been looking for a reason to fire him for months, and after tonight, despite the little boss's attempts to keep him in suspense, Ah-Jack knew he was out. But it was hard to look at his work and feel any desire for more. Why else had he let go of that plate of lamb? He hadn't overestimated his ability; he had known exactly how weak he'd become. He'd wanted to free himself. In that moment, two questions had sprung into his head, so powerful that they had overridden his duty toward his wife. Would he have to work until he died? How long would that take?

Letting go of that plate hadn't swept those questions away. They had grown louder in his head. Now he would have to start looking for a new job tomorrow. He would have to work more for less. The entire ride, Nan had ground her teeth at every stoplight. But this wasn't what had stopped him from asking her these questions. She had an unlimited patience for telling him what he needed to hear. But she also always had the right answer. The idea that Nan might have already wondered how long he could work, already worried about him dying . . . He would rather have no answer at all. When she pulled up to his house, they said goodbye without lingering.

Outside, the air was spongy with humidity and the smell of cut grass. Lawn clippings stuck to his leather shoes as he cut across his small front yard. Michelle never reminded the neighbor's boy to bag the grass after he finished mowing. Ah-Jack reached behind the rainspout on the side of his garage and pulled out an old sneaker. He fished a stale cigarette from its toe and lit the bent end. Taking a puff, he leaned against the edge of his garage door. Michelle would kill him if she saw. She was rabid about doctor's orders, but he enjoyed having a few secrets from her. How else could they have stayed married for five decades?

Americans. They believed a strong marriage came from knowing their partner's every shadowy thought. But it was knowing too much that killed love. A strong marriage came when the wedded stopped trying to plumb their partner's depths. Life became easier when one passed the years with an amiable stranger and not a mirror that reflected back all of one's flaws.

Marriages were torn apart by empathy; to look into her eyes and find pity was to discover *what* she pitied in the first place. Intimacy was not to know but to wonder. Eyes that searched in their staring were the hallmark of every lover's gaze. And if the search was lazy, unstructured—a slow, easy stroll rather than a rush to the finish—then in this stretch of time, forever might comfortably rest.

After he'd forced himself to finish the entire cigarette, Ah-Jack threw the butt into the carton and put everything back in its hiding place. Michelle had forgotten to lock the door again. A pile of bills waited for him on the end table. He was so bone-tired that after looking up the flight of stairs leading to his bed, he considered settling for the living room couch. If his wife hadn't fallen asleep there first, as she used to do. But of course she hadn't. Ah-Jack stayed in the living room after he'd switched off the light, his eyes focused, through the dark, on the empty couch.

The first time she'd been diagnosed with breast cancer, his wife had been too weak, or apathetic, to make her way up the stairs of their townhouse. He'd often found her curled up on the couch, her naturally flared nostrils quivering as they whistled in her sleep. Back then he'd had some vitality left in his bones, and he'd carried her to bed, moving carefully so as not to clip her head or ankle while he rounded each corner. Barely five feet and denser than her height suggested, his wife had never been a slight woman. She was even less so after her treatment started. They had expected her to waste away; instead, the steroids caused her to balloon.

Maneuvering her up two flights of stairs, he'd relished not just the eventual pleasure of unloading her weight, but the knowledge too that when she woke up the next morning she would understand that he had done right by her. All the doctor's visits he couldn't drive her to, all the clumps of hair she'd swept away herself, the absence of his hand on her back while she vomited vinegar and foam into the toilet, might be briefly blinked away. Ah-Jack sometimes believed that his wife had let herself fall asleep on the couch all those years ago because she trusted that his arms would be willing and strong.

The continued absence of her body on the couch sent relief through him, and also shame for this relief, and shame again, of a slightly different shade, at the notion that this time around she was forcing herself to climb those stairs because she thought, even after she'd unexpectedly lost so much weight, that she might spare him the embarrassment of dropping her. This was what a wife was for. To save her husband and in doing so magnify his humiliation.

Worse, if Ah-Jack remembered correctly, this Monday was three days after his wife's most recent chemo treatment. She would have been completely drained of energy. Yet she had managed to crawl up those flights of stairs and tuck herself into bed. As he started his own climb, he allowed himself a few full seconds of loathing, not for his wife, per se, but for their situation, which was essentially a repeat of the worst year of their marriage, only even more terrible. He hadn't expected to be in the same place in his seventies as he had been in his forties. Only now he didn't even have his health. His left foot burned and prickled with every step.

Finally on the third floor—he cursed his younger self for buying a townhouse with one more story than he could afford— Ah-Jack quietly slipped into the master bedroom. The room smelled faintly of mildew, even though the humidifier was turned off. A nightlight shaped like the Bay Bridge revealed the swell of his wife's body, lying beneath four quilted blankets. He went on into the adjoining bathroom.

He was startled to find the toilet water dyed red before remembering that chemo changed the color of his wife's urine. She had forgotten to flush a few times in the past, and each time, the surprise drove his heart crazy, the red tapping into some animal instinct to flee. He put down the toilet cover before flushing.

He should shower. He stank. But the overtime hours had leeched so much from him that he couldn't imagine standing for another minute. He sat on the lip of the tub and struggled to get his ankle onto his knee. His doctor forced him to examine his feet for cuts, ulcers, and sores at least once a day; otherwise, his diabetes could take them with no greater warning. This was no treat. His feet were ugly to look at: yellow-crusted along the sole from a lifetime of waiting tables, his nails gnarled and calcified because he had trouble reaching down to trim them. Once every month, his wife cajoled him into the bathroom, where she would squat at his feet while he sat on the covered toilet. She would cut his toenails, then cover his dry, flaking feet with petroleum jelly.

He slowly peeled off his socks, the edge of the tub digging into his tailbone. When *was* the last time his wife had taken care of his feet? More than a month ago. His nails were longer than he'd ever seen them. And not just long but jagged, with pointed corners that had worn small lacerations into the sides of his toes. He couldn't feel the cuts, and he was suddenly frightened by the numbness in his toes. He couldn't blame his wife, weak as she was, but who else could help him with his feet? He'd had to dwell many times on a future without her, but he had done so abstractly: an empty house, a grave to visit, an anniversary of death. Who would cut his toenails? Who would clean the house? Who would ask him how his day had been, and who would take his hand gently when he didn't want to answer? Such practical matters had slipped from his impractical mind.

He left his dirty socks balled up on the tiled floor. He tried not to think of how they might remain there, untidied, one day.

In his bedroom, across the hall, Ah-Jack finally shucked his uniform. He took off the gold chains he wore as bracelets; he left on the ones around his neck. He yawned so fiercely that tears sprang from his eyes. But before he turned out the lights, he took a second look around. Something was different about his room. His twin bed was neatly made. The tops of the furniture gleamed. The tissues he'd used to clear his nose and throat the night before had disappeared from his nightstand, and even the plastic shopping bag that lined his trash bin was new. Not just replaced but from a "Fresh Farm Market," a store that Ah-Jack had never been to before.

Ah-Jack sank onto the edge of his bed and bumped his knees together. How could his wife, who couldn't flush the toilet most days, who had neglected his broken feet, still be cleaning? Running errands? Michelle almost never left their house. She was afraid of going out alone, and even with a companion at her side, she was painful to watch. Like a bird trained only to fly from one perch to another, she reacted to the slightest change in her scenery with a flurry of panic. Once, when the bank teller had tried to promote a new deal for a debit card, his wife had grown so overwhelmed that she'd abandoned depositing his tips and gotten lost exiting the building. The only time she was at ease with others was on the telephone. She had two contacts nowadays: her second cousin, Yu, who lived in San Francisco, and Nan.

He continued to grip his knees; even if she did have the strength and the conviction to keep house, why was she going to a new grocery store? Fresh Farm Market was not a place along his wife's familiar routes.

He was intrigued by the idea of his wife hiding secrets from him. A little frightened. He'd known her since they were kids; she'd been his classmate in Mian Yang, their small southern town. They were too old to be changing. They had lived separate lives for decades, divided by his restaurant work, but she was still the girl who had followed him around, with her plump cheeks and untamable hair. The girl who was never singled out by the teacher for making a mistake, her palms never marked by the slap of a ruler. Even her penmanship was certain, every stroke in the right place. Her voice had rung out louder than others only during arithmetic recitations. He was the boy unworthy of her attention, who had carried on anyway, his charm making him fearless. He had learned to take his falls early, before he'd grown too big for the tumbles to hurt. He had purposefully pushed boundaries, showing up late to class, talking his way out of trouble, then showing up even later the next time, until he found the point where no amount of charisma could save him from a whipping. He did the same in conversations, saying whatever came to mind, telling the dirtiest jokes. The first time he'd talked to his wife, he had brought her to tears with his bawdiness. Soon, he'd had her laughing again.

What could his charm do for him now? Could it chase away whatever had possessed Michelle to run from routine? His wife was still the same person, and yet, was she the person he had understood her to be? Ah-Jack fell back on his bed. A rustling noise made him sit back up. He pawed around the blanket for a moment, before unearthing a pair of newly purchased compression socks from the end of his bed. His wifey had gotten him a present! The long black socks looked like the ones soccer players wore. The packaging promised relief for aching legs and feet. He felt another kind of relief when he saw that the price tag had "Fresh Farms" stamped at the top.

He struggled to pull the socks on, expecting the squeeze to be painful, but instead he was surprised by how well supported his feet and legs suddenly felt. The aching muted. Ah-Jack wiggled his toes. He pictured his wife speaking to a salesperson, struggling to overcome her shyness to ask about the benefits of these socks. Her thoughtfulness made the careless loss of his job all the more shameful, and finally, the panic he'd been expecting all night arrived.

Creeping out of his bedroom, he slipped through Michelle's half-open door. He padded as quietly as he could to her bedside.

Clumsy man, he tripped over a water glass she'd forgotten at the foot of her bed. The glass skittered out from his foot, hitting the nightstand with a loud *clack*. Ah-Jack squinted at the lump on the bed. When nothing moved, he started breathing again. Poor wifey, she'd tuckered herself out. He gently pulled down the quilts, searching for her forehead, her lovely fat cheeks.

But from the nest of fabric, a thick pillow emerged. Confused, he pawed the quilts down farther. He grew desperate to see her tufts of hair and chilled scalp, her familiar, clammy skin, but still more pillow showed. He tore the bed apart, throwing sheets onto the floor, and only when the mattress was bare did he stop. His wife was not home. He had no idea where she'd gone.

7

Nan called out for her son as she pulled her key out of the lock. She missed the days when he would drag his blue beanbag chair to the front door. When she got home from work, her first sight would be his sleeping figure slumped deep into the chair. Now she was lucky if he was home by the time she returned. He grabbed a ride from one nameless friend or another to get to and from the Duck House, barely telling her when he left in the morning, and sneaking out of the restaurant at night. In high school, he'd started getting invitations to study groups and parties. She used to wait up for him, before she decided she was too tired to spend those hours half dozing in front of the TV. She had gone to bed in an empty house and woken up after Pat had already gotten himself to school, unsure if he had even come home the night before. How quickly this had become routine.

She couldn't remember when she'd started letting her son live his own life. She wanted to believe it was because she trusted him. Because Pat was a good boy. Even after the sudden dip in his grades (despite the study sessions), the calls from school, his shocking expulsion, she'd chanted this like a prayer. The other part of the truth was impossible to bear—she was just too tired to stop him.

She might as well have been one of those divorced American fathers who saw his children on alternating weekends and the occasional holiday. At least those parents used their limited time to spoil their children, with trips to amusement parks and arcades. Nan was tempted to sleep straight through her one day off a week, and the times she'd taken Pat to the movies, she'd nodded off before the trailers ended.

"I can go on my own," Pat had said after she'd slept through another one of the *Batman* movies. "We shouldn't buy two tickets if you're not going to watch."

Tonight, small blessing, he was at home when she opened the front door. His backpack hung from the staircase. The microwave whirred as she shut the door behind her. She approached the kitchen, her movements careful. Pat was waiting while a frozen pizza made circles in the microwave. He had a new phone in his hand, and her stomach ached at the sight of it. He must not have heard her come in. She should have made more noise. Now she'd have to try to confiscate the phone, just as she had with his last one. When would she fit in her apology for slapping him? She'd never learned that maternal skill of showing love through her scolding, of acknowledging both their faults in her apology. She was always too cruel or too kind.

She rustled the plastic bag she'd carried inside. Pat jumped from the counter. He stashed his phone behind him in his waistband.

"I get you Slurpee," she said, taking the domed cup out of the bag and pushing it toward him across the kitchen table. She'd spent half an hour driving around, looking for an open 7-Eleven. "In case you thirsty."

"How'd you know I drink Slurpees?" He seized the cup with both hands. With a decisive squeeze, he popped the plastic cover off and examined the insides with the long, shovel-ended straw. "Coke and blue raspberry. I like these flavors."

"I pay attention." She massaged her lower back against the edge of the counter. "To my favorite son."

"I'm your only son."

"My only favorite son."

Pat gave her a small nod. He was a good boy; he let her have this joke every time.

She wasn't lying when she said she paid attention. She'd noticed the empty Slurpee cups in the trash and the colors that pooled inside the bottom ridge: brown and blue. Just as she had noticed, last month, that he went through the frozen macaroni and cheese faster than the spaghetti and meatballs. She'd made the adjustment the next time she went grocery shopping. She knew when, earlier this year, Pat had started having his friends over, because of the overripe smell of teenage-boy deodorant in the living room, and she knew when the contents of her dusty liquor bottles had started smelling less and less like alcohol. Perhaps these were the same boys who'd talked him into setting that fire, but at the time, she had only stocked the pantry with more chips and salsa and popcorn. She hadn't asked Pat who his friends were. He wouldn't have told her the truth.

When she'd first entered the house, she'd spoken her most careful English, different from what she used with customers in the restaurant. She had lowered herself in this uncertain tongue to let him know how sorry she was. But as he drank his Slurpee, she switched to Chinese.

"Where did you get that phone? I took yours away."

"What phone?"

"Don't try to lie to me."

"One of the busboys lent it to me." He reached back to pull the phone out of his pants. "Filipe."

"Why would an amigo do that?"

"Don't call them that," he said, tucking the phone into his pocket in case she tried to take it. "They have names."

"You work there one month and you think you're their savior." She shoved the 7-Eleven bag under the cupboard and closed the door with a bang. "The amigos can take care of themselves."

"Whatever."

"Give me that phone." She held out her hand.

"I have to give it back to him tomorrow."

"I'll give it back for you," she said. "You're not allowed to have a phone."

"I need one."

She kept her hand open in front of his face.

"This doesn't have to be so difficult," she said.

"Okay." He took the phone out again. Instead of handing it over, he resumed whatever game he'd been playing before. He leaned his elbow casually against the tiled counter. The pizza in the microwave was bubbling over. Nan took a step toward him and Pat took one back, not looking up from the screen. His thumb had stopped moving over the keys. He was feigning interest in a blank screen. The microwave beeped and neither of them moved to open it. What was her son reducing her to? She made a halfhearted lunge for the phone. He moved easily out of her way.

Before Nan was forced to try again, her doorbell sounded out a flurry of rings. She poked her head into the hallway. Pat popped the pizza out of the microwave and followed her out of the kitchen.

"I'm not through with you!" she called over her shoulder. His feet stomped up the stairs.

Without checking to see who was outside, Nan wrenched her front door open. The person behind it fell through, colliding into her arms. Ah-Jack!

She patted him down, looking for an injury. "Are you hurt? Are you okay?"

He quickly straightened up, and she got a good look at his face.

"I'm great!" His voice was loud but hollowed out at the same time. His eyes bulged out of his thin face, rimmed with red. "Never better."

"I don't need more liars in my house," Nan said.

"I'm not lying." Ah-Jack stumbled through the house, into the kitchen. Pat had left the Slurpee on the table, where a ring of condensation gleamed under the light. Ah-Jack seized the cup and sucked thirstily from the straw. "My blood sugar is a little low. But I'm fine, really."

"Why are you here in the middle of the night?" she asked. "I know something's happened, and the longer you keep it from me, the more worried I'm going to get."

"For you, to think is to worry," Ah-Jack said, still drinking the Slurpee.

"Does Michelle know you've left the house?" Nan pulled out a chair for him. "If she wakes up and you're not home, what's she going to think?"

"She's not home either." He ignored the chair and ground his knuckles into his temple, grimacing from the chill of his drink. He went over to where Nan kept her liquor.

"Is she okay? Where's she gone?" She intercepted him as he went to grab a tumbler for his whiskey, taking the bottle away from him. She didn't want to explain why the whiskey had been replaced by brown-tinged water.

"Stop minding my business," Ah-Jack protested, but he finally sat down. "I don't know where she is. I came home and she wasn't in bed. I called her and when I asked her where she was, she told me she was sorry, but she wasn't coming home tonight. Then she hung up, and she won't answer, no matter how many times I call. Now you know everything I know! Are you happy?"

"Of course I'm not." Nan squatted beside him, her hands balancing on his knee. "Don't jump to conclusions. I'm sure Michelle has a reasonable explanation. She's a sensible woman."

"I don't know what kind of woman she is anymore," he said. "Fifty years of marriage, and not a single problem."

"You're exhausted." Nan stood and pulled Ah-Jack up with her. "You're staying here tonight. I'll set everything up in the living room, and then you just sleep. Everything will look better in the morning."

"As if I can sleep now." He fought back a large yawn.

"Don't be stubborn, old man." She pushed him gently into the living room. "You stay right here. I'll get you some clean sheets."

They barely spoke while Nan made up the pullout bed. Her mind moved so quickly that it grew clumsy as she tried to figure out where Ah-Jack's wife had gone. Michelle was a devoted woman, and very sweet, but she was hardly as simple as Ah-Jack seemed to believe. This was the woman who, after Ah-Jack was diagnosed with diabetes, had thrown out all the flour and sugar in her house. Who, to keep Ah-Jack on his diet, had eaten the leftovers from every meal, gaining over twenty pounds in three months. Nan had never thought a day would come when Ah-Jack was no longer in Michelle's care.

"Now get in," Nan said, holding up the blanket for Ah-Jack to squirm under. He'd changed into a pair of old pajamas that Nan had found in the back of her closet, so old she couldn't figure out if they had belonged to her or her husband. She thought she'd thrown out everything of Ray's after he'd moved to California, but her husband had a tendency to insert himself into the cracks of her life.

Ah-Jack lowered himself onto the bed, bouncing lightly, as if to test the springs. Nan watched how gingerly he moved and fought the urge to help. She laid the blanket over him and gave his hand a small squeeze.

"I'll be right upstairs if you need anything," she said, lowering her voice as she turned out the lights. "Good night."

She was almost out of the room, already thinking about what she would do with Pat, when she heard Ah-Jack crack one last joke.

"This has absolutely ruined my day off." His voice was muffled beneath the covers. An old slyness had returned, off-key.

She laughed. It was what he wanted.

Nan was nearly at Pat's door when she heard a noise from out on the street. She didn't understand what the sounds were—an animal? a car honking?—but an unrecognized instinct kicked in. Pat was about to escape. She had to stop him.

Her eagerness to move made her paralysis all the more painful. Every breath she took marked another moment she might catch her son. One breath, and she could grab him by the elbow; another breath, his hand; yet another, by the collar of his shirt, wrenching him back from the window. A small grunt of effort came from inside; Pat was lowering himself down into the bushes. Her body unlocked.

She crashed into the door. Pat had shoved a stack of clothes and blankets up against it. The door kept catching on the pile, barely opening. She wrestled with the fabric. Finally eking out a space wide enough to get her foot through, she kicked the bundle out of the way and pushed into his room. Only to face an open window.

A warm breeze blew in, fluttering the pages of a comic book he'd left open on his desk. The bells of the good-luck charm she'd nailed over his bed hung silent. Nan gathered the pile of blankets on the ground. She dropped them in a heap at the end of the bed. The outline of a body wrinkled his sheets.

8

When his GPS announced that he'd arrived at his destination, Jimmy double-checked the address. The street he'd pulled onto was short and cramped. No more than a sliver of room existed between houses, thin paths barely wide enough for a person to slide through. Trees along the curb were spindly, newly grown. A steady stream of cars rumbled across a nearby highway bridge.

Jimmy had always assumed that Janine's calculations carried a queenly detachment. She sold houses to pass time, subdued men for the same reason. Her office was in the middle of downtown Bethesda. She drove a car that cost more than most people's salaries. Once, while searching for one of her cell phones, she'd pulled a Rolex out of her purse and tossed it like a tissue onto the table. But her house didn't even have a garage. Her Mercedes was parked on the street.

Jimmy cut across the stubbly lawn, dawdling on his way to the door. He was angry he hadn't thought of the possibility sooner. What if Janine worked not *with* Uncle Pang but *for* him? What if she was caught in the same bind that had held Jimmy and his father? How helpful could one trapped rat be to another?

Sweat pricked the backs of his ears. Last week, like an idiot, he'd suggested the possibility of a future without Uncle Pang.

But who could blame him? At his lowest point, she'd made him feel untouchable, materializing as if his heart had summoned her. He'd come back to the Duck House from the bank, having overdrafted his account by ten thousand dollars, and there she'd been, waiting by the bar with a bottle of champagne.

Hopping off a stool that a waiter must have dragged over for her, Janine told him that she wanted to make a toast. In his cramped office, she popped the champagne.

"Gan bei," she said. Her fingers caught the strings of froth slipping down the dark-green glass. He could practically taste her perfume in his mouth. "To starting anew."

"Hello, future," Jimmy said. He hid the sudden crush in his lungs. His bank account had loomed back onto the horizon.

They'd clinked their flutes together and Jimmy had prepared for his first taste of alcohol in over a year. Little bubbles jumped from the glass and fizzed against his wrist. The sweet fumes tickled his nose. Weeks of sleepless nights caught up to him. He fell into his office chair with such a *thud* that he sloshed champagne onto his leg. When Janine asked him what was wrong, he ignored her, opening and closing his desk drawer without taking anything out.

"Are you hurt?" she tried, and then, "Are you sick?" He expected her to keep pushing and prying. She'd clapped her hands in front of his face instead.

"If you won't tell me what's wrong, then stop making a fuss."

Jimmy stared up at her. She'd scolded him, as if he were a child.

"You're not acting like yourself," she added more gently.

The anger growing in Jimmy's throat died down. These would have been empty words from anyone else. He put his champagne down and laced his fingers together in his lap. Janine, who didn't seem invested in anything, was invested in him.

"I'm a little overwhelmed." He picked his words carefully. "This isn't what I imagined."

Janine took a sip of her champagne. Her lipstick left a faint imprint on the glass. "What's different?" she asked.

"Too many goodbyes. And not just the Duck House." He counted on his fingers. "My old customers. My employees." He hesitated. "You."

Janine's eyebrows barely lifted, but she sat down on his desk and crossed her legs.

"I have a confession to make," she said. "The toast was a front." She traced the outline of her mouth with a finger, smiling behind her hand. "I wanted to see if you would consider me for future projects. I think we work well together, don't you?"

"Of course we do." Jimmy leaned closer. Seconds ago, he'd had no future projects in mind. Now he did. Janine had that effect on him. He grew bolder. "I think we would work even better without Pang in between us."

"Middlemen should be cut out," she had said, her hand crossing the foot of professional space that had always separated them. "That's just good business."

Janine's eagerness to part with Uncle Pang had felt miraculous. The unexpected weight of her hand on Jimmy's arm had stunned him further. He hadn't asked any questions.

Studying her neighborhood again, Jimmy couldn't believe it was so different from what he had imagined, from what, he could swear, Janine had pretended it to be. He kicked a brown clump of grass on her lawn, digging his toe into the dry sod until he'd worked a hole in the ground.

At the door, he rang the bell with his thumb. Before the button could decompress, he pushed it again. This time, footsteps followed the muffled ring.

"Coming, coming," Janine yelled from inside. The door opened and the chill of her house hit his face. Vapors of a finished dinner hovered in the air. Her house was small on the inside but airy, all warm wood, mirrors, and soft lighting.

To his disappointment she was in her business clothes, with her makeup freshly applied. Almost eleven o'clock and her voluminous perm was not the least bit deflated. She looked no different than she had on the first day they'd met, when she'd aimed her gleaming car into a Duck House parking space with frightening speed and accuracy. Her ever-moving face still flustered him.

She was even wearing heels. On another woman, the shoes would have looked like torture, but Janine's hummingbird frame seemed to put no pressure on her feet. Following her into the kitchen, Jimmy was reminded of the Barbie dolls his niece, Annie, used to leave all over the place, their feet permanently molded into severe arches. He spotted no toys scattered around Janine's home; she must have tidied before he came.

"Will you get out of those shoes?" Jimmy tried to tease but sounded fussy instead. He'd slipped out of his shoes—force of habit—at the front door.

"I like to hold myself to a dress code," she said, but she stepped out of her heels and lined them against her oven. "Are you feeling better? You sounded so unlike yourself over the phone."

He tried to think of an answer. She pushed him into a chair and went to her pantry.

"I've got just the thing to loosen you up." She pulled out a fat glass bottle of baijiu and set it in front of him on the kitchen table.

He twisted the cork out and sniffed the bottle's opening.

"You drink this shit?" He wrinkled his nose at the searing sweetness.

"Same calories as vodka," she said. "But twice the kick."

Moving to the cupboard, she rustled up two ceramic cups, no bigger or deeper than his thumb. She sat down across from him and took the bottle out of his hand.

"We can't have a proper business meeting without a toast." She filled each cup. "Gan bei."

"Gan bei." Jimmy pushed his cup across the table with his finger to clink against hers, then knocked the liquor back. The taste filled his mouth with sour saliva. It reminded him of stealing too many shots from his father's basement bar. When he slammed his cup down on the table, he saw Janine taking small, finicky sips from hers.

"Are you fucking serious?" he said, suddenly remembering that he was already a little drunk.

"I don't do shots," she said.

He poured another cup and swallowed it. Heat crept up from the collar of his shirt. Soon, his eyes would be bloodshot. Janine did not say anything when he started laughing. She gripped her cup with both hands like a baseball pitcher.

"You're a fraud," he said. He turned the cup upside down and put it over his thumb like a hat.

"Jimmy." She sighed out his name. "What are you talking about?"

"You said Pang was a middleman," he said. "But he's your fucking boss."

"I don't understand," she said. "Pang is hardly my boss."

"He owns you."

Janine sat up straighter. "I've got no idea what you're talking about."

"Just admit it," Jimmy insisted. "I know how he works. He controls your client list and he probably takes a cut of every sale you make."

Janine's jaw shifted back and forth.

"How much does he take from you?" He wanted to nail her to her seat. "Ten percent? Twenty?"

Janine pushed away from the table and Jimmy took a breath to steady himself. He didn't want to lose her entirely.

His father's secret slipped out of him so easily, it was hardly a betrayal: "The Duck House has owed him a kickback every year it's been open."

Janine leaned her elbows on the table. "Are you sure you're okay?"

NUMBER ONE CHINESE RESTAURANT · 83

Jimmy was laughing again. "Haven't you been listening?"

"So he set up the same deal with the Glory," Janine said. "Is that why you fired him?"

"I fired him," Jimmy said, watching her carefully, "because he was planning to burn down the Duck House."

Janine's face twitched with too mild a surprise.

"You knew!" He stabbed his finger at her. The cup fell off his thumb and clattered against the table. Janine moved to plug up the baijiu, but Jimmy put his hand around the bottle. "I guess Pang tells his little girlfriend everything."

"Don't be disgusting." She crossed her arms and leaned back. "Did you think I just drove you around gesturing at buildings? I saw your finances." She gripped her body tighter. "I know what Pang's capable of." The high slope of her cheekbones caught the kitchen light, throwing her eyes into shadow. Behind her hooded lids, he saw arrogance.

"People like you are the worst kind of people," he said. The liquor was eating through his thoughts like acid. "You pretend you're better than everyone else, but you're a leech. Stop trying to hide! It's not flattering."

"What's not flattering is a man with two businesses and a mansion in Potomac acting like he's the victim." She took a sip from her cup. "People like me? You saw this house and this neighborhood and you think I lied to you."

Though Jimmy's throat was tight from shouting, the tension in his body dipped. Had he managed to wound Janine? Had he wanted to? He slumped over in his seat. "Why should I trust you?"

Janine stood up, took his empty cup and hers, and placed them in her sink.

"My ex-husband is the reason Pang is in my life." She turned on the water and rinsed out the cups. When she faced him again, her shirt was wet from where she'd pressed against the sink's edge. "He liked gambling, among other things. Pang helped him get what he wanted."

"I forgot about your ex," Jimmy said. The kitchen was small enough that Janine didn't have to raise her voice, but there was another reason she was speaking softly. On the counter, a small race car peeked out from behind the fruit bowl.

"Easy enough to," she said. "He's back in Shanghai. Pang had him deported, and he can't step foot back into the States."

"I'm sorry."

"Don't be. He left his Mercedes."

Jimmy started to laugh again.

"Pang got me started in real estate. He's kept my client list full. But my son cried for months. I've been doing everything I can to stand on my own."

Jimmy grabbed the salt and pepper shakers at the end of the table. They were two porcelain pigs, joined at the lips by a magnet. He pried them apart and let them clunk back together. He'd been right about Pang taking a cut from Janine. He smacked his lips lightly with satisfaction and put the shakers down. He liked that Janine had opened up to him. But hadn't her little speech sounded too much like the sob stories Johnny ate up? Jimmy couldn't let himself be distracted by her tricks. If they were tricks.

"I'm tired of talking." He rested his arms on the table and nestled his head, hot and sweaty, into them. The desire to trust her beckoned to him, like sleep in the middle of a snowdrift. "You talk me into circles."

She walked to his side and bent down, crouching on the balls of her feet.

"I'm sorry you're scared," she said. "But you're going to find the money without Pang. I saw your potential. I saw you doing great things."

Her confidence pissed him off. That air of entitlement was pure performance. She didn't have anything besides her cleverness. When she started to rise, Jimmy grabbed her by the arm. Without hesitation, she pinched the fingers of his left hand together, twisted sharply, and stood up.

"There's no point in talking when you're in this state," she said. "You should go home."

Mouth tight, Jimmy curled his fingers gently and rubbed them with his thumb. The clock on the oven told him he'd been there for less than half an hour. The drive over had taken longer. He couldn't leave without a plan. He had no idea what to do, besides set the restaurant on fire himself. Why did Janine think he could find the money? Was she trying to get him out of her house without a fight? Or had she overestimated his abilities? She thought he had a mansion in Potomac. But it wasn't his; it was his mother's.

"What if I sell the mansion?" he blurted out. The solution was so obvious it was as if Janine had planted it in his head.

"If you could sell the mansion, why did Pang need to burn down the Duck House in the first place?" Her tone couldn't disguise the curiosity in her face.

"Burning down a restaurant would be easier." Jimmy pinched his nose. "Look, the house is technically my mother's. And she'll fight me, but she's getting older, and she hasn't been the same since Dad died. I can get the house." He found that he was mimicking Janine's brisk tone, the one that had convinced him she knew what she was talking about.

"When do you want me to start looking for buyers?" She tilted her chin up, daring him to refuse.

Jimmy thought that for once he might see her face clearly. Not a centimeter of her twitched or changed; not even the vein in her forehead seemed to pulse. But he could not discern if she was beautiful. He knew her too well. Her face had taken on the blurring soft glow of a faded photograph, well worn by thumbs.

"Let's go, then." He pushed himself to his feet.

"Go where?" She began playing with her sleek necklace, the pearls no doubt warm from her skin's heat. "I can't leave Eddie."

"The boy is almost seven." Jimmy nabbed her heels from under the oven. The inside leather was moist to the touch. "He can spend an hour alone."

Janine followed him to the front door, her body magnetized to his. Did she like seeing him this full of steam?

"I have to move fast. I need to know you're on my side." He put her heels down on the floral doormat. She watched him struggle to balance while he wrestled on his shoes.

"Last chance." He willed her to bend to him. "Think—with this sale, you'll be free of him. We both will."

"Just—" She looked up the stairs. Jimmy looked up as well, relieved not to see her son clinging to the railing. If he never saw the kid, he might as well not exist. "Just let me call my neighbor. I know she's still up and she owes me."

Jimmy pumped his fist behind his back. "I'll be waiting in my car."

"No way." Janine reached into a ceramic bowl next to the staircase. She tossed him a set of keys. She couldn't quite keep the excitement out of her voice. "I'm driving us. You need to sober up."

Hadn't she wanted him to drive himself home? He shuffled out the door and dropped down on the cement stairs to fix his shoes. He had no plan to convince his mother to sell her house, but he didn't need one. All he had to do was get Janine on the hook. She was an ambitious little weasel, and figuring this out about her had opened a secret window into her head. If he couldn't come up with a way to sell the mansion, she would. As long as he got her to tour the place, she would do everything in her power to get the listing. He almost hoped for a struggle from his mother. The longer the ordeal, the more time he had left with Janine.

He rose from the stoop. The neighborhood now looked friendly, scattered fireflies blinking against the black night. He raised Janine's keys over his head and unlocked the Mercedes, relishing the sound of the front doors, then the back, clicking open. First her house, and now her car.

"So what do you think?" Jimmy whispered. He flipped on every switch he passed. The mansion blazed with light. His mother was in the house but sleeping, cocooned in the labyrinthine basement. Jimmy reassured Janine that ever since his mother had broken her leg a year ago, she took a sedative twice a day, once for her afternoon nap and once at night. A few weeks ago she'd slept through an entire construction crew tearing down the house next door; her dose was that strong. Janine did not look convinced, and she startled when his phone rang, her stilettos sounding out sharply against the marble tiles. Jimmy silenced his cell phone through his pocket. Janine slipped out of her heels.

"You grew up in this place?" She marveled at the sky-high ceiling that the open foyer offered up. A chandelier the size of a small child dangled at the center. By the spiral staircase, a large china urn overflowed with plastic cherry blossoms. "No wonder you act like such a spoiled brat sometimes."

He knew she was teasing, but he couldn't help saying, "We moved here when I was almost in high school. Even after we unpacked, most of the rooms stayed empty."

"Can I see the rest of the house?"

He hooked her by the elbow. "Follow me."

They finished the first story of the house quickly. Janine was too nervous to do more than peek her head into a room before moving on to the next. She skipped the library altogether, the entrance to the basement too close for comfort. But by the time he followed her up the stairs, she began to relax.

"This staircase is beautiful," she said. Her fingers traced the wood railing. "A bit dusty, though." She laughed and brushed off her hand.

She began trotting up the stairs, her stockinged feet whispering against the wood. Her behind twitched with every step. He could have planted his face right into the heart of her ass. Too soon, they reached the top. He showed her the master bedroom, with its adjoining office space; his brother's old room, untouched since Johnny had left for college; and his own bedroom.

"They turned this into an office?" Janine said, when he turned on the light. They stared at the boxes and crates filling out the corners of the room.

"More like a storage unit," he said, hovering at the door. He hadn't been in his bedroom since his father had died.

When Jimmy had lived in the house, his bedroom was where he'd spent most of his free time. After years of sharing with Johnny, he'd been overwhelmed, at first, to have his own room. But soon this bedroom became his refuge from the house around it. The mansion's largeness, the dark woods outside, the empty hallways filled only by his father's explosive sneezes: The new house had been too grand to ever be comfortable.

Now Jimmy—or, rather, his ex-wife—had a house in Fairwood, a neighborhood that was the clone of his parents', right down to the stone fountains and massive gates. Directing Janine into Belle Terre, he'd felt none of the awe he remembered from his adolescence. While she'd cooed over the spread of land and the hedge of oak trees that guided them down the winding community road, he'd sat back and enjoyed her eagerness.

Then to see his room filled with boxes and cabinets. He hadn't realized how deeply he'd craved a return to its security. He took a step back, and the floorboards creaked. Janine looked over her shoulder, and Jimmy quickly shifted forward again. He forced himself to walk farther into the room and didn't stop until he'd reached the wide windows. The curtains and sheer linings were the only familiar items left from his past. He ran his hand along a gauzy panel, wishing he could wrap himself tight inside the fabric as he used to do when he was bored, or lonely, or afraid of his boredom and loneliness. From inside this opaque cocoon, the world outside his window had softened. He would smell the staticky odor of the panel, the dust that spun out from all his twisting, and he would grow calmer, until he unwound himself and returned to whatever homework or video game he'd paused. Now he could only wrap his hand in the milky fabric. The chandelier light threaded the white with unexpected glints of color.

"Are you okay?" Janine was at his shoulder, her hand covering his wrapped one.

"Just a little irritated." He took comfort in the one emotion he had any control over. "She didn't tell me she was remaking my bedroom."

Janine's hand squeezed his.

"Now," he said, "I won't feel half as bad for putting this house on the market."

"This place will sell for three times what your parents paid." Her other hand went back up to her pearls. "This community has the right amount of prestige and accessibility. Perfect for anyone with new money looking to trade up."

"A nice commission for the real estate agent," Jimmy said.

Janine smoothed back the hairs curling at her temple. "Not many agents would know where to find the right market," she said.

With a quick swirl of his wrist, Jimmy bound Janine's hand tightly against his with the sheer drape. Their palms pressed together through the layers of cloth. For a long moment, neither pulled away.

"You think I'm just going to hand this house over to you?" he said softly.

Janine slipped her captured hand free. She walked away to examine the room's crown molding. "You aren't going to make selling this house easy, are you?"

"What can I say?" He sneezed from the dust. "Money makes people unpredictable. 'Just like women,' my dad always said."

"Everything is like women." She blew a strand of her hair away from her face. "How clichéd. Like father, like son."

Jimmy swung his leg back and kicked the nearest box of folders with the side of his foot. The impact made a hollow and resounding noise, like an echo, and Janine jumped a little. He kicked another box, then another, hard enough for the cardboard tops to pop off and settle crooked.

"Stop it!" she hissed.

"This fucking house is too quiet." He knocked over a row of binders stacked on a metal cabinet. "It's always been too quiet."

"What are you doing? Your mother!"

"She's not waking up." He rapped the side of the cabinet with his knuckles. "You might as well join me, because I'm not stopping."

"You're making a huge mess."

"This was already a huge mess," he said. "You think because something is neatly filed away it's not a huge fucking mess?"

She retreated to the doorway, one foot on either side of the threshold. Her toes curled and uncurled inside her sheer stockings, looking for a grip. Jimmy felt a sudden meanness overtake him.

"Let me wash your feet."

"What are you talking about?" Her toes shrank back and did not uncurl.

"If you let me wash your feet, I'll let you sell this house." He leaned against the cabinet, elbow pressed into the dull edge.

"Why should I trust you?" She stood on her tiptoes, flexing her calves. For the first time, she looked unsteady on her toes.

"It's a little risky," he said. "But what do you lose?"

"You'll have to sell it eventually," she said slowly.

"My mother will find somewhere else to live," he agreed. He'd heard her surrender, but if she needed him to let her play the game out, he was willing.

"Your brother might intervene." She stretched herself taller, holding her hand out for balance.

"You're a single working mother. He'll consider it one of his charities."

"You have a foot fetish?" She extended one pointed foot, forming a graceful curve. "Just take a picture."

He came over and bent down, lifting the foot higher with a finger under her heel. The skin was rough beneath the sheer satin of her stocking. "I just want to see what it feels like to wash your feet."

"You're a sick boy." Her voice didn't sound teasing, but she lifted her foot up to his downturned face, as if she wanted him to kiss it.

"I saw my father do it once."

"To your mother?"

Jimmy paused, remembering. "To his mother."

Janine's foot reached up and tapped his right cheek.

"It's the only memory of this house that I kind of like." He straightened. "Sometimes you just want to do something to see, okay?"

"This is strictly business." She stepped back to let him through the doorway.

"I think you'll enjoy it," he said.

He brought her back into the master bedroom and through the double doors that opened into the bathroom. The counters were cluttered with pill bottles and opened packages of panty hose and skin cream. His mother had been obsessively neat while his father was alive but had clearly relaxed her strict routines since his death. Jimmy pushed past two walk-in closets that sat kitty-corner to each other. Janine seemed to gather strength from their size and expense. Through another set of double doors, they came upon the toilet, the shower, and the Jacuzzi bath.

"Sit here." He gestured to the pink marble ledge bordering the bath.

He cranked the taps, struggling with the handles, which had not been turned in who knew how many years. The bottom of the tub was fuzzy with dust, which the gushing water washed away. He tested the water temperature, wetting his hand every few seconds, first under the faucet and then, after he'd plugged up the tub drain, by dipping his fingers into the rising pool. Janine sat, legs crossed, and watched him work. Her hands were folded on her top knee.

To pass time as the tub filled, Jimmy spoke of his grandmother, the one person his father had truly loved. His father had hated leaving his mother behind in China. He'd argued constantly with Uncle Pang about getting her a green card, one that the old woman, according to Jimmy's mother, didn't even want.

Toward the end of her life, his grandmother had acquired a visa to come stay with Jimmy's family for a month. Jimmy saw the washing, by accident, on the third night of her visit. On his way up to his bedroom, he'd heard a curious splashing on the first floor and looked through a crack in the guest room door.

Jimmy knew his father led his grandmother to her guest room every night—Jimmy had assumed because the old woman was scared of their large house. But through the door, he'd seen his father's back hunched over a plastic tub of steaming water. His grandmother sat in front of the tub, her slippers discarded on the carpet. His father was gently washing her feet. His cupped hands cascaded water over her pale, floating arches. Her eyes were closed in pleasure. Jimmy had stumbled back from the door, his insides squirming with unnamed emotion. The man had never touched Jimmy's mother in front of the family except to nudge her out of the way. He used his hands to cuff Jimmy on the side of the head, and even Johnny got only a hard, stiff clap on the shoulder for his achievements. But for Jimmy's grandmother, his father's hands transformed into tender creatures. Jimmy had avoided that part of the house for the rest of her stay.

"How beautiful," Janine breathed, breaking into the end of his story. "Maybe one day my Eddie will treat me so well."

Jimmy pointed at her stockings. "Will you take those off?"

Janine slowly shimmied her tights down to her knees, then folded the nylon down each calf. Her bare foot emerged, nails shining but unpolished. She kicked the stocking off her left foot. The wrinkled, fleshy hose looked at once normal and obscene.

Jimmy reached out and cupped the backs of her calves, swinging her legs over the ledge of the tub and into the water, which had been turned opaque by froth and heat. "I should give you a kick in the face," she said, but she rested her legs solidly in his hands. He liked the weight of her calves.

He shut off the faucet when the water lapped against her ankles. Kneeling against the steps to the bath, he lifted one of her feet just barely out of the water.

Her hands gripped the edge of the tub, framing her seat. "Don't you dare look up my skirt."

She had pressed her knees together, but her fitted skirt offered a small, dark hole through which, if he peered at just the right angle, he might see. Jimmy dipped his head down and lifted his eyes up, smiling.

Janine started to giggle—not laugh, *giggle*—and the harder she tried to stop, the harder her body shook. Her cheeks turned pink and a drop of sweat slipped down the side of her face. She looked as if she couldn't believe she'd gotten herself into this mess. He copied the cupping–spilling motion he had caught his father using years ago. When he switched to her other foot, she quieted down. The only sounds were of water falling against more water and their even breaths.

"This is nice," she said, her voice faraway.

Her mouth had relaxed, falling open a sliver. He wanted to slip his tongue into that space, to catch her bottom lip between his teeth. Would Janine let him kiss her if he tried? Would he forgive her for her desperation if she did? He didn't know. But if she kissed him back while laughing that big, frightening laugh of hers? He would forgive her in a heartbeat. Because then he would know that she was submitting to this washing out of curiosity, out of daring. That she wasn't just humiliating herself to sell a house.

A series of muffled sounds came from downstairs.

"What is that?" Janine whispered, upsetting the water as she plunked her feet onto the tub floor. "Is that your mother?"

"It can't be." Jimmy refused to panic, as if by acting nonchalant he might will the noise to stop. The sounds grew louder.

"Jimmy!" His mother was awake and howling his name. "Jimmy!"

Jimmy and Janine whipped into action, jumping away from the tub, careful not to get the floor too wet. Janine grabbed her stockings and Jimmy pulled the bath's plug.

"I'll lead her into the kitchen," he whispered loudly. They hurried out of the bathroom. "Let yourself out and go home. I'll get a cab."

"We'll do lunch tomorrow," she said. She slipped behind the bedroom door and he ran downstairs.

His mother was at the bottom of the stairs. She looked crazed. Her hair was falling out of her pink rollers and she had a phone clutched to her chest.

"Mom," Jimmy started to say, moving her away from the foyer.

He was frightened by her chattering teeth. How could his unannounced visit have upset her this badly? He dragged her into the kitchen.

Before he could continue, his mother began to wail. Jimmy clutched her shoulders, so startled that he almost slapped her. He'd never heard her make this much noise before, and he felt sick as the sounds coming out of her grew louder. Her hands scratched at the sides of her face, clobbering the phone against her cheek.

Then as suddenly as she started, she stopped. She regarded him curiously, as if wondering whether or not to share her news.

"What is it, Mom?" he asked. "What's wrong?"

"Your restaurant's on fire," his mother announced, dropping the phone. "Someone burned it down to the ground."

9

The first two decades of Jimmy's life, he believed cooks didn't talk in the kitchen. Waiters could shout, dishwashers could flirt with the duck carvers, but the cooks stood silent over their woks. They were like the old horses Jimmy had once seen on a duck farm in Long Island, with their sloped backs and long, motionless faces. They looked too miserable for words.

He was a few months shy of twenty when he walked into Koi's pristine lobby on the first day of his stage. He passed the indoor waterfall and rock garden, through the restaurant's sunlit dining room. He assumed he was about to enter an equally soundless kitchen. The chef, a white man named Alfred, led the way.

"I don't usually let people stage who haven't worked in a kitchen before." The chef glanced down at the over-packed knife kit in Jimmy's hands. "How many résumés did you fax me again?"

"A lot," Jimmy said. "Chef," he added.

"Sixty résumés. And not a single one with relevant work experience." Chef Alfred knocked back a double shot of espresso. "But you have passion. That's something you can't teach." He thought for a moment. "You can use a knife, though, yes?"

Jimmy nodded. He'd been practicing on crates of onions filched from the Duck House, and he'd gone through so many that the amount of missing produce was driving his father crazy. Jimmy's father had no idea who to blame, and when he wasn't on the phone with the produce supplier, he was interrogating every person on staff, from the prep cooks to the little girl who poured water on the weekends. Served him right, the asshole. If Bobby hadn't thrown him out of the Duck House for wanting to apprentice at Koi, Jimmy could have afforded to buy his own practice onions. The tips he'd saved had run out with his rent check, and stages didn't pay. He felt too young for the knives he was holding. He was nineteen and had never been broke in his life.

"Knife skills, we can teach," the chef was saying. "But we'd rather not."

"Thank you for this opportunity," Jimmy said. They approached the kitchen doors, and excitement replaced his dread. Two months ago, after his mother insisted they go for her birthday, he'd eaten here for the first time. His world had split open, as neatly as an apricot. His father had not enjoyed the meal.

Chef Alfred put his hand on the kitchen door and pushed his way in. "You're free labor," he said, before the sound of pans crashing together swallowed his words. The noise was sudden and explosive. Jimmy didn't realize most of it was coming from a stereo in the back.

"Shut that fucking death metal off, Ronny!" Chef Alfred screamed, his pale face growing mottled as he battled the volume of the music. "Or I'll fucking gut you!"

The kitchen was full of stout men with sleeve tattoos and wild, unfocused looks in their eyes, but to Jimmy's surprise, Ronny turned out to look not unlike himself. Strolling to the stereo, Ronny turned the volume dial a scooch to the left, looking at the chef with what Jimmy's father would've called a smack-me face.

"Hurry it up." Chef Alfred was tasting the stock. He rapped the spoon against the edge of the pot. Ronny held up a long finger and continued his slow turning.

"I'm trying to find the perfect compromise, Chef." He wrinkled his nose to push up his John Lennon glasses. "Not too quiet, not too loud, just right."

"I'll shove that tape up your ass, how's that for a compromise?"

"I can't work without my music," Ronny said, his voice a playful whine, but he turned the volume dial from 10 to 6. The caterwauling of the Norwegian vocalist died to a medium yowl; he sounded as if he were coughing up phlegm now rather than blood.

"That's our fish cook, Ronny," Chef Alfred said. "I don't know why I haven't cut him yet, but you'll be helping out at his station."

"Chef, I got that eel." Ronny came up to them with a plated terrine of unagi over toasted rice. The smell of mirin, sake, and sesame oil, the holy trinity of fragrance, hit Jimmy's nose. His stomach grumbled, loud enough for both men to hear. He'd been living off onion sandwiches for a week.

"Little dude is hungry!" Ronny clapped Jimmy on the shoulder.

Chef Alfred carved a spoon through the tower and chewed. He began to hum softly. A dreamy look settled over his face and he leaned against a steel prep table.

"That's it." He sucked the sauce off his teeth. "That's why you're still here."

"Butchered it myself," Ronny said, then he turned to Jimmy. "Want a taste?"

Jimmy grabbed the chef's spoon and shoved half the terrine into his mouth before he realized his mistake. The two men looked at him with shocked faces.

"Shit, that was for the rest of the kitchen," Ronny said, looking at the plate.

"We taste in the kitchen; we don't eat," Chef Alfred said.

Jimmy knew he should be embarrassed, but the eel was buttery and sweet in his mouth, flaking against his tongue like snow, and the toasted rice cut through the softness with a nutty crunch. His stomach filled with warmth. He reached out for the plate again, before Ronny could pull it away, and plucked a crisp half-moon of cucumber to clear the unagi sauce off his tongue.

"That was amazing," he said, picking a sesame seed out of his teeth. "Like, one of the best things I've eaten in my entire life. Can you teach me how to make it?"

"Where the fuck did you find this kid?" Ronny asked. "He just hoovered my dish."

"Reminds me of you," a passing cook said, stockpot in his arms.

"Yo, that's racist!" Ronny called over his shoulder. Then he pushed the plate into Jimmy's hands. "What's your name?"

"Jim—"

"Gonna call you Hoover." With that, Ronny brought Jimmy around the kitchen, introducing him to the other cooks and kitchen staff. Jimmy quickly learned that Ronny was the unofficial ambassador of the Koi crew, untethered by kitchen hierarchy. He not only knew everybody—prep cooks, line cooks, and pastry chefs alike—but had recently partied with, schemed with, or owed money to each person who shook Jimmy's hand. He reminded Jimmy of a cruder, cooler version of his own brother.

"This racist fucker is Key." Ronny grabbed the white cook with the stockpot by the back of his neck. "He's the saucier. Don't ever let this man drive your car. And over here"—he fist-bumped a Hawaiian man with three skull rings on his hand—"is Lewis the grill man. You ever need a fake license, you call him. You still do passports, Lew?"

Ronny finished the tour with the dishwashers, a trio of Hondurans who looked at the empty plate in Jimmy's hands with open disgust.

"They usually get a taste after the rest of the kitchen," Ronny whispered, bringing Jimmy back to his station. "Look, we'll get you back into everyone's good graces." He reached under his prep table and pulled out a big blue bucket. Something was thunking against the plastic. Jimmy looked down to see a swirl of freshwater eels, their gray-and-white bodies thick and tangled in the low water.

"You ever butcher an eel before?" Ronny put on a blood-spotted fillet glove. He stuck his hand in the bucket and pulled out a wriggling eel by the head, its thin, muscular body almost the length of Jimmy's arm. "I made this contraption myself." He pointed to the wet board on his table, a screwdriver sticking out of the wood.

"How do you butcher an eel?" Jimmy asked. A strange floating sensation clouded his head. He realized his hands were sweating.

"Easy," Ronny said. In one fluid motion, he slammed the eel onto the board and stuck the screwdriver through its head. He hammered the driver down with the flat of his knife, then stuck the blade below the gills, running it down the length of the eel until he'd butterflied it in half. Jimmy started breathing hard through his nose, black spots dancing in his vision. Ronny spread the eel open like a book, and as he was dragging the knife back down, peeling the translucent white flesh off the skin, Jimmy felt his eyes roll up in his head. With a strangled curse he went down hard.

He came to when he felt someone's clog push against his ribs. He rolled up into a seated position, clinging to the leg of the prep table while the blood rushed into his head. Blinking up at Ronny, he felt like crawling out of the kitchen and into the busy street.

"You shit yourself?" Ronny asked, as if Jimmy were a toddler he didn't particularly like. He scratched his nose with the side of his glove. "Look, why don't you go gut those tomatoes?"

His knife pointed to the stack of crates by the walk-in fridge. "Can you handle that?"

Jimmy nodded, his face still clammy. He stood up on his own, Ronny having already turned back to his butcher board. He'd finished off four eels while Jimmy was passed out. The fillets were curled up like sausage casings, piled next to a stack of emptied skins. Jimmy slapped his cheeks and moved toward the tomatoes.

"The tomatoes aren't bleeding," Ronny shouted after him. "It's just juice." He turned to the other cooks, cackling. "Yo, you see that, Lew? When's the last time any of you fuckers passed out like that?"

The cooks traded stories, the noise in the kitchen growing again; Jimmy sliced tomato after tomato. He was so mad at himself that he squeezed a few to bursting, and he hid those beneath the seeded guts he'd scraped from the others. With Chef Alfred no longer in the kitchen, Ronny turned his music back up, head-banging while he ripped his way through the rest of the eels. The flaps of his bandanna flew, wild; his glasses grew splattered with water and blood. Jimmy watched him from the corner of his eye, fighting the queasiness in his stomach. So this was what a real cook looked like, sounded like, moved like. If the cooks at the Duck House were workhorses, then Ronny and the rest of this kitchen were demon dogs, wrestling their prey and each other to the ground. Dogs with finesse hidden even in their most violent, butchering acts. Dogs who could fucking cook.

Jimmy wondered where he might go to get his hands on some live eels.

It took Jimmy two months, working behind Ronny every single night, before the fish cook bothered to speak to him outside the instructions he barked during prep and service. That night, a packed Saturday service, Chef Alfred finally called Jimmy up to assist. He took the scallops while Ronny worked the fish, and together they built a rhythm that made Jimmy's veins feel lit up beneath his skin. Every inch of him vibrated with fear, yet he did not come undone. Instead, with every passing hour, his movements grew sharper and faster. He couldn't believe he had managed to harness this awful energy. He felt invincible, as if he'd managed to take the loose, liquid sand that made up the inexplicable world inside him and pack it until it ceased its shifting.

At the tail end of the dinner rush, while craning his head to see Chef Alfred's reaction to the scallops he'd just plated, Jimmy grabbed a hot sauté pan without a towel in hand. He yelped. Ronny, without turning to look, asked Lew, who was on the grill opposite, if he had some burn cream. The grill man grinned through the sweat dripping down his nose. The chateaubriand in his tongs spat hot oil.

"Fuck burn cream," Jimmy shot back, though his hand was so tender that the heat of the air made it sting. "Put that shit on your pussy. Fix that burning sensation when you pee."

He'd never spoken this loudly in the kitchen before. His first few weeks, he'd kept getting stepped on for standing too quietly. But he'd been absorbing the crack and cadence of the cooks' bravado, their complicated insults and even more convoluted retorts. Jimmy waited, watching his scallops, to see if he'd hit his mark.

"Hoover *got you*!" Lewis howled, leaning his shaved head back.

"Who did Hoover get?" Key asked, on his way back from presenting the tea-egg appetizer to the chef.

But Ronny gave only a thin smile and bent his head over his sea bass. His refusal to play along starved the oxygen from Jimmy's little ember. Lewis went back to his grill. Key fired up a new miso glaze.

After service ended, however, and Jimmy had finished cleaning up the fish station, Ronny waved him over to the restaurant bar.

"Saved you some of the family meal." Ronny jutted his chin at the plate of cold pasta on the counter. He'd also gotten Jimmy a glass of iced tea, with a thick wedge of lemon bobbing in the center. Parched, Jimmy took a big gulp. He nearly choked. The iced tea was almost all vodka. For a second, he held the glass to his mouth, watching the man in front of him. Then he swallowed half the glass down.

"Guess you're coming out with us tonight," Ronny said.

Ronny had Jimmy drive him and a few of the other cooks to a Korean restaurant right outside Chinatown. A jittery neon sign read, OPEN LATE. They ordered a round of Kirin before they'd even sat down. The beer came out with a cluster of small plates, holding kimchi, pickled radish, potato salad, and tiny sardines. Ronny, who knew the owner, had him bring out a mystery dish, which turned out to be raw blue crab smothered in Korean chili paste and green onions.

"It's a fucking delicacy!" Ronny shouted, bullying the more squeamish cooks, but Jimmy needed no pushing. He was the first to suck the sweet, slippery flesh straight out of the crab. By the time the bowl was emptied, he had a tingling ring of red around his mouth, cracking up everybody around him. They dubbed him "Hot Lips," then "Crabs," before settling on "Suckee Long Time." Jimmy left the sauce on for so long that when he finally wiped the ring off with a napkin, the skin underneath was puffy and inflamed. At half past two, the cooks started settling their checks, throwing crumpled bills on the table, which was littered with empty beer bottles, stained napkins, and crab shells. Ronny dug through his pockets and cursed. He'd left his wallet back at Koi.

"I can cover you," Jimmy said. Since Uncle Pang had taken pity on him and given him a side job, his wallet had become too fat to close. He'd worked a house party last night and made two thousand dollars. He took a couple of twenties out to add to the pile.

Ronny eyed the money for a long moment. Then he lumbered up to lead the group out of the narrow little restaurant. "We're making a few more stops," he said, over his shoulder. "Hoover's paying!"

The cooks around Jimmy cheered. Lew squeezed his shoulder and Key whooped right into his ear. Warmth sloshed around Jimmy's chest. If he'd been sober, he might have been embarrassed by his own delight. He pumped his fist into the air.

"Let's get fucked up!" he shouted, waving his key over his head. The cooks piled into his parents' old Lexus, scuffing the leather seats with their dirty clogs, pushing and jabbing for space. Jimmy adjusted his rearview mirror. The cooks were arguing over who would have to crouch in the trunk. In the passenger seat, Ronny leaned over and shoved a dirty key under Jimmy's nose. It smelled brassy and chemical. A small white mound perched on the central groove.

"You're first," Ronny said.

Jimmy pinched one nostril down, then sniffed hard and leaned his head back. He closed his eyes and listened to Lew hefting his heavy body over the back of the second row. There was laughter. Lew shouting, "Let go of my pants, fucker!" Someone else yelling as Lew's clog clipped him on the side of his head.

Jimmy knew then that he would pick up every check these cooks could think to make. Anything to be part of this exclusive club of outsiders and freaks. To be able to nod at each of them in the kitchen the next morning, meet their bloodshot eyes with his and say, "Crazy fucking night." To know he had paid for it to be possible. They, in turn, would teach him how to cook, to eat, to party, to hustle. How to carve an eel to shreds and burn his hand into an unfeeling piece of meat. How to fill a room with terrible snarling music and hear no shit from anyone. He would finally learn what it felt like to be untouchable. He would pay any cost.

10

_____

Annie honked her horn, waited five seconds, then honked twice more. She fiddled with the air-conditioning until she saw Pat emerge from the bushes on the side of his house. The clock read half past twelve, but Annie was wide awake. It might as well have been the afternoon. The radio played a discordant mix of techno. A flurry of bats swept down from a nearby tree.

Pat climbed into her car wearing a backpack, which jangled when he shifted it onto his lap. She tried to ignore how childish he looked holding on to the pack. At least he'd changed into a tight white shirt.

"Hey there." When she turned her head, she let her hair fall over one eye.

He leaned in, grabbed her behind the neck, and kissed her. The kiss ended sooner than she expected. He tapped her steering wheel. "Let's go."

"Bossy." The throbbing between her legs was distracting. "Where?"

"The Duck House," he said.

"You're kidding."

"I have something I want to show you." He played with the zipper on his pack.

"You're sure you can't show me in the backseat?" She shifted her car into neutral and let the wheels glide on their own momentum.

He reached over and pushed the gear back into drive.

"Trust me."

"What do you have in the backpack?" She tapped her foot on the brake.

"Fireworks." He gave her a big, wet kiss on the cheek, laughing when she wiped at the spot. His energy filled the car and lapped at her body. Her left leg danced up and down.

"It better wow me."

"Just drive." Pat's tone was teasing but impatient.

Annie wanted to pinch his cheek until it bled. Show him that a high schooler couldn't bully her. She pressed hard on the gas instead. The car shot forward, wheels whirring. Pat's backpack hit his chest with a *clank*.

Pat directed her from the Duck House to the sprawling apartment complex behind the back lot, where he had her park. Running out of the car, he opened her door for her. His apology. She accepted it, and his hand; his thumb lingered on her skin. She knew she had the softest skin of anyone. He kissed the back of her hand before letting go.

"Come on." He slung his backpack over one shoulder. "Over here."

They approached the apartment complex, which held seven buildings, each at least four stories tall. The outsides of the structures were clean and well maintained. She spotted a small playground between two of them.

"This is where the amigos live?" She'd pictured someplace grimmer.

Pat gave her a look. Maybe she wasn't allowed to use the term outside the restaurant. Her neck and cheeks heated up, which made her dig her heels in harder.

"They look so poor and dirty." She walked up a set of white concrete steps. In the yellow lamplight, chalk drawings appeared. "I thought they lived in tents."

To her surprise, Pat grabbed her and lifted her up in the air.

"You're so fucking evil." He set her back down and tugged on a lock of her hair.

"I can say whatever I want." Her ribs ached where his arms had been.

"Sure." He grabbed her wrist and pulled. "Come on, fireworks."

She followed him to a low chain-link fence that cut the apartment complex in two. Pat scooped her up in his arms and carried her bridal style over a sagging drop in the fence.

"Here we are." He set her down on top of a large stump. Wood dust sprinkled the surrounding grass.

"You are so full of shit," she said. "Where're my fireworks?"

"We have to build them first." He unzipped his pack and pulled out a bottle of baijiu and a fifth of rum. He opened the rum and tipped the liquor out onto the grass.

"What the hell are you doing?" She grabbed the bottle and held it away from him.

"I need them half full." He held out his hand. As if she'd give it back to him now.

"Fuck that." She took a big swig, her lips burning where the alcohol touched. "Every time you spill a drink, an angel loses its wings."

"We can't drink all that." He scratched at the corner of the baijiu label. "You won't be able to drive."

"Whatever, we'll call a cab."

He made another grab for the rum, but she held it over her head and skipped out of reach.

"We can't do that," he said. He was working hard to keep something off his face. He was *nervous*.

"What's wrong with you?" She handed the bottle back to him and felt for the keys in her skirt pocket. "I'm going home."

"Hey, no, come on." He fumbled with his backpack. The distant sound of a baby crying came from an apartment building. Annie was trying to find which one when Pat took out a wad of something she couldn't quite make out. She leaned in closer. The smell hit her first. For a moment, Annie was a child again, playing with her grandmother's hands while she counted out the restaurant register.

"Why do you have that?"

"I got a part-time job." He pointed to the lot. "Setting that dumpster on fire."

Annie had to laugh, one loud syllable cracking out of her chest. Who was this kid? She'd had boys take her out to five-star restaurants, sneak her into clubs, and, once, fill a room with rose petals, but nothing like this.

"What am I?" she asked. "Your getaway car?"

Pat put the money away. "I was going to ask what you wanted." He held up the baijiu.

She grabbed the bottle. How had Pat known that she wouldn't storm off as soon as he revealed his plan? That instead she would feel an urge to rise to his unstated challenge? Most times, his intuition flattered her, but there were moments, like now, when he anticipated her thoughts before they'd crossed her mind. She wanted to throw her arms up in front of her face to block his view.

She focused on opening the bottle and taking another swig. The pungent liquor flooded down her throat. She felt warm and brave. The night opened up around her.

"If you want my help," she said, almost believing the confidence in her voice, "then we do things my way."

Slowly, Pat lifted his bottle up to his lips. He waited for her cue.

"Gan bei," she said.

They drank until their throats could no longer muscle the liquor down. They lowered their bottles, gasping and making faces at each other. She checked the liquid left. They drank again.

A light sleeper—more so with every passing year—Ah-Jack stirred at the screeching of tires outside Nan's house. He woke up completely when the lock slid open. By the time Pat crept past the living room, Ah-Jack was sitting up on the foldout couch.

"Late night?" He cleared the phlegm from his throat.

Pat jumped and bit back a yell. Ah-Jack forgot that his presence was a surprise.

"Why are you here?" Pat asked. He was coughing from inhaling too sharply.

"Locked myself out of my house," Ah-Jack joked.

Pat started to walk down the hallway, his steps no longer so careful.

"You should be happy you have such a nice home to come back to." Ah-Jack made his voice stern. "You really worried your mother."

"I'll get better at sneaking out, then," Pat said. He had a nervous edge to his words, which pricked Ah-Jack's ears. His godson, in his blackest moods, had always been polite with him.

"Are you okay?" He struggled off the couch and walked over to the boy, who backed up into the kitchen.

"I'm fine."

"You're shaking." Ah-Jack flipped on the kitchen lights. Pat covered his eyes with his hand. His shirt was torn. The remaining fabric rippled over his trembling body. "What happened?"

"You mean, what did I do?" Pat's voice cracked at the end.

"You stink," Ah-Jack said. "I don't . . . It's only . . . why do you smell like smoke?"

"Maybe I was smoking." Pat moved away from him again, putting the kitchen table between them.

The boy needed a tranquilizer, and Ah-Jack, who'd started drinking when he was much younger than seventeen, knew what might calm him. He went to the liquor cabinet to grab the whiskey Nan had confiscated earlier, but Pat was already at the freezer, his arm poking around inside. He unearthed a small pint of off-brand bourbon, half empty, and shook the frost off his hand. Pat grabbed an extra tumbler for Ah-Jack, filling both glasses. His politeness had reappeared.

Ah-Jack grabbed his glass from Pat's side of the table. "Cheers," he said.

Pat sat down and knocked back his glass in two thirsty gulps. Ah-Jack hadn't even wet his lips.

"My God, it's whiskey, not water!" Ah-Jack teased. He refilled Pat's glass.

"You can go back to sleep," Pat said.

"I've got the day off tomorrow. I can get a little wild tonight." Ah-Jack looked over to see if Pat had cracked a smile, but the boy had sunk his head into his arms.

"I thought you could handle your drink better," Ah-Jack said. He shuffled over to Pat's side. His godson was fighting back tears. "What's wrong?"

"Leave me alone," Pat managed through gritted teeth. "I'm fine."

"Your problems are my problems." Ah-Jack gripped him by the shoulders.

"I barely know you." Pat lifted his red face.

"That's nonsense! Do you want me to get your mother?"

"Don't!" Pat started up from the table, nearly knocking over his chair. "Don't tell her anything."

"I'm sure she's awake," Ah-Jack said. "Waiting up for you."

Pat laughed and grabbed for his bottle. He planted his sneering mouth right on the lip and drank. "She never stays up anymore."

"Let's go and find out, then."

Faster than Ah-Jack could blink, Pat was in front of him, his hands out as if ready to shove Ah-Jack back if he tried anything. The boy had forgotten to take off his sneakers; they squeaked against the tiled floor.

"Stay out of our business," Pat said.

"Why are you acting this way?" Ah-Jack tried to reason with the boy. "Let me out. Your mother doesn't need this."

"How do you know what she needs?" Pat puffed up his body, filling the space in the doorway.

The boy wasn't quite big enough, and riding the wave of an impulse, Ah-Jack pretended to slide through. He'd barely gotten his hand across the threshold when Pat grabbed him by the arms and threw him across the room.

The force of the throw sent Ah-Jack falling back. Unprepared, he went much farther than either of them expected. Tripping backward, watching the room shift around him while his body plummeted, Ah-Jack sensed before the thought could enter his frozen mind that a fall this big might break him for good. When he hit the kitchen table instead of the floor, the impact knocked the air out of him and left him breathless with relief. Pain crackled along his back and he rolled off the table, which had tipped over from his weight. The floor greeted him kindly. He heard, retroactively, the incredible racket his body had caused.

Pat ran over to help. He was apologizing, whispering too quickly. Ah-Jack couldn't parse the English. Disoriented, he kept pushing Pat's hands away, not because he wanted to help himself up but because he was scared, for the first time, of this boy, and he was not yet calm enough to hide his fear. Nan's footsteps padded down the stairs.

"What the hell is happening down here?" Her voice reached the kitchen before she did. She let out a little shriek when she saw him on the ground, furniture and broken glass scattered around him. Pat leapt out of the way, and Nan knelt down beside Ah-Jack. He finally got his bearings when her face became all he had to see. Her hair was matted on one side and her left cheek was wrinkled from sleep.

"A small fall," he said, which Nan dismissed immediately. She whirled around to look at Pat.

"Are you drunk or are you crazy?" she said. She stalked over to him.

"It was an accident." Pat was getting upset. "I said I was sorry."

"Sorry? You nearly killed him!" Nan was making Pat angrier by exaggerating, and Ah-Jack reached up to stop her.

"Please." He eyed Pat in case he lashed out again. "It's late; he's sorry. We should all just go to sleep."

"This is what sorry is supposed to look like?" Nan pointed at Pat's face, which was clenched so tightly that Ah-Jack worried he'd bite through his own teeth. "I don't know who you are anymore!"

"He got in the way," Pat snapped.

Nan took a few stuttering steps back from her son. She raked her hands through her hair. "You're drunk," she said. Pat opened his mouth, but Nan cut him off. "I don't want to look at you anymore. Go to your room. We'll talk in the morning." Then, as if seeing him for the first time, her voice softened. "Oh, Pat, what did you do to your shirt?"

"Nothing." Pat left the room with heavy footsteps, which resounded up the stairs. He slammed his door.

Ah-Jack pulled himself up using the fallen table. The throbbing in his back had deepened; his skin had taken on its own pulse. He couldn't help grunting. Quick like a dog, Nan returned to his side.

"I'm so sorry," she whispered. She led Ah-Jack back to the living room. "I don't know what to do anymore."

"It's not your fault," Ah-Jack said. "You're doing the best you can."

"That's one way of putting it." Nan snorted. She covered her mouth, as if surprised by the rude noise.

Ah-Jack settled himself onto the pullout mattress. He grimaced, more out of habit than actual pain. When was the last time he hadn't grimaced while sitting down, or standing up, or moving at all for that matter?

But Nan said, "You'll sleep in my bed." She was already pulling him back up. "I'll sleep down here."

"I won't allow it." He moved his butt from the mattress to the arm of the couch. "You're the lady of the house. I'm fine. It's just a bump."

"Don't be ridiculous." She had the crook of his elbow in her hand. "We can share. It's a big bed." She made the suggestion ironically, to highlight how stubborn he was being, but by the end, the suggestion had turned serious and, in its quiet way, urgent.

Ah-Jack was drawn to the idea. To accept would be improper, but if Michelle had already stepped out of their marriage, shouldn't he be allowed to do the same? He hadn't shared a bed in months.

Nan was chewing on her bottom lip, creating those little ridges of skin that Ah-Jack only saw when she drank red wine. He could stop that chewing, with a word. His body sent out the memory of another person's heat against his back. Would this bed smell like Nan? Did he want it to?

"You sleep in my bed, and I'll sleep here," she blurted out, putting an end to the possibility. This time, Ah-Jack had to agree. He hadn't expected to feel disappointed, but he could hardly insist they share a bed now. The short trek up the stairs was lonely and strange. He kept looking behind him, though he knew that Nan had not followed. His stomach flipped when he tiptoed past Pat's door.

Her bed did smell like her, deeply of her, and she'd left a few strands of hair on the pillow and in the creases of her bedsheets. Her blanket had been thrown off to the side in her rush to get out, and he settled it back over the bed. Out of respect—For Nan? For Michelle?—he slept on the side that Nan did not favor.

He certainly hadn't been so shy the last time they'd shared a bed. He'd jumped right in. Of course, it was more accurate to say they'd shared a mattress. After Ah-Ray had left for California, they'd gone to trade in her queen for a full—the first time they'd been alone together since Nan had gotten married. She'd agonized over the rows of mattresses for an hour, forgetting the feel of one as soon as she tried the next in line. How could someone so sure be so helpless? It was as sexy as it was maddening, like watching a woman in a crisp dress shirt suddenly lose all her buttons.

Finally, determined not to spend his entire day off at a Mattress Warehouse, Ah-Jack forced Nan to lie down on a mattress and close her eyes. She refused, until he flopped down on the bed and pretended to snore. Scolding him, she eventually gave in. They lay side by side, as they might have tonight, and rested their eyes.

"It's perfect," she whispered. Her voice was thick.

He knew, even with his eyes closed, where her hand would be. He reached down, found it clenched at her side, and placed his hand around her fist. Like a mollusk, it opened. Her fingers rose up to nestle, just barely, in the space between his, and they stayed like this, pretending to be asleep, until a salesman came by and asked how they were liking the full-size Comfort King.

What a shock it had been to open his eyes, awakening to a world that wasn't quite the same. How strange he'd felt for the rest of the day, so strange that when Michelle asked him if he'd bedded any women in the warehouse, he hadn't realized she was repeating a joke he'd made right before he'd left.

"Of course not!" he'd said before he caught his mistake. Thinking quickly, he'd turned his head into his shoulder like a wounded woman. "None would have me."

Testing the springs with an elbow, Ah-Jack was glad he'd found Nan a comfortable bed. Even with his bruised back, he had no trouble drifting off. But though he found sleep easily, with Michelle back in his thoughts, peace was hard to come by. Bad dreams seeped into his head. His sheets grew sweaty and tangled around him. He kept waking during the night—a little frightened of the strange place he found himself—before falling asleep again, the wakefulness a chronic hiccup in his rest. When he finally woke up on his day off, on Nan's side despite his trying, he could not say that he had slept well at all.

11

It was two in the morning when Jimmy drove up to the Duck House in his mother's SUV. The building crackled, as if shifting its bones, but stood upright, enclosed. Jimmy was relieved—his mother always exaggerated. There were no flames. His fears might be unfounded after all.

"Thank you," he said, approaching the man operating the fire truck's pump.

"Nowhere near the end yet." The fireman's voice was hoarse from smoke. "Fire's got itself in the roof structure."

"What fire?" Jimmy saw only the fire truck's flashing glare.

"See that black smoke?"

"Sure."

"That's the fire." The fireman cleared his throat and spat over his shoulder. "Fire ain't just flames."

"That's nonsense!" Jimmy wanted to step on the big hose to get the fireman's full attention.

"Excuse me," said a voice from behind. "You the owner?"

Jimmy turned. A short, unappealing woman stood with a notepad in hand. Her hair was pulled back, showing off a muscular neck. Her skin was as thick as a gargoyle's. She was wearing the same coveralls as the firemen.

"Jimmy Han." He stuck out his hand.

"I'm the fire investigator. Laura." She spoke in short, direct bursts. "Follow me. We'll go through some questions."

"I've got a lot of questions—"

"Let's start with mine first," she said.

Jimmy followed Laura to her car. They walked through a crowd of amigos, who'd been woken up by the sirens and pulled out of bed. A few had their phones out.

"So, Jimmy." Laura leaned her hip against her car. "When did you leave the premises tonight?"

"The usual time," he said quickly, then clucked his tongue. "No, actually, I left an hour earlier tonight, to visit a . . . I left around ten."

"You didn't close the restaurant?"

"No, but I almost never do."

"You know who did?" She paused in her note-taking to snap a few pictures.

"My manager. Nan Fang. Or if not her, then she'll know who."

"What time would that have been?"

Jimmy blew air out of his mouth. "Eleven, eleven-thirty. What started the fire?"

Laura glanced at the restaurant, a look of consideration passing over her craggy face. "Firefighters said the back lot's dumpster was full of garbage. It was pushed right up against the wall."

"A dumpster fire?" Jimmy studied the crowd of amigos. Despite himself, he felt hopeful. No way Uncle Pang could have moved this quickly.

"Not quite," Laura said. "If anything . . ." She cut herself off, her mouth closing into a stern line. "Anyways. You're the sole owner?"

"Technically," he said. "My brother works with me, but he's more involved with the front of the house. Johnny Han. He's out of the country."

"No matter," Laura said. "I'll need written permission from you. I need to reaccess the building after the fire's put out."

"Of course," he said. "Has anyone been inside? How does it look?"

"The bottom level is covered in a light haze," she said. "I went as far as the kitchen. Your safety nozzles failed to activate. Any reason why they stopped working?"

"We had them checked last week." He wiped the corners of his mouth, his saliva gummy. Something was wriggling around his tired brain. "How soon until I can get back in there?"

"No one's allowed in until the police take a look at the scene."

Jimmy noticed the two police cars hidden between the fire trucks. An officer was eyeing the crowd, a loudspeaker in his hand.

"But that's just the back lot. I have a business to run!"

"The entire restaurant is a crime scene." Laura underlined a word in her notepad.

"Some kid vandalizes my dumpster and I have to shut everything down?"

Laura made another note. "We noticed some interesting flame activity around the area. Especially on the back wall. Blue flames, for one." When Jimmy didn't say anything, she added, "Smelled strongly of gasoline."

"This wasn't an accident," Jimmy said. The seed in his brain burst open. Uncle Pang had made him get his sprinklers checked last week. His heartbeat was suddenly in his ears. How had the man done all of this in so little time? And for what? Pure spite?

"Somebody burned down my restaurant," he said. "My family's restaurant," he stressed, when Laura did not move to comfort him.

"I don't make any claims until all the evidence is in," she said. Jimmy realized she didn't trust him. He couldn't remember what he'd already told her. Had he said anything incriminating? Was this part of Uncle Pang's plan?

"By the time you get all the evidence in, everything will have been destroyed." Jimmy yanked at his collar. The air tasted burnt in his mouth.

Laura shook her head. She made a soft noise, one that wasn't sympathetic but pitying.

"There's a lot left after a fire," she said. "That's what surprises people."

Before it became a restaurant, the Duck House building had been a pharmacy, a real estate office, and at least a half dozen other businesses in between. In the process of these transformations, the structure had accumulated a number of roofs, each layered over the ones before, and within these unseen structures, the fire hid.

"This is going to take days," was the firemen's consensus, so when the backhoe rumbled into the parking lot, Jimmy didn't at first understand. But when it began to approach the restaurant, he hurried over to the nearest firefighter.

"Somebody stop that thing." He gestured at the hideous yellow machine. "It's going to run into my restaurant."

"That's the idea," the fireman said. His tired face offered nothing.

"We're going to take out the walls," another, younger fireman said. "The roof's gonna collapse anyways. If one truss goes, they all go." He adjusted the hose on his shoulder.

Jimmy could barely speak. "No, please no."

"Once the roof goes, the fire'll show itself," the first man said. He lifted his helmet to scratch his head. "Then we smother the sucker."

"Can't we wait and see if the roof collapses on its own? You said it could happen any time." Jimmy stopped short of tugging on the fireman's sleeve.

"We're not going to stand around all night," the older one said. "We don't have time to leave and come back to fight the same fire."

Jimmy rubbed the hinges of his jaw, his fingers traveling up around his ears, desperate to plug them up.

"It's really for the best," the younger fireman said. "We're not being over-aggressive."

With a crash, the backhoe rammed into the front entrance. The screech of metal against brick against glass sent Jimmy stumbling back.

"You can wait this out in your car," the older man shouted. "It's all standard."

"How close can I get?" Jimmy asked.

"Best you stay here, or farther." The front wall crumpled and fell in. The roof tipped down, the noise deafening. Jimmy's imagination paled in front of the real deal. How could they do this to his father's restaurant? How could he have let them? Jimmy lurched toward the building. He wanted to rush in, grab whatever photographs he could, save the seating chart, or the carton of duck pins in the back, or even the fucking obituary.

Breathless, he loosened his tie. He was still wearing his work uniform. One glimpse at the dancing ducks on his tie, and he was overcome by emotions he couldn't parse or wrangle. Releasing the catch on the duck pin he'd worn every day of his adult life, he ran toward the restaurant, ignoring the firemen's shouts. Pulling his arm back, he threw the pin into the rubble. The black recesses of the Duck House swallowed the glinting metal up. Someone grabbed him from behind and hauled him away from the building. Wrenching around, Jimmy swung blindly at the person who'd put his hands on him. More hands appeared: Osman, William, Filipe, Jose, Saul. The amigos who'd once filled his kitchen surrounded him. Their bewildered faces dodged his fists, then disappeared as they ducked down. Together, they hugged the trunk of his body into a tackle that slowly brought him to the ground.

Back in his borrowed car, where the fire investigator firmly suggested he stay until their work was done, Jimmy called his older brother.

Twelve hours ahead, Johnny picked up, loudly sipping a cup of coffee.

After Jimmy shared all the information he'd gathered, Johnny took two slow breaths and then, just like that, regained his composure.

"I'll be back out on the soonest flight," Johnny said. "You need to call the insurance company right away. Both policies are at my house; just ask Christine. I'll handle everything with the press. Any reporters contact you, have them email me, okay?"

"The fire's already happened," Jimmy snapped. "You don't have to butter them up."

"I can hint at a new Duck House. Make it less a tragedy and more a PR push for when we reopen." Johnny's voice didn't break in tone or rhythm, but there was an extra layer of calm cemented over the new cracks in his patience. "Everything will be okay."

After Jimmy hung up, he tried to get a little sleep, but his eyes refused to stay shut in his mother's car. He remembered how Johnny's old room had looked earlier that night. The framed certificates for honor roll and garlanded track medals still nailed above Johnny's dresser. His old baseball glove on the night-stand. His bookshelf filled with impressive thick-volume books. Surrounded by his brother's cultivation of generic excellence, Jimmy found that he had not outgrown his adolescent drive. He wanted to torture his brother without having to touch him, the way Johnny had once tortured him. For once, his brother would feel the chill of Jimmy's shadow and wander, angry and blind, through the shade it cast.

Jimmy sent an email asking Johnny to be on Skype in twenty minutes. Lowering his car window, he called to the fire investigator that he was going home to freshen up.

The picture quality on his computer was sharp enough for Jimmy to make out the beads of sweat dotting his brother's upper lip. Johnny had never looked more toadlike.

"What have you done?" Johnny said.

"Now you have an actual restaurant for the reporters I send your way," Jimmy said. "I bought the place when you left town."

"You don't have the money." Johnny's jaw firmed back up. He'd grasped upon a weak point.

"The insurance will pay for everything." Jimmy improvised with the energy his body hadn't burned through. "But if that takes too long, I'll sell Mom's house. You've been bitching forever about Mom being too old to take care of it. I found the perfect agent."

"You've figured everything out." Johnny sucked desperately at a bottle of water.

"You're used to making all the plans," Jimmy said. His brother's face looked pained as he drank. Water dribbled out of the corner of his mouth. "I understand if this is uncomfortable."

"I don't understand," Johnny said. "Why didn't you tell me? I would have supported you."

Jimmy minimized his brother's video. How boring, how stable. He was like the inflatable cone-shaped clown that you punched, only to have it bounce right back up. Jimmy couldn't be the only one overflowing with despair. Johnny deserved some too.

"I didn't burn down the restaurant," Jimmy said, bringing the video up again.

The froggy look washed back over his brother's face.

"Stop it," Johnny whispered.

"I hired a man instead. I'm not sure if he did it. I told him the deal was off, but who knows." Jimmy leaned back in his chair, dizzy, almost exhilarated by his confession. For once, he was glad to have a brother whose opinion he cared nothing about.

Johnny collected his empty bottle and stood. He'd taken the Skype call in a crowded café. The sound of the metal chair against the tile made Jimmy want to reach through the screen and slap his brother. He never took Jimmy seriously, but now Jimmy had shown him.

Johnny stooped back down, his hands holding up his weight. His face was angled above the screen. Jimmy felt like he was actually looking up at his older brother.

"You are no longer my family," Johnny said. His face did not quite know how to look angry, but the deep blackness of his eyes stopped Jimmy from laughing. "You've destroyed everything Dad worked for, and for what? Your own restaurant?" Johnny leaned his face even closer to the screen. "There's no way in hell you're getting a single cent of that insurance money. I'll make sure of that."

The thin fog of tolerance that had enabled Jimmy to work with his brother seven days a week for seven years lifted.

"I'd like to see you try," Jimmy said, ending the video call.

By the time he'd returned his mother's car and collected his from in front of Janine's house, he was too exhausted to call the insurance company. Jimmy got into bed, fully clothed, and lay there until his normal wake-up time. The dull, almost negligible ache in his belly and the solid beating of his heart felt oddly familiar. After his father's funeral, he'd also gone to bed in an uncomfortable suit. Lying down, arms tight at his sides, he'd tried to imagine himself in that position for an eternity. How was tonight any different? Jimmy's eyes watered. Something hot slid into the thick grooves of his ears.

At nine, he palmed his shrill alarm clock, sat up, and rubbed at the new wrinkles in his trousers. He changed into a fresh suit and tie and wet a comb to pull through his oily, smoke-tinged hair. His reflection looked sloppy but well rested. Would his lack of dark circles be suspicious? He could only hope that Uncle Pang's rashness had kept the man from planting any more clues against him. How angry was he? Angry enough to take the Glory down too?

Jimmy started his long list of calls, twisting his piercing until the top of his ear ached. To the insurance company, he told the bare minimum. They recorded their calls, and in his current state he didn't know what might slip out. He thought about calling Nan to break the news to the rest of the waiters but called May instead—she was the bigger gossip. When the waitress tried to ask him questions, he hung up. He called his mother, who didn't pick up, no doubt already re-entombed in her basement bedroom. He called his brother's wife, Christine, who was also the Duck House's accountant; she volunteered to talk to the insurance reps. He called the IT guy who ran the restaurant's website, to put a notice on the front page and to email everyone on their mailing list. He called the restaurant itself and changed the voicemail message. Finally, he had only Janine left to call but no energy to dial. He couldn't handle any more questions, any more sympathy. He would see her at lunch.

He wasted no time getting into his car. The Beijing Glory's soft opening would have to be pushed up, but the building didn't even have a new sign. He hadn't contacted the new servers, most of whom had probably lied about their work experience. The printed menus were arriving this morning; the silverware was still covered in factory dust; the seafood distributor was hounding him for cash on delivery. He couldn't dwell on the past, not when the future was this precarious. He had a duty to the Glory. There was nothing he could do for the Duck House now. He wouldn't give Uncle Pang the satisfaction of wasting the day to mourn a pile of rubble.

He ticked past his extensive to-do list while he navigated through traffic. He steered mindlessly, and on instinct he pulled off the Beltway many exits too early. But he didn't turn the car around. He'd begun to wonder what his father's restaurant would look like in the morning light. He was a block away when the smell of smoke wormed its way into his car through the air-conditioning vents. He held his breath when the strip mall next door came into view.

Surprisingly, the bones of the restaurant were still intact, though the place was scooped out like a melon. Two of the remaining brick walls stood tall around the piles of iron and collapsed roofing. Caution tape held the small crowd back. Jimmy recognized many of the same faces from the middle of the night. Didn't they have anything better to do? The waiters, who could have at least come to show their support, were nowhere to be seen. This was loyalty. No doubt they hadn't even put down their phones before racing over to whatever nasty takeout joint would have them.

Jimmy was working up a good head of anger when he glimpsed Ah-Jack, Nan, and Nan's son in the crowd. *They* were not fair-weather employees; *they* had not run off for still-standing restaurants. A scheduling blip popped into Jimmy's head. Ah-Jack was even here on his day off. A good thing he'd held off on firing the old waiter. He made a note to hire them all at his new place. He could pay back his gratitude and plug some of the remaining holes in his employee roster. He'd stick Nan and Ah-Jack in the back, maybe as duck carvers, but the kid could be at the front of the house, as a busboy or a runner. He could even be a waiter.

Jimmy parked and went over to join the crowd. Feeling a surge of electric affection, he put his arms around Ah-Jack and

Nan. Both jumped underneath his touch and jumped again when they turned to see him behind them.

"Jimmy." Nan was the first to speak. "I am so sorry. How awful."

"This a true crime." Ah-Jack shook his head. His loose gray hair whirled around like a sheepdog's.

"I'm touched you all are here." Jimmy released his employees. "Incredibly touched." His knees wobbled. He nearly reached out again to steady himself.

"We got feeling so sad," Nan said. Forgetting herself and slipping into Chinese, she cried, "It's like a death in the family. We saw you grow up behind these walls."

"At least my father did not live to see this day." Jimmy's Chinese was so awkward and reverential that he shut it off immediately. "There's nothing we can do here. It's in the fire department's hands. I need to check in on my new restaurant. You three can follow my car."

"Your new restaurant?" Nan's voice was tentative, unsure if she'd misheard or he'd misspoken.

Jimmy had forgotten that the Glory was technically a secret, but like all good liars, he pretended he'd revealed nothing out of the ordinary.

"Yes, it's going to be an Asian fusion restaurant."

"Where is it?" Nan asked.

"In D.C. On the Georgetown Waterfront."

"Wow, so nice," Ah-Jack said.

Jimmy started to lead them away from the damage. In that moment, he believed that if he did not get them folded into his new restaurant, he would lose them forever. Their phones would ring on the hook, their houses sold or abandoned, and he might never see Nan or Ah-Jack again. Days earlier, he had sickened looking upon their faces, listening to their mincing English. But he'd never really imagined a world where Nan and Ah-Jack were not steadfastly, irritatingly present.

"A woman, she asking us questions," Nan mentioned, peering over her shoulder.

"Yes, Laura, the fire investigator," Jimmy said impatiently. "What did she want?"

"We don't know," she said. "She talk to us each by ourself. Pat too, who only work one month. She talk to Pat longest."

"She try ask you on date?" Ah-Jack jostled Pat.

"She just wanted to know what time I left the restaurant last night," Pat said.

"She say she want talk to you too," Nan said to Jimmy. "You go find her."

"Another time." Jimmy was in no mood to face the investigator and her clicking camera. He had to get his story straight. Maybe he could convince her to interview him another day. She'd given him her card last night. Surely she had other people to interrogate. The sun was already high in the sky. Cars on the road slowed as they passed; some pulled over for a better look.

"Come with me," he said. "We're wasting daylight." He strode off, the boss again. But a few steps later, his confidence flagged. He checked behind him. No one was there.

He spotted them a few yards away, heading in a different direction altogether. "Where are you going?" he shouted, panic creeping in. He started to chase after them, arms flapping, but stopped himself just in time.

The threesome was walking toward the back lot, curving around the caution-taped left wall of the restaurant. Even with the Duck House burned down, Nan and Ah-Jack had parked in the back, leaving the front parking spaces free for customers. Jimmy couldn't believe they'd remembered his rules after all this madness. It was like finding the crosswalk signals flashing after the world's end.

"Pull around!" Jimmy cupped his hands around his mouth as they disappeared behind the building. His relief was unrelenting, almost painful in its power. "I'll wait!"

*

At the Glory, Jimmy assigned a few of his tasks to his three employees. He had no idea what he was forgetting to do, whom he was neglecting to call. No one had taught him what to do if his restaurant burned down. What to do if he was the primary suspect. Johnny was the one built for moments like these. His older brother always acted like he had the instruction manual to life. Jimmy knew how stupid he was being, but he silenced his cell phone anyway and walked down the waterfront to meet Janine for lunch. She'd picked an Italian place called Antonio's, texting him the plans the night before. He hadn't thought of canceling.

"I heard about the fire," she said when she saw him. She stood up and held his hands in hers. "I'm so sorry. I didn't think you'd show up."

"The fire's already happened," Jimmy said. "I've still got to eat lunch." They sat down. Jimmy didn't let go of Janine's hands, and she didn't pull away either. "Besides, I like to see something beautiful after something so ugly."

"You're being brave," she said, as a reprimand. But she squeezed his hands.

"I'm being an asshole." He let go when their waiter approached with the breadbasket.

They ordered whatever the specials were, with appetizers that the waiter recommended, none of which entered Jimmy's short-term memory. Each plate, shining and luxurious with olive oil, was a surprise. The food tasted expensive, its tenderness and fragrance created not by the chef's mediocre skills but by material so good it only needed to survive the haphazard spice.

"Where did you get this chicken?" he asked the manager, who was floating around.

"Antonio has a farm in West Maryland." The manager pointed to a photo on the opposite wall: A cluster of spotted chickens pecked around a field. "He oversees the raising and treatment of all the meat we serve, including the veal."

"Amazing." Janine stabbed into her veal parmigiana. "That's so committed."

"Antonio loves food," the manager said. He whipped out a silver scraper and cleaned the crumbs off their table. A passing waiter refilled their crystal water glasses.

"A fucking farm," Jimmy said, after the manager left. "What a fucker."

"What do you mean?"

"Not to quote Dad, but only an American would be so precious with his food." Jimmy threw down his knife and fork and wiped his mouth.

"What's wrong with a farm?" Janine ate a triangle of veal. "And I think Antonio is Italian."

"What's wrong with a food distributor?" Jimmy used his napkin to wipe his entire face. "What's wrong with playing the game like everybody else?"

"Oh God." She rested her chin against her hand. "I know you're nervous, but you're going to be a hit."

"Not with Farmer Antonio down the street." He took a big drink of water and nearly choked. "I'm buying a farm. I'll get authentic fucking seeds and grow my own fucking spring onions. I'll raise the ducks too."

Janine signaled for the waiter with her credit card. Jimmy was too busy trying to control his breathing to steal the check from her. Soon they were out on the waterfront, shielding their eyes from the sun.

She looped her arm through his and dragged him upright, forcing his lungs to expand. "You're not okay right now," she said. "You probably haven't been okay in a while. But you're going to survive this."

He couldn't look at her. The sun was piercing holes into his eyes, and the milky blue of the sky was immense and suffocating. All around him were restaurants that were out of his league. The pizzeria boasting eight-hundred-degree ovens and ninety-second Neapolitan pies; the sushi restaurant owned by a Japanese chef with a show on Netflix; the French bistro with tasting menus starting at $145 a person. What would the Glory have? Peking duck carved tableside, like on a fucking Carnival cruise!

Only Janine's arm in his grounded him. Jimmy tilted his chin up and locked his knees. He wanted to launch himself into the atmosphere until the pressure and the cold popped him like a balloon.

"Come on, I've got something that will help you breathe," Janine said. She led him away from the water. Only after she'd pushed his head in did Jimmy realize that he was in her car. He closed his eyes. He hoped she was driving him somewhere promising.

The sex was startling. Not so much satisfying as it was natural, surprising in how unsurprised he was by the way Janine looked and felt naked. He couldn't have lasted more than three minutes, and she didn't make much noise, which he appreciated. It had felt honest between them.

From the waterfront, they had gone back to her office in Bethesda, which was really a small apartment she was renting with a spare bedroom.

"What're you doing?" he'd asked, when she'd started to undress. But when she began to pull her zipper back up, he'd nearly torn his shirt off.

They'd gotten into bed, on top of her covers, all without talking. She'd sucked in a great bubble of air the moment he pushed in, and he had inhaled sharply too, at the small miracle that his skin did not snag on hers, that she was wet enough to guide him through. She'd murmured into his ear and rubbed his back in long, slow strokes. The gentle rhythm of her sounds and stroking overwhelmed him. He finished on her stomach, while she caressed his forearm, bent by the side of her head.

His mind was clear and buzzing. Janine had managed to yank him out of his downward spiral. His entire body was subdued, like a boat rocking on a lake, and while he listened to her shower, he flexed and stretched all his parts. He felt the blood rushing through his muscles as he looked around the room. The bedroom was sparsely decorated, and what few items it did hold looked out of place, too impersonal but also too private. A bird-shaped wrought-iron clock hung by the door. On the vanity, a silver picture frame, the photo inside just out of view.

The shower stopped. Jimmy's senses were so heightened that he swore he could hear her toweling off. He hoped she might come out with nothing on, or with just a short hand towel wrapped around. But Janine emerged from the bathroom swallowed up by a thick terrycloth robe. Water droplets dotted her chest, but above her collarbone, her skin was dry. Her makeup was untouched.

"Quick shower," he said.

"Wanted to freshen up." With her robe half on, she pulled on her earlier outfit. He caught a flash of her naked back, the shoulder blades pushing out coils of muscle, before she slipped into her silk blouse. He stayed naked, a corner of the sheet covering his lower half.

"You're in a hurry," he said.

"Some open houses." Her voice was frosty. But then she twisted around and touched her cheek. "Lunch went a little later than planned."

"Kicking me out so soon?" he said. "No cuddling?"

She laughed as she fastened her earrings.

"That's what happens when you get involved with a working girl," she said. "We don't exactly get to take breaks."

"Write this off as a business expense."

Janine came over and sat down next to him, slipping into her shoes. She cupped his face, and he leaned into her touch.

"This is really weird," he said. "But I can't stop thinking about my dad."

"That's not weird," she said. "Well, a little. But I get it. You feel like he's died all over again."

"Sure." Jimmy didn't like the way the words sounded out loud. "But also I can't stop thinking about something he said once. He said, 'If you go, you kill the Duck House. You kill me.' I thought he was overreacting."

"You can't blame yourself," Janine said. "I think he would be proud of you."

Jimmy had forgotten that Janine had little context for his life, just as he knew few of the small, dramatic scenes built into her story. Had she ever considered what his family was like? Or what he was like within his family?

"I did leave the Duck House for a few months when I was nineteen," he said. "That's why he said that to me. I tried to apprentice at another restaurant in D.C."

"But you came back," she said. "Did you not like the other place?"

Jimmy rolled onto his back to stare at the ceiling. How could he convey to her the beauty of Koi's sunlit dining floor? Or the black magic of the fuming kitchen, hiding in the back? He would step through those double doors, and his heart would start pounding so loud he could almost hear it over the noise of the cooks working and sparring inside. Those swearing, sweating men had taught him how to wrap the most delicate spring rolls and pipe the smallest drops of wasabi cream. A month in that kitchen and Jimmy could plate a fillet of sea bass with the precision of a violinist drawing his bow. Two months and he could roll cigarettes better than Ronny. He could cover for Lew when his girlfriend called and even withstand the stench of Key's farts, which he'd cup in his hands and release under the nearest unsuspecting nose. By month three he'd learned how to work on two hours of sleep, how to stop a nosebleed, how to cut his coke with baking soda from the kitchen pantry to hide his losses. His hands trembled too badly to wrap the spring rolls and pipe the cream. The sea bass fell apart on the spatula. But Ronny had promised that Jimmy would get a job on the line when his stage ended. He'd promised to get Chef Alfred to put Jimmy's bulgogi burger on the menu. He'd promised he would pay Jimmy back—they all would—as soon as paychecks came out. Jimmy had believed him. He hadn't given those promises a second thought, until the day Uncle Pang showed up at his door.

"People have been complaining," Uncle Pang had said, pulling off his gloves. "They say you're selling them flour." He'd riffled through the stack of bills Jimmy had handed him. The counting was an act; he could tell by weight alone. Jimmy was five thousand dollars short. A week late.

"They're full of shit," Jimmy said, stone-faced.

"You make some new friends?" Uncle Pang asked.

Jimmy bristled at the change in subject. "I don't have time for friends," he said.

"They have time for you." The doublespeak tickled Jimmy's brain like a spider's web. "Time, but not money."

"They're going to pay me back. It's good business to front old clients."

"I suppose you're telling me it would be good business to front you as well." Uncle Pang dropped the stack on the table, where it made a small, light sound, barely audible over the noise from the street. Jimmy had thrown all of his windows open. His apartment stank from last night's party.

"You know I'm good for it." Jimmy had half an hour before he was needed at Koi. "I'm going to see those guys now. If you'd let me know you were coming over, I would've been prepared."

A thin line appeared between Uncle Pang's eyebrows. Jimmy blinked and when he opened his eyes, he was on his back, laid out flat on the floor. His mouth filled with blood. His tongue probed the gap where his right canine used to be.

"Blame me again, and I'll take the rest of them." The heel of Uncle Pang's polished dress shoe crushed the tooth, which had landed near Jimmy's head. "You've really disappointed me," he added. He peered down at Jimmy like a dentist. With a vicious twist, he pinched Jimmy's nose between his fingers. "I see the coke inside your nostrils, little piggy."

Jimmy wriggled out of the man's grip. Warmth bloomed inside his nose.

"You even bleed like a pig." Uncle Pang headed toward the door. "Get the money to me by the end of the weekend, or we'll get your father involved."

Jimmy was trying to find some hole to breathe through, trying to swallow, trying not to choke on his own blood, but those words made him bolt up and scramble on all fours. Uncle Pang let the door close right in his face.

When Jimmy showed up to work, Chef Alfred was waiting at the door. Jimmy touched his lip, which sagged in the space where his tooth had been. A wad of tissue hung out of his left nostril. The chef was pinker than he'd ever seen him.

"You're not coming in here." His finger pointed at Jimmy's chest. Behind him, the restaurant shone in the late-autumn light. "I take you in and you deal to my kitchen? You're fucking fired."

Jimmy's stomach lurched. He felt so defeated he didn't think to deny Chef Alfred's accusation. "Please don't do this," he said. "Don't fire me for one small mistake."

"One mistake?" The chef laughed. "You've been fucking up every plate you put your hands on. I was going to fire you in a few weeks anyways."

"But Ronny said—"

The chef blew out his lips. "Ronny's a liar. A user. And a cheat." He wiped a drop of sweat from his temple. "But at least *he's* a good cook."

Jimmy's face filled with heat. He was a good cook. A great fucking cook, who'd scarred and scorched his hands for the sake of Koi's fresh-shucked oysters; its flambéed octopus legs; its chilled sea urchin, cracked open and served with spines intact. Worse, he'd been a good friend. The designated driver at night, the coffee bitch in the morning, the eager target of every kitchen prank. He gave away his blow for free, for fuck's sake, thinking that a favor given was a favor owed, thinking that surely, after this, Ronny and the others would have to give him a proper place at the table. He'd truly believed that he'd found his people.

He rounded back and stuck his battered face right in Chef Alfred's.

"I can cook!" he screamed. Their noses bumped. Jimmy's balled-up tissue touched the other man's upper lip, and the chef pushed him away. Jimmy shoved him back hard in the chest, hard enough to send Chef Alfred falling against the gleaming glass doors behind him. Jimmy's mouth was too dry to swallow. He was breathing hard and then he was running.

"You piece of shit," Chef Alfred yelled after him. "Get back here!" Jimmy ran faster. He tried to outpace the voice sprinting after him. Rounding the corner, he scraped his elbow against the brick wall. His shoe cracked against an empty cardboard box. But even after the shouting turned into unintelligible noise, Jimmy understood. The chef's words burned into his back: "You'll never work in a kitchen again."

Jimmy wanted to bury his face into the pillow and smother the memory out of his head. Some stories not even Janine would get to hear.

"I liked it fine, but I got blackballed for dealing to the staff," he said. The pressure in his chest released. "You embarrassed that you slept with a coke dealer?"

Janine registered his dodge.

"Not at all." She recalibrated to match him. "This was lovely."

"Let's get lunch again," he said. "Soon."

When Janine dropped him off at the waterfront, she let him kiss her goodbye. Jimmy had to stop himself from clapping strangers on the shoulder on his way into the Glory, but when he saw Ah-Jack sitting at a booth near the entrance, he couldn't help shaking the old waiter lightly by the arm.

"Hard at work!" he crowed. Ah-Jack stood up immediately.

"I take small break." He started wiping down the booth. "One minute."

"That's fine," Jimmy said. "We all need breaks. In fact, it's your day off. You should go and enjoy the rest of it."

Ah-Jack was out the booth and through the doors before Jimmy could think to take his favor back. The old waiter's face looked grim when he walked past the front windows, as if he were annoyed that Jimmy had taken this long to release him. Jimmy went to inspect the kitchen. He made a note to treat Ah-Jack more harshly tomorrow.

He nearly ran into Pat when he rounded the waiter station.

"What's your hurry?" He grabbed the kid above the elbow. He tried to apply pressure, but his fingers couldn't close around the bulk of Pat's arm.

"Sorry," Pat said. He let his arm drop instead of pulling away, forcing Jimmy to hang on like a child. "I was looking for you."

"Well, you found me."

"I want to thank you for giving me this opportunity, but I can't take the job." Pat scratched at a zit on his chin. The skin around it looked inflamed.

"You have something better?" The one thing Jimmy hated more than giving out favors was having them thrown back in his face.

"No—"

"Then what's wrong with this job? You think you're too good to wait tables?"

"No, I just don't think I'm the right person." Pat stuffed his hands in his pockets.

"If I say you're the right person, then you're the right person." How had someone like Nan produced a son this stubborn and stupid?

"I'm sure you can find someone else, someone more qualified."

"Don't tell me what I can do." Jimmy stepped closer and lowered his voice. "I'm doing this as a favor to your mother. Haven't you tortured her enough?"

Pat reared back. The kid looked like he might head-butt Jimmy in the face. Then he slumped into his shoulders.

"Okay," he said. "Thank you, Mr. Han."

"You don't make it easy to help you," Jimmy said. He slapped Pat on the back and walked away. For a brief moment, he thought he sniffed a thread of acrid smoke coming off Pat's hair, but then he was past the kid and standing in his favorite part of the restaurant: the direct center. From there, he could turn around in a tight circle and take in every furnished inch of the establishment—from the lush brown sectionals that made up the ground seating; to the high-backed chairs in the raised upper section; the stained-glass lanterns suspended from the mahogany ceiling beams; down to the bold-patterned carpet, its own paisley galaxy.

His thumbs tucked into his belt loops, he surveyed the wide space of his new restaurant. Sunlight streamed through the floor-to-ceiling glass front.

12

Johnny had enjoyed his time away. Hong Kong in the summer was remarkable, the humidity a revelation! His students had called him Superman, because he never seemed to sweat. Secretly, he'd sweat plenty—he just never complained. Johnny's rule was that if he didn't belong, then he would behave better than those who did. He'd planned to spend the last weeks, after his classes ended, traveling around. Maybe see his birthplace, Beijing, for the first time, though his mother had refused to put him in touch with any family there. He hated to admit it, but running the Duck House had become stale. The same customers, questions, jokes, dramas. The hiatus had refreshed him. A few more weeks and he'd have been ready to return.

The news of the fire was a brisk wake-up call. He'd known to some degree that he was the one who kept his brother in check. But now he was certain, and duty bound him back to Maryland. He'd made some harsh threats to his little brother over Skype, but they had been necessary ones. Jimmy couldn't depend on his family to bail him out forever; he was far too old to be acting out this way.

Johnny fully intended to see his promise about the insurance money through, but he was struggling to come up with a plan. He called himself a co-owner, but this wasn't technically the truth. His name wasn't on the contracts. Legally, he was no different from any other Duck House employee. Their father had been a symbolic man. He hadn't added Jimmy's name until his brother had worked at the restaurant for ten years, the same amount of time it had taken to open the Duck House. Their father couldn't be convinced, even after he was hospitalized, to make an exception for Johnny. But Johnny was no less the rightful owner than Jimmy. For God's sake, all the Duck House paperwork was at *his* house: the insurance policies, the W-2s, even the contract. His little brother couldn't be trusted to run a business on his own. He was impractical, impulsive, and held himself to nothing, not to his word and least of all to his responsibilities. Their father must have known this. Why else would he have let Johnny start out as manager and skip the years of waiting tables that Jimmy had had to go through? Even the employees and customers preferred Johnny, which was perhaps why he had decided to let Jimmy lord over the place for three more years. What had seemed like an easy way to keep the peace had backfired, wildly. Now he had no say in the insurance matters. Without a restaurant, he had no say in anything.

Once Johnny cleared the security line, he called his mother to let her know he'd be back a few weeks early. Jimmy would have accused him of trying to show off the sacrifice he was making, which showed how little his brother understood about their family. When had their mother ever noticed a sacrifice that wasn't her own? Johnny had been paying her bills and looking after her finances for over a year, and had he ever gotten a word of thanks? He was happy to help, but on principle, favors should be appreciated. Then again, his mother hadn't been in the best condition since his father's death—the shock of the fire would be another hit to her health. He needed to be gentle.

But his mother made such a task impossible. "Jimmy has ruined your father's life," she announced when she picked up his call.

"Dad's dead," Johnny said. "I don't understand."

"He's selling my house! Right from under my nose."

"Ma, calm down." He stopped perusing the duty-free cologne. His brother certainly moved fast. "What did Jimmy actually do?"

"That's it! His real estate agent called me. She sounded so fake. There's nothing worse than a country girl pretending to be educated."

"When is Jimmy selling the house?"

"I don't know." His mother made a sharp noise, as if reprimanding him for asking a question she couldn't answer. "But he's bought an outrageous new restaurant in D.C. He didn't tell me or anyone. He was probably going to tell us opening night! Fire us all too!"

Many Chinese women spoke with voices so melodious and bright that the language sounded like a gentle, teasing song; his mother was not one of those women. She emphasized every word as others might slap a table. When she was allowed to talk without interruption, the effect was like waiting out a rainstorm under a tin roof.

"He's not abandoning Dad's restaurant," Johnny said. His mother's haranguing made him want to defend Jimmy. "He's moving it to a new location."

"Don't you know your brother by now?"

"Ma, you're making yourself crazy."

"He's probably not even going to serve Chinese food." Her volume was unbearable. "Why are you in Hong Kong? You don't speak Cantonese. You're supposed to be at home watching over your stupid little brother."

"That's why I called. I'm coming home. My flight leaves in half an hour."

"You come straight to my house," she said, registering no surprise or relief. "That's if your brother hasn't sold it already!"

*

Eighteen hours later, Johnny was rolling his baggage out of Dulles Airport. His daughter, Annie, was waiting by the exit to drive him home. He didn't know if he should give her a hug, but before he had to make the choice, she was walking in front of him.

"Thank you for picking me up."

"Hey, Dad." She didn't turn her head as the automatic doors opened. "I'm kind of in a hurry."

"You're very busy." He struggled to keep his breathing steady while he jogged to catch up. "I understand. How was the rest of freshman year? How's work?"

"Fine," she said. She'd left her little car idling outside the terminal. A security officer circled the car ominously. Before Johnny could intervene, Annie stepped in.

"Sorry," she said. "My dad just ran off and I had to chase after him. It's his first time in America." A harried look hung over her face. "I think all the buses scared him."

The officer looked over at him. Johnny straightened up and raised his chin. He was offended when the man appeared convinced by his daughter's ridiculous story.

"You need any help getting him in the car?" the officer asked.

"No." Annie reached over to touch the man's arm. "But thank you."

"Where'd you learn that dirty trick?" Johnny grumbled, opening his car door.

"Uncle Jimmy," Annie said, smiling for the first time.

In the car, Johnny wished he'd taken a taxi home. He'd felt a rush of love when he'd first seen his daughter, who was as lovely as a nineteen-year-old girl should be. But how had he forgotten the tension between them? He'd hoped that his absence might make her a little sweeter, but she was even moodier than when he'd left five months ago. Couldn't she see how tired he was? Didn't she care about the terrible news?

Annie sped past a slow-moving car, jolting Johnny sideways when she swerved back into the lane.

"Jesus, will you slow down?"

"He wasn't driving the speed limit." She spoke sluggishly, mocking his own speech patterns, but Johnny would not rise to the bait. His early years in China had made his mouth inflexible to certain sounds, and he had to slow his words to be understood; Annie said this made him sound more like a stage actor than a real person. Better that than how Jimmy sounded, with his machine gun for a mouth.

"I bought you this car," Johnny said while Annie continued to jump lanes. "When you pay for your own car, then you can wreck it."

"Okay, fine." She checked her eye makeup quickly in the rearview mirror. "I'm dropping you off at Grandma's. She wants you to drive her car to Uncle Jimmy's."

Annie's attention to her eyes made Johnny curious. Her lids were puffier than normal. The black lines she drew close to her lashes didn't quite disguise the fat wrinkles that formed when she widened her eyes. The end of her nose was red. Johnny's chest panged, not in an unpleasant way. He wasn't the reason she was acting so touchy after all.

"Everything okay?" He reached out and touched her hand.

"Dad!" She jerked the steering wheel in surprise. "Everything is fine. Stop being weird."

"Are you having trouble at the restaurant? Or with friends?" Johnny tried to check how eager he sounded. "Or is it boy troubles? Don't be embarrassed."

Annie drove past one exit, then another. The silence between them was doughy with possibility, but slowly, surely, it stiffened. The drop in his stomach was familiar. He should've been used to the ways his daughter liked to punish him by now.

"I was seeing a dishwasher, from the restaurant," she said suddenly.

Johnny stared at his daughter, as if expecting fingerprints to appear on her skin. She kept adjusting her steering wheel, making the car wobble left and right. He had to close his eyes. "An amigo?" he asked.

"No, you don't know him. He's new. We had kind of an embarrassing incident in the storage closet. I wanted to tell you before you heard the gossip."

Johnny swallowed and realized his mouth had gone dry. Annie had finally found a response more punishing than silence. If she'd wanted to shut him up, she'd gotten her wish. He leaned his head against the window, the glass cool and painfully hard against his temple.

With Annie, Johnny didn't think of where he had gone wrong but rather of where he had lost her. His mother used to nag him about having more children, but during the years when their family had room for another child, he shrank from the idea of splitting his attention. Annie, from birth, had been so greedy for his time, weeping when he had to leave her and throwing herself into his arms when he came back. She devoured him, and in her constant consumption he felt bottomless. He had always thought she would be the one to grow tired of his affections. He was terrified of that day. Children grew up and lost interest and life went on. This was what his mother had warned him, while he dangled Annie over his lap, her chubby legs bowed out as she tried to find footing on his thighs. Have more children, his mother had continued. Slow down time. He only hugged Annie tighter.

"You're the one for me," he sang to her.

But when Annie was maybe twelve, he got distracted. Johnny had no other way of describing what happened in those years, after he left his research lab and joined the Duck House. His father, stomach cancer still undiagnosed, had needed an extra hand. Johnny had had no intention of doing more than his duty. He'd always disliked the family restaurant, which was like a monument to his father's greed. He used to wish, as a kid, that his father

were a lawyer, or a doctor, or even a postal worker, just someone whose job had a larger purpose than filling a bank account.

Even the food they served suited his father's pockets. Everything a person might find at a takeout joint they could find at
the Duck House, under a fancier name, at three times the price,
and served on a nicer platter. Black pepper beef became Beijing
Steak. Fried shrimp transformed into Phoenix Prawns, named
for their extra-golden color, like the outside of a corn dog.
Seafood pan-fried noodles kept their name, but got "Gourmet"
tacked in front and came hand-tossed tableside by a waiter.
Was it tasty? Sure. But was it authentic? Was it anything to be
proud of? Only the Peking duck fit the bill. His father, not for
want of trying, had never figured out how to prepare the duck
faster than the traditional way, with the fowls shipped down
from Long Island, their skin air-dried then brushed with sugar,
and finished off with slow heat in a rotisserie oven. Everything
else on the menu was a scam.

Johnny had only meant to stay a year. Then Jimmy had
gone to rehab. His father's health had started to suffer. Duty
transformed into something else, something close to pride. No
one was more surprised than Johnny. He found that he liked
greeting old VIPs and introducing himself to new ones; he felt
in control in the dining room, as he never had in his lab. The
food didn't grow on him, but he couldn't deny the pleasure with
which people attacked their fried rice. After a year of working
with his father, Johnny began to piece together the original vision
for the Duck House. The early press; the old pictures of the
restaurant's cooks dressed in toques and fake medals; the stories
of presidents renting out the private party room. All pointed to
the same dream—his father had wanted prestige. Johnny only
had to update his father's vision slightly to fit his own.

When his father was finally hospitalized, Johnny took a hard
look at the Duck House. By then there hadn't been a new visit
from a celebrity or politician since the restaurant's first decade.

Who would come back once the bribe had been paid and the meals were no longer free? His father had no foresight. You couldn't expect people to think highly of you when you sat them practically cheek to cheek. When the food you overcharged for didn't, at least, tell a story. More customers pulled Johnny aside to complain about the greasiness of the lo mein than to ask about what the president once ordered. They quizzed him about MSG and asked if there was a senior discount. Slowly, people stopped ordering the Peking duck; the ones who did complained without humor about the price.

Johnny did what he did best. He studied his father's restaurant and told a story he could be proud of. It turned out their homemade garlic sauce wasn't a cheap way to use up ancient garlic but an old family recipe from his mother's side. The relative quickness of Chinese cuisine wasn't one that any rookie with a wok could create; half a second over high flame was the difference between meat and jerky. And the old waiters weren't feeble and hard of hearing; they were storied professionals.

"You've got yourself a Duck House historian here," he'd say to any new customer who raised his eyebrows at being served by a man with gray hair tufting out of his ears. "Ah-Sam has so many years of experience, he can wrap your duck in his sleep."

Johnny's aboveboard savvy elevated the restaurant in ways that his father's methods never could. Using his wife's trust fund, he made a few impressive donations and started a scholarship, all in the Duck House's name, and soon invitations to charity events and black-tie galas poured in. He called up journalists and reviewers. He went to other restaurant openings and met the chefs. He invited the owners to a free meal at the Duck House. While Jimmy accused him of shirking his job to eat dinner and gab with the VIPs, Johnny saw himself as raising not just the restaurant but the Han name.

"This place needs some dignity," he tried to explain to Jimmy. "*We* need some dignity."

"We *had* dignity until you started whoring us out," Jimmy said.

"Think what you like." The real story would surface in time.

In all his excitement, as he made more connections, with generals and senators and actors, and as more photos were framed for the restaurant's wall of fame, Johnny lost Annie. Or, as it might have seemed, he lost interest in her. He stopped dropping her off at school and picking her up from softball practice. He forgot the names of her teachers and her friends. He forgot to speak to her at all some days. But a stubborn part of him refused to bend down to the blame she placed on his shoulders. He was making something of his family, a family that included Annie. The very fact that this mission absorbed him contradicted all claims of lost interest. He had not done any of this for himself.

All he could hope for now was that Annie would grow to love him as he had grown to love his own father. Things would have been different if Annie had been a boy. A boy wouldn't take his father's distance so personally. A boy would one day come to understand his father, when he became a man himself.

His own father had spent most of his time at the Duck House while he and Jimmy were growing up. Johnny didn't really meet his father, as a man or a parent, until he started working with him at the front of the house. He used to think his father did nothing besides terrorize and charm. He was always shaking hands with people who had selective power, in that sliding way that meant a small square of money had been tucked into the lines of a waiting palm. They never had to wait for a table at restaurants. A C– on Jimmy's report card was changed to a B+. The one time his father attended one of Johnny's track meets, the boy who placed first was mysteriously disqualified. Johnny, who was second, inherited the gold medal, smudged with the winner's oily fingerprint.

But within the Duck House, the full story emerged. Johnny saw that rather than his father being the worm inside an apple,

Bobby was the worm and the apple also. He raked in money, year after year, enough not only to afford a mansion in rich white Potomac but also the permission to live there. Yet he barely got to sleep inside the house for which he'd worked so hard.

The profits grew, multiplied, and were never enough; his father's health slowly shattered. Johnny began to love if not his father then his father's body, which would not quit even as it was. He disdained his father for always wanting more and better, but he loved his father too, because his body did not let him get away with his own greed. The worm, in devouring the apple, devoured itself.

Johnny had not wanted his father to die, especially not as he had, from stomach cancer, slowed down to its most painful pace by money. He hadn't wanted the signs of stress to show so undeniably in and on his father's body—in ulcers, in sores, in deep worry lines—and Johnny took no pleasure now that his little brother was deteriorating at the same implacable rate. He had beseeched both of them to slow down. Neither listened. But Johnny, for better or worse, needed the world to be fair. Even in the face of disaster, he felt a certain satisfaction that the world still turned in the same direction. He'd once been yanked from one culture and transplanted into another, his five-year-old roots too grown to fit into this new plot. When nothing had made sense for so many years, his faith in a just world sometimes felt like the only thing tethering him to this earth. To budge even an inch away from his perfected system was to lose his grip on everything.

Annie merged sharply onto the highway off-ramp. Her dad kept pretending to sleep against the window. Or he was actually asleep. When she was younger, Annie had been frightened by how her dad could fall asleep anywhere, disappearing into a realm she couldn't disturb.

She supposed she was acting in character by rebuffing him. They were both used to her chilliness. To hug him hello after months of absence, to tell him how much she'd missed his voice, would have raised his suspicions. Her tears blurred the highway lanes. All she wanted was to reach over and hold his hand.

Why didn't she tell him about the fire? It would be easy to blurt out the words. She knew he would act rationally, like he had when she'd been caught shoplifting last year. He'd get her lawyers; he'd make a plan; he'd act as if hired for the job instead of sentenced to it. But the secret had grown too big to squeeze out of her throat. What would she say when he asked her why? Asked her how?

Would she tell him that she and Pat had done a fair number on their bottles before she'd finally let Pat pour the rest of what they didn't need out onto the wood-dusted grass? That she had been buzzed enough to exaggerate the unsteadiness in her legs, bobbing back and forth until Pat had thrown his backpack over her shoulders and hefted her onto his back, grabbing her thighs to shift her higher?

She'd wrapped her arms around his sweaty neck and whooped at him to giddyup. Her skirt had fallen back; she'd pressed herself into his spine.

He carried her past the apartments, past her car, and into the Duck House's back lot, where he set her down. She reached out to steady herself against the open dumpster. When she glanced back, Pat was busying himself with their half-empty bottles. He poured what smelled like gasoline into each one until the liquid filled three-quarters of the container. If she breathed too deeply, the smell made her head swim.

"What're you doing?" she asked, when Pat shucked off his T-shirt.

"I need to make wicks," he said. He tore off the bottom third of his shirt with a loud rip that made Annie's breath catch.

"Use mine too," she said. "We're partners."

She pulled her shirt over her head and handed him the soft pink fabric, faded from washing. It ripped easily in his hands. He put his shirt back on, his exposed stomach tight and cut by the shadows. She was ashamed now, remembering how turned on she'd been. But at the time, she couldn't take her eyes off Pat while he stuffed the fabric into the bottles' necks.

"Where'd you learn to make those?" she asked.

"The Internet," he said. "It's pretty easy, but you can make dumb mistakes." He grabbed a roll of duct tape from his backpack and taped the necks. One end of the fabric floated in the liquid, and the rest streamed out like a ponytail. He made sure the openings were well plugged.

"Almost done." He had a bottle in each hand and curled them up and down.

"Wait!" Annie patted her skirt pockets. "Damn it, I forgot my phone in my car."

"Just use mine." Pat's tone was impatient; he was getting skittish. He jutted a hip out at her and she pulled a slim flip phone from his pocket.

"Cool phone," she couldn't help saying.

"Sorry; my parents don't own a restaurant," he said.

"I didn't mean—"

"Come on, take the picture." He lifted the bottles to his shoulders, arms in a "W."

"Okay, sexy boy," she said, and snapped one. The flash blacked out his surroundings and nearly obscured the bottles in the picture, but as clear as a shadow on a bright day, there was Pat, hamming it up with his Molotov cocktails.

"Your turn." He handed her the bottles.

Laughing, she put them up by her face and puckered her lips at the phone.

"Who's the sexy one now?" He looked approvingly at the photo.

"I was always the sexy one." She held the bottles away from her and pulled a face at the smell leaking out.

"Do you want the first firework?" He pulled a long-stemmed lighter out of his bag.

"I'll watch and learn," she said, pushing both bottles into his arms.

He grabbed her by the hand and took her a couple of yards away from the dumpster. He pressed the trigger on the lighter and a long flame shot out. His hands were shaking. The flame circled the cloth but refused to latch on.

"Hold this." He dumped the bottle into her hands. "Don't let go." The bottle felt warm between her palms. The amber liquid looked oddly delicious.

The fabric finally lit up. The flame flared from the cloth and Annie shoved the bottle back into Pat's hands. She expected him to tease her again, but his eyes were focused on the burning wick, which grew until his face turned a different shade in its light. Her face must have also become this dusky shade of red, sinister and unborn. Without warning, he whipped his arm back and shot the bottle at the dumpster.

"Fuck you!" He held out the words until the bottle smacked into its target.

The glass hit the broadside of the dumpster, the sound of its breaking drowned out by the metal clang, and a *whoosh* of flame briefly engulfed the front of the big green container. A puddle of fire continued to burn, but after a few seconds of holding her breath, Annie saw that it was harmless. The sight was surprisingly beautiful, and she told Pat so.

"I promised you fireworks." He was panting softly from excitement.

"Don't fuck up my dad's restaurant," she warned, but she ran a finger down his neck. "My turn!"

Pat fidgeted with the leftover bottle. "I think I know the problem with the wick."

He took out the canister she'd seen before—it *was* gasoline—and doused her pink shirt. A bloom of fruity odor wrapped around her head and sent her staggering.

"Aim for inside the dumpster," he said.

"Give it, give it." Her hands grabbed at the air. She'd never been this nervous before, or this excited. The one time that had come close was when she'd shoved that bottle of perfume into her purse. She'd walked out of the store, feeling not just good but gorgeous, basking for once in her invisibility. Then she'd turned around and seen the mall cop behind her.

"Ready?" Pat clicked the lighter.

"So ready."

Pat lit the wick, and before Annie could blink, the flame devoured half the length of the fabric. She bit back a scream, wheeled her throwing arm back, and let it rip.

They watched the bottle sail straight into the propped-open lid of the dumpster, where the glass broke and fell into its gaping mouth. The bark of fire was much louder this time. Flames rolled over the mounds of black and white plastic.

"Nice fucking throw," he said.

"I played softball in high school." Her heart was zipping around in her body, her chest as expansive as the sky. She pulled Pat's arm over her shoulders and nestled her head into his neck, smelling the musky spot right behind his ear. Instead of kissing her, he stared ahead, taking in the fire.

"I wish I could let this burn forever," he said softly.

"There's enough garbage," she said. "This dumpster could keep burning *for centuries*." She pitched her voice low and spooky, but Pat gave only a small chuckle. His attention had slipped out of reach. She was about to knock his arm off her.

Out of nowhere, an explosion flashed out of the dumpster, spitting flaming embers into the air.

Annie screamed and clutched her ears. "What the fuck!" Pat stumbled back, nearly pulling her to the ground with him. Three more sharp explosions followed, and like a walking nightmare, the bits of fire that had sprung from the dumpster landed on the dock and multiplied, spreading to the back wall and snatching at the garbage bags that hadn't fit into the dumpster. In one moment, the flames had become an uncontainable force.

"What did you do?" Annie pushed Pat in the chest again and again so that she didn't have to look at the restaurant.

"I don't fucking know!" His eyes were wide, terrified. A few more pops sounded out, and Annie screamed again.

"We have to go." He pulled her arm. "We have to get out of here."

Their eyes were watering and Annie started coughing too hard to say anything else. For whatever reason, they didn't run from the fire but trotted back to the car, barely lifting their knees. She was crying and shaking so hard that at first she thought she was jostling Pat's arm, which he'd draped over her shoulders. Then she heard his teeth chattering. His entire body shivered while the air grew hotter around them. The smell of burning wood and plastic filled her head.

She shoved her car into reverse and peeled out of the lot, scraping against the Jeep on her left. The white gash in the green paint job stood out brilliantly, like a flash of light. They drove away from the Duck House, neither of them looking into the rearview mirror. Annie took her phone out of the cup holder to call 911. Pat grabbed her by the back of her neck. She dropped the phone down the crack between her seat and the console.

"Let me go!" She tried to elbow him in the ribs without driving them off the highway ramp.

"The fire might not spread," he said. "If you call, we're going to get caught."

"We?" she said. "I'm not part of this."

"What are you talking about? You're the one who threw the fucking bottle!" He let go of her neck and dropped his head into his hands. "Come on, don't make this a big deal. No one is going to think it's us."

"You burned down my dad's restaurant. My grandpa's restaurant!"

"They probably have insurance," he said, with almost enough confidence. "We did them a favor. If we just keep quiet, it'll blow over."

"This is too much." Annie used her firmest voice, forcing her breaths to stay even. "I *have* to tell my dad." When Pat didn't respond, she counted the conversation over.

"Look, I have pictures," he said, after a long stretch of highway. "Of the both of us. So don't think I'm going down without you."

She slammed on the brakes and stopped the car in the middle of the interstate. Cars and trucks swerved out of their lane and honks pierced the air.

"Get rid of those pictures," she said.

"No."

"I swear to God I'll shove you out of the car," she said.

Pat laughed without much enthusiasm. "You push *me* out? You'll hurt yourself trying—"

She reared back her arm to punch him on the chin, but he leaned away in time. Her knuckles grazed his jaw. She pressed down on her horn and started screaming for help. Pat grabbed her again and held her against him.

"What are you afraid of?" he said into her ear. "Me?"

"No," she said. She wanted to bite into the side of his neck.

"You afraid of getting caught?"

"No."

"Admit it." He loosened his grip. "You liked what we did. You had fun."

"That's what you want me to say," she said. A bodiless semi whined past them, the driver leaning into his horn.

She was confused by her own adrenaline, so scared her groin

pulsed with a persistency she could almost mistake for pleasure. *Did* she like it?

"You wanted to throw that bottle more than I did," he said.

She sank her teeth into his skin, but she stopped herself from closing the bite. His neck vibrated in her teeth. His arms released her.

She pressed on the gas and restarted the drive.

"Just wait, please," he said, when their exit approached. "We can talk about it tomorrow morning."

"I have to go to work," she said automatically, and choked on the last, hard "k."

She hated him with her entire body in the silence that followed, and she vowed that if he laughed, she would ram the car's passenger side into the median divider. He covered her hand with his and together they squeezed the hard bulb of the gearshift.

"Restaurants burn down all the time," he promised, pretending not to see her cry.

A tear slid an all-too-familiar path down her cheek. Annie wished she could undo the past. She hadn't expected the intensity of the past two days. The terror felt like a sharp stabbing. Worse was the bitter dread that slipped down her chest and pooled in her belly. She'd slept all day to escape the feeling, but each moment of waking dragged her right back.

In his seat, her dad stirred, shifted his shoulders, then stilled. If he had opened his eyes, he would've seen no distress on her face. Annie had swiped the tear off her cheek, so fiercely that she'd scratched the skin a little with her nail. After years of wanting him to see her, what she wanted now was for him to keep looking past.

At the intersection, she braked for a red light. In front of her, four teenagers suddenly spilled out of their car. Tripping over their laughter, they raced one another around the idling vehicle, clinging on to the edges of their thrown-open doors to round the corners. Annie was transfixed by their game. The kids made one lap, then another. On the third round, one of them shouted something. The passengers dove back in the car, squirming into their seats. The four doors shut. Annie blinked. For all their gleeful running around, the teenagers had ended back in the same positions they'd started out in, as if they'd never left the car at all. How stupid they looked, laughing in their seats. The light turned green, and the driver, struggling with his seatbelt, didn't notice. Annie slammed the heel of her hand against her horn until their car shot forward. The passengers looked behind them, confused.

"What was that all about?" her dad asked, rumbled awake.

"My hand slipped." She gave him the breeziest smile she could muster. "Go back to sleep."

Johnny's mother was waiting for him when they pulled into the circular driveway. Dead leaves, leaves that his mother usually cleared away in the morning, surrounded the weeping willow in the center. His mother's small face was visible from behind the side window. She did not wave or otherwise acknowledge the car.

"We're going to talk about your new friend when I finish this," Johnny said, opening the car door. "I'm glad you felt comfortable enough to tell me about the relationship, but we need to go over your behavior. And his."

"Dad, close the door." Annie pressed the lock button prematurely. "You're letting in the heat."

He shut the door with more force than necessary and instantly regretted that both his mother and daughter had witnessed his frustration. His mother's face remained in the side window until he walked up the front steps. The sheer drape sprang back into place and her face disappeared. Seconds later, he heard the heavy click of the deadbolt, and when he pushed the door open, he felt her pulling from the other side. His mother couldn't even let him open a door without interfering.

"Good, you're here," she said, when he stepped into the foyer. The temperature of the house was in the eighties, a sucker punch after the heat outside. His mother appeared to be wearing at least five layers of sweaters. The extra cotton padding swallowed up her thin body. If he asked about her health too directly, she would accuse him of wanting his inheritance early, but it was his responsibility to make sure she wasn't a danger to herself. A year ago she'd slipped on the stairs and broken her leg. He and Jimmy had looked into some retirement communities after the accident, but they hadn't committed to anything.

"Ma, how are you; have you eaten?" Johnny slipped out of his shoes. She'd laid out his father's old sandals, which were made of hard plastic, with nubs meant to massage the feet. Every step pinched his skin. He followed her into the kitchen.

"This is what happens when you run off to Hong Kong and leave your family behind," she continued, ignoring his niceties. "Did you forget you're a grown man? You looked ridiculous. At least you stayed out of Beijing and didn't saddle my family with your nonsense. You missed so many charity dinners while you were gone. You could have made some connections for the restaurant. Now you don't even have a restaurant to make connections for!"

"I'm back now," Johnny said. He felt a dull stab of worry at the mention of his unemployment. "You need to calm down. You'll give yourself a heart attack."

"This boy goes and teaches one class and now he thinks he can lecture his own mother." She looked off to the side, addressing the invisible audience that witnessed all their family's disagreements.

"Sit down and I'll make tea," he said. He pulled a chair out for her.

The kitchen counter was dull and sticky, lacking the perfume of bleach and lemons that once followed his mother everywhere. He'd been right to worry about the upkeep of the house. When he was younger, he'd never wondered how the mansion was kept so spotless, every corner free of dust and cobwebs, and every toilet, of which they had eight, scrubbed clean. Once, a friend had asked what maid service they used, and when Johnny said that his mother did all the cleaning, the friend had called him a liar. Keeping their house clean on her own, when she worked nearly full-time, must have required superhuman strength. But his mother was no longer superhuman. She was just human now, a senior human at that, who could no longer keep even the kitchen island clean.

At least the hot-water dispenser was full. Johnny filled the teapot, packed loose tea leaves into the strainer drying by the sink, and grabbed two mugs.

His mother had gotten up soundlessly. Surprising him, she took the mugs and teapot out of his hands.

"Ma, let me." She was already setting the items down on the table.

She looked him over while they waited for the tea to steep.

"You've gotten fatter," she said.

"I'm just puffy from the flight," he said. He tugged at the waistline of his pants, which were tighter, but not, he reassured himself, uncomfortably so.

"You're looking older too. You need to sleep more. You'll catch a cold."

"I would be sleeping now if you hadn't asked me to come here immediately."

His mother made a sucking noise with her tongue, as dismissive as an eye roll but with extra juice. Johnny grabbed the teapot, scalding his fingers, and filled their mugs.

"The tea isn't ready!" she scolded. The liquid came out a pale, translucent green.

"You're clearly freezing." He pinched the sleeve of her sweater. "You need something to warm you up."

"The heat is good for your health." She inspected her cup petulantly. "This is why Americans die young. Their houses are too cold."

Talking to his mother was like talking to a toddler. Her reasoning didn't take steps; it leaped and bounded with strides too long for any person to follow. She was steadfast in her opinions, and the only person more stubborn was Jimmy. No wonder Jimmy was her favorite, a piece of knowledge that sometimes made it easier for Johnny to be patient with his mother and sometimes drove him to tell her he was the only one who cared.

"You shouldn't be sweating in your own house," he said. He warmed his already hot hands against the teacup. "Does Jimmy know I'm back?"

"He doesn't answer my calls. Who knows if he listens to my messages?" His mother sniffed and turned her head. "What did I do in a past life to deserve these sons?"

Something about the way his mother addressed her invisible audience sounded different. Her voice had taken on the goading tone she'd used to get his father's attention when he was alive. Had his mother replaced her audience with his father?

"Are you lonely?" he asked her. "Do you miss Dad?"

She recoiled at his questions. A puff of breath shot out from her mouth.

"I'm fine." She rooted through her pockets. "You ask useless questions. More like the baby of the family than the oldest. I should've kept trying for a girl." She pulled out a small tin of mints and crunched one between her teeth. "A girl would keep her mother company. A girl would've made your father smile, even in his grave, instead of making him weep in the dirt."

Johnny quickly drank down his tea and walked his cup to the sink. The extra distance dampened his mother's volume. He was tired from traveling, too tired to absorb the shock of his brother's actions, his daughter's behavior, and certainly too tired to listen to his mother's accusations. Even her wishful thinking was hostile. How could one woman be so hateful and yet so clearly obsessed with love? He turned back to face her, leaning his waist against the sink. She'd let the gray take over her hair. He didn't like the look. The gray didn't so much age her as sharpen her. His mother didn't need to look more severe and put-upon. Even so, she seemed to be shrinking behind the large mahogany table, dwarfed by the high back of her chair. She was too small for such a big house.

"Why am I driving you to Jimmy's?" Johnny asked.

"We should've already left." She checked her watch. "But you had to make tea."

"If you wanted to leave, you should have said so."

"Don't pout." She poured her tea back into the pot. "You were always too sensitive. At least your brother's got thick skin."

"I spent the past six months teaching lecture halls full of college kids," Johnny said, following his mother into the garage. "I don't think a sensitive man could've handled that."

"Only a sensitive man would surround himself with children who don't have an original thought in their heads," she shot back. She ducked around to grab his shoes from the foyer.

"You are impossible to talk to!" He was a teenager again, surly because his mother had forced his hand.

She set down his shoes, fussing with a small scuff on the leather. "Jimmy is expecting us," she said. "Apparently he's brought over his real estate agent. I bet she's a real looker."

Johnny brought up his most recent image, from almost ten years ago, of Jimmy's ex-wife, Helen: painfully thin, with an impossibly large chest, and big teeth that showed whether she smiled or scowled. Jimmy had, of course, met her at a club.

"Be nice," Johnny said.

"I raised two fools," his mother yelled over the crashing groan of the garage door. She zipped herself into a large puffy jacket, looking like a sleeping bag with legs. Walking toward the hulking SUV she'd picked out for her birthday a few years ago, she paused at the passenger door. "Now help Ma into her car. My hip is too stiff to use the step."

13

Johnny and their mother were minutes from arriving, but Jimmy was more preoccupied with every step Janine was taking in his condo. He'd lived there since his thirties, hiding out after his divorce. He'd signed the lease as a temporary solution—until he found a good woman to take pity on him, his mother liked to say. But the years had passed.

He'd forgotten what it was like to re-see his space through a lover's eyes, and Janine's eyes in particular did not gloss over details. Her head swiveled while she walked around his living room, taking in every thoughtless choice he'd made. The condo had an industrial design: exposed piping, useless pillars, and cold concrete floors, which he'd minimally covered with a few rugs. His TV was large and thin, like a slab of black ice. A leather couch curved around the room, ugly and brown, but so comfortable that he'd spent many nights curled against its back. The coffee table was crowded with remotes, and an old, stained coaster teetered on the edge. Janine took a seat at the end of the couch, anticipating but unable to stop the rude squeak of the leather.

"What a place you've got here," she said, hands on her knees.

"I'd show you around, but my cleaner is on vacation," he said. His mother had trained messiness out of the entire family, but better to save the rest of his apartment from scrutiny.

"How're you planning on telling Johnny and your mother?" She was still looking around the living room.

"I'm sure Johnny's briefed Feng Fei," he said. "We just need to make sure they don't team up."

"Divided they fall," Janine agreed.

"Leave it to me," he said. "You talk business and profits."

"The sexy bits," she said, crossing her legs.

Jimmy sat down next to her and skimmed his hand up her thigh.

"I can't wait to get ahold of *your* sexy bits." He tucked his fingers under the hem of her skirt. She pushed his hand away.

"Stay focused," she said.

"Just a small handful," he said.

"I'll give you more if you just wait."

They were both aware of how unappealing her promise sounded. So Janine was nervous. She placed a soft kiss on Jimmy's neck, an apology for allowing her performance to slip. His discovery of her gambits had cast a penetrating light on their interactions, but it hadn't reduced the pleasure he took in her attention. He didn't enjoy her more; the enjoyment was just more intimate. The way that laughter at a joke and laughter at an inside joke took on separate registers felt different in the throat.

The doorbell rang and a flurry of knocks sounded against the wood. His mother's signature greeting. Jimmy burrowed his head into Janine's chest, murmured that he needed the luck, before going to let his family in.

"You gain weight," his mother said when he opened the door. She always spoke English to him and Chinese to Johnny. Unless she was very angry. "You need new pants. I pick some up for you." She went to check his size on the inside of his waistband, but he stepped out of reach.

NUMBER ONE CHINESE RESTAURANT · 163

"Good to see you," said Johnny, following close behind.

"Nice of you to come all the way from Hong Kong," Jimmy said. He inadvertently took a step back when Johnny approached. To cover, Jimmy swept out his arm, as if displaying his apartment, which was neither new nor impressive. "Anything to drink?"

"Ma, do you want tea?" Johnny asked.

"I can make tea." Janine jumped up. His mother looked at her as if she'd appeared from thin air.

"This is Janine, my real estate agent." Jimmy put a hand on each woman's shoulder and pushed the two of them a little closer together.

"Nice to meet you." His mother switched to Chinese as she shook off his hand. "You're from China?"

"Yes," Janine said, also in Chinese. "Like I said on the phone. Beijing, originally."

"A Beijing girl." His mother adjusted her Cartier watch. "Rare to find these days."

"I haven't gone back in a while," Janine said. "What about you?"

"Not in years." His mother sat down. Disliking the sinking cushion, she relocated to the sofa's arm. "Do you have that pu erh tea I bought you?"

Jimmy started slightly. His mother was talking to him.

"It's on the shelf above the toaster."

"I'll find it," Janine said. She seemed unruffled by the abrupt end to the conversation. All three of them watched her leave the room.

"A Beijing girl," their mother scoffed. She preferred to tear people down in her native tongue. "Putting on airs when she lisps like a Southerner. As if I can't hear the difference!"

"I think her family is from Beijing," Jimmy said. "Her ex-husband is from Shanghai."

"She's divorced?" His mother looked pleased and scandalized. "No wonder she has to be a real estate agent."

"Mom!" Jimmy would not permit his mother to stick her thorns into Janine. "She's a professional and the best in her field."

His mother looked up at him like a startled child. Then she turned her head toward Johnny and her crowd of unseen supporters.

"Your brother is in love with his real estate agent," she said. "My grandchildren will have country blood."

The hot-water heater bubbled and clicked in the next room. Janine came out with a tray.

They sat in a semicircle on the couch, no one truly facing anyone else.

"What we do here?" his mother asked.

"The police are deciding whether or not to get involved," Jimmy said. "But the insurance company is almost certain it was arson, and as long as they think I had something to do with it, I can't cash in my policy."

"You did have something to do with it," Johnny said, as if forgetting their mother was in the room.

"Then why haven't the police interrogated Jimmy as a suspect?" Janine said.

"Luckily," Jimmy interrupted both of them, "my new restaurant is opening soon, and we can make up the lost wages with the Glory. But I need money until it starts making a profit. Mom, be reasonable: You don't need that house, and I do."

His mother stood up from her perch and slapped him on the side of his head.

"You be reasonable!" she yelled. "You ungrateful idiot."

"We'll find you a better place," Jimmy said, his head stinging. "In D.C. Near the restaurant."

"Like I'd want to eat at your trash heap. You don't even have the family specialties."

"Jimmy's restaurant is high class," Janine said, taking a few liberties to defend him. "The buzz is already incredible. The money will be repaid."

"And my house?" His mother stood over Janine, whose professional veneer remained solid as ice. "Will my house be given back to me? The house where I spent my last years with my husband? The house that represents all our hard work and suffering?"

"That house is overwhelming you," Jimmy said. "I saw how cluttered and dusty everything was. You need a smaller place or you're going to hurt yourself." He gestured toward Johnny. "We were already planning on moving you somewhere else, before this fire business. Janine thinks we'll get triple what you and Dad paid."

"So that's why you were in my house in the middle of the night!" His mother screwed up her face. "You brought this stranger into my house while I was sleeping?"

"Of course not," Jimmy said easily. "I told you, I was trying to find paperwork."

"Jimmy's right. We were already planning on moving you," Johnny said, swerving them, to Jimmy's complete surprise, out of danger. "Ma, it's not safe for a woman your age to live by yourself in a house that big."

"And were you planning on letting me live with you?" she asked, her voice sharp and yet, at the end of her question, vulnerable.

"My place is under renovation—"

"My own children." Their mother sank back down and dug her nails into the couch. "Hire me a housekeeper. Or a part-time nurse. If you really cared about my well-being and not your own pockets, you would never sell my house." Her teacup tumbled out of her lap and broke against the concrete floor.

"Ma, you're shaking." Johnny grasped her thin shoulders. "We've worked you up. You need to lie down." He tried to haul her up.

"You can take my bed," Jimmy offered.

"I'd rather sleep in a pigpen," his mother snapped. "I can't stand to look at you. Any of you! I'm going to the car."

"Let me walk you down." Johnny tugged the car keys from his pocket.

"Leave me alone." She grabbed the keys. "Stay up here and keep plotting with your worthless little brother and his 'real estate agent.'"

She slammed the door behind her. Janine bent down to pick up the ceramic pieces from the floor.

"You can just leave that," Jimmy said distractedly. Janine gathered all the pieces and went to the kitchen.

"Are you happy?" Johnny asked. "You've probably taken five years off her life."

"If you're going to lecture me, you can leave," Jimmy said.

Johnny sipped his tea, then settled into the cushions and crossed his legs. "I meant what I said on our last call," he said. "You're not getting the insurance money. But the situation has changed. You saw Ma's place. Strangers probably wouldn't notice a difference, but we do." He uncrossed his legs and leaned forward. "She's not what she used to be. I think it's time we admit that. You're not selling the house for the right reasons, but I think the house should be sold. Ma will need some of the money to offset the cost of a retirement community, but her finances are solid. I think we can work this out."

"What happened to 'You are no longer my family,'" Jimmy taunted. "What happened to 'Over my dead body'?"

"I don't think I said the second thing," Johnny said. "But I had an eighteen-hour flight to collect my thoughts. I can't watch you bury yourself. And the more we fight about this, the less chance we have of rebuilding the Duck House."

Jimmy leaned into the sofa. For all his talk about family and duties, what Johnny really wanted was his kingdom back. He was nothing without his little pedestal.

"The Duck House is dead." Jimmy glanced over at the kitchen. Janine should've come back by now. She must've overheard their conversation and stayed busy. Sure enough, the sound of the faucet running came from the next room. "It's been cremated."

"I'll resurrect it." Johnny took a breath. He had a speech prepared. "It was never right for Dad to leave my name off the contract," he began. "I might not have worked there as long as you, but I helped make the Duck House what it . . . was."

Jimmy made the hurry-up gesture with his hand.

"Do we still own the land?" Johnny said.

"We haven't looked for interested buyers yet."

Johnny clasped his hands together in his lap. "Now you have one. Give me the Duck House. Put the contracts under my name. When the insurance works itself out, I'll take over. If the insurance company doesn't give us the payout, I can find investors. It's what Dad would have wanted. Ma will be happy."

"Mom is never happy," Jimmy said, but he scratched his neck in thought. "So what do I get?"

"I'll help you sell the house," Johnny said. "After she broke her leg last winter, Ma gave me power of attorney. She didn't feel capable anymore. I pay all her bills."

Johnny answered the look on Jimmy's face. "She wanted it to be a secret. You know how she is with information. She still hasn't told her relatives in China that Dad is dead. We don't even know who our relatives in China are."

"Looking out for dead Dad and strung-out Mom." Jimmy knew sarcasm didn't reach his brother, but he persisted. "Even when you're helping, you're insufferable."

Janine came out and put a damp hand on Jimmy's shoulder.

"Looks like you two have come to some agreement," she said, as though she hadn't been eavesdropping. Jimmy knew he hadn't left a single dirty dish in that sink.

"I think we have." Johnny reached out his hand. Jimmy slowly extended his as well. Their hands were the last identical parts of their bodies. Thick but agile fingers, meaty palms that could withstand hot plates and strong handshakes, and hairless wrists. They were hands that could bow at customers and shame employees. Now each hand grasped its mirror image.

"Admit you're doing this for the money," Jimmy said.

"Admit *you're* doing this for our family." Johnny squeezed hard to stop Jimmy from wriggling out of the handshake.

Janine looked on approvingly. "I wish I had siblings," she said, when Johnny finally released Jimmy's hand.

"It was nice meeting you, Janine," Johnny said, getting up with a stretch. "Good seeing you too, Jimmy."

"If Mom sells, I'll change the contracts," Jimmy said.

"The house will be snapped up as soon as it hits the market," Janine said. "I'll make sure of it."

At these words, Johnny looked over and held Janine in his gaze for a second too long. Janine stood up a little straighter. A jolt ran through Jimmy's gut, but then Johnny was at the door, slipping into his shoes.

"Hopefully, Mom hasn't driven off without you," Jimmy said.

Johnny lifted his hand and smiled. The door clicked shut behind him. Janine dropped down onto the couch immediately, letting out a great gush of air.

"What a tense meeting," she said. "You do not get along with your family."

"What're you talking about?" Jimmy stood up and paced the room. "That *was* us getting along." He sank back down next to Janine. "Ready to kick an old woman out of her mansion?"

"So all your brother's talk about family?" Janine dipped her chin into his shoulder, a knowing smile on her face.

"Total bullshit." He kissed the top of her head. "I've never felt closer to him."

"Do you want to feel closer to me?" she asked. She nibbled the collar of his shirt.

He jumped on top of her. Their bodies bounced lightly on the couch, their skin sticking and smacking against the leather.

The cushions were still warm from the weight of his family's bodies.

Waiting in the car, which she'd had a hell of a time hoisting her stiff body into, Feng Fei allowed herself a minute to fume before she got straight back to work. She'd never been lazy, nor was she the kind of woman who would allow the creatures she'd created to bury her under their self-interest and neglect. Ever since her youngest had dropped his plans on her head, she'd been considering her options. Then her oldest had come flying back, further disrupting her strategies. Now she had two sons to manage, and as with most ill-mannered children, they only ceased their fighting to fight her. Johnny, for all his peacocking, was more like his father than he realized, and it wouldn't surprise her if he'd already leveraged his control over her finances to get what he wanted. Jimmy, like a drowning rat, would gladly seize the option, regardless of how cruel the consequences, because he still, at his core, believed his big brother was a hero. How she regretted signing over her freedom to Johnny in that period of weakness. Grief and pain had made her want to throw out her own ambition; she was rooting through the garbage for it now. But she was not without one last ally to call.

"Long time, Feng Fei," Pang said when he answered his phone.

"Ah-Pang," she said. Nostalgia came into her like new breath. How many times had she said those words to him? How many favors had they traded over the phone? This was why one kept old friends, even rotten ones. "You're repeating your old tricks. It's like you wanted me to hunt you down."

"Why replace an old trick if it keeps working?" His laugh crackled through the connection. He'd always had an old man's laugh, yet now that he was finally an old man, all Feng Fei could think of was Ah-Pang in his twenties. Back then, self-conscious about his missing finger, he'd strapped on a steel prosthetic. He used to dip it into the hot broth they used for the wonton soup and trace it along the back of her neck, stinging her like a scorpion. He was the worst when he was bored. At his best, he fixed all her problems. As long as he got to tell her about the slick and violent routes he used. Powerful enough that he clung to secrecy like a security blanket, Ah-Pang spoke exclusively to her about his plots, shutting even Bobby out of the loop. Because of their private chats—or, rather, Ah-Pang's whispered monologues while she worked—her husband was always suspicious of the two of them.

"I don't give a damn about that sneak," Feng Fei used to have to say. "He clings to me like a duckling, and the only thing worse is you boohooing like the last unmarried girl in town."

Truthfully, a part of her had enjoyed Ah-Pang's confidence, had felt, in his recognition, a sensibility inside her that set her apart. He gravitated toward her because, like him, her meanness came not from greed but from the constant fear that life had never and would never respect her. She had to demand respect from life, or it would try to pass her by.

"You and my husband," she said. "You don't know when to retire."

"You're sounding mighty friendly, considering what you're accusing me of," he said.

"I only hold grudges when they benefit me," she said. "Unlike some people."

"I don't understand why you're calling," he said. "Unless you're asking me to do something unsafe to my livelihood."

"Who do you take me for?" she snapped. "My sons are idiots. You know this. Forgive Jimmy like I've forgiven you." She turned the car on and cranked up the air-conditioning. For the first time in a while, she was too hot.

"None of them take after you, little Feng," he cooed. "None of them got your business sense." His tongue clucked against his teeth while he considered her offer.

"Perhaps I was a little rash," he continued. His voice disappeared from her phone and rematerialized over the Bluetooth speakers. "You know my temper is hard to manage."

"I also know that you never have fewer than three Plan Bs."

They'd switched to talking in code, speaking about events that had remained unspoken for so many years they'd lost the language. The most immense moments of their lives—coming to America, Bobby's first restaurant, Jimmy's possession charges—had been diced up and scrambled into the same shorthand.

"I need your help," she said. "They're planning on selling the house out from under me. And they've got some flimsy little real estate agent helping them. I assume she's your girl, so call her off."

"I never told her to sell your house." Ah-Pang's voice turned throaty with indignation.

"You always had a hard time controlling your women," Feng Fei said. "Even without her, they'll sell the house. You know what a good location that place is. Jimmy needs his money."

"I can fix the insurance," Pang said. The speakers crackled from his breathing. "But you'll have to let me deal with Jimmy as I please. I know he's your darling baby—"

"He needs to grow up sometime," she interrupted. "His father did." She thought, with some relish, of the decrepit takeout joint Bobby had owned before the Duck House, how he'd presented it to her, newly in America, as if it were the greatest gift the country could ever bestow. How easily the greasy walls had burned.

"Everyone should have a mother like you," Ah-Pang said.

"And an 'uncle' like you."

14

Ah-Jack's wife officially introduced him to her new lover at the second-best hotpot restaurant in Maryland. After Jimmy had let him leave early, Ah-Jack had spent the rest of his day off waiting for Michelle to come home. He'd called her so many times that the phone started sending him automatically to voicemail. Ironic, then, that this was how she finally chose to contact him. He woke up Wednesday morning to a long message from Michelle. He couldn't bear to listen to it until he was in the car, on his way to pick up Nan—then, he could not bear not to. At the end of the voicemail, she'd asked him to come to Li Wah's, where she and the other man would be until close. He should've just driven into a tree. At least Michelle cared enough not to book the meeting at his favorite hotpot joint. Li Wah's was stingy with their fish balls, and their vegetables were unclean. He was happy to give the place up.

By the time Ah-Jack showed up at the restaurant, Li Wah's was mostly empty. Jimmy had kept refusing to let him take his lunch break, even though the new staff had finished all his remaining tasks. Now it was almost two. Waiters were eating their family meal at a round table in the corner. Michelle was easy to spot in her headscarf. Beside her in the booth was her new lover. The other man was younger, his face generously creased around the eyes and mouth but nowhere else. He was dressed casually, but his hair looked freshly combed. Ah-Jack could smell the man's recently applied cologne. Michelle also looked younger—or, rather, newer. But when she stood to greet him, the healthy glow on her face revealed the marks of makeup. She rubbed nervously at the line of her bottom lip, painted an unnaturally rosy color. Her cheeks were a similar shade, and the soft down above her upper lip glimmered with translucent powder. The one thing unenhanced by makeup was the eager, hopeful look that came into Michelle's eyes whenever she glanced at the man next to her. Ah-Jack wanted to bring a wet washcloth to her face and scrub everything, down to that terrible look, away.

"Order whatever you like," the other man, who called himself Gary, said. "This one's on me."

Gary was acting as though the late lunch were a normal event. He tried to make small talk that, given the circumstances, came off as perverse, even malicious. After they'd ordered, Ah-Jack pretended to keep reading the menu. He was secretly studying Gary, trying to find what was so appealing about him. Gary was a fat-cheeked man whose clothes looked too new, as if he'd swiped his outfit off a store mannequin. His speech was to the point, lacking any finesse or tact; based on the coarseness of his manner, he was most likely from some mountain village up North, where the men were known for eating too much meat and beating their wives. The other man clearly lacked any real intelligence and was so petrified of silence that he didn't allow any gaps between his sentences. He prattled on as if practicing a play to a mirror. Ah-Jack would have hated Gary even if he hadn't stolen his wife.

Michelle stared at the soy sauce bottles near her left hand, unable to meet his eyes across the table. She had the look of a defenseless animal who, rather than curling into a tight ball, laid itself out flat, ready for the blow. But watching her over the roiling hotpot, Ah-Jack couldn't muster the strength to hurt her back—only a wounded tenderness, and a desire to trace the sunken sockets around her dark eyes.

"You look well," Ah-Jack said. He'd interrupted Gary mid-sentence. "How're you feeling?"

"I feel fine," Michelle said. "Thank you for asking."

"Don't thank me!" Ah-Jack was aghast. "I haven't done a thing that requires thanking."

Michelle looked down at the table, then at Gary.

"If you need to yell at anyone, yell at me," Gary said. He moved his body in front of Michelle's and put his hands firmly on the table. Ah-Jack was once again reminded of Gary's big-ness. He'd mentioned in passing how he used to practice judo, and though the muscle had given way to fat, he'd retained an athlete's ability to fill up the space around him. "I'm to blame for this mess. I'm the one who pursued Michelle."

Ah-Jack wanted to reach over and flick Gary in the eye. He knew, from the voicemail, all about how they'd met—in an overcrowded hospital lobby, while Michelle filled out paperwork and Gary waited for a doctor to set his dislocated shoulder. He knew about the friendly lunches that had turned into secret dinners. Worse, it was Gary who'd accompanied Michelle to her doctor's visits; who ferried her to the pharmacy for her meds; who distracted her from her nausea. The other man's worst crime and greatest power was that he'd simply been there. Where did that leave Ah-Jack?

Their waitress moseyed over with a tray of raw beef, fish balls, glass noodles, cabbage, and radish. Ah-Jack shooed her away before she could dump all the items into the hotpot, and, standing up, he started dropping the fish balls in from too high a distance. The boiling broth splattered onto Gary's broad hands.

"Shit!" Gary wiped his hands on his chest. Red patches bloomed on his skin.

Ah-Jack didn't stop there. From the same height, he used his chopsticks to push the bundle of noodles into the pot, then the hunks of cabbage. The thick rounds of radish cannonballed into the soup, sending up geyser spouts. The vinyl tablecloth grew wetter as the broth rolled, unabsorbed, across the surface. He finished with slices of beef, which barely unsettled the waters. By then he'd calmed down. The beef, turning rapidly brown, floated, shriveled, above the broth.

"Are you finished?" Michelle demanded. She cleaned up the mess with her napkin.

"You can have the townhouse." Ah-Jack stayed standing.

She started to refuse.

"I don't need our home," he continued. "Nan is going to let me stay with her."

He was throwing this information at her spitefully. But if Michelle had betrayed him, he should at least be allowed to intimate that he could do the same. Nan hadn't actually offered him a place in her house. She didn't know Michelle had left him. But when had Nan refused him before?

"You're staying with Nan?" Michelle said, as Gary asked, "Who's Nan?"

"She's a good friend," Ah-Jack said. "A great friend."

"She has no room for you," Michelle said. "What're you doing, burdening her and her family?"

"What Nan and I do is none of your business anymore," he said. "Where do you think I went after I found you gone?" He stopped himself short of revealing which bed he'd filled. Why hurt Michelle with false allusions?

He sat down and ladled whatever looked cooked into his bowl. He mixed in too much shacha sauce and wolfed it all down, the biting saltiness of the sauce and the heat of the food making his nose run. Soup ran down his chin. He snuffled and chewed and swallowed until his bowl was empty.

"Eat, eat!" he said. "There's enough for all three of us." Michelle and Gary sat motionless, watching him.

"You must be hungry, waiting so many hours for me to show up." He nearly gagged on the mass of food in his mouth. "How rude of me!"

He was fully exposed before his wife and her lover. They shouldn't be allowed to watch him eat. No one who ate with any pleasure looked human, and for them to stare at his churning jaws while they fiddled with their chopsticks was to feel completely animal.

"Stop it." Michelle sounded frantic. She'd switched off the hotpot. The bubbles that had moments before threatened to brim over settled down. "You're going to choke yourself to death."

"This was a bad idea," Gary said. The simpleton.

Ah-Jack continued to eat. He let his cheeks bulge obscenely. He opened his eyes as wide as they could go, showing his whites like a demon. If they wanted to stare at him, he would leer back. He would show them their own reflection with his face, show them what he pictured, the sickening lewdness of his images, where they touched and grabbed and stroked each other. He could feel their thighs overlapping in the booth, the press of their flesh. What had Michelle's leg felt like under his thumb? He could only vaguely bring up the skin, soft and cool, the sparse hairs, the raised spots. She was the one who always did the touching. He bit the inside of his cheek by accident.

"If you're not going to eat, then leave." Ah-Jack sprayed flecks of food at the couple. "Who comes to a lunch and just sits there? You son of a bitch, you're paying but not eating? What're you trying to make me?"

"This was a bad idea," Gary said again, but this time he stood and tugged Michelle gently up with him.

"Is there a problem?" Now, of all times, their waitress hurried over.

"We have a doctor's appointment. I'll pay at the front." Gary slipped an over-generous tip into the waitress's hand.

How did the other man already know Michelle's schedule? Did her doctor know who Gary was? How many people had known before him? Ah-Jack had not asked any of his questions.

"Are you finished as well?" the waitress asked Ah-Jack.

"Me, finished?" Ah-Jack's voice was a touch too loud. "When there's so much food left? I would never waste a beautiful lunch like this."

"No hurry," she said, but she took away Michelle and Gary's table settings. Where their plates had been, there were two dry circles, untouched by the broth.

"I'm sorry," Michelle said, after the waitress showed Gary to the register. Her body was already drifting in his direction; her world now tipped downhill toward Gary. "Please tell Nan to call me."

"Why would she call *you*?" he said.

"She's my friend too."

"Because she had to be," he said. "Because you were my wife. But now you're nothing to both of us."

Michelle stepped back and tightened the knot on her headscarf.

"Tell her to call me." She was already picking up Gary's bad habit of repeating himself. "Goodbye."

"Enjoy our home," Ah-Jack called after her. Gary put an arm around Michelle's shoulder and steered her out the door. Ah-Jack stretched his neck to see. Outside, their heads were close together, almost touching. They talked without smiling, but their relief was palpable. Their new lives could begin now that they'd ended his.

The last time her bowels had seized up and bent her body in half, Nan had just said goodbye to her husband, Ray, who'd promised he'd call when he was settled in San Francisco. Now, hiding in the new restaurant's wine closet, the same sharp pains had returned. But she had to call her husband, no matter how her body resisted. She didn't have much time before Pat finished waiter training. Shifting on top of a box of chardonnay, she muscled through the discomfort.

Checking the time—it would be one in San Francisco—she dialed the phone number, rusted in her memory. Ray worked seven days a week, but he owned the small dim sum shop he'd opened ten years ago. He'd take her call even during the lunch rush.

"Yes?" he said, answering on the second ring. He sounded impatient, but Ray could sound impatient soaking in a bathtub. In the background, orders were being shouted in Cantonese. Nan had never set foot in the restaurant, or even in California for that matter, but she could piece together the shape of the room and the movement of the crowd based on pictures Ray had once sent her. She saw the scuffed linoleum tile, the polished glass counter, the paper menus taped against the wall. The line that sometimes snaked out the door and down the block.

"Pat can't stay with me," Nan said. The longer she took to get to her news, the worse her husband would react. She'd already delayed news of Pat's expulsion by months. What could Ray do from across the country? But now she told him the most important details, keeping her voice neutral. Pat, hard to wrangle before, had never, until two nights ago, been physically violent. Who, with goodness in his heart, could throw an old man to the floor? She truly didn't know her son. Watching him banter with the other waiters today, she feared what the new money would twist him into. One day it might be her, thrown to the ground at the slightest provocation. She was already only one woman. But her husband was a man who could train a dog that had bitten him. Her husband bit back; sometimes he bit first, a predilection that had led to his firing from the Duck House all those years ago. But her husband never did as she expected. So she recited all of Pat's troubles, and then she waited.

Over the line, Ray's breathing grew labored. The background din quieted as he moved to a private place, perhaps the bathroom. When he spoke, an echo sounded out.

"You've done the best you can," he said. "He takes after me. He's a piece of shit."

"You'll take him?" she said. "I wouldn't ask unless I thought he was really in trouble."

"The schools are good here," Ray said. He was probably holding his body in his thinking pose: elbows cupped in his palms, legs also crossed, teetering slightly as he stood. This was the one time her husband looked vulnerable. "He can work for me until the school year starts, then finish high school."

"Thank you." She rocked through another elongated stomach pain. Far from relief, she felt so nauseous that sweat sprang out from her hairline, tickling her scalp. She almost didn't hear what Ray said next.

"You could come too," he was offering, softly. Nan pressed her hand hard against her aching stomach. Her husband hadn't brought up a move in years. He barreled on while she wiped the sweat from her forehead. "There'd be no problem if you both lived with me."

Nan caught her breath in the back of her throat. She wanted to remind him that *he* was the one who'd broken up the family. But while her husband had mellowed out over the years, he was still the kind of man who could easily take back a favor just granted.

"Think about it," he said, exasperated by her brief silence. "Call me when you decide. I can take Pat in, but he'll never forgive you if you abandon him." The line clicked. He had hung up.

Ray, or Ah-Ray as she'd called him for far too long, disrupted everything he touched. He'd hounded her for years at the restaurant until she agreed to go out with him, talked her into marrying him four months after that, and knocked her up right after they'd decided not to have kids. Not even Ah-Jack could keep up. "Your husband knows how to wear me out," he'd liked to say.

When Pat was five, Ray got himself fired for throwing change at a customer who'd left pennies for a tip. He'd chased the woman outside, pelting handfuls of coins at her car. The only explanation he gave was that something in him had finally snapped. He packed his bags weeks later in a delusional journey west to find his fortune. But thousands of miles of country hadn't dampened the ripple effects of his impulse and will.

If Nan did go to San Francisco with her son, both of them forced to start over, would they know better than to repeat their old mistakes? She believed as much as she dared that once the momentum of his youth passed, Pat would regret how he'd hurt her. She could practically see, ten years into the future, Pat visiting with her first grandbaby, fat-legged and gurgling, all of them browner from the sun. Maybe she might get more than one day off a week. She and Ray could even scrape together a weekend every now and then. Nan couldn't remember the last Saturday she'd had at home or a single Sunday afternoon she'd spent sipping hot soy milk at a dim sum joint. She cared for Ray; he excited her, and age should have made him less temperamental. Or, if not age, then owning his own establishment, being his own boss. He'd never brought up divorcing her, though they'd been separated for twelve years. She was his wife. Divorce wouldn't change this.

But here she had Ah-Jack.

Her fear of the unknown and her dislike of change were merely passive knots, waiting to be undone. Ah-Jack, however, was a tugging grip on her wrist. She would have to cut a piece of herself off to loose his pull.

Too soon, she heard a knock at the wine-closet door.

"Come in," she said, her throat clogged. The door opened only after she repeated herself.

She scooted onto a crate of merlot. Her son picked his way through the cramped storage hold.

"What do you want?" He shouldered his backpack. "I'm about to grab a ride."

"I spoke to your father," she said. She'd wanted to use English, to make sure Pat understood what she was saying, but the language had scrambled to nonsense in her head.

"That asshole?" Pat said.

"Don't be vulgar." She stalled. "This was a very hard decision, but as parents, we have to do what's best for you, our son."

"What's he want? To yell at me? Screw him."

"He wants you to live with him," Nan blurted out. "You'll like San Francisco. You've always loved the outdoors."

Pat took a step back and nearly tripped over a box. He looked so ludicrous in the small space. Her chest ached.

"You already decided." He moved his hands around his collar like he was overheating. "You're shipping me off. I knew it."

"I might join you, in a few months." Nan wished her words could be stronger or at least make better promises. "When I make sure I've settled everything here. I'll come to California. We can be a family." She told herself she wasn't lying. Ah-Jack needed her now more than ever.

Pat crouched and rolled onto the balls of his feet. He cradled his head in his arms.

"You're never coming," he said. His nose made snuffling sounds.

She got down onto her knees and grabbed his wrists.

"Of course I'll move to California with you and your dad," she said. "You'll see. You'll be happier out there. You can start over. We both can."

Pat shot his arms out suddenly. Nan stumbled back to avoid being shoved. Instead, he gripped her tightly around her waist. His grasp was painful, accidentally digging into her ribs, but she would've rather broken them than shift her body in any way. She'd expected her son to be relieved, or indifferent, or angry, but not frightened, inconsolable. He was still a boy. She couldn't forget this. But as much as she cherished the contact, the fierceness of his embrace forced her to understand how her son could be both—a boy and a man—or, rather, something in between: a grown boy. Wasn't this the reason she was sending him away? She could not help him in this in-between time, when he was young enough to want his mother but big enough to break her too.

"What's keeping you here?" he asked, his head buried in her side.

"Jimmy is going through a rough time with this new restaurant and he's depending on me," she had to say. "I can't leave him now. Once I've made sure he's settled, I'll come to you and your dad. I promise."

Pat began to relax his grasp. It pained Nan to admit this, but he shouldn't have bent under her hollow reassurances. She should've taught her son how to ask for more. The fact that he didn't was what made him hers; they were genetic mirrors, with identical weak spots in their bones. She loosened her grip in perfect tandem with him. By the time they had their arms back at their sides, it was as if they had decided together when the embrace must end.

Ah-Jack packed his bags and left them piled in front of the door for Gary to trip over, in case the man dared enter his home before he'd properly left. He drove back to the Glory to finish the workday. He wondered how he would tell Nan.

At first, he couldn't locate her whereabouts. The new, young American waiters had no idea who Nan was, even after Ah-Jack described her. Useless, all of them. He was growing worried, a departure from his nature, when he remembered Nan's odd quirk of hiding in moments of panic. He checked the remote corners of the restaurant, looking in the walk-in fridge, the freezer, the pantry, and the bathrooms. Following a hunch, he finally found her sitting in the Glory's wine closet, her body rigid, rooted in place. She didn't seem to notice he was there, and he couldn't help but announce: "I have some news."

He always felt a spark of pleasure when he looked at his old friend, who had aged yet not aged in the thirty years they'd known each other. Overlaid on top of her current face were the faces she'd worn each time she'd rescued him from his life, until the current wrinkles and age spots faded out, leaving the exact same expression to shine through. One of worry, affection, frustration, and grudging patience.

"What did you do?" Nan said.

Bewitched by that beautiful expression, Ah-Jack let the account of the hotpot lunch roll out of his mouth. He was ashamed of his selfishness. But when he finished his story, a change came over Nan's face. She regained her sureness. She demanded he stay with her for as long as he needed, radiant with certainty. Overcome by relief, Ah-Jack grabbed one of her hands and kissed the middle knuckle, which was as large and speckled as a river pebble. All day he'd been stalked by a terror so large he had not dared to name it. But he invoked it now. She was not going to leave him. He would not grow sick alone and die forgotten. Nan would always be by his side.

15

After Ah-Jack dropped her off at home, Nan ventured into Pat's bedroom. The room was neat, which gave her a superficial surge of pleasure. Her son, at least, picked up after himself. How many mothers could say the same? But soon she found the item she'd been looking for, the dirty ripped T-shirt from two nights before. She lifted the shirt to her nose and inhaled. The smell of smoke was impossible to mistake, and after years of washing her chain-smoking husband's clothes, Nan knew the smell didn't come from cigarettes. The unspoken thing, wedged in the back of her throat all day, uncurled itself. She swallowed hard to keep it from wriggling out. With her hands, she tore the shirt into shreds and went downstairs to throw the fabric into the trash. She took the trash outside, put it in her garbage, then hauled the bag back out and crossed the street to shove it down her neighbor's can. She could still smell the smoke somehow. It had rubbed onto her hands, and with her palms lifted to her face, she nearly screamed into them. But already she was spreading doubt, like cooling lotion, over her wild thoughts. Perhaps the smoke—she sniffed her fingers again—*was* from cigarettes. She hadn't washed Ray's laundry in over a decade. How did she know what cigarette smoke did or didn't smell like? What made more sense? That her son had gone to a party, smoked, and torn his shirt in a fight, or the alternative? She scolded her mind for hearing zebras instead of horses.

In the house, she scrubbed her hands until the skin burned. The front door opened, then slammed. Her son was home. Guilt scalded her; she hid her hands behind her back.

"How was the rest of training?" she asked, when he came into the kitchen. He went to the freezer and pulled out one of the microwave dinners he ate between meals.

"Fine," he said. "Tiring." They were both acting bashful, their way of acknowledging the conversation they'd had in the wine closet.

"Restaurant work wears you down," she said. "How're your feet?"

"Throbbing," he said.

"When I started waiting tables my fingers ached so badly from lifting all those plates that I couldn't untie my shoes. How're yours?"

"All right," he said. "I still can't balance a tray."

"You'll get there," she said. "The first time I carried a tray, I spilled a beer down a customer's back. Luckily he was already drunk."

Pat flicked his eyes from the microwave timer to her face. "Funny," he said.

Nan didn't push the conversation. They were out of practice with each other. With every prodding question, her son would slip further beneath his ill-fitting skin. She wanted to preserve the tentative sense of family between them. If she could keep this lukewarm feeling alive, they might be able to have an honest conversation. She might ask him about two nights before.

Carefully, as she would with a difficult customer, she made suggestions.

"Maybe you can stay home tonight," she said. "Rest."

Pat sniffed loudly, eyes back on the microwave. He was making macaroni and cheese. He'd forgotten to cut a slit in the plastic wrap.

"If you have too many late nights, you'll get sick. This new job will be hard on the body. You've seen me." She was joking, but her back strained when she tried to straighten it.

"You look fine." He turned toward her, holding the steaming tray of macaroni between his fingertips. "I was already going to stay in. Tomorrow's training starts at six."

"I'm glad," she said, but she could have sung. She was breathing something better than air. She walked toward him, about to inspect the orange noodles he'd pulled from the microwave. A series of knocks sounded out from the front hall.

"Who could that be?" she asked, irritated at the disruption. Then she saw, through the window, Ah-Jack's car in the driveway. She hadn't meant for him to come tonight. How could she have forgotten that for Ah-Jack, an offer began as soon as it was spoken? To her horror, Pat was already down the hall, striding to the front door. Ah-Jack pushed the door open with a bang.

"Are you here to welcome me home?" He reached up to put his hands on Pat's shoulders.

"Uncle Jack," he said. "Are you visiting?"

"You could call it that!" Ah-Jack looked over at Nan as she hurried down the hall. His face registered her panic. "Your Uncle Jack has run into some family problems. I was going to ask your mom if I could stay a few nights."

Pat saw, at Ah-Jack's feet, the pile of suitcases.

"Looks like you've already asked." Turning to his mother, he said, "Is that what you meant by settling things?"

Before Nan could think of an answer, Pat had pushed past Ah-Jack and thudded up the stairs. His broad back disappeared behind his bedroom door. Nan's tongue was heavy in her mouth. She wanted to whip around and slap Ah-Jack across the face.

How dare he interrupt her life like this? But by the next breath, she was sorry for her reaction.

"I can leave," Ah-Jack said. "It won't be a problem."

"He was already in a bad mood," she said. "I'm sorry. You should stay."

"I can find a hotel."

"Stay tonight, since you're already here." She grabbed his suitcases and hauled them in. She had to cover her eyes with her hand, the light of her house suddenly too bright to bear.

Nan knocked on Pat's door. When she didn't hear a reply, she set down the tray of milk and cookies—Oreos, his favorite—and pushed her way through. The door caught on the blankets piled behind it. He'd snuck out again. She didn't blame him. She started untangling the blankets. Why didn't he just use the front door? He must know that she wouldn't have tried to stop him.

"Is there trouble?" Ah-Jack asked from the doorway. Nan hadn't heard him walk up the creaking stairs.

"Pat's broken out." She lay on the bed, her feet lifting off the carpet.

He walked over and sat down by her head. His fingers found their way into her hair. They combed through her scalp, stopping at her bun. He'd never touched her this way before, but his hands felt natural in her hair. She reached up and undid her bun, sighing when Ah-Jack shook out the tight spiral.

"What a troublemaker," he said. "I'm sure he'll be fine. He's a smart boy."

"Clever, not smart."

"Even better. Clever boys can always find their way out of trouble."

"Smart boys don't find their way into trouble in the first place." Nan had never been in this position in front of Ah-Jack before. What must she look like to him, to anyone who might peek in on this scene? An old woman having her hair stroked like a child, an even older man doing the stroking. She thought, suddenly, of Michelle walking in on them. Of the look that would be on her face: confused, but not angry, a small smile ready, in case it was her mistake. Nan had seen that look before. The vision was so intense that Nan nearly knocked Ah-Jack's hand away from her temple.

"Nan," Ah-Jack had said to her one day, in their first month at the Duck House. "I have a favor to ask you." They were sitting in a booth, folding napkins into fans.

She'd leaned in before drawing back again, when she felt her knees brush his.

"Of course," she said. "I'll do it."

"You haven't heard the favor." He laughed and unwrapped a sour candy from his jacket, crunching it between his molars. He threw the plastic onto the carpet, for a busboy to sweep up. "Michelle has been feeling better lately. But now she's restless, stuck in the house all day. She wanted me to ask you to come over for lunch on your day off. A girls' lunch. I didn't know how to say no."

"You talk about me with your wife?" Nan twisted the napkin in her hand. She wished it were paper.

"Of course," Ah-Jack said. "Your stories make her laugh." He looked down at her hands. Nan quickly shook out the napkin. "Forget it. I shouldn't have asked. My wife can find her own playmates."

"It's just lunch," Nan said. "I'd like to meet your wife." She grabbed a pen from her pocket and wrote herself a note, digging the point into her hand. "Have her call me."

Ah-Jack held his napkin up to his face, forming the cloth into a big beige smile.

"You've made someone very happy," he said.

*

Ah-Jack lived in a narrow, three-story townhouse, with stairs so steep that Nan had to pull herself up by the railing, as if she were climbing to temple. Ah-Jack's wife navigated the same steps with no trouble. She was so translucent she reminded Nan of a tadpole.

"I'm so happy you could come over." Michelle dipped her head to avoid the potted fern guarding the top of the second floor. "I'm on house arrest."

"No trouble at all," Nan said, out of breath. She swatted at the plant, which she'd forgotten to sidestep. "Can I help with lunch?"

"Absolutely not," Michelle said. "You just wait upstairs in the dining room while I bring everything up from the kitchen. Don't lift a finger!" She pointed Nan up the last flight of stairs.

Alone, Nan moved slowly. The carpet covering the steps suddenly felt too plush under her feet. The air grew warmer as she climbed, perfumed by the sharp odor of muscle balm. The top floor had an open layout, flanked by two windows and four closed doors. The dining table, in the middle of the room, rested atop a thick Persian rug. Michelle had already set out the plates.

After a moment's hesitation, Nan wandered over to the cluster of doors. One was too narrow to lead to anything but a supply closet. A quick peek confirmed this. The second she opened slowly, certain that the hinges would creak and give her away, but the door revealed that she'd wasted her time on a coat room. The third door she opened boldly. She found a guest room, barely furnished. The last door was where she needed to be.

Nan was about to shut the third door when she caught a whiff of something familiar. Why would a guest room smell like Ah-Jack? She stepped inside. She found the clothes he'd worn to work the day before in a small laundry hamper by the door.

The hamper was nearly full. Nan walked over to the vanity. She didn't know what she was looking for. A sign? A hint of how she fit into this place, this life? His mirror was dusty, and without thinking, she wrote her name carefully in the dust. She quickly wiped the characters away. Her palm left a streak of clean glass behind. She remembered herself and looked away to forget.

Ah-Jack's bed was neatly made, but his pillow held the indent of his head. She went over and picked up the pillow, carefully fluffing out the depression. After a few seconds of stillness, she set the pillow back. A magnet in her gut drew her down with it. Before she knew it, she was on the bed, and in the next moment, her face was on his pillow. The worn cotton felt oily against her cheek. She breathed in and found a spot of sourness where his mouth must have been.

"What are you doing?"

Nan jerked her head off the pillow. Michelle stood by the open door.

"I—" Nan touched her cheek. "I was looking for the bathroom. And I got dizzy."

"There's one in the master bedroom," Michelle said. Her tone was brittle and cautious, like a child deciding whether she'd deserved the slap. "We don't usually have guests use our private bathroom."

Nan stood up, holding her head. She didn't have to pretend to be nauseous.

"I didn't mean to come in here," she said. "I'm sorry."

"So why did you?" The serving spoons in Michelle's hand clicked together.

"I don't know," Nan said. "I've never done anything like this before."

"My husband told me you only came over a few months ago."

Nan couldn't look at Michelle. She stared instead at the top of the other woman's scalp, at the black fuzz that had grown back in. Nan's own head began to itch as she waited for Michelle's accusation.

"You must be lonely," Michelle said instead. Nan's eyes suddenly filled with tears, as if needles had punctured them. She'd been hiding those words in the pit of her stomach for months. How had this strange woman pulled them out? Where was the timid wife Ah-Jack had described?

"I'm the same," Michelle said, to Nan's surprise. "I understand."

She led Nan out into the dining room. The air now smelled like rice starch and braised pork. They sat at the table, Michelle at the head and Nan at the corner.

"Jack likes you," Michelle said. She began to polish the spoons with a cloth. "I see why."

"It's nothing."

"It's not nothing." Steam rose from the rice bowl, wispy strands tangling into clouds. "He's a silly man. But you make him better. He drinks less since you started carpooling. Stays away from the racetracks more. You keep him safe."

"I didn't tell him to do any of that." Michelle's fingers were long and delicate. They made the spoons she was polishing look expensive. Nan sat on her own hands.

"He likes talking to you at work," Michelle said. "He doesn't need any other distractions."

Nan clutched the corners of her chair. "We should eat." She took the polished spoons out of Michelle's hands and placed them by the dishes she'd brought up. "The food will get cold."

"I followed him to Taiwan." Michelle stood up. "I followed him here. But I can't follow him everywhere. He's his own person."

"He's yours," Nan insisted.

"How can he be mine when I never see him?" Michelle picked at a loose thread in her brocade tablecloth.

"I'll take care of him for you." Nan felt steamrolled by the fierceness of her own promise. "We'll take care of him together!"

192 · LILLIAN LI

Michelle let out a tinkling laugh, which all the girls from the south seemed to have.

"You're so young," she said. "What're you doing pledging yourself to someone else's husband?"

"Because it's the only way." The words snuck out of Nan without her permission. She'd gotten this far without confessing to Ah-Jack's wife, but now it was all over. She could have smacked herself. He'd never speak to her again.

Michelle only rubbed the patchy velvet on her skull. She seemed not to have heard. "Life is long," she said. "We should be friends. But first"—her dry lips cracked into a smile— "let's eat."

Life was long. She and Michelle were friends. And Nan had done nothing wrong, not a single indiscretion since her cheek had touched Ah-Jack's pillow. Michelle couldn't blame her for indulging, just this once, not when Michelle had indulged in so much more. She had lost her rights to Ah-Jack. Let her see them on the bed. The comfort was unparalleled.

"Getting Pat that job was smart," Ah-Jack said. "Or clever, whichever you prefer."

"I don't know." She pressed the top of her head into his leg. "All that loose cash. What's he going to do with a hundred dollars flopping around his pocket? It's dangerous."

"Maybe," he said. "But we turned out all right."

"I was always going to turn out all right." She turned her face up to smile at him. "But you were saved from a life of sin."

"I could've been a small-town gangster," he mused.

"Instead, we're civil servants." They both laughed, jostling the mattress.

"Not much longer for me," Ah-Jack said. "Now that Michelle's bills are on some other fellow's back."

"I'm sorry," she said.

"What've you got to be sorry for?" He tugged on the top of her ear. "What if I got a job at one of those carryout joints? I could sit in front of a fan all day and play with the owner's granddaughters. I'm a bachelor again. I don't need much."

"You'll go back to the horses in a heartbeat!" Nan sat up suddenly. "Haven't you learned anything about yourself, old man?"

Their eyes met. Nan felt her blood jump against her neck. She willed herself to keep her chin lifted. She would not look away first. If she did, California waited, yawning and sunny and hopeless.

Ah-Jack didn't look away either. Unexpectedly, his eyes grew teary.

"What will my life be now?" he said. He grabbed her hands off the mattress, which nearly sent her tumbling back onto the bed.

"Whatever you want it to be." She leaned her weight into him, to show him his own strength.

"It's not polite to tell lies," he said. "I hear you laughing at my limitations."

"How am I laughing at you?" The air conditioner's breeze blew Nan's hair into her mouth. "You're not dead yet."

"I can't even cut my own toenails!" He pinched his lips together. His breath grew quaky. "What can I do?"

"Anything." She readjusted her hands until they grasped his fingers back with equal strength. Without thinking, she brushed the hair out of her mouth with his hand. "I'll help you. I promise. You are my family."

"I can't ask you—"

"I don't give a shit!" She pulled him off the bed. "Let's go."

"Where?"

Nan stopped at the threshold of the bedroom. She hoped Ah-Jack couldn't read her expression. He'd always said she was at her most transparent when she worried, and she didn't want him to know that right now she was worrying about him. She wanted to calm him, to ground him with practicalities.

"The bathroom," she said. "I'm going to take a look at those toes of yours."

"They'll stink you out of your own house." Ah-Jack rubbed his big toes together.

"I'll hold my nose."

Nothing he said could dissuade her. She refused to be discouraged. She wished she could just tell him that she wouldn't find his feet too ugly to bear. But that would only make him feel more exposed. In the bathroom, to ease his self-consciousness, she groused while she hitched up the knees of her slacks, acting as if her joints were greatly inconvenienced. Crouching down before him, she slipped off his tight, shin-high socks.

"You're still breathing!" Ah-Jack couldn't help teasing her when the first sock fell. He pretended to fall into the toilet she had him perch on, and they both laughed at the absurdity of their situation.

Squatting on her heels, examining Ah-Jack's feet, Nan now remembered her son. Her stomach retightened as the guilt hit her. She hadn't been worried about his whereabouts or his safety. But looking up at this beloved man's face, brightened by the fluorescent lights, Nan could not blame herself for forgetting. She could only allow herself to forget again.

Ah-Jack watched his friend squatting in front of him, his ragged feet in her hands. Perhaps this was love. What he had with his wife had been perfunctory. Even the way Nan held his feet was different. Michelle cut his nails quickly, leaving sharp corners that grew back to prick his toes. Nan made many small snips, rounding out the nail until it looked manicured. He'd never questioned his love for his wife, but maybe this was because he rarely associated what he had with Michelle as love. She was a comfort and at times a crutch, and he could be sure that she saw him in this same light. Their relationship was symbiotic but detached, like separate animals in the wild. And while Michelle was his wife, wasn't Nan his companion? She was slathering Vaseline on his feet, the gentle pressure of her fingers tangible through his nerve-damaged soles. When she thought he wasn't looking, she took quick peeks at his face, gauging his comfort. Michelle was his cane, her help inanimate and impersonal, but Nan was his little thermometer. She moved as he moved, a constant measurement to the heat he gave off. Who could blame an old man for pulling her up and giving her a hard kiss on the mouth?

He was already apologizing when she stood and backed away, a sleepy look on her face.

"We need to get our rest," she whispered, and he accepted the rejection as coolly as he could. He let go of her hands, the disappearance of her touch a shock to his heart.

He was about to heft his body off the seat, when her hand came back down to help him up. Wordlessly, he took it. He followed her out of the bathroom and down the hall. He let her pull him into her bedroom.

16

———

Annie tried her best to get out of working at the Glory. She claimed she was busy preparing for her sophomore year, and she was possibly anemic, and she was having boy troubles, but her parents were adamant. Her uncle, opening his restaurant a month ahead of schedule, needed hostesses. Annie would have to grow up and help out.

"Do you think I want to handle insurance investigators?" her father asked, crossing his legs so that the openings of his Bermuda shorts flared wide. "Do you think your mother wants to go through all her accounting files? Do you think your grandmother wants to sell her house?"

Annie tried her mother next. "You don't even like Uncle Jimmy," she said. "Why are you helping him?"

But her mother only said, in her dreamy way, "Family is family." Annie pinched her around the waist, where a soft layer of fat had formed over the years. Her mother never spoke against her husband's side of the family. She was a daughter-in-law, and it was as if these hyphens closed her mouth like stitches.

"We never help out with your family," Annie said.

"My family is in China." Her mother swayed her midsection away from Annie's hands. "And *they* send *us* money."

"So can't you just send him money and let me enjoy the rest of my summer?" Annie heard herself begin to whine, which meant she'd all but forfeited. Even while she continued to argue, a part of her was already accepting that she would have to work at the Glory, with Pat.

Two and a half weeks after the fire, the Thursday the Beijing Glory opened for friends-and-family service, Annie was back at work. Her heart thumped as she parked in a garage and walked toward the entrance. She usually changed into her hostess uniform at the restaurant, but today she was already wearing her qipao. She didn't want Pat seeing her in normal clothes. She wanted to appear hardened, a waxy professional, even though underneath her uniform she hadn't showered since the night of the fire. She'd barely left her bed, sleeping sixteen fitful hours a day. She smelled bad, muddy. A bit like dirty ketchup. Her hair, slicked back in a bun, clung to her scalp. She was treading a dangerous line, but no one in her family had noticed.

She entered the Glory with her head down and walked quickly to her hostess stand. She barely looked up from the seating chart for the next few hours. She expected every passing body to be Pat's. Her paranoia grew until she stopped pretending to guide diners to their table altogether. She directed each party from the safety of her stand.

At the top of the lunch hour, her uncle came out of his office and looked her over. He told her to fix her makeup but pretended not to see her point an elderly couple to their table. She could've laughed in his face. Who would have thought that she would prove to be more volatile than her uncle? She was deeply tempted, right then, to tell him about the fire. If he knew that she'd held that flaming bottle before it was pitched into the dumpster, what would he do? Would he throw her out of the restaurant? Would he have her arrested? Would he spit in her face? The same cycle of thoughts had rolled through her mind a hundred times, applied to every member of her family, down to her grandfather. And with every turn of the cycle, she hated Pat a little more. He'd taken away her family. When he had no family of his own, not a real one, to suffer for.

She heard Pat before she saw him. His laugh. He was with a group of waiters at their station, eating the restaurant's family lunch—a stew of leftover chicken and rice. They were in that lull between lunch and dinner service. He caught her looking over at him. How was it possible for him to look so normal? He gave her a wave, as if they were friends standing on opposite sides of the street, and then he was striding over to meet her.

"Long time no see." He leaned an elbow against her stand and smoothed his lower lip with his thumb. "Where've you been?"

"Trying to get out of this job," she said. The Glory's hostess stand was a wispy little podium, with fake birch branches stuck on the sides. She felt exposed behind it.

"That sucks. How much you getting paid?"

"Twelve an hour. Before taxes."

"No tips?" He reached into his blazer pocket and pinched a roll of bills. "Thought you had the family connection."

"I don't want to serve people." She bent the edge of her newly laminated seating chart. "I'd rather save a little dignity."

"Your dignity must be expensive." He leaned in closer.

She leaned in too. His face registered her smell. He took his elbow off her stand.

"You look stressed out," he said.

"How about deleting those pictures of me?" she said.

If Pat had touched any part of himself, his pocket, his blazer, she would have pounced and torn through the fabric to get that phone back. But he stayed still, with his arms crossed. She bit the tip of her tongue as hard as she dared. She wouldn't cry.

"I think I'm going to keep them," he said. "But you can trust me."

"You can trust me too," she said. "Just let me see the pictures."

"You want to see if you look good?" His voice was teasing, but his eyes were restless. He lowered his voice and gripped her shoulder. "Look, they just want to close the case."

"But what if they want to talk to me?" Annie was having trouble breathing. "I can't lie to them. *Shit!*"

"Come on." Pat put his hand against the small of her back. "You're taking your break."

He bought her a pack of cigarettes from a convenience store on M Street. They sat on a ledge across from the movie theater. They hadn't been alone together since the fire. Their smoke drifted over the late-afternoon traffic. Annie counted two typos on the marquee.

"I don't usually smoke," she said. "Except at parties."

"Some party this is," he said. A mosquito buzzed a figure eight around their ears. "Are you feeling better?"

She said yes, though she couldn't meet his gaze. It was easier to be angry with Pat than to admit that she also missed him. He was good at noticing her in moments when she was certain no one was watching. Even the cigarettes he'd bought were the menthol ones she liked to bum off others. His attention didn't just flatter her; it used to make her feel safe. If she ever went missing, he'd know. She wanted to lean into him and her stomach turned from her own desire.

"What if I never feel better?" she said, after a couple of slow drags. "What if I crack? I don't want to, but—"

"Then you'll go to jail." His tone was abrupt, and cold.

Annie sprang back and dropped her cigarette. Her cheeks burned. She regretted every second of softness she'd felt toward him. "You'll go away for longer."

"I'm a minor." The way he held his body, hunched and shrinking, made him appear as though he were apologizing to her. "You're nineteen with a record."

"How do you know about that?"

"The whole restaurant knows about the shoplifting."

"I'll say you forced me to." She was thinking in bursts. "My family can get me the best lawyer in the state."

"You can't be serious." He reached out to touch her hot cheek. She turned her head away, and his fingers ended up in her hair.

"I fucking hate you," she said.

She wrenched her bun out of his hand, but his grip tightened.

"Careful," he said. "What've I got to lose?" He held up the Bic he'd used a minute ago to light her cigarette.

Suddenly he withdrew his hand. A look of pain crossed his face. It was as if her body had moved on its own to strike him. But Annie hadn't budged an inch. Pat backed away from her. He shoved a fist into his pocket and pulled out a thin gold chain. A green-gemmed pendant swung at the bottom of the loop. He thrust the necklace into her hand. His clammy fingers pushed her dry ones closed. He turned sharply and walked away, disappearing down the first alley in his path. Annie looked around for anyone who was watching, but the faces in traffic looked ahead, bored and disinterested. Her image reflected off a storefront's side window. Her hair stuck out in odd tufts; her mascara had melted onto her bottom lid. She looked alien in her hostess dress, her body wrapped tight in a cocoon-like sheath of unforgiving fabric. She undid the clasp that was constricting her throat and massaged the spot.

Dangling Pat's present in front of her nose, she tilted her head back and opened her mouth. The heavy pendant clacked against her teeth, then hit her tongue with a brassy tang. The chain came next, pooling on her tongue. She swallowed, but the pendant stuck to the back of her throat. She coughed it out into her hand. She picked the necklace up and fastened it carefully.

Dragging her feet, Annie headed back to the restaurant. All around her were one-way streets and souvenir shops. The glinting jewel bounced once against her skin, then stuck to her throat, sweat and spit adhering. The strange roads were already turning familiar.

Pat didn't recognize where the alley had taken him, but he had to keep moving. Of course Annie would hate him after what they'd done. But a part of him had hoped that maybe, since they were the only two people who knew what had happened, they would be bonded for life. Losing Annie meant losing the one person who might keep him from going insane.

For the past week and a half he'd been out every night, drinking and getting the level of stoned that guaranteed a black, dreamless sleep. When he woke up, with no idea of how he'd gotten home, his clenched jaw would ache from nightmares he couldn't recall. His sheets would be wrapped around his neck. His work didn't suffer. His hangovers didn't last past noon. He could, theoretically, do this forever. But picturing a future of unremembered nights shot panic through his body. His lungs became too squeezed to let air in.

The one thing that helped was walking. He walked miles to get to his friends' parties. He imagined he must have walked those blacked-out miles to get back. The constant movement calmed him, or at least distracted him. He'd developed the trick in kindergarten, when he'd be the last one left at after-school care. His mother's lunch service didn't end until four-thirty, an hour after his class. He cried the first time, when he looked up to find all the other children gone. But when his mother finally did show up, her dress shirt untucked and stained, she took one look at his tears and made a face so tired he immediately stopped crying. The next day, when he found himself alone again with the teacher's aide, he got up from his chair and walked the perimeter of the small room. He repeated this square loop, soothing himself, until his mother came and he could collapse into her arms.

Would they let him walk in prison? Or would he have to pace the tiny quarters of his cell until he tumbled over? He played out these scenarios while trying to find his way back to M Street, sweat dripping down his armpits. But the late-afternoon sun felt too good against his face; the usual dread failed to overwhelm him. He must have tortured himself with these thoughts before. He couldn't remember when; he just felt their familiarity, like worry beads still warm from his touch. Then the Glory sprang into view, the waterfront a dirty mirror. The knotted muscle of memory opened.

The day of his first fire, the one with the garbage can, Pat had forgotten his cigarettes at home. The principal found this most suspicious, as if a lone book of matches revealed sinister intentions.

"What were you planning?" the man kept asking Pat in his office.

Pat didn't feel like explaining that he used matches because he liked the hiss of sulfur hitting the air when he lit them. He sure as hell wasn't going to admit that the smell made him think of birthday parties. Pat and his friends had been in this foreboding office a number of times already. None of them had ever been suspended. So he didn't think to defend himself; he didn't think to lie.

The truth of why he set the fire was obscure even to him, but the truth of how he came to set the fire was not. He'd been cutting English class. He'd wanted to leave school, but a security guard was waiting by the exit, staring at him as if he'd been shown a picture of Pat's face. Pat had turned around and dipped into the bathroom. At least it beat a PowerPoint on whatever dead poet they were reading. But being in a stinking boys' bathroom for nearly an hour was worse. The stalls were painted puke-green; clumps of paper towels had been stuck over the mirrors. He started lighting matches to do something with his hands and to make the smell go away. He would watch the flame burn down the wooden stem, holding on for as long as he could before dropping the match in the garbage. Each time, a small flame bloomed up from the mass of paper towels in the can, but each time, the flame put itself out. He came down to his last match. Easy to drop it, like all the others; easier to leave his fingers unburned.

Maybe he didn't think the fire would catch. But then it did, and all he had to do was run to the sink and throw water on the flames. Still, he stood there. He wasn't frozen, at least not by fear. He could move; he just didn't want to. He wanted to watch. He wanted to let it grow out of control. The smoke grew heavier. It tasted awful. Tears streamed down his face as he coughed and coughed. He had to be dragged away by the same security guard who had forced him into the bathroom in the first place.

Security had him change into lost-and-found clothes after he was partially doused by the fire extinguisher. When his mother showed up an hour later and spotted him in a lime-green hoodie and too-big track pants, she looked almost hopeful. She said his name like a question. Then her eyes found his face. Pat had no such near-mistake of thinking she was anyone but his mother. She'd come to school wearing her work uniform. But he had wished for a stranger also.

Sitting behind a big, cheap desk, the principal couldn't have been a less intimidating figure—thick in the middle, with a short neck and round face, he looked like an egg perched on top of a larger egg. The students called him Principal Humpty. To Pat's surprise, as soon as his mother sat down, her body seemed to cower. She bore no resemblance to the woman in Uncle Jack's stories, the one who could shut down even the most difficult customers.

"This one woman brought an old piece of meat and snuck it onto her plate when the carver wasn't looking," Jack once said.

"Told everyone she'd been served this duck. It looked more like a piece of steak."

"Anyone can eat at a restaurant," his mother had said, sharing a smile. "The poor carver kept trying to reason with her, even offered to get her a fresh duck. With some people, you can't be so nice."

"But Nan here." Jack wrapped Pat and his mother up in the cozy blanket of his story. "She pointed out that the old meat was the twenty-ninth slice on the plate. All ducks offer exactly twenty-eight slices. So there was no way that slice came from our duck. Even if it did—and here, she grabbed the thing and threw it right onto the carver's tray—well, didn't that solve everything? I swear I saw that woman smile. Tell your son how much she left you as a tip."

"Ten dollars on a forty-dollar bill."

But whatever powers his mother had over other people clearly faltered when she left the confines of the restaurant. She apologized to his principal and guidance counselor so effusively with her terrible English that Pat couldn't tell if the two men were embarrassed by what she was saying or how she was saying it.

"Pat is a good boy," she kept repeating, when she was at a loss for words. "He do a bad thing. He need the best principal, best teacher to help him be good."

Pat wanted to tell her to get out of the office. Every word that came out of her mouth made his skin hot. He itched all over from invisible pinpricks. He couldn't sit still, and he didn't know if he was angry or mortified. Finally, he shot out of his chair.

"I set the fire on purpose to get out of class," he said, just to shut them all up.

He left his mother behind in the principal's office, left the school, and walked the six miles home. Kicking rocks into the street, he entertained thoughts of punishment that he knew, with flippant certainty, would never come to pass. Yet if they threw him in prison, how unfair it would be! His offense would pale in comparison; he would be the victim. His mother would cry buckets, and then she would have to stand up and fight for him. She couldn't leave him behind bars and go to work or look the other way and pretend he was at summer camp. He would finally get to see her at her most ferocious, all for his sake.

The entire time he was playing out his liquid fantasies, he kept an ear ready for the hum of approaching wheels. Car after car zoomed past without stopping. After the first few miles, he stopped looking over his shoulder. His daydreams stopped too—gone stiff and clumpy, like cold oil left in a pan. His mom wasn't at home. She'd gone back to the Duck House.

The next day, with two weeks left of school, Pat was expelled. A few weeks later, after his hearing, he was at the restaurant. Now he was here—so many miles away that he could walk all day and still not find his way home.

17

The first unofficial night and the Glory was unexpectedly packed. Familiar faces dotted the open dining room. Jimmy had sent out a soft-opening invitation to the Duck House mailing list a few days earlier, expecting a small assortment of guests to show up on Thursday. Who would drive in from the suburbs and brave the city's weeknight traffic? He didn't need many, just enough to iron out any kinks in the days leading up to the grand opening. But a trickle of customers at the start of the dinner hour had fattened into a stream, and now nearly every table was full. Jimmy should have been pleased by his old customers' loyalty, but he was just as equally bothered. Had these people shown up for his sake or his father's? Worst of all, the Glory could not turn any of them away.

Already, the kitchen was backed up. The food was not even that complicated. The chef Uncle Pang had been in the process of luring away from a trendy Thai bistro in Adams Morgan had started screening Jimmy's calls, and he'd had to simplify his dream menu to a shell of its former self—one appetizer, three entrees, a dessert, and the duck. Jimmy worried about the few D.C. locals who had wandered in, attracted by the activity inside. They did not have nostalgia to soften the edges of their impatience. Jimmy checked his phone. Janine's dinner reservation was not for another fifteen minutes. He sent two busboys to sweep around her table one more time.

She'd said she was bringing a date, which meant she was bringing her son, Eddie. For all Jimmy knew, the boy would hate Chinese food, hate duck, and hate him on sight.

"If I find a single scrap over there," he said to Osman, the Duck House's former head busboy, "I'll make you vacuum the entire restaurant, including the seat cushions."

Osman nodded as he went to put the broom away. He was the one amigo who'd agreed to commute to D.C. If he was upset about his demotion, he'd yet to express it.

Jimmy walked over to Janine's table in the center of the dining room, obliged to chat with each table on the way.

"The Mister and Missus," he said to a couple who'd waved him over. Names were Johnny's domain. All Jimmy knew was that the woman was finicky, always asking for paper napkins to blot her food. The man tipped well only after his third scotch. "Thank you for considering the Glory this Thursday."

"It's too bad you didn't keep the Duck House's menu." The husband wiped his mouth on the napkin his wife handed him. "I was really craving your kung pao shrimp tonight."

"Oh, he's teasing," his wife said. "This is a lovely new space."

"New space, new menu." Jimmy planted his hands on the edge of their table. "Expand your culinary horizons, right?"

He set off before the uneasy laughter died down. The next three tables made similar small talk, and each time Jimmy said the wrong things.

"Why would you want pork lo mein?" he said, while faces grew tight around him. "Try the miso-wasabi frog legs. Or the grilled ginger tofu."

But the guests continued to ask if they could order off the Duck House's menu, their tone growing icy and clipped when Jimmy politely refused. By the end of the first hour, in an attempt to decongest the kitchen, Jimmy was forced to oblige. The most popular items on his father's menu took no more five minutes to prepare. He had to feed his customers. He supposed he should feel lucky that he had forgotten to cancel the Duck House's deliveries last week—though what was the point of a soft opening if no one ordered from the new menu?

He kept an eye out on the few customers who had gotten their food on time. One of them had finished only a quarter of her bulgogi burger before pushing it aside. She filled a small saucer with her date's fried rice. Jimmy beelined for their table.

"What's wrong with your burger?" Jimmy knew he was standing too close. "Not to your liking?" A sticky puddle of brown sauce had pooled under the bun.

"It's fine, it's great." The woman smoothed the cloth napkin in her lap. The lamps above gave everyone's skin a sallow cast. "I'm just taking a little break."

"Don't fill up on that fried rice," he said. The woman's eyebrows shot up. "But if you do, the burger is great the next day. Perfect as leftovers."

"Actually, would you mind boxing this up for me now?" She pushed the burger plate toward Jimmy. "I'll save it for lunch tomorrow."

"Certainly," he said, through clenched teeth.

Jimmy was about to hand the plate to a passing busboy, but something told him to take a closer look. He'd demonstrated each new dish to his cooks, had them replicate the recipe once, and the taste had been fine. But was the burger in front of him the same one he'd invented during his time at Koi? What if the flavors didn't match up under the pressure of a busy service? He carried the plate into an empty waiter station, and after looking around, he tore off a piece for himself. Chewing slowly, he hoped for a problem, missing salt or too much sesame oil. But it was the exact burger the cooks had made for him in demonstration. The only difference was that, at the time,

Jimmy had cared only that his staff could make the burger. On such short notice, he had had to hire his cooks through a less-than-reputable Chinese agency. With the clock racing and no chef in charge, he had settled for good enough. Now he had to admit that the flavors were there, but they were muddy. Clumsy. Unrefined. He could come up with a hundred words all saying the same thing, which was that he'd hired a bunch of fresh-off-the-boat village boys to make a gourmet meal. He shoved the burger into a takeout container, wishing he could throw it in the trash, where it would be the next day anyway. He intercepted Annie and told her to rewrite the menu, scratch everything that hadn't been at the Duck House. She could alert the waiters and the kitchen while she was at it. Then he circled back to drop off the woman's burger.

"Excuse me," she said, before he could leave. "There's something off about the fried rice. You can take it away."

The back of Jimmy's neck prickled.

"I'm so sorry." He grabbed the half-finished platter. "I'll get a new one made for you. It will only be a minute."

"No thanks," her date said. "We're actually pretty full."

"Just the check, please," she said.

"I'll let your waiter know. The fried rice is on the house." Jimmy hustled into the nearest waiter station and shooed away a busboy packing up a barely eaten order of kimchi nachos. Snatching the serving spoon out of the busboy's hand, Jimmy dug into the plate of fried rice. He almost spat out the lumpy spoonful. How could something be oversalted and flavorless at the same time?

Hindsight yanked him back hard. He hadn't shown the kitchen how to cook something as basic as the Duck House dishes. Any Chinese cook could stir-fry protein, vegetable, and sauce. Had he hired cooks so new that they couldn't even make what this country called Chinese food? Were the other Chinese dishes coming out of the kitchen this terrible? It had never occurred to him that the food at his restaurant might fall short of his father's. He looked around, trying to study the people around him, people he'd spent so many meals with that he could intuit their appetites with a glance. The tables that had gotten their Duck House entrées seemed to be not only eating the food but also enjoying it. Maybe this fried rice was a one-off.

He checked his phone again. Janine was minutes from arriving. What would she say about the food? And what about her damn son? Back at her table, Jimmy grabbed the steel RESERVED plate and rubbed fiercely at the smudged fingerprints. He pulled the tablecloth one way, then the other, then put his nose close to the seat cushions to check for crumbs. He was balancing on the balls of his feet, peering under the table, when he smelled her perfume and nearly came undone.

"Here's the table our owner has set aside for you," he heard Annie recite. "Though I don't know what he's doing right now."

"Something wrong with our table?" Janine asked.

Jimmy spun around. Janine was dressed professionally, but her hair was relaxed, in loose curls that he wished he could wrap his fingers around. Her son was at her side. He was small for his age, delicate like his mother, and pale, as if he didn't see much of the sun. Already grim-faced, he looked like trouble.

"It's perfect," Jimmy said.

"Isn't that nice, Eddie?" she asked her son, who reached out to hold her hand. "Uncle Jimmy gave us the best table in the house."

"You can watch the chefs work." Jimmy pointed to the semi-open kitchen. He didn't know whether to bend down or hunch over the kid. He leaned against the seat back.

"Thank you for getting us in," Janine said. "It's so crowded! You must be thrilled."

A few tables over, someone clapped. Visible from the kitchen window, a cook flambéed bananas, the fire electric blue in his saucepan.

"It's only the first night," Jimmy said. "Once I trash the Duck House menu, who knows who'll come back?"

"Stop assuming the world is full of cheap bastards." She whispered the last word conspiratorially. Eddie squirmed past Jimmy's legs to climb into his seat. The little boy's shoves were surprisingly rough, and Jimmy nearly pushed back.

"I'm going to be your waiter this evening." Jimmy fixed his plain patterned tie and took the menus from Annie. He almost faltered, struck by a funny smell coming off his niece. But he recovered quickly and dismissed her with the butt of his hand.

"How special," Janine said to her son. She'd settled into the chair next to Eddie. "Did you hear that?" She leaned in, touching her head to his.

"Yeah," the boy said. He was pretending to be distracted by his chopsticks, which were made of laminated wood. He let them fall from his fingers, until they finally rolled off the table.

"He's used to the lighter, break-apart kind," Janine said.

"I'm sure the carryout station has plenty of those," Jimmy said. "I'll send over some drinks and be right back with your utensils, sir." He tousled Eddie's hair, or, rather, his scalp, since his hair was buzzed short. The boy gnashed his teeth at Jimmy's hand. Janine grabbed her son by the point of his chin and gave him a light shake. Jimmy wished she had been a little harsher.

The duck arrived soon at Janine's table. Jimmy had ordered the kitchen to jump the line. Nan was their assigned carver. Jimmy took a seat across from Janine and the boy.

Nan was clumsier than the other carvers, who'd spent years practicing at the Duck House. Her hands were still sensitive to the hot grease that spurted from the duck. They were red underneath her plastic gloves and she sprang back, if only a few centimeters, each time the fat burned her.

"Doesn't this look yummy?" Janine asked her son.

The boy reached out and took a strip of skin, so quickly that Jimmy almost didn't see his hand move. He stuck the piece in his mouth and sucked on it.

"You should wait to put that on a pancake," Jimmy said. "Then you can use the plum sauce and the green onions."

"Don't they wrap the first pancake for you?" Janine asked. "You should wait, honey, for the nice lady to show you how it's done."

"He his own master." Nan put the first plate of meat in front of Eddie. She knew better than to tell Janine that waiters wrapped the first pancakes.

"He's very independent," Janine agreed.

"I can wrap your pancakes while Nan keeps working on her carving," Jimmy said.

"So generous. Eddie, watch an expert at work."

The boy continued to suck on his strip of skin, which had gone limp in his hand. He looked intently at his plate. Jimmy grabbed a hot pancake from the silver serving bowl and dotted the dough with plum sauce. He grabbed a few sprigs of cut scallions with his chopsticks, as well as a slice of duck meat and a slice of crispy skin. Then he wrapped the pancake closed like a burrito and handed it to the boy.

"He touched it." Eddie shrank away from the pancake as if it had hissed at him. "He didn't wash his hands before he touched it."

"Of course I did." Jimmy dropped the pancake on the boy's plate and held his hands up in front of him.

"Stop making a fuss," Janine said. She took the pancake and made a show of biting into it. "It's very tasty. You don't know what you're missing."

Nan had finished carving the duck and was waiting awkwardly. Jimmy stood up and whispered for her to bring him three serving spoons.

"If Mr. Eddie doesn't want me using my hands, I'll go old school." He planted himself at the front of the table. His thighs pressed against the edge. Nan came back around quickly, her hands freed from their plastic wrap, and passed on three medium-size oval spoons. He wove two through the fingers of his right hand. He held the remaining spoon loosely in his left.

"Wow!" Janine was already applauding. She'd put down her hand-rolled pancake, which slowly came undone on her plate.

Jimmy hadn't assumed this server's position in well over a decade, and he fumbled a few tries before the spoons fit into their grooves and became makeshift tongs in his hand. He pried a pancake off the pile and onto a plate; pincered the meat, skin, and scallions; and dolloped sauce with his third, free spoon. The entire process was going smoothly, though for some reason Nan was hanging back. As if her presence jinxed him, he pressed his spoon a little too hard against the pancake's belly. The thin dough split; plum sauce oozed out.

"It's been a little while." He put down his dirty spoons and Nan took over. She'd brought a second set. As always, her preparedness left Jimmy defused when he'd rather have exploded. He couldn't watch her correct his shoddy job. He muttered an excuse about checking in with the kitchen.

He didn't even get halfway there. At table 10, a waiter was cleaning bones off a customer's plate with his bare hands. He seized each chop as if he were about to pick it clean. It seemed to Jimmy that half the tables were still waiting for their food, that customers were tripping over one another to get to the bathroom. The layout of the seats was slightly imprecise; people couldn't push out their chairs without colliding straight into others. The tables themselves were meant to hold much smaller plates, and with no lazy Susans outfitting the larger groups, people dipped their shirtsleeves into their soup when they reached across the table for wonton chips. One peek into the kitchen confirmed it. Nothing fit together. Food was dying under the heat lamps. Order slips were on the ground. The new amigos couldn't communicate with the Chinese cooks, who couldn't understand the American waiters. The Duck House's ecosystem had always seemed haphazard to Jimmy, but he now realized it had had an internal logic, one he had not thought to construct for the Glory. His father would have laughed in his face. It was easy to imagine what else his father would or would not have done.

His father wouldn't have hired amigos who'd never worked in a Chinese kitchen or Americans with tongues too lazy to learn the sounds that came from the back of the house. His father wouldn't have gone into debt for a flashy space surrounded by restaurants far more comfortable in their flashiness. The new place was everything his father distrusted. The outdoor patio would bring vermin and beggars. The partially exposed kitchen made even less sense. Who wanted to watch a fat cook scratch his ass and bang his wok? The floor plan was too open, the lighting too bright, and where, pray tell, was Jimmy going to find the time to clean all those windows? "Why do people need a view?" his father would have asked. "They'll be sitting in their seats for hours."

But his father had been blocked in by his own golden bricks, his dreams compressed like a watermelon grown in a cinder block. Jimmy had different plans. *He* was not going to be so obsessed with monthly returns; *he* was going to focus on the big picture. He was finally going to get his hands on the status that had eluded his family, rich as they were, or had been. He was going to grow that intangible capital that reached where money couldn't go. But in this strident difference, would Jimmy elude the money as well? Would his restaurant drag him down, taking his apartment, Janine, his family, his livelihood, with it? He'd spent his entire life working in a restaurant; he'd never graduated from college. If they charged him with insurance fraud, he would have a record on top of everything. How could a restaurant this fucking big feel so small? A fist formed around Jimmy's lungs. Steel fingers crushed the air out as soon as he sucked in. Yet with each cruel squeeze of his chest, there followed an opposite reaction. One of expanding heat, energizing heat. Anger built deep in his gut, until his body hummed from the need to do some necessary violence.

He set off for the waiter with the tray full of bones, a moon-faced white boy named Tom. He pulled him into the nearest station, where the other new servers could overhear. Grabbing Tom by the wrist, Jimmy forced him to look at the greasy print on his palm.

"Are you an animal?" Jimmy asked. Tom shook his head. Jimmy grabbed the plate of bones off his tray and threw it to the ground. "Use your spoons to pick up the bones, like I taught you." He left Tom on his knees, spoons clinking together. The waiters who'd stopped to look quickened their pace.

Swinging by the coat closet, Jimmy hung up his jacket and pushed up his sleeves. Then he headed toward the kitchen. He threw the first cook—a large, stooped man with one bloodshot eye—off the line. Taking his place in front of the flaming wok, Jimmy motioned for the others to give him their tickets. He gave half to the one veteran cook in the entire kitchen, a grizzled man who rubbed the white stubble on his chin as he received the tickets with an otherwise neutral face.

"Throw out your food," Jimmy shouted in wooden Chinese. He tied on an apron. He had the cooks gather as closely around the wok as the narrow space allowed. "Pay attention. Then you cook like me."

He cranked the burner as high as it would go, until the air in front of his face shimmered with heat. Then he dropped his ladle into the drum of peanut oil by the wok, pouring it straight into the pan.

"Always more oil," he demanded. "More, even more."

He swirled the oil around in his wok, coating the entire surface, then poured the oil back into the drum. Filling his ladle partway again, he wet the wok with one more splash of oil and cracked eggs into the gleaming puddle. Stirring the yellow around, he grabbed a container of rice, dumped it in. Mixing the rice into the oil and eggs, he lifted the wok with his left hand. One heavy flick and the rice transformed into a wave, cresting over the edge of the rim and breaking back down into the center of the pan.

"Again." He tasted sweat as he flipped the fried rice three more times. "Do it until your wrist breaks." While he rested his hand, he pressed the rice down with the back of his ladle, until each individual grain was crisping in oil. He handed the wok back to its owner, instructing him to toss the rice until he saw it dance. Then he took over the next wok, refilling his ladle with oil.

He moved down the line, wok by wok. He left a new cook to finish each dish he started. He showed them how to boil vegetables in a spider perched over hot water and how to measure everything with their ladle, from salt to soy sauce to green onions. He demonstrated kung pao shrimp, instructing the cooks how long to fry the peanuts and how to jostle the frying cage to make sure the oil dropped off the nuts. They saw how to coat thin slices of flank steak with cornstarch for extra-crispy Mongolian beef and how to precook chunks of chicken in deep oil in their woks. By the time he reached the veteran cook, taking just over fifteen minutes, his line was busy again and he was free to wipe the sweat from his eyes.

"Give them back their tickets," he told the old cook, clapping him on the back. Around him, the kitchen was alive with fire and fragrance. Iron clanked against steel, and the smell of sizzling meat turned heavy in the air.

The first cook, the one with the bloodshot eye, finished his dish. He presented his plate, his nose running from the heat.

Jimmy grabbed a nearby spoon and carved into the mound of fried rice. He barely tasted the perfect combination of salt and grease before he bit down hard on the spoon, his teeth aching against the metal. Dirty tasting spoon in mouth, he was the spitting image of his father.

Dizzy from the heat of the burners, Jimmy stumbled out of the kitchen's back exit and onto the alley street outside. He needed air. But the cramped Georgetown quarters were no less claustrophobic. Three pairs of shoes hung on the telephone wires above his head. Graffiti tagged the high brick walls. He got down into a crouch, feeling his pants stretch dangerously, and tried to count out his breaths. He reached back for something to prop himself against. He settled for a locked bike. Why was he panicking? The first night was always a terror. The first year, even. Once his mother gave up the house, once they caught the fire setter, he would feel more like himself. He would redesign the menu, retrain the staff, and throw out anything and anyone who didn't fit. He would take the chef position until he found someone suitable. With the house on the market, he could remake the restaurant in his own image and not his father's or Koi's. That was all he had to do. He focused on the patch of moss growing from where the brick met the pavement. It was nothing. Truly nothing.

Out of nowhere, a four-fingered hand reached down and brushed a hair off his shoulder. Jimmy lost his hold on the bike's crusted wheel.

"How's your opening night?" The corners of Uncle Pang's eyes wrinkled.

"What the fuck?" Jimmy gasped; he'd lost whatever grip he'd had over his breathing. A fat diamond of pain inserted itself between his eyes.

"Your mother called," Uncle Pang said. A black BMW idled next to them against the curb. How had Jimmy not seen it on his way out of the restaurant?

"Why is she calling you?"

"I'm a friend of the family."

"You're not my friend." Jimmy struggled to right himself.

"You always say that. But I'm afraid you inherited me." Uncle Pang offered a hand. Jimmy ignored it; he felt safer crouched.

"My father's fault."

Uncle Pang flicked Jimmy hard on the knobby tip of his nose.

"Don't speak ill of the dead." He'd switched to Chinese for his superstitions. "Especially not the dead who raised you."

"What do you want!" Jimmy clutched his nose. "Do you want the Glory? It's going to be a giant, money-sucking hellhole, just like you said. Happy now?"

"I'm surprised you're not more thankful." Uncle Pang smoothed his black tie against his chest. A breeze brought the smell of the marina into the alley.

"Thankful?" Jimmy cooled the heat in his voice. His nose throbbed.

"I don't let many people try to screw me more than once."

"Thank you." Jimmy's mind was whirring. What did Uncle Pang want? Jimmy bowed his head as if facing an angry customer. "You're a generous man."

"Don't disrespect me with your dog-shit words." Uncle Pang looked down at him with lazy disdain, like a cat batting at a half-dead mouse.

The bike tire flexed beneath Jimmy's grip. "I've learned my lesson, I promise," he said.

"Then listen carefully." Uncle Pang patted down the greasy shell of his hair. "I'm going to tell you who set your restaurant on fire."

The cityscape around Jimmy expanded and shrank. "You're not serious."

"I'm always serious." Uncle Pang smiled stiffly. "Everything depends on how serious you are. I have the evidence to put them away, but I'm only giving you the name. What you choose to do next is up to you."

Jimmy stood up and brushed the mud off his hand. "Who burned down the restaurant?" he asked, expecting a riddle back. Uncle Pang would draw the news out.

Instead, a strange look crossed the man's face. "A boy named Pat," he said, after a pause. "Your girl Nan's son."

"Pat?" Jimmy's heart felt like it was stuttering. Sweat squeezed out of the bottoms of his feet. "He's right behind those doors, working, right under my fucking nose."

"That's the thing about young boys." Uncle Pang scratched the side of his jaw with one finger. "They'll sell their souls for a couple thousand dollars. Don't feel too bad. I picked Pat weeks ago."

"Why him?" The borders of Jimmy's face felt fuzzy. He thought he could hear a distant car alarm.

"You never thought to ask Nan why her boy was expelled." Uncle Pang looked dismayed, then delighted, by Jimmy's mistake. "You've always had this problem. You think you're too good to listen to the people underneath you."

"How could he have burned down an *entire* restaurant?"

"I helped things along," Uncle Pang said. "Once I got you out of the restaurant. A little gasoline on the walls. Some toggling with your sprinkler system. Aerosol cans in the garbage. What Pat did was childish vandalism. He might have gotten your back wall ashy." His eyes sharpened. "Of course, if you mention my name to the police, you will regret that decision. Pat knows better than to link me to the fire."

Jimmy made a foolish zipping motion in front of his mouth.

"It's nice to be back on pleasant terms," Uncle Pang said. He turned toward his car, then swung back. "One more thing. I assume you're going to be using Janine as your real estate agent to sell your mother's house. But have you ever wondered why Janine invited you to her place that night?" He offered his hand for a shake.

Jimmy gripped Uncle Pang's hand before he fully absorbed the words.

"I'm the one who called her." Jimmy took his hand back and pressed it hard against his leg.

"You don't have to believe me," Uncle Pang said. "Although you must have realized how . . . ambitious that woman is. She was eager to help."

"She told me she hated working for you," Jimmy said. "She said she would do anything to get rid of you."

"For a suspicious son of a bitch, you'll trust any woman who gets into bed with you," Uncle Pang said. "She *didn't* tell me that, by the way."

Despite the ebbing heat of the evening, Uncle Pang pulled out a pair of black leather gloves. The ring finger of the right one was lopped off and sewn shut. He caught Jimmy staring.

"Do you want to know how I lost this finger?" He held up his right hand and wiggled the stump. His tone was unreadable, but there was that strange look again. Pity.

Ever since he'd first felt that callused stub press against his palm as a child, Jimmy had imagined the most violent scenarios.

"Tell me," he said.

Uncle Pang examined his hand, expression blank. He seemed caught in a memory.

"Lost it to an infection," he finally said. He pulled on his gloves. "Swam in a river with an open cut, and it was gone the next week."

"Unlucky," Jimmy managed.

"What did I tell you about young boys," Uncle Pang said. "Old boys, at least, know better." He got into his car, signaled something to the driver, and pulled the door closed. Jimmy watched the BMW enter the flow of traffic. Around him, brake lights lit up, red and angry. Past the intersection, he lost sight of the car.

18

Either Ah-Jack's memory was slipping or someone had taken his blazer while he was in the stall. He liked to hang it on the restroom coat rack—a finicky habit—but today when he reached for it, his hands swiped air. He checked under the sinks and the other stalls. Had someone been in the restroom with him? The classical music taunted him, playing overhead.

"Fuck," he said under his breath. Why couldn't he have waited to take a shit until after dinner service?

At the Duck House, Jimmy might have yelled at him for entering the dining room without his uniform, but at the Glory? His position was already a charity. Who had ever heard of a staff translator? His hands were too shaky for duck carving, and he was good for nothing else. He might as well be suspended over a cliff, with Jimmy holding on to his fingertips.

Someone approached the bathroom from outside. Ah-Jack slipped into a stall. He peered through the space between the door. To his mixed relief, Pat walked in. The boy stopped to check his reflection in the mirror.

"Pat," Ah-Jack whispered through the stall.

"What is it?" The boy didn't even jump.

"It's Uncle Jack. I misplaced my blazer. Can you find it? Or a spare? I can't leave here without one."

"Where do you think you lost it?"

Ah-Jack grasped his hair. "Maybe the waiter station? Or behind the bar?"

"I'll try," Pat said, continuing to preen. Then he was out the door. The entire time he'd looked only at his mirrored self.

Ah-Jack sat down on the toilet and palpated his lower back, which didn't know whether to be thankful for the seat or to continue grousing.

"Don't you feel better?" He addressed his body as if it were a sulking friend. There was no point panicking. He rested his elbows on his knees, propped up his head, and closed his eyes.

Some time passed before the door thumped open again. The bang startled Ah-Jack out of his short nap. Pat's shoes appeared under the stall door.

"Here," Pat said. A blazer shot over the door and landed on Ah-Jack's head.

The smell of vinegar pierced his nose before the damp fabric hit his face. Pulling the blazer off, he checked and found his name tag.

"Someone must've thought it was a rag," Pat said, as if he could see Ah-Jack's face through the closed door.

"Thank you," he said.

"No problem." Pat's shoes retreated. The door closed behind him.

Ah-Jack struggled to his feet and shook out the blazer. It had been doused in black vinegar. Who would mistake a blazer for a rag? He tugged it on and exited the stall. The mirror reflected back a limp and wrinkled version of himself. He didn't even have his nice leather work shoes, which he'd forgotten at home. He'd had to buy a discount pair of black tennis shoes at the Payless near Nan's. In all his years working, he'd never looked so defeated.

Nan was re-pinning her duck carver's hat when he found her in the kitchen.

"Dear God!" She pinched her nose while she circled him. "What'd you get into, old man?"

"Someone used my blazer as a mop." He waved his arms to dry the cloth. "It's not that noticeable, is it?" A waiter squeezing past them coughed into his elbow.

"Go grab a new one from Jimmy. But tell him a customer spilled on you. Otherwise he'll use *you* as a mop." She pulled on his hair, then tucked the strands back behind his ear, the thoughtless, tender act startling them both. They took a step back from each other.

"He'll say I should've watched where I was going."

Nan raised herself to full height and lifted her chin. "After decades of Jimmy yelling at you, you're not prepared to take a little more?"

Ah-Jack plucked at the lapels of his sodden blazer. "He's always been a little tyrant, but he's been worse lately, torturing an old man like me."

"Your mind's scrambled," Nan said. "It's the same medicine. Now go take your medicine before Jimmy shoves it down your throat."

Jimmy was nowhere to be found at first, but a second hard look around the dining room revealed him. The little boss was hanging around by the entrance, chatting with customers eating at the bar. Something was off about his greetings; they carried a hard edge, like artificial sweetener, and he left each person he talked to looking unsettled. Before Ah-Jack could hide himself, Jimmy was upon him. The little boss flared his nostrils, sniffing the air, before hustling Ah-Jack into the coat room.

"What is the matter with you?" Jimmy's face was so close to his that Ah-Jack felt Jimmy's breath on his neck. The small space smelled like mothballs and carpet cleaner.

"Vinegar spill on me." Ah-Jack shrugged out of the blazer.

"We can't get you a new one," Jimmy said. "You'll stain it."

"I keeping wearing mine?"

"Are you insane?" Jimmy stroked his brow, strangely distracted even as he glared at Ah-Jack. His anger should have been a straight line, but it seemed bent at an unexpected angle. Like a knife half submerged in water. "You know what you can wear? The duck carver's uniform. You're not a waiter anyways. It's confusing. People keep trying to ask you for extra drinks—"

"I got them drink," Ah-Jack tried to cut in.

"That's not your job," Jimmy said. "It gunks up the system. Put an apron on."

"Shirt have stain too."

"No one will notice." Jimmy turned to organize the coat rack. "You owe me fifty dollars for that blazer." He dismissed Ah-Jack with his back.

On his way back to the kitchen, Ah-Jack ran into Pat. He'd been running into Pat a lot lately. The tray of drinks Pat was carrying barely tipped, but all of a sudden the front of Ah-Jack's shirt was drenched with Coke.

"Aw shit, Uncle Jack." Pat toed the fallen cup. "Will you clean this up? I'm behind."

"Okay, fine." Ah-Jack bent down to grab the cup. He shivered when a shard of ice slid its way down his chest.

In the kitchen, Nan had finished putting on her hat. She was sharpening her carving knife while she waited for her duck to come through the kitchen.

"Another accident?" The worry she tried to hide on her face tugged forward fiercely, like a dog on a leash.

"Just a clumsy idiot here," Ah-Jack said. "Baby manager wants me to wear an apron. Food stains and all."

Nan reached up to grab at a stack from above the jumbo rice cookers. The thick yellowed fabric, damp from rice steam, covered Ah-Jack's entire front, down to his ankles, like a butcher's apron.

"Looks like I'm here to slaughter the ducks." He fumbled to tie the strings behind his back. Nan came around and batted his fingers away.

"I knew your vanity would ruin you one day," she said.

"If I dress like a beaten man, that's what I become," he said.

She spun him around to straighten out the front. She started rolling up his sleeves.

"At least you get the little hat," he said.

"It's so I look better in the pictures they take."

"Where can I get my hands on those pictures?" He gripped her playfully by the forearms, sliding his grip up and down.

"The Internet," she replied, smiling. "Where you get all your pictures."

"Can I get by?" Pat barreled through their arms. He tossed four soup bowls onto his tray. Ah-Jack hurried over to the cut garnishes and grabbed a handful of green onions. He began sprinkling them into each bowl while Pat ladled hot broth out of the steam table. The boy's movements were clumsy, and broth spurted out of the bowl.

"Careful," Ah-Jack warned.

"My bad," Pat murmured, without changing a thing. The last ladleful spilled out of the bowl and cascaded over Ah-Jack's thumb. He let out a hiss.

"What happened?" Nan rushed over.

"My fault." Ah-Jack shook out his hand. Pat had already set off with his order.

"You never burn yourself," she said. "Did Pat hurt you?"

"No!" The air between mother and son was polluted enough without him adding his own suspicions. "Look how hard Pat is working. You should be proud."

"He's like a different person," Nan admitted. "But it's early. Maybe he's only learned how to be trickier."

Ah-Jack picked at something yellow and crusted on his apron string. "Good crowd tonight. The Hans have the magic touch."

"They're our old customers," Nan said.

Ah-Jack sucked his teeth. "Of all days to wear a stained apron!"

Nan touched her paper hat lightly. "Yes."

Ah-Jack slapped himself on the cheek. "Forgive a foolish, brain-dead old man."

"You forgot vain," she said.

"Yes, of course. Incredibly vain."

The kitchen had been filling with waiters, calling out orders and smacking together soup and rice bowls. The noise and people didn't bother Nan and Ah-Jack, who were accustomed to switching their attention on and off. Even so, Ah-Jack noticed that the kitchen was more chaotic than usual, or, rather, that this chaos lacked logic. Waiters kept breaking into his and Nan's idle conversation to clarify which plate of brown slurry was theirs. For some reason, Jimmy had changed the menu in the middle of service and the American staff needed Ah-Jack to tell them the difference between Mongolian steak and pepper steak, curry chicken and kung pao chicken. The cooks, who could not read English, shouted at him to translate the waiters' orders through the commotion of metal and flame. But restaurant work was heavy in his blood. He needed no extra thought to organize the orders and the servers. Nan, whose position was the only one overstaffed, helped guide the waiters as well. Finally her turn came back up, and she scooted a duck, pinwheeling in its own grease, onto her silver platter. He sent her out of the kitchen with a pat on her rear.

Not long after, Pat came in, though he'd only called out an order a few minutes before. He was killing time, striding around on his long legs, like Ah-Jack used to do when he was that age and found hard work more boring than exhausting.

"Did someone take my shrimp in lobster sauce?" Pat peered at the cooks through the stainless-steel divider.

"Not ready yet," Ah-Jack said. Against his will, his body stiffened, remembering the small attacks upon it since he'd moved in with Nan two weeks ago. A toilet flushed while he was in the shower. An accidental elbow in the hallway. The chair he'd been sitting in moved back an inch while he fixed a snack in the kitchen. He could forget—he was a star at forgetting—but his body would not.

"You mixed the orders up, didn't you?" Pat said.

"Of course not."

"If you weren't so busy talking, you wouldn't have screwed up *my* order." Pat came closer to Ah-Jack. What was the boy doing?

"I can talk and watch at the same time," Ah-Jack said.

Just then Pat's plate, brimming with cloudy-white gravy, spun out onto the divider. Ah-Jack reached out at the same time as Pat; they grabbed the plate together. Ah-Jack knew, before his fingers touched the plate, that it was steaming hot, the fresh gravy heating the cheap china with every second. But before Ah-Jack could call out a warning, Pat had yanked his hand off the plate. Unbalanced, the plate tipped up and the lobster sauce spilled onto Ah-Jack's bare arm. He dropped the dish with a shout.

"Shit, that's hot." Pat was shaking out his fingers.

Ah-Jack, trembling but calm, wiped the burning sauce off his skin. His forearm was bright red, tender, and swelling in front of his eyes. He would need to soak a towel in soy sauce. Otherwise his skin would blister and split like a hot tomato.

"Oh shit!" Pat had noticed the fallen plate. "You're fine, right? Shit, I needed that." Ah-Jack looked down as well, and his chest tightened. The plate had landed right on top of his cheap cloth shoes.

"Tell the chef to rush your order," Ah-Jack said. He couldn't feel anything, and his fear came out as impatience. "Five minutes if he rushes. Maybe three. It's all the same quick garbage." Ah-Jack caught a cook's attention and shouted, "You saw what happened. Make the boy another number four before he shits himself."

"All right, all right!" The cook started cleaning out his wok.

"What did you say to him?" Pat asked. "Did you tell him it was your fault?"

"What are you yelling at Uncle Jack for?" Nan said, pulling off her plastic gloves as she entered the kitchen. She tossed her dirty tray to a dishwasher and came between them. Suddenly she was on the ground, her voice thin with panic.

"Your feet! Get your shoes off now!" She scooped the food off Ah-Jack's feet and into her apron.

"He dropped the dish on himself." Pat widened his eyes over his mother's head.

"Yes," Ah-Jack said. If his feet didn't hurt, then they couldn't be burned. "Get up. I barely feel anything."

"You don't feel this?" Nan waved her hands at the steam rising from the gravy. "Are you crazy?" She finished scooping and threw the full apron at her son.

"What am I supposed to do?" He held the apron as if it were a used diaper.

"Tell Jimmy I'm taking Ah-Jack to the hospital." She stood up and handed Pat the ruined cloth shoes as well.

"I don't need the hospital," Ah-Jack said.

"You can't leave," Pat insisted.

"Don't be selfish," Nan snapped. She tugged on Ah-Jack's unburned arm.

Looking into Nan's eyes, a sense of calm came over Ah-Jack. The world around him narrowed into pinpricks, framing the fretting woman in front of him.

"I don't feel a thing," he reassured her. "Honestly, I don't."

"Wait, Mom." Pat reached out for Nan, his fingers digging into her collarbone. She turned around and shook him off.

"What has gotten into you!" She massaged her shoulder.

Pat's hand went into his pocket and pulled something out. He unfurled his fingers and they all looked down at his palm. A braided gold chain pooled softly across the lines of his hand. At the end: a luminous pearl teardrop. He must have been holding on to that necklace all day; why give it to his mother now? Ah-Jack wanted to tell him to stop, to wait for a better time. But he'd glimpsed in Pat's face what he'd seen that night out on the loading dock, right after Nan had struck the boy's cheek. Sadness without surprise. Pat already knew what was going to happen; he offered his cupped palm anyway. He moved closer to his mother, teardrop at the center of his hand. She took a step back.

"Don't waste your money." Neck stiff, she turned and walked away. The other waiters, who'd been watching by the kitchen entrance, came in to fill their trays. Ah-Jack followed Nan but kept his eyes on Pat, who'd looped the chain loosely around his fourth finger and pinky. His fellow servers rushed around him. The chain swaying from his hand, Pat went to collect his new order of shrimp.

Right before Nan led him out of the kitchen, Ah-Jack spotted the necklace sliding from Pat's fingers, dragged down by the weight of the pearl. Ah-Jack's shout of warning was in his throat when the teardrop fell straight into the waiting cracks of the steam table. The chain followed, a golden tail, disappearing soundlessly into the stainless steel.

After he'd sent Ah-Jack away—what had he even shouted at the old waiter for?—Jimmy stayed in the closet, tempted to squirm under the coats and hide beneath the hems. But Osman, the lone Duck House amigo, came in to collect a broom, startling Jimmy back into the dining hall. He did a cursory lap around the room. The restaurant had regained its balance. Dishes were coming out of the kitchen on time and his father's customers kept calling out to him to pay their compliments. He ignored them all, ending at Janine's table. The Glory would be fine without him for a few hours.

"I've got to head out," Jimmy said. Eddie had been happily eating one of his pancakes, but he sucked in his breath and held it when he saw Jimmy. He wished he could punt the small child into the air like a football.

"Is there a problem?" Janine asked.

"I just need to find my mother." He could barely turn his face toward hers. "I'm really sorry. I'll get you the next-best waiter." He spotted Pat heading out of the kitchen with a tray full of soup bowls. His body locked up. He caught the boy's eye with a sharp gesture and waved him over.

"What's up?" Pat rested the tray on his shoulder. Forcing the boy to wait on Janine wouldn't keep the two of them from disappearing while his back was turned. But Jimmy didn't care. He had to leave.

"Take care of these VIPs for me," Jimmy said. "I'll hear back if the service is anything but perfect." He smiled over Janine's head and took her hand briefly, before lowering it back onto the table.

"Sure," Pat said. "What's the order?"

"Everything," he said. "Give them every dish on the menu."

"That's too much!" Janine said, but Jimmy said, "You deserve it." He smiled to keep his teeth from clenching. "This is all because of you."

Janine quirked her mouth to the side. She'd detected the black thread of anger beneath the milky sweetness of his words, and this made her cautious, conciliatory. "We can always take the leftovers home," she said. She raised her face up for a kiss. He pressed his lips quickly to hers, resisting the melting feeling in his stomach.

"Great meeting you, buddy," he said to Eddie, who again held his breath.

"When am I going to see you again?" Janine asked.

Jimmy was already heading toward the door. "I'll come by tonight," he said over his shoulder. For once, no customers called to him. Janine's eyes tugged at his back as he let himself out. So this was how you got a woman's attention.

The drive to his mother's house was slow and ugly, all highway except for the last five minutes. An accident on the freeway forced his car to a crawl; his mind only raced faster. Why had his mother reached out to a man he knew she detested? She must have really wanted to keep that dusty old house. Problems kept popping up in his life, as insidiously as the canker sores in his mouth. As soon as one began to heal, two more would erupt.

The trouble with life was that life needed trouble. That was what Janine would have said. A woman that clever—why was he surprised that she couldn't be trusted? She was right, of course. A year ago, he had been alone, rotting in his father's restaurant, working under his big brother, and serving customers whose every dietary request he could, by pure reflex, anticipate. He had been collecting stores of useless information, a basin of stagnant water that continued to fill. He ate the shit staff meals the kitchen churned out, no longer for appearance's sake, as his father had once commanded, but because he'd stopped caring about how his food tasted. On his days off, he had done nothing but drink and smoke in his apartment. He had been able to sleep for fourteen hours straight, suppressing hunger, thirst, the urge to piss, until his brain stewed in its container. Now he could not sleep three hours without stirring. He could not sit still, and he could not eat, but the bites he managed to swallow were vibrant and nourishing. For the first time in years, he was truly alive. It did not feel good at all. But at least it felt like something.

His mind fumed and boiled inside his car, but when he reached the circular driveway to his mother's front door, his thoughts grew quiet. The top of his head tingled when he saw the light shining from the kitchen window.

His mother was at the door, peering out. Jimmy forced himself out of the car. He tucked the back of his shirt in and hitched up his pants.

"Hello, traitor," she said, opening the door. "Have you eaten?" She let him into the foyer. The marble tiles shone, freshly polished. If she had started cleaning again, then she really was ready to root her stringy self to this house's foundation. She looked more like she had before his father passed away—back straight, trousers sharply pressed. She'd even touched up the color in her hair, the black gleaming near-purple under the chandelier light. Jimmy reluctantly followed her into the kitchen.

She had known he was coming. She had piled the dining table with platters of food. All his favorites, dishes he hadn't eaten in years. True home-style fare. Jimmy's mouth watered despite himself. He thought of the food he'd had in mind for his restaurant. He knew so little about what people actually wanted to eat. He grabbed a handful of roasted peanuts and littered the floor with their casings.

"Why did you go to him?" he asked with his mouth full.

"Why you go to him?" she parroted back. "You stupid boy."

"I wanted my own place."

She knelt down on the floor, picking up the crispy skins with a pinched napkin. He dropped a few more peanuts to spite her. She smacked the back of her hand against his ankle. "He is dangerous man. You made such big mistake."

"At least I tried to get our family out of his grasp." He plunged his fingers into the bowl of sticky spareribs, sucking the meat off the bones. He was resorting to methods that he'd used as a teenager to gross her out. His pettiness added to the satisfaction of seeing her squirm. "He was asking for more money. He's always been a parasite. I was the only one who was going to stand up to him."

"Stand up!" She struck the glossy wood table with her palms. "Only a snake thinks he's standing up when he's hiding in the grass. I didn't raise you right. I made your life too easy. You should get on your knees and beg for his forgiveness."

"That gives you the right to throw me back to him?" Jimmy always wanted to laugh when his mother scolded him in Chinese; the impulse had landed blows to his head when he was younger. He grabbed more food to suffocate the feeling. His mother shoved a bowl of rice into his hands.

"You eat like a barbarian," she said. "You don't think I begged your father to kick that man out? But I'll tell you what he told me: You get rid of Pang, you get rid of the money." A neat row of his mother's prescription bottles lined the short edge of the table. Jimmy wanted to knock them over.

"We have enough money." He shoved his chopsticks deep into the steaming mound of rice. "That doesn't change the fact that we work in a shitty Chinese restaurant."

He expected his mother to screw up her face and scream about how ungrateful he was being. He was ready to scream right back. Instead, she pincered a few choice pieces of spareribs with her chopsticks and dropped them in his bowl.

"My baby boy," she said. "Where do you think you got all your big ideas? You always think you're the first one to have a thought in his head, but I gave you everything. Don't you remember how often I told your father the words you just threw at me? You're nothing but an eavesdropper." She wet a rag in the sink and scrubbed at his sticky fingers.

The food in Jimmy's mouth turned to glue. She was lying. How could an uneducated woman—someone who had married a dishwasher, for fuck's sake—know anything about ambition? He tore his hand out of her grasp.

"You know nothing about your own mother," she said. "You'll see. I'll get Johnny on my side. We'll sell my house together, and not a cent of it will go to you or that country girl. You're going to have to turn that poor boy in. You're going to have to get your hands dirty. And while you learn how to take care of your stupid self, I will rebuild your father's restaurant and stand at the front of the house."

"You belong in the back," he said. "That's how you get your hands dirty, counting what you didn't fucking earn." His mother used the damp cloth to rub at a grease stain on the table. Jimmy put his bowl down with a sharp *clack*. "Did you forget you gave Johnny financial power? This house is no longer yours to sell."

His mother shook her head in a way that dismissed everything without needing to say a word. But his mother always did the needless thing.

"The thing to know about your big brother is that his mind is rigid but his spine is weak," she said. She started wringing out her towel, squeezing drops of dirty moisture onto her slippered feet. "He calls himself the family so he can say he thinks of the family first. He'll do whatever looks best, no matter what he did the day before." The blue-green veins in her hands bulged from the strength of her grip. "And you, you are equally transparent." She seemed to compose herself, but then she threw her rag on the floor.

"Get out of my house," she said.

"No." Jimmy squared his stance as if his mother were about to bulldoze through him. "I'm not done talking."

"How dare you treat your family this way," she said. "You respect nothing!"

She grabbed the nearest plate of food—a bowl overflowing with shrimp in red sauce—and moved with it to the garbage can. Before Jimmy could stop her, she'd dumped the entire bowl into the trash. She went back to the table, grabbing the spareribs, the baby bok choy, the green beans and pork. Cascades of fresh, still-warm food fell into the white bin, becoming, in an instant, inedible. Trash.

Jimmy hadn't thought that he could be shocked by his mother's actions anymore. His entire life, she had been a woman who did and said what she felt in the moment, relishing the act without finding relevance in the consequences. She was the kind of mother who, if she thought he was wearing unflattering pants, would find a certain pleasure in saying, "I never noticed how stubby your legs are—like a baby elephant's," because her words were accurate, because they had a rhythm and sting. And as her son, the frequent target of her love's shade, he was no longer disturbed by what came out of her mouth. But this wanton discarding made him ill in a way that had not happened since he was a child, when his mother had come down with a terrible flu and could not stop vomiting. She had lost control of herself. The act of throwing out good food—food that she had spent hours creating; this pure waste of resources from a woman who had once fished his dumpling from the trash and eaten it, hunched over the bin, in front of him—showed how far his mother was willing to go to teach him a lesson. The last dish emptied its contents, leaving only tracks of sauce.

"Mom, you've gone crazy."

"Say whatever you want." She brushed the hair out of her face with both hands. "I'm going to bed."

With that, she departed. Her steps descended the stairs to her basement bedroom, where the air was cool and the darkness a consistent dusk. She'd left the rag on the floor and the ventilator over the stove running. Jimmy bet that if he held his hand over the burners, they would still be hot.

Alone again—what a relief to be alone—Feng Fei thought of what she hadn't told her son, to console herself over the secrets she had. She'd said more than she'd planned to. Her youngest could build the froth of her rage so high it blocked her sight. But he still believed, like everyone did, that Ah-Pang was Bobby's friend. That she had no role in the Duck House's success. That she was harmless, the husk of a self she'd willfully turned into after Bobby's death. This was her greatest strength: how easily

she was underestimated. Ah-Pang had taught her this unbal-
ancing trick. But she'd taught him plenty too. She'd taught him
to pretend at a snobbishness he didn't believe in. She'd taught
him how to take advantage of coming from nothing, how to
spin that nothing into mystery and play with the imagination
of those above him in station. Most important, she'd taught
him, or perhaps they'd taught each other, how to tell the best
story. In a world without fairness, the best stories rose to the
top. So the Duck House was a diamond in the rough, with the
most authentic Peking duck, attracting powerful and influential
people. The Hans were hardworking dreamers who had carved
an indelible place in this country. Ah-Pang was their beloved
uncle, a constant guardian. Beautiful stories she told. She loved
the way words sounded in her mouth.

Now her sons had become preoccupied with other stories.
What if Feng Fei couldn't win them back? After all, they—the
thieves—had inherited from her the ability to shape the world
around them. Johnny, with his nobleman's pretensions, saw himself as the patron saint of their family. She had to admit that after
Bobby died, her eldest son's story had worked like a numbing
draft. But he was useless, to the family, to the restaurant. The
charm, the diplomat's accent, the face and showy intelligence
that worked on his customers, never worked on his family. Even
Bobby, who wasted little time thinking about his sons, had once
remarked that Johnny was flimsy as a paper doll. But paper
was sly; it left the smallest burning cuts. If Johnny took over
the Duck House, as neither she nor Bobby had ever wanted, he
would quickly find the restaurant work, the back of the house,
beneath him. Contradictory to the story he told about himself.
He would leave to find "more meaningful work," abandoning
the place that had elevated him to this insufferable level.

The back of the house *was* demeaning, but, more than that,
Johnny was incompetent when a task asked that he make himself
unlikable. As was the case with many first sons, their Johnny

grew up to be a trophy that needed to be polished daily by others' hands. Jimmy, on the other hand, had no reservations about smelling unsweet. From childhood, he'd been a little whirl of fury, collecting slights on his skin like balls of burr. In China, while Johnny had corralled the neighborhood children into doing his gentle bidding, Jimmy bit and scratched whoever tried to play with him. She'd had to spank him raw, but part of her had enjoyed having a child who would fight back. In America, the schools had civilized him, but they'd also dulled the edges of his personality, turning him, if not timid, then taciturn. Only when he began to work in the Duck House did that vein of anger pulse again. He had ruled the back of the house. He was the one who'd created the infamous "vacation," one week of forced unpaid leave, like slapping a dog on the nose and locking it up. He was the one who'd strong-armed the waiters into improving their phonetic English, until the customers no longer had to ask them to repeat the specials. Unfortunate that Jimmy got his story mixed up in his head. He'd had to go against his essential nature to force his plain face out into the dining room. She could have told him how ridiculous he looked, parading around like Johnny, just as she could cut Johnny down to size for thinking he had any clout in the back. She was most disgusted when faced with a person who did not understand his own limitations. When she saw such behavior in her sons, she could have wept from disappointment. She had tried to teach them the only way she knew how, with an old fable she'd read in a translated book. She'd repeated the story so many times.

"One day," she always began, "a donkey wandered out of its stable, attracted to the sound of its owner laughing." At this, Johnny always started laughing as well, and Feng Fei would shout at him to stop acting like an idiot.

"The donkey saw that his owner was watching a monkey dance on the roof of his house." Feng Fei would make the fingers of her right hand flutter on her sons' noses. "So the donkey climbed onto the roof with the monkey and started dancing too." Feng Fei's left hand would follow her right. "But the donkey was too heavy for the roof. Its hooves broke through the plaster, making a large hole. The owner pulled the donkey outside and beat it until it cried, 'Why did you laugh at the monkey but not at me?'"

She always paused here, waiting for her sons to chorus the moral of the fable back. But they would already be distracted. She would have to slap their hands to get them to listen.

"'Because you are a donkey, and it is a monkey,' the owner said, bringing the stick down on the poor, dumb donkey's hide."

"Which ones are we?" Johnny would ask, desperate to be part of the winning team. "I'm a monkey, right, Ma? And Jimmy's a donkey!"

"I'm not!" Jimmy would protest.

"That's not the point," she'd say. "The point is that what some can do, you cannot. What you can do, others cannot. Get it?"

Sometimes, as if it were a cosmic joke, the parent was the best combination of the children. Johnny got her charm, Jimmy her spine. Johnny got her restraint, Jimmy her anger. They both got their father's pretensions. They both got his determined disdain for her, his dismay when she proved that without her, none of them would have been anything.

Without her, her stories and her tenacity in retelling them, Bobby would still be in the back kitchens of Chinatown. She and the boys would still be abandoned in Hong Kong, blacklisted from Beijing because her husband's uncle had owned too nice a restaurant. She'd made sure Bobby remembered to bring them over, when he was spending his new money on things that let him forget. She wrote to him every day, finding his new addresses when he moved to cheaper apartments, pestering him with news of his children, and when that didn't work, she began to hint at the rumors she could spread. Not of his unfaithfulness, or his drunkenness, but of his total failure, of his inability to get even a dishwasher's job, the position he'd started in in China, and one he hadn't deigned to hold in years. "Even if you become a millionaire," she wrote to him, "I will make it my mission to convince your family and friends, your old rivals and lovers, that you are a fraud. A wife holds all your secrets. Even the ones that aren't true."

Then she'd sent her cousin his way, writing to Ah-Pang to shape up her gutless husband. Ah-Pang had been the reason Feng Fei knew about America at all, while all those around her believed Beijing to be the heart-center of the universe. From her aunt, she'd heard of Ah-Pang's success abroad, how much money he was sending back to his family, often once a week, and without alerting the village officials that remunerations were coming from abroad. In their childhood, she'd played with Pang-Pang in the countryside, where his family lived. To this day she remembered the afternoon she saw him wringing the neck of an injured bird. What had stuck with her was not the bird's limp body or the sound of the snapping bone. It was the bored look in Pang-Pang's eyes when his hands went around the flapping bird's neck. It was the slight pleasure in his voice when, after he'd carried the dead bird into his mother's kitchen, he asked her how they might cook it. So pleased by results yet so cold about the painful routes to achieve them. He might be the only man who could bring the Hans to America and help them thrive. Then again, perhaps this was just the best story.

Feng Fei had tired herself out, thinking about her family and how they continued to find new ways to torment her. But this was a different kind of exhaustion than the one that had kept her in the basement all year. This tiredness would lift, like a curtain blind. It was merely a reminder of her power, which could suck the energy right out of her. She sank into bed, kicking off her slippers. She didn't bother to take off her clothes. She had missed feeling this tired. She had missed the sensation of sleep not for escape but relief.

19

Nan pulled Ah-Jack through the restaurant, keeping an eye out for Jimmy, who was, mysteriously, nowhere to be found. Ah-Jack held her hand all the way to the car.

"I'm sorry," he said, after she'd started the engine.

"Don't forget your seatbelt."

"It was all my fault," he said. "I thought I could handle the weight."

"I should've been watching out for you," she said.

"Please," he said. "Let's stop hogging all the blame."

She looked over to find him smiling at her.

"What will we do?" she said. Then, "We'll get you to a doctor."

"If anything, the heat cured my athlete's foot!" he said as she started to drive.

"You have to be extra careful with your feet. Infection. Nerve damage."

"My feet are fine," he said, but when they reached Urgent Care, he got out of the car without prodding.

The doctor's face was placid while examining Ah-Jack's feet, until Nan told him about the diabetes.

"Better safe than sorry," the doctor said. He was an Indian man with chubby cheeks and beautiful eyes, sunken from sitting behind thick glasses.

"That's what I tell him." Nan shoved Ah-Jack with the point of her elbow. "He never listen."

"Listen to your wife," the doctor said, scribbling on his prescription pad.

"Wife know best," Ah-Jack said. "Happy wife, happy life."

The doctor laughed and ripped off the prescription, handing it to Nan with a wink. She had been the one to claim she was his wife, in case they barred her from the examination room. Yet she was flustered by how easily Ah-Jack leaned into the lie. What did they look like to the doctor, to the nurse out in the waiting room, to the three other patients, who peered at them from behind old *Time* magazines? In China, they would have seemed a strange couple, with Ah-Jack clearly decades older than she was and both of them dressed in stained formalwear. But in this waiting room, they belonged together if only because they were both Chinese.

Or if it hadn't been their shared skin then perhaps it was the comfort with which they'd sat side by side. Strange as she'd felt in his presence all day—really ever since they'd begun sharing a bed—Nan hadn't known how awkward she'd been acting until tonight's emergency had returned them to their old, familiar roles. Ushering Ah-Jack back into the car, she realized she didn't know more than one way to be around him.

Nan picked up the burn ointment at the CVS near her house, throwing in a pair of slippers. She forced Ah-Jack to stay in the car, practically locking the doors to keep him from following. Standing in the checkout line, the bright, disorienting lights making her eyes dance, she felt the giddy confusion of wanting to laugh and cry at the same time. Finally she had what she'd been too afraid to ask for. She knew what his mouth felt like on hers, on her skin, and the weight of his hands, how they differed from the weight of his head, his arms, his feet. She not only knew but was growing accustomed to the smell of his breath in the morning and the noises his body made in the middle of the night. Suffused with all these fresh experiences, her love should have been transformed into something new. But her feelings hadn't changed. It was as if they were cut from the same dusty cloth as the old, original love, the one that had flowered thirty years ago. A love so perfectly petrified over time—could it possibly have been real and organic to begin with?

Perhaps, though, their problem was simple. Her feelings hadn't changed because they hadn't yet gone to bed. Not truly. At night, they touched purely for comfort. Their relationship was in limbo, too skittish to be strong. They couldn't be timid with each other for much longer. She returned to the car, eyes still blinded, now by the absence of those bright lights.

"Here you are." She slid behind the steering wheel.

Ah-Jack took the taped box with nodded thanks. In his woozy state, he could not figure out how to open it. He scratched helplessly at the packaging, denting the thick cardboard. Nan could not help herself. She took the box back out of his hands.

While Nan tried to peel back the silver foil latched over the mouth of the ointment tube, Ah-Jack relished the bound, tingling sensation in his feet. The doctor had done a wonderful job of dressing them—more of a precaution than a necessity, Dr. Gupta had assured him—and Ah-Jack's feet had never felt so clean and sterile. Like they were in their original packaging. The quarter dose of Vicodin he'd sweet-talked from the nurse didn't hurt either. The heavy, floating quality of his body, like a fish ball bobbing in warm broth, was like sleep without the sleepiness.

"Wonderful," he murmured, when Nan finally succeeded in un-foiling the tube with her teeth. "You're wonderful."

"I have to be to deal with you," she mumbled. The foil was stuck between her lips.

He reached out and brushed the metal off her mouth, pinching it between his thumb and middle finger.

"I've got the reflexes of a cat," he said.

"A lazy cat." The warmth in her smile was delightful.

"Laziness is not so bad," he said. "At our age, we can both be a little lazy."

She made a noise halfway between a scoff and a laugh and started the car.

"After a night like this, I'm thankful." He wanted to pull her gaze off the road and back onto him. "When I look at you, the world quiets down."

"We have a poet in the car." Nan shot a little glance at him that he found supremely sexy. "Were you so effusive with Michelle?"

Ah-Jack puffed out his cheeks, distracted by the sensation of his skin stretching.

"Poetry just sneaks out of me, like passing gas," he said.

"How is she?" Nan said.

"I thought you were *my* friend, not my wife's."

Nan laid a cool hand on his. "Michelle is still my friend."

"You get in bed with all your friends' husbands?" He spoke not with anger, which the medicine blunted. In this moment, everything was matter-of-fact.

Nan had been about to speed through a yellow, but she slammed on the brakes instead. They both rocked forward, seatbelts straining.

"Don't be nasty." She looked intently at the stoplight.

He briefly rose out of his fog. "Michelle was only friends with you because she was suspicious."

"Okay, fine," Nan said. When the light changed, she sped out as if racing the car beside her.

"I can't wait to lie down." Ah-Jack slid as far as his seatbelt would let him. He was already forgetting what they had been talking about. The even heaviness of his body was pure pleasure. He'd been turned into peanut butter and spread over a piece of toast.

"Perhaps we should go to bed when we get home." Nan's voice was strange, but not strange enough to fully penetrate his bubble. "After a shock like today, we need to rest. Together."

"Wherever." He flopped his hand around. A near-thought formed in his head, concrete enough for a wolfish smile to bloom. "As long as I can be horizontal."

As soon as she shut the front door behind them, Nan was seized by a swirling panic strong enough to suck her down with it. She hurried up the stairs, faster than Ah-Jack could handle. Without turning around, she started to complain about her job, hoping to disguise her coldness toward him, which had come over her so quickly she felt poisoned. If only she hadn't suggested that they go to bed together. If only she'd convinced him to sleep on the downstairs futon, just for tonight.

"You look very sexy in your duck-carver outfit," he said, trailing her up the stairs. He was alarmingly bright-eyed after his nap in the car. "Especially that little hat. It looks so delicate but sturdy at the same time. Just like you!"

"You're not listening." She was out of breath. "I feel like a servant. I can't even talk to the customers. Jimmy says it's unprofessional. No one wants to hear me open my mouth."

"He'll relax his policies." Ah-Jack's hand rubbed her back. She slipped out of reach again. "Remember when he wouldn't let us speak Chinese at the Duck House? The same will happen with this rule."

"But he's right." Nan tried again. "The customers don't want to talk to me. They want me to pose for their photos. Or try harder to scrape the duck fat off the skin."

"Your old customers will want to talk to you," he said. "And as for the others, who cares about talking to them? That's not your job anymore. Your job is better. You get to sit down, take turns. You don't even have to memorize which table is ordering your duck. It's as close to retired as you can get!" Ah-Jack had a habit of ending all his last sentences louder than the rest: an emphatic stamp sealing his missives. Nan suddenly detested how easily he could shout.

"I was a manager!" she shouted back. "Jimmy didn't even tell us that he was buying a new restaurant, that we were two months away from no job, no money, nothing. But he tosses me a small scrap, and I'm supposed to be thankful? I gave that family thirty years of my life. What's even keeping me here?"

Desperate for any kind of delay, she threw the comforter off her bed and went to work smoothing the bedsheet. Ah-Jack walked over to the other side and held on to the corners, pulling them taut to keep Nan from yanking the sheet completely over to her. In his silence, the echo of her frustrated words rebounded back to her. He would never say what he was thinking right then, but she saw in his downturned face the question: What about me?

And since she could pluck the thoughts straight out of his head as if they were worms wiggling from his ears, wasn't she responsible for reassuring him? For answering the question he was too afraid to speak?

He should ask his own damn questions. Nan was done playing her part. She was tired. She was mortified by her job, her age, her son. She couldn't get Michelle, her kind, round face, out of her head. She wanted to scold herself, her nervous body.

The bed made to her exacting standards, she looked around for something else to tidy. Before she could attack the mirror with a damp cloth, Ah-Jack came around the bed and softly rubbed her arms. His hands went up and down, brushing the dry points of her elbows and rounding the curve of her shoulders. He was pushing air back into her chest, reminding her to breathe and be still. In her stillness, her heart beat and her breath flowed; the weight of her body pressed down into the floor. The bed was so close. Their calves grazed the cotton duster. She kept her eyes peeled on the journey his right hand was making on her left arm. Age spots speckled the hand, as if someone had spilled seeds over the skin. It was not the same hand she had shaken when they had first met. It was a hand that trembled, sometimes, and dropped what it tried to hold. But his hand was not shaking now.

She closed the gap between them and laid her head on his chest. Thirty years too late she heard the hitch in his breath. His arms went around her and his fingers danced a steady beat over her lower back, where she was her strongest. Her hands went up to his shoulders, forearms hooked underneath his armpits. She felt for the knots of muscle near his neck.

Slowly, with a little hesitation, they allowed their hands to drift. Nan was surprised when Ah-Jack began to lower into a crouch. His hands traveled down her legs. She raked her fingers through his hair and traced the bumps of his skull. He touched her thighs through her pockets and explored the terrain of her knees.

"There you go!" He gripped her ankles and unbalanced her into bed.

"You never change!" she shouted, but she was laughing too hard to protest.

He joined her on the bed, which bounced from his weight.

"To think, you made this bed for no reason." He began to unbutton her shirt.

"If I hadn't made the bed, you wouldn't be trying to seduce me in it," she said, returning the favor. "The only time you move off your lazy ass is to make a mess."

"The only time you move is to clean up my messes."

They continued to tease and snap while they slowly removed their clothes. At some point, Nan reached up and shut off the light.

"I've gone blind!" Ah-Jack moved his hands over her in wild pantomime, and she laughed, barely realizing that he'd gotten on top of her until she felt his knees press the outsides of her legs.

"You haven't gone blind." She pushed her legs out. His knees relocated to bump against her inner thighs. "You'll go senile before you go blind. You need your sharp eyes to look for little misses to harass."

"You were always my favorite little miss to harass." His mouth was both dry and wet against her skin, and she only realized he was whispering from the sensation of his breath.

With pleasure growing, she forgot to keep the teasing up, and in the soft-breathed silence, she saw their old bones rubbing up against each other. Her body tightened.

"Maybe we're too late." She started to move out from under him.

He dropped down on his elbows and pressed his entire body against hers.

"I like being late." His voice was airy all of a sudden. With a start, she realized where all the blood in his speech had gone.

She finally slid the elastic of her underpants down, then reached up and tucked her fingers under the waistband of his. There, she hesitated. He rested his forehead against hers, their noses bumping lightly. He waited. His quiet patience won her over.

Ah-Jack was breathing deeply beside her; Nan could not get her eyes to stay closed. Her body prickled with shame over what she had just used it for. She had slept with someone else's husband. *Michelle's* husband. She could get no more than a few shallow sips of air. Why had she thought that sex would make things easier?

Carefully, she got out of bed and took her phone into the hallway. She thought she might be feverish, but when she pressed her hand against her forehead, the skin was chill and clammy. In the hall, Ah-Jack's breathing was still audible. The phlegm in his throat shook with every inhale. Guilt drove a heavy cylinder into her chest. Ah-Jack—she couldn't stop referring to him in that brotherly way—would never forgive her if he woke up and found himself in another empty bed. She dialed Michelle's number anyway.

Unexpectedly, a man answered the other line.

"Hello?" His wariness barely dampened what must have been a booming voice.

"Hello," she said. What did Ah-Jack say was this man's name again? "This is Nan. Michelle's friend. I was hoping to check in on her."

"She's in the bathroom right now." He was crass but friendly. "But I'm sure she would love to hear from you."

"How about I come over, then." Nan looked down the hall, at her bedroom door. "If it's not too much trouble."

"I think she'd like that."

"I can be there by ten-thirty," Nan said. She hadn't been home this early in years. "If that's all right."

"That's fine. We'll see you then."

After stopping at a Starbucks to buy the last of their pastries, Nan parked in Michelle's driveway. She sat in her car, listening to its little clicks after she'd shut off the engine. She pressed the box of pastries hard into her lap. She hated the lingering rawness between her legs. She hadn't thought this plan through at all. How shameless to visit Michelle right after sleeping with her husband. Who barged in on a sick woman with stale Danishes while her own body recovered from the aftershocks of sex?

Before she could stop herself, she was out of the car and at the front door. She stared at the chipping doorknocker. It was too late to turn back now. Regardless of her intentions, she was doing the right thing. Her hand found the doorbell.

To her muted surprise, a larger man than she'd imagined answered the door. He was like a granite statue softened and plump. His face was fleshy and oily and therefore youthful even though gray flecked his hair. He clasped her hand in both of his before taking the box of pastries.

"Come in." He threw the door open wide. "Michelle is in her bedroom."

"If it's too late I can . . ."

"No, no, we call it her 'office' now." He smiled at his own joke, but his eyes were tired. "She's always up there. Please, go right up the stairs. I'll be up soon with tea."

His assumption that she knew the floor plan of the townhouse was endearing. He seemed like the kind of man who made many assumptions, always flattering if a little too forward. He and Ah-Jack were eerily similar in spirit. But unlike Ah-Jack, this man could focus his vigor and good humor. He no doubt owned his own business, something that had him outdoors but didn't make him sweat. A landscaping company, possibly. And in his free time and conversation, he probably preached the value of hard work. Nan rounded the last flight of stairs. All these judgments from one encounter. As if by criticizing this man, she might undo the pain she was causing Ah-Jack. Had she ever hurt him before? Not in all their years.

The door to the master bedroom was open a crack. A yellow light seeped out, the kind that hurt your eyes if you read under it. Nan knocked and Michelle called out a greeting. Nan pushed open the door. She nearly gasped.

Michelle had lost a ghastly amount of weight. The last time Nan had seen her had been months ago, and she barely looked like the same person. Ah-Jack had mentioned that this time around, Michelle's treatment had made her lose, not gain, weight. But the transformation was startling. Michelle's body was barely visible beneath her comforter. Her head was propped up by a pile of pillows. Because her face was no longer joyfully plump, the full spheres of her eyes were visible; they looked reptilian as they blinked up at Nan. Only her smile was unchanged: wide, bright, and nervous.

"Get over here," she said, biting at her chapped lower lip.

"How are you feeling?" Nan perched at the foot of the bed. She was forced to scoot closer when Michelle reached out to grab her hand.

"Fine," Michelle said. "And you? I hope Jack isn't too much of a burden. I told him he shouldn't be bothering you, but you know he doesn't have a clue."

Nan was tempted to fall back into old patterns. She and Michelle didn't have much in common, and teasing Ah-Jack was easy. But she couldn't pretend she was Michelle's friend after what she'd done.

"Actually." She squeezed Michelle's dry hand. "Jack and I . . . We've grown closer. It wasn't planned." Her words tumbled out. "It just happened. I'm so sorry. Please know we didn't want to hurt you." She took a deep breath, unable to look up from Michelle's hand. "I understand if you never want to see me again."

Michelle quietly leaned her head back. She blinked, and two tears fell down her cheeks, down the length of her neck, disappearing into her nightgown. Nan put her hands back in her lap and waited to be asked to leave. But when Michelle lowered her head again, her face was calm.

"I'm not surprised," she said, crying with a small smile. She looked like rain on a sunny day, miraculous and ordinary. "I know you and my husband have always been special to each other. I knew from the first time he said your name. That's why I invited you to lunch all those years ago. Made you eat with a strange woman you'd just met."

"I'm sorry." Nan was also starting to cry, but she bit her tongue. She didn't have the right. Michelle leaned forward with a grunt and took her by the arm.

"I know." Her eyes were encouraging. "Of course I know. But he left me long before he met you."

Nan nodded before she could stop herself. She hated being disloyal to Ah-Jack. But he had never done enough to help his wife grow into this country. He was too comfortable being the absent sun to her tiny world.

"I have no right to keep you two apart," Michelle said. "Perhaps I should thank you. With you there to pick up the pieces, I was allowed to leave. To be with Gary."

"Gary." Nan took the time to memorize his name. "He seems like a good man."

"A little young for me, and sometimes too childish," Michelle said modestly. "He's always carrying me up and down the stairs. I tell him I can walk! But he doesn't listen. Men are never happy unless they're carrying something too heavy for a woman to hold. He's paying my hospital bills. I didn't want that. But he feels a duty. They all do." She smiled shyly to herself, as if wondering whether to tell Nan a secret.

"You know, he taught me the most interesting thing." She played with the tail of her headscarf. "I was always so afraid of going outside. I couldn't stand being confused. Not knowing how to ask for help. He told me, 'Just laugh. Everyone wants to help a woman with a beautiful laugh.'" She beamed up at Nan. "Now I can go shopping at the mall. I can order at restaurants. It's so easy!"

"You look happy," Nan said, because this was the truth.

"I was always happy," Michelle said. "But now you can be too."

Nan hated to break the translucent shell of Michelle's joy, but she couldn't leave without addressing the biggest problem in the room.

"I think you should speak with your husband," she said. "He needs to know that you're not feeling well."

Michelle lunged forward with surprising strength, her head-scarf slipping back to reveal new inches of scalp. Her fingernails were thin and splintered.

"Don't tell him." She struggled to roll onto her knees. "Promise me."

"Don't get up," Nan said. She settled Michelle back into her pillows and looked at the agitated woman. "Why don't you want him to know?"

"I have Gary to take care of me," Michelle said. "Why does Jack need to know? Then everyone feels bad. Worse, everyone feels responsible. I want you both to be happy."

"If this is really what you want," Nan said. "As long as you get better."

Michelle smoothed the covers over her lap.

"Even if I don't," she said. "Even if I die. Swear to me that you'll take care of him."

"Die?" Nan hated the feeling of the word hissing out of her teeth. "You're not dying. Don't exaggerate."

"Look at me." Michelle stretched out her bony arms. "Jack and Gary, they both refuse to see what's in front of them. They'll break into pieces if they even try. I'm telling you because you're strong enough to see. The doctors say that everything is okay, but I know what okay feels like."

Her fingers plucked at the pilling cotton. Then she looked up with an eager glint in her eye. Gary opened the door with his elbow, holding a tray.

"You are such a bad host," she teased. "Making our guest wait for so long."

Gary apologized good-naturedly and settled the tray onto the bed.

"I didn't know what kind of tea Nan wanted." He gestured at the three small teapots cluttering the tray. "I have oolong, chrysanthemum, and jasmine."

"I just remembered." Nan was already off the bed, which felt love-worn and intimate with Gary sitting there. She couldn't be in the room another minute. She shouldn't have visited. Her tongue stuck to the roof of her mouth; her throat was so dry it hurt to speak. "I have to pick Pat up from a friend's house. I'm so sorry to drop in unexpectedly and then leave this soon. I'm a terrible guest." She looked at Michelle over Gary's large head. "I'll make it up to you."

"I know," Michelle said. She yawned to excuse the tears leaking out from her eyes. "You always keep your promises."

"Are you sure you can't stay for a cup of tea?" Gary said, standing up to shake Nan's hand. His pleasant face was broad, like a big dog's. She wanted to tell him to take care of himself. To take care of Michelle. She gripped his hand in both of hers and told him that next time she would.

Halfway down the stairs, she sat on a step and leaned her elbows into her knees. Her breathing sounded hoarse as it bounced off the tight walls encasing the staircase. The words Michelle had spoken so casually rebounded, with extra force. Michelle was dying. She was in great pain. She was in love.

Nan let herself out. She got into her car, but she didn't feel like she could drive. She couldn't stop thinking about Michelle's forgiveness, her grace, her skeletal frame. Bad behavior didn't rattle Nan anymore. After working for the Hans, marrying Ray, raising Pat, she was too comfortable with people acting out. In tantrums, the true desire revealed itself. But when people acted graciously, as Michelle had done—when they acted through goodwill, or sacrifice, or charity—Nan felt out of her depth. What did these people want when they said they wanted nothing but her happiness? Nobody was without motive or desire. Yet the only thing Michelle asked was that Nan take care of her husband for her.

Michelle was right. If Ah-Jack knew, he would be duty-bound to come back, even as Gary's presence turned him into a shadow.

But if Nan stayed quiet and he found out about her visit, about their alliance to keep him in the dark, he wouldn't know how to heal himself. The easy happiness that made him such a treasured man would leave him. He would learn to mistrust his friends and suspect the intentions of strangers.

Nan started the car, embarrassed by her thoughts. She might as well be talking about a child! Ah-Jack was a grown man, an old man. Old men didn't get their hearts broken. She didn't either.

When she pulled away from the curb, she thought she could see the bedroom light go out on the third floor of the townhome. She hoped that Michelle might sleep through the night, without pain. That in the morning, Gary would be waiting, arms open, to carry her down the stairs.

20

Jimmy pounded on Janine's door, ringing her doorbell with his other hand, until she appeared. At the sound of her lock turning, he shoved the door open, pushing her back. She had to grip the staircase to regain her balance.

"What the hell, Jimmy?"

"You know who I just had a reunion with?" He closed the distance between them.

"Of course not," she said.

"I think you do." Jimmy gripped her by the shoulders. He wanted to feel her body snap and buckle in his hands. "He gives you his best."

"What are you talking about?"

"I'm talking about Pang," he said.

"You saw him? Was he here?" She tried to go to the window, but Jimmy blocked her way.

"You'd know better than me."

She sucked in her cheeks, her eyes drifting to his left earlobe.

"I promise you," she said. "I don't know what you're talking about."

"You thought you could trick me," Jimmy continued, as if she hadn't spoken.

"Of course not," she said. "Please calm down. Tell me what he told you, and I'll tell you the real story."

"Tell me why you invited me over the night of the fire." Jimmy let her go and began to pace. The floor creaked beneath his feet. "Did he tell you what he was going to do? Did he give you money? A job?"

"Nothing," she said. She didn't try to misunderstand this time. "He told me nothing. He gave me nothing. I'm the one who owes him. When Pang asks me for a favor, I do it, no questions asked." Jimmy didn't say anything, too preoccupied by the snakes burning tunnels through his gut.

She sank down on the second step of her staircase, tugging him down by the hand to sit next to her.

"I used to drink too much," she said. "After my ex-husband left. The police pulled me over one night and I failed the Breathalyzer. I was going to lose my license, which basically meant I would lose my job. Pang stepped in. He knew the judge. But I promise you, I'm trying to get out. Selling your mother's house is the first step to getting my own client list. Then I'll never have to listen to that hateful man again."

"Who doesn't he know?" Jimmy chipped a flake of paint off the banister. "He wants something from you, and he wants to destroy me."

"I'm your alibi! I'm the reason the police haven't questioned you yet. I swear I didn't know what Pang was planning. When I heard what he'd done, when I saw you at Antonio's, I wanted to die. I feel fucking terrible. I'll do anything to help you, I promise." Janine pulled her legs up and rested her chin lightly on her knees.

"Will you stay over?" She looked up at him. "I dropped Eddie off at the neighbor's. We have the house to ourselves." Across the hall, a row of candles glowed softly from the living room.

Jimmy got back on his feet. The awkward, halting way she'd spilled her story was unrehearsed. She was desperate that he stay. But she was also desperate that they sell his mother's house together. He thought of her son, how unappealing he found Eddie yet how deeply Janine loved the boy.

"I don't think I can." He pressed his tongue against the roof of his mouth and tried to bore a hole into his skull. "I don't trust you. I can't let you sell the house."

"Do you honestly think I'm talking about the house?" she said. "What kind of woman do you think I am?"

Jimmy grew flustered, no longer certain he knew the answer.

"I don't know my own family, and I've lived and worked with them my entire life. I've known you for a year, and you've kept your distance the whole time."

"Because I'm scared," she said. She started unstrapping her shoes, nearly ripping apart the thin leather. "I have no one else looking out for me or my son. I can't just do whatever I want and not be afraid."

"I'm afraid." He was angry that she'd forced him to admit this out loud. "You see how little you know me? We're practically strangers. If I had really lived my life, I wouldn't be here. And Pang wouldn't have my fucking number."

"Stop blaming him for everything." Janine's voice hit a level of feeling Jimmy had never been able to access before. He stepped onto the welcome mat. He hadn't even taken off his shoes.

"Fine," Jimmy said. "Maybe I shouldn't be making my own choices, then. Maybe you tell me, should I stay with you or should I leave?"

"Did you only want me before you found out all my problems?" she said.

"Your problems are your problems until the solution is to make my life hell," Jimmy said. "What if I become the one thing standing between you and what you want?"

Janine stood on her flat feet, her arches collapsed against the ground. She looked unbalanced, and her fingertips touched the knobbed end of the stair railing.

"You don't have children," she said. "If my success means that Eddie can go to a good school or live in a better neighborhood, then—"

Jimmy interrupted her before she had to finish exposing the outward bounds of her ambition. His last generous act toward this woman he loved.

"I don't have children," he said. "But I have a family. And you're right. I thought I would give up everything just to have you. I would have bought a hundred more restaurants. I would have given you my mother's house, even without the fire." He felt cornered by his own confession, by his deep desire to forget everything and walk straight into her arms. He opened the door and backed out, stumbling over a small shoe. He would never let himself get this weak again. "If only you hadn't slept with me. You meant more before I got you."

He watched her face crumple and the flood come as she lost control of her beautiful, liquid features. His own flood he locked inside his chest. He shut the door behind him, knowing it would never open for him again.

He wasn't, in the end, that generous. Generosity, after a certain point, was just another word for self-destruction. Jimmy had only himself to watch out for.

The waiters closing up the Glory told Jimmy that Pat had grabbed a ride to a Mexican bar back in Maryland.

"He's getting pretty wasted." Tom reached past Jimmy to show another waiter a series of texts from Pat. "Guess he made bank tonight."

"You always talk to your boss this way?" Jimmy snatched the phone from him. "You'll get this back in the morning. There're tables to clear." Tom picked at the corner of his eye with his twiggy middle finger but walked away.

The new waiters were forever forgetting their place or, worse, forgetting Jimmy's place over them. He didn't want to hear about their weekends, their relationship dramas, their sick-day excuses. He missed the peace of the old waiters at the Duck House, whose passions had coagulated over the years. Their arguments passed like morning fog.

Scrolling through Pat's texts, Jimmy found the address of the bar, in the crowded shopping center a block from where the Duck House used to be.

"COME ALrrDY,,duCCKkcing BASTsdard." Pat was indeed getting drunker. Jimmy, against his nature, obeyed.

Guadalajara looked, from the outside, like it was packed to the gills. Loud, horn-heavy Mexican music pounded through the thick-glass storefront, and flashing neon lights streaked onto the pavement outside. Inside, the restaurant and bar was patronized by only a handful of customers, all men, and almost all amigos.

Pat, the glaring oddity, banged a Corona he shouldn't have been served against the bar counter. The boy was talking to one of the waitresses, who was dressed, oddly, in lingerie and heels. At the karaoke machine in the corner, a familiar man was belting Julio Iglesias, fighting to be heard over the DJ. It was Osman. Around Jimmy, other faces clarified and focused from the dark corners of the room. Almost all the ex–Duck House busboys plus a few members of the kitchen staff had gathered near Pat. They were also drinking Coronas, pelting one another with lime wedges. Jimmy could barely meet the former busboys' eyes when they nodded hello. He pushed back the feeling of their hands gripping him, yanking him away from the Duck House wreckage. Funny how they'd gone on living their lives, only to be pulled back together by the boy who'd splintered them in the first place.

"Jimmy, what are you doing here?" Pat yelled over the music. His eyes blurred when Jimmy came closer and took the stool next to his.

"This is my favorite bar," Jimmy deadpanned. "What are you doing here?"

"Osman took me." Pat offered his half-drunk Corona to Jimmy, who politely refused. "I didn't know you guys had the same favorite bar." He was slurring but coherent.

"Are you drunk or stupid?"

"Bit of both." Pat nodded sagely. "You're not so scary when you're out of the restaurant. Cool earring." He'd noticed Jimmy fiddling with his cartilage ring and leaned in to take a closer look.

Jimmy said, "I came to talk to you, but you're not in any state."

"Why would you want to talk to little ol' me?" Pat ordered another beer and clinked bottles with everyone within arm's reach.

"You remind me of me," Jimmy said, not because it was true but because he didn't know what else to say. He didn't want to stay, but he had to figure out what to do with Nan's son. He cursed Uncle Pang and ordered a tequila and seltzer.

"No offense, but you've only known me a month," Pat said.

"I've known your mother for most of my life."

"Don't rub it in." Pat stuffed his lime into his mouth and grinned at Jimmy, a grotesque green-gummed smile that made him want to punch the wedge down the boy's throat. Jimmy's anger only seemed to bead up and roll off Pat, like water on wax.

"She's too good for you." Jimmy made to stand up. His decision was set.

"Yeah, I know." Pat surprised him into sitting back down. "Of course I know. She's probably never fucked up."

"She married that dad of yours." Jimmy regretted the comment, even after Pat started to laugh. It had been Jimmy who'd fired Ah-Ray twelve years ago.

"He's not so bad." Pat wiped his sweaty forehead. "Or, he could be a lot worse."

"You see him much?"

"Sometimes he calls. I guess I'll be seeing more of him soon."

If Ah-Ray was moving back East, maybe Jimmy could get him a job at the Glory. The fabric around his armpits kept sticking to his skin.

"You're young," Jimmy said. "You can get over anything."

"Nothing can touch me!" Pat boasted. "You know, don't you? You're the fucking boss."

"Of course I am."

"Damn right." Pat nodded heavily.

"You've probably got all sorts of plans for the future." Jimmy hoped for the opposite. "Now that you're out of school, what's next?"

"You know, I would've said I was going to have fun for a while," Pat said, "if you'd asked me a few weeks ago. But I need to grow up and—"

"What's wrong with taking things easy?" Jimmy grabbed at his drink, nearly putting his hand in it in his hurry to keep Pat from talking. He didn't want to hear about Pat straightening out his life. "Sounds perfect for a guy your age. I should've had all my fun in my twenties. But I kept going until my thirties, when I had much more to lose."

"I think I'm done." Pat stripped the label off his beer and tore it into small pieces. "You're right about my mom. She doesn't deserve more shit. I'm going to try college. I looked up the ones in Cali. I think I can do it."

"California's good." Jimmy's stomach started to hurt. "My brother went to Berkeley. But the University of Maryland is just as good."

"No, man," Pat said. "Why would I come all the way back to Maryland for school?"

"All the way back?"

"I'm going to be in California, with my dad," he said. "You know, new start. Or else my mom just wanted to get rid of me."

"Nan's sending you to California?" Jimmy's mind struggled to find a grip on this information. Already his thoughts were spinning out of control, gathering so much speed that when they finally collided into a realization, the power of the impact shattered all doubt. Nan had found out about Pat. She was doing everything she could to save him. The tequila crawled its way back up his throat, painting Jimmy's tongue bitter. "When?"

"When did she decide, or when am I going?"

Jimmy waved his hand sharply, clipping his fingernail against Pat's bottle. "Whichever. Both."

"I don't know when she decided. Maybe when I got in trouble at school. But she told me a few weeks ago."

"Was it at the Duck House? When you were working there?"

"Actually, it was a couple days after—" Pat gulped the words back down, a strange hiccup bubbling out instead.

"After what?" Jimmy leaned back in his stool to hide his impatience. His arm scrabbled for a hold on the counter to keep himself from tipping over. A waitress put her hand on his shoulder, but he brushed it away.

"When . . ." Pat's eyes darted around, over-blinking. "When I got caught with Annie in the storage closet."

"My niece? That Annie?" Jimmy had to laugh at the confession, which had Pat cringing in his seat yet also undeniably proud. "Isn't she older than you?"

"I'm sorry about that." Pat scratched his chest, right above his left nipple, as if clutching at his heart. "She's a super-sweet girl. I don't think she likes me very much right now. I'm an asshole."

"Apologize to her." Jimmy cleared his throat. "Girls get over shit."

"Maybe," Pat said. "Anyways, I'm leaving in a few weeks. I just wish she knew I didn't mean to hurt her. I didn't mean any of it."

Jimmy had stopped listening. Pat had reminded him of the urgency of his visit, and his body reacted as if attacked. He wanted to run. He had to act. The two impulses ran amok inside him. Gravity pulled him into his seat; everything was sinking downward. If he did not move now, the weight of his panic would drop over his head.

"Everything will work out." He threw a few bills on the counter and knocked back the rest of his tequila. "You're young." He didn't know if he was trying to reassure the boy or apologize to him.

"Hey!" Pat called after him. "Can I get a ride?"

Jimmy rounded back and slipped a wad of cash into Pat's hand.

"Call a cab," he said. Then he leaned in until his mouth was by the boy's ear. "I know what you did," he whispered, the air whistling past his teeth. "But I forgive you. I hope you forgive me too."

At the front of the restaurant, Osman hit a high note. His friends whooped and clapped their hands against the bar.

Pat's sodden brain was already erasing Jimmy's words. The chili-pepper lights dangling over the bar reflected in the boy's hazy eyes. Soon the entire evening would be a blacked-out smudge sitting in his head. But the transcript of the world had recorded Jimmy's apology. This would have to be enough.

Jimmy hated his brother's house. Cruising up the long driveway, Jimmy had no idea why he'd decided to come here. Johnny's place was pretentious, uncomfortable, smug, and, thanks to Christine's trust fund, quite a bit more expensive than the house Jimmy had once owned with his ex-wife. The tall Colonial pillars out front appraised him like Greek-statues-turned-doormen.

So of course, when Johnny opened his front door, Jimmy told him immediately, and not for the first time, how awful everything looked.

"Looks like someone hasn't eaten," Johnny said. "Christine can make you a plate."

"I can't stand that health-food crap," Jimmy said.

"Did you drive here?" Johnny let him in.

"I've only had one drink." Jimmy looked around the foyer. His brother's double spiral staircase loomed at him like an illusion. "Is your cigar room ready?"

"Finished a few weeks ago," Johnny said. "But I've been too busy with the insurance company."

"Well, what are you waiting for?"

He followed Johnny downstairs to the basement. In the cigar room, a walk-in wood-and-glass-paned humidor sat against the back wall, the color of pale honey. When Jimmy stepped into the contraption, the smell of cedar hit his nose and he sneezed twice.

"I don't have much of a collection yet." Johnny traced his finger along the shelves. "But I have a nice Montecristo."

"Sure." Jimmy was already pushing his way out of the humidor. "Your choice."

While Johnny selected their cigars and sawed off the ends, Jimmy settled into a slick black leather chair. He propped an elbow on the arm and rested his head, studying the framed diplomas Johnny had hung up on the wall. Ever since Uncle Pang had told him about Pat, he'd been trying to find a loophole. Even he was not so cold that he could throw a kid into prison, arsonist or not. Why was everyone—his own mother!—insisting that Jimmy turn him in? Why was this the fire in which he had to be forged? His questions laced around a subterranean suspicion and pulled it from the earth: Uncle Pang had no intention of forgiving him. Jimmy had been the one to hire Pat just a month before the fire. To turn in the boy might implicate himself. Why trust that snake now? Jimmy couldn't even trust his own family.

"Here you are," Johnny said, shutting the humidor. Jimmy took his Montecristo and the butane lighter that Johnny swore was the only way to light a cigar. The toasted, spicy smoke coated the lining of his mouth with a tingling sensation.

"Not bad," he said, after a few puffs. His voice felt wobbly and he was worried his brother had noticed. But Johnny only lit his own cigar, before filling Jimmy in on the insurance proceedings. He listed off facts that Jimmy barely registered as important before they evaporated from his head. Everything was turning into white noise.

Suddenly, Janine's name sliced through the wall of sound. "I said, 'How's Janine?' " Johnny repeated. Jimmy was paying attention now.

"I might have fired her." The cigar smoke had made his mouth taste like soot. He wished he had thought to ask for a glass of water.

"That's too bad. I was thinking of contacting her to put Ma's house on the market."

"You can do whatever you want." Jimmy looked around for an ashtray.

"Well, if you fired her, she couldn't have been very good." Johnny placed a bronze ashtray, ugly as sin, on Jimmy's knee.

"She's fine. I just didn't trust her. She's sneaky."

"I didn't get that sense of her when we met."

"You only met her for a minute." Jimmy had a sudden vision of Johnny calling up Janine. The two of them laughing on the phone, then Johnny in her Mercedes. The image alone was enough to make him want to put his cigar out on his brother's cheek.

"It's a moot point if the police don't catch the fire setter," Johnny said. "When're they finally going to find a suspect?"

Jimmy tapped his ash into the tray, if only to cover up some of that hideous bronze. Smoke had filled his head; he was floating, barely tethered to his problems anymore. A familiar sensation.

"What if I found out who did it?" he said.

"Yeah?" Johnny leaned in, uncrossing his legs.

"It might have been Nan's son—you remember him?"

"You're kidding." Johnny took his cigar out of his mouth. A sprinkle of ash dotted the leg of his khaki shorts. "How'd you find out?"

"I can't reveal my source," he said. "But I have evidence."

"Enough to go to the police?"

"I don't know what to fucking do." Jimmy lowered his head. Suddenly, all the soft spots on his body felt open to attack.

"Who knows what the right thing to do is in these situations?"

"You do." Jimmy glanced at those gleaming diplomas again. His words sounded like an accusation.

"Why would he do it?" Johnny demanded. "We've been nothing but kind to him and Nan. This doesn't make sense."

Should he tell his brother about Uncle Pang? Johnny understood the man's seedy influence on the family. But, kept safe at the front of the house, he'd never been dragged under by the riptide of Uncle Pang's anger. Johnny might try to go after the man himself.

"The kid's disturbed," Jimmy said. "He almost set his school on fire—that's why he was expelled."

"I *have* heard of people who set fires compulsively." Johnny reached up to smooth the wrinkles on his forehead.

"He's still working at my restaurant," Jimmy said.

"They'll think you paid him off," Johnny filled in.

"I just found out he was a firebug," Jimmy said. "I didn't know."

"And you were planning on burning the restaurant down anyways."

"I'm fucking screwed." Jimmy took a long pull of his cigar.

Johnny also puffed on his. Jimmy was reminded of when their father was alive. The few times all three Han men had shared their small office, they would work in this sort of silence, which was not so much comfortable as tolerant. Every so often, their father would let out a loud, sputtering fart, which the boys were not permitted to laugh at. But once, Jimmy had caught his brother's eye and Johnny had wrinkled his nose in response.

"You want me to turn him in for you, don't you?" Johnny said, cutting through Jimmy's thoughts.

Jimmy blinked hard. Against his will, his body squirmed, as if he were a child again, caught sneaking into their shared bedroom, which Johnny used to lock to keep Jimmy from touching and breaking his things.

"What do you mean?" Was that why he'd come to Johnny's house?

"I mean you've always been this way," Johnny said. "After every fight you had with Dad or Ma, you'd slam your door, then wait for me to calm them down. At the restaurant, when a waiter or customer got on your nerves, I was there to apologize for your behavior. Now I'm the one dealing with the insurance company, the fire investigator, the police."

"I never wanted you to step in." Jimmy bit the end of his cigar. So these were the stories Johnny told about him. "You inserted yourself."

"You know, I'm happy to be the older brother and apologize for you," Johnny said. "That's my responsibility. But what always got to me, what honestly pissed me off, was that you've never had the respect to ask for my help."

After forty years of confusion, Jimmy finally understood exactly what his brother was saying. He'd read between Johnny's mild lines. His brother wasn't worried about being connected to the arson or even about Pat. All Johnny wanted was to hear Jimmy say that he needed him. As if Jimmy hadn't spent his entire life defined by this need. As if he hadn't tried to clean up his own messes in the past, only to buckle as soon as Johnny stuck his nose in. The cycle had spun uninterrupted since childhood—Jimmy fucking up, Johnny saving the day. Rescue had become a habit so ingrained that Jimmy no longer thought to fight it. Wasn't his constant submission enough for his brother? Did Jimmy really have to speak it aloud?

He spread his fingers out in front of him, cracking them with his thumbs. After so much prostration, what was one more small humiliation? He stared down at his hands. Johnny was going to win this ancient war between them.

"All right, fine." He didn't need to fake, at least, his reluctance. "I'm a huge fucking mess. I'm selfish, I'm impulsive, and

I've hurt our entire family." He couldn't keep his words from sounding sarcastic. His brother remained unmoved.

Barely believing himself, Jimmy lifted the ashtray off his leg and placed it on the ground. Slowly, he slid off his chair and onto his knees. He hung his head, his face so hot that he almost felt the shame he was pretending at.

"Please." His voice was a whisper. "I need your help."

In a blink, Johnny was right there, pulling him up by the armpits. His brother's face was radiant. He looked like he might try to hug him. Jimmy stiffened even as Johnny sat back down.

"You didn't have to do that," Johnny said. Jimmy could have spat in his lying face. "I'm your family. Of course I'll help. All you had to do was ask. "

"You will?" Jimmy's anger transfigured so quickly into joy that his voice cracked.

"It'll be tough," Johnny mused. "It's often hard, doing the right thing."

The two of them breathed in the haze of smoke filling the room. Jimmy's plug burned down; his exhilaration also lifted into the air, draining out of his body through the top of his head. He was left with tired, heavy limbs. He missed Janine, in a grudging, reluctant way; he had been since Johnny brought her up. Maybe he'd moved too hastily. He missed her loud laugh, the reason he'd fallen for her in the first place. He missed her quicksilver face and biting comments and the two cell phones she could text on simultaneously. If he left now, he knew he would drive right back to her house, and he couldn't let himself do that. Not out of any pride or sense of principle, but because he didn't want to set himself up for certain failure.

"Is your guest room under construction?" He scratched a thin white line on the inside of his chair.

"No," his brother said. "We're working on the outdoor pool, so we're leaving the guest room alone. Why? Do you need to stay the night?"

The word "need" raised Jimmy's blood pressure again. But he was tired, and lonely, and out of ideas.

"I need to stay," he said. "I'm not feeling well."

"I'll let Christine know," Johnny said. "She can whip you up the best green smoothie. You're under a lot of pressure. You need to watch your health."

"Thanks." He didn't know if he was being honest or still playing the part. "You're a good brother."

Johnny looked taken aback. For the first time, he was agitated out of his calm, and he shifted around in his seat.

"You would do the same for me." He studied the end of his cigar. "Even if you refuse to admit it."

The brothers looked past each other at the wall. Jimmy felt looser, the melancholy leaving him. He was like a wind chime, blown by gusts of emotions that made him sound out wildly, whipping about, only to round back to a hollow silence.

"I'll let Christine know about the guest room." Johnny brushed off his knees and hefted himself up out of the chair. He bent to drop his cigar in the ashtray. "She'll want to change the sheets and whatnot."

"I don't need that."

"She can't relax until she's played the perfect host." Johnny headed for the door.

"I'm just family!" Jimmy shouted at his brother's retreating back.

"Exactly," came his answer, already muffled by the growing distance.

Jimmy was left alone with his sputtering cigar. The house kept him company, its strange whistling ventilation, the grumble of the humidor, the muted thuds of footsteps a story above. They were familiar, the sounds his old house might have made, and this made them all the more haunting. If only he could have silence. But what was silence without peace?

21

_____

Ah-Jack woke up for work in a recently emptied bed. He rolled onto his back and rubbed his belly. He'd finally taken Nan to bed. His first new woman in fifty years. His body was like a forgotten object finally turned on. Colors seemed brighter. Sounds clearer. Even his rotten morning breath tasted sweet. Had Michelle felt this way too? Had she buzzed all over with energy? Or had she been hit by an awful, crushing guilt? Hers more awful because her betrayal came first.

He clapped his hands above his head, as if killing a mosquito, and got up. No bad thoughts allowed after such a magical night. The room itself held no evidence of their fun. They'd gotten re-dressed after the act, and he'd fallen asleep almost immediately. Everything was where it should have been. No clothes were draped over chairs; no lamps had been knocked over. Well, he was an old man. Anything more rollicking might have sent him to the hospital.

Only Pat was downstairs in the kitchen, drinking a Coke and watching a frozen scallion pancake make circles in the microwave. Nan was nowhere to be seen. Ah-Jack fought the impulse to climb back up the stairs and wait for the boy to leave. The past few days, Pat had rarely been home. His presence now felt like an intrusion.

"Good morning," Ah-Jack said, striding into the room. Pat stank of stale cigarette smoke and sweat. "All right there? You didn't come home last night."

"Surprised you noticed," Pat said.

"Of course I noticed. Your mom has been worried sick." A small lie, but Pat perked up. Ah-Jack felt the same strain of guilt that had nearly overwhelmed him in bed.

"I told her where I'd be," Pat said.

"Even so, she'd prefer you be at home with her."

"I'd prefer you be in your own home too." Pat's hangover softened the bite in his comment, but Ah-Jack still felt the teeth. He'd seen the boy when he was only a day old in the hospital, had watched him grow up, and now, seventeen years later, the young man hated him on sight.

As if his hangover made him sensitive even to the hurt feelings of a man he couldn't stand, Pat relaxed his stance. "About last night." He glanced down at Ah-Jack's bandaged arm. "I'm sorry. I was stressed."

"Stressed"—what was that word? Americans used it all the time, and Ah-Jack always translated the word in his head to "pressure," which made more sense. They were all under a lot of pressure with their new jobs and new living arrangements. Happy as these changes had made him, the weight of the newness was crushing. He couldn't imagine how Pat must feel, the painful imprints the pressure must have left on his reluctant form. He forgave Nan's son then. He'd been angry with the boy all this time, he realized, and as his anger left him, his spirit ballooned up.

"I barely remember last night," he said. "Doctor gave me very good pain meds."

"Cool," Pat said. The timer beeped and he opened the microwave, grabbing the thin pancake with his hands. He juggled the hot disc between his palms before dropping it onto the kitchen table.

Ah-Jack picked up the pancake with his fingers. The skin on his hands was like steel. Though that hadn't been a problem with Nan last night; his fingertips could still feel certain kinds of heat. Wicked thoughts to be having in front of her son!

"Decades of practice," he crowed. "Should be cool enough for you to handle now."

"Keep it." Pat backed away from the pancake.

"You'll feel better if you eat." Ah-Jack took a big bite. A limp piece of scallion squeaked between his teeth. "Get that sour taste out of your mouth."

"I'm fine." Pat crushed his Coke can between his hands and tossed it in the trash. "My mom said to tell you she's running errands. She'll be back to drive you to work."

"What a busy woman." Ah-Jack's smile bumped up against the curve of the pancake. Pat noticed.

"She's probably getting us ready for our California trip." Pat burped into his hand, then fanned it away from his face. "We're leaving pretty soon."

"California?" Ah-Jack stopped chewing his mouthful. "To visit your father?"

"Not quite." A rare smile spread across Pat's face. Ah-Jack wanted to slap it away.

"My dad wants us to move in with him," Pat said.

"That's not going to happen." Ah-Jack sank into a seat. The words Nan had spoken in frustration last night—"What's even keeping me here?"—came back to him. "Your mom has a life here. She's not planning on leaving."

"Go and ask her, then," Pat said, louder than either of them expected. "That's her pulling in." He grabbed his work blazer off the back of his chair and slipped his cell phone and wallet into his pockets. "My ride's here."

He headed toward the back door to avoid Nan, whose key

was clinking its way into the front-door lock. Ah-Jack wanted to grab Pat by the shoulder and drag him back into the kitchen. He was tired of feeling like the messenger between mother and son. But Pat was too quick, and besides, Ah-Jack knew his idea was a fantasy. If a man as unobservant as he could see the ways Nan and Pat reached for and missed each other, then there was something more selective behind their blindness.

He hurried over to the door, anticipating shopping bags, but Nan held no trace of the errands she'd run. He went to embrace her. She stopped him by snatching the pancake out of his hand.

"You shouldn't be eating white flour," she said. "That's a restricted food." She held the pale, floppy pancake between her thumb and pointer and shook it. "It's not even cooked right. Did you microwave this? You lazy man."

She gave him back the pancake and moved into the kitchen. She grabbed the package from the freezer and turned on the stove. While she waited for the wok to heat, he came up behind her and kissed her on the back of her head. He inhaled the still-sleepy musk of her hair.

"I had a wonderful time last night," he said.

"I know," she said, face hidden. "You already told me."

"I wanted to tell you again. In fact, I think I'll tell you every half hour today."

"Since when have you followed a schedule?" She threw a pancake onto the pan. Her sass was a little shaky. She hadn't been this shy around him in decades.

"My body is like a clock!" He knocked on his chest to get her to laugh.

"The only regular thing about you is when you go to the bathroom."

"You were such a lady last night. Now you're bringing up my shitting habits?"

She flipped the scallion pancake with one hand and slapped at his leg with her other. He danced out of reach, enjoying his nimbleness, which reminded him of the secret games of tag he used to play with the Duck House busboys during service.

"Maybe this job kept me young," he mused when she handed him his pancake on a flat wooden spoon. He tried to pick it up with his fingers but quickly dropped it onto a plate when the golden dough singed his fingertips. Good thing Pat wasn't around to see. Nan passed him a pair of chopsticks, then went back to stand by the stove.

"You kept yourself young." She had a strange note in her voice. "You kept me young too."

"You're *still* young. But I will take all the credit, thank you!"

"You're an amazing, amazing man," she said. From the way she spoke, she should have been wrapped up in his arms. Instead, she stayed, stubbornly, all the way across the kitchen from him. He found the moment strange but also precious, as if they were separated by a gulf and had to holler their sweet nothings at each other.

"You're the amazing one," he said. The scallion pancake was crispy and flaky. An oniony fragrance lifted off the plate. The alchemy of this woman! "This delicious pancake is only a fraction of how delicious you are."

She laughed and crossed her arms, a sight so familiar that his chest fluttered. Thirty years ago, he'd looked down from his ladder to see this same pose. Had he known from the start that he cared deeply for her? Or had he kept such an idea out of his own reach until Michelle finally set him free? He'd certainly guessed that Nan had had a harmless crush on him at the beginning. He'd been flattered and, he could be honest now, invigorated by her attention. But as the years passed, their friendship had deepened, until it became its own category, impossible to compare and therefore impossible really to understand. Stepping outside his marriage, never a true possibility, no longer seemed relevant. Their relationship existed outside the worlds he'd always known. His love for Nan was his outer space. He finished his last mouthful of pancake. Good food from a good woman could certainly make him blossom.

"We're going to be late for work," the good woman said, clearing the table.

All that poetry and fragrance had completely distracted him from asking about California! This was the problem with indescribable relationships. They had no limits but also no rules, no boundaries. The only thing holding them together was the strangeness and majesty of their love. Was this enough? He opened his mouth, then closed it again. He didn't want to know. He used to think that he wanted the answers to all his questions, but his recent experience with Michelle had made him reconsider. He'd survived her honesty, but Nan had been the real shield, not his less-than-tough skin. If Nan was leaving him—he had to believe not because she wanted to but because she had to—then he didn't want to know. He would take his last days in ignorance. The only knowledge he ached for now was not if she would go but how to make her stay.

"Actually," he said, getting a sudden, dazzling idea, "let me deal with the plates. You've been working hard enough and I just remembered something I have to do. I'll take my car today."

"Are you sure?"

"Yes, you go. I'll see you at the restaurant." He pecked her on the mouth. "Don't miss me too much."

Once he heard the front door shut and her car drive away, he ran up to the bedroom and nabbed one of Nan's rings. He studied the ring he'd grabbed—a cheap yellow thing that looked suspiciously like an old wedding band—but only for a moment.

Then he was out the door, his unbuttoned sleeves flapping. The August morning contained the glitter and heat of a baking rock, but Ah-Jack sucked in the roasted air as if it were a refreshing drink. He plucked a flower from the edge of a neighbor's yard and stuck it behind his ear. Nan was right; he did know how to stay young. He got into his car and peeled out, heading toward the strip mall he passed every time he drove from his place to Nan's.

The jewelry store he'd thought he'd seen in the strip turned out to be a pawnshop. A used pool table sat in the center of the long, narrow room. Antique swords and electric guitars hung on the wall. Luckily, the store had a good selection of engagement rings.

"What size?" the man behind the counter asked. He was pot-bellied, over-cologned, and wore a stained white button-down tucked into black slacks, not unlike the uniform Ah-Jack was also wearing. Bending their heads over the glass counter, they must have looked like two monkeys in tuxedos.

Ah-Jack took out Nan's ring and gave it to the man. The man took out a series of finger-like cones and slid the ring onto one.

"An eight." He gave the ring back while grabbing a case from the bottom of the counter. "We've got several. Usually from mature marriages. Fingers get thicker the older you get."

"She have thick finger, all right," Ah-Jack said. "Maybe more thick than mine."

"You can get yourself a nice ring too. We have men's engage-ment rings. And wedding rings. Might as well get the entire collection; save you a trip in the future."

Ah-Jack fingered Nan's old wedding band. "Just ring for her. She can say no."

"To a sharp-looking man like yourself? I think you've got this one in the bag."

"I know her thirty years."

The man whistled through the gap in his teeth. "Jesus. My wife made me buy a ring after five."

"She is patient." Ah-Jack looked through the selection of rings, hoping that one might jump out at him. "What is good?"

"Who knows? They're just rocks to me."

"I like this one." Ah-Jack pointed to a square-cut ring that had a modest but bright diamond. He could see it glittering in the dome of the security mirror.

"It's a beauty," the man agreed. "A real steal at $2,399."

Ah-Jack balked at the price, but he'd heard that a ring should cost even more than that, something like one month's salary. Nan deserved a nice ring. *He* would not have waited thirty years to end up with himself. He patted around his blazer for his wallet.

"You take Visa?"

The ring and its box didn't weigh more than a bundle of tips after a busy night, but Ah-Jack felt every gram acutely. He sweated through his shirt on the car ride to the Georgetown Waterfront. He didn't usually get nervous, but he had no idea what to expect. He hadn't proposed to Michelle. They were married in a community square, no rings, no party. Would Nan expect him to get down on one knee? What if he couldn't stand back up! Forcing himself to focus, he managed to parallel park without clipping the cars sandwiching him.

Walking toward the restaurant, Ah-Jack took quick looks around. Had any of the people on the street noticed the extra weight in his pocket? He realized that he wanted someone to ask him what he was carrying around. He wanted to share the news of this day, a day when everything would change and yet also stay the same. He was going to make his indefinable relationship official. He was going to guarantee that Nan would stay by his side until the day he died.

He slapped his cheeks lightly to get the morbid thought out. The gust of air-conditioning that greeted him when he opened the restaurant door put him solidly back in good spirits. When he saw Nan in her carving uniform, he nearly got down on one knee right there, and he was sure that one look at his dopey face would reveal everything. But Nan merely glanced over and gave him a little wave before returning to her conversation with the other carvers.

If it were up to him, he would make a big, public production of the proposal. He'd get the staff to serenade Nan, as if it were her birthday. Maybe he'd hide the ring in a slice of cheesecake or, even better, in a duck she was carving.

But Nan was a quieter person, quick to control a scene that was getting out of hand. She wouldn't appreciate a loud celebration, especially if she was the center of attention. Ah-Jack couldn't remember her ever being the loudest person in a room. Even her sneezes were silent.

He walked through the kitchen, picking up a bowl of mixed noodles from family breakfast. He looked for a private spot he might be able to lure Nan to. On a whim, he cracked open the walk-in fridge and looked inside. His breath turned visible. Back at the Mayflower, and in the early days of the Duck House, he used to find her in the fridge sometimes, perched on a crate of produce.

"I'm cooling off a bit," she always said. "I'll be out in a second." A few times, he'd spotted a trail of tears that had dried shiny on her cheek.

Something about this memory struck him as poetic. The walk-in was the perfect place to propose! They would both cry freezing tears of joy while the frigid temperatures saved their hearts from exploding. Their embrace would keep them warm. He even spotted a bare pallet that made the prospect of getting down on one knee less daunting.

Pushing out of the walk-in, he spotted Pat, who looked no less terrible than he had hours earlier. Ah-Jack in his youth, after a night of heavy drinking, needed only to throw up or take a shit to bounce back to his usual handsome self, and he wasn't unsatisfied to see that Pat couldn't handle the same level of abuse. They didn't make young people like they used to.

"No improvement?" Ah-Jack slurped his noodles as he approached.

"Stay there." Pat crossed his arms, careful not to touch any part of his stomach.

"You're missing a delicious breakfast," he said. "The Glory cooks really know what they're doing."

Pat had been about to drift toward the other waiters. "What're you so happy about?" he asked, squinting at Ah-Jack. "I thought you'd be a little . . . quieter."

A part of Ah-Jack shrank back in shame. Pat was the only one who might put the puzzle together, which was that the ring was a bid not only for Nan's love but also her presence. Pat happened to be fighting for the same things. A larger part of him, however, stood up taller. Pat was nearly grown; he didn't need his mother anymore. What Ah-Jack and Nan had was singular and special. Worth saving, even through desperate ways. He wasn't marrying her to keep her from going to California. He was marrying her because they loved each other and had for thirty years. What he'd told that pawnshop owner was the truth. Nan had waited long enough.

Ah-Jack shifted and the ring box moved in his pocket. He had yet another flash of inspiration.

"I have something to ask you." He put down his noodles. "Can you come outside with me for a moment?"

"I'm going to be late." Pat looked around for Jimmy. "But I need to smoke. My head is fucking killing me."

Outside, a line of boats bobbed a few feet away. Red and blue cloth umbrellas stood below large bronze pillars that doubled as lights. A small yacht pulled out of the marina, spitting up brackish water. Ah-Jack was so jittery that he asked Pat for a smoke. Pat passed him a slim dark cigarette from an engraved box Ah-Jack hadn't seen before. They smoked and watched the foot traffic, both waiting for the other to start talking. Finally, Ah-Jack took a steadying puff and pulled out the ring box.

"Pat, I'm going to ask your mother to marry me."

Pat looked at the black velvet box as if Ah-Jack had whipped out something pornographic.

"You've got to be fucking kidding me."

"I'm not." Ah-Jack flipped open the box. "Do you think she'll like it? I didn't know what kind of ring to get."

"She's married! You know that, right? My dad is still her husband."

"I know. But they haven't been in the same state for years. Your mother deserves someone who wants to be by her side forever."

Pat whipped his cigarette into the street. He fished out another one and lit it, sucking deeply.

"Why are you showing *me*?" he asked. He reached out to grab the ring, and for a moment, Ah-Jack thought he would throw it just as he had with the cigarette. But Pat merely put the ring up to his eye and squinted at the square diamond at the center. He gently replaced it in its velvet slot.

"I'm showing you because I want to ask for your blessing. I'm not just marrying your mother. I'm becoming part of your life too."

Pat snorted but didn't interrupt.

"All I want is for everyone I care about to be happy," Ah-Jack said. "That includes you. I never had a child of my own, and from the first day I saw you, I wanted to be your guardian."

"What do you want me to say?" A woman walking her dog looked curiously at the two of them.

"I want you to be okay with me in your life. Your mom's life."

"You're pretty sure of yourself." Pat looked out at the water. "I've always hated that about you."

Ah-Jack tucked the box back in his pocket, disappointed but not surprised. But when he turned to go back into the Glory, Pat touched his shoulder lightly.

"You didn't buy that ring today, did you, Uncle Jack?" he asked, his voice strange but not unnatural. "You didn't do all this just because I told you about California?"

Ah-Jack was going to tell him the truth. After all, his intentions were pure. But then he understood why Pat's voice felt so familiar. This was how Pat had sounded when he'd been a child. Ah-Jack hadn't heard this high, clear tone in years.

"Of course not," he said instead. "I've had this ring for a couple of weeks. Who knows, your mom might not even say yes. She's the catch, after all. And if she does say yes, maybe we'll go to California together. Nothing's set." He'd gone too far in consoling Pat. The boy had sniffed out his pity. The vulnerability in his face disappeared in a blink.

"What do I care?" he said. "Go ahead. Marry my mom. Make a whole new family. Have a ton of babies while you're at it." He laughed rudely, as if trying to draw yellow phlegm up from his chest.

"Thank you," Ah-Jack said anyway. "You've made me very happy."

"Whatever." Pat slouched back to let a pair of joggers huff by, his cigarette clenched in his fingers. Ah-Jack took one last look at the boy. Heaviness plumbed through his elation. He went back inside before he was dragged down entirely.

He couldn't get ahold of Nan until an hour before the dinner service. As soon as the lunch shift ended, she'd dashed out to buy Pat some new shoes. When she came back, she was still fluttering around, organizing and fussing with her bags in the coat closet.

"He's worn holes the size of quarters into his old shoes!" she kept saying, while Ah-Jack tried to get her attention. "What is that boy *doing*?"

He finally had to snatch her by the wrist, which smelled of department-store perfume.

"What is it, old man?" she asked with a crooked smile. "You want a little fun in the afternoon?"

He knew he couldn't fool her, so he had to push some truth into his lie. "What an accusation!" he cried. "Your son has holed up in the walk-in fridge. He wants his mom."

Nan's eyes widened in alarm, and Ah-Jack instantly regretted his words. It was true what she had once accused him of: He was only good at careless living. He tried to keep up with her on her way to the walk-in. He told his pounding heart that they would all laugh about this in a minute.

Nan threw open the heavy fridge door as if it were nothing but a curtain. "Pat?" she said, into the mouth of the walk-in.

A chilly mist swirled around their feet. Scales of frost covered the metal walls. When she saw no one else in the fridge, she wheeled around, mouth twitching in panic.

"He's not here," she said. "Where's he gone? Did he look scared?" She leaned her hand against a plastic container of chopped green chilies, her head bent.

"I wanted to get you somewhere private," Ah-Jack said quietly.

Nan's head shot up. "You don't lie about something like that!" She smacked his arm, a good bit harder than when she was teasing. "You don't use my son as bait."

Ah-Jack crashed down to one knee, banging it badly against the frozen metal floor. The faster he got the ring out, the faster he could turn Nan's mood around, but he hadn't expected how badly his knee would hurt. Or that Nan would think he'd fallen. She let out a small gasp and tried to bend down to tend to him, but he pushed her back up.

"No, this was on purpose," he said, trying to keep the pain out of his face. He fumbled with his pocket, his fingers wooden from the cold. He'd never been an especially bright planner.

"What are you doing, you fool?" she said, making disapproving noises, but she stopped mid-word when she saw the ring box emerge from his pocket.

He struggled for another moment to locate the seam on the box. He snapped it open in front of her.

"Will you marry me?" he asked, all versions of his speech whooshing out of his head. "Please?" His knee had gone numb against the floor.

Nan's mouth had fallen open and was forming strange shapes, but no noise came out. Craning his neck back, he nearly lost his balance. His body lurched from side to side.

"Please get up," she finally said. She grabbed him by the arms and tried to heave him to his feet. He stumbled and grasped the vegetable crates, pulling himself up slowly. He focused on the throbbing in his knee instead of on the answer she still hadn't given.

"When did you get the ring?" she asked. The disastrous result of his last lie made him incapable of telling another.

"This morning."

"That's why you wanted to take your car. I bet you came up with the idea this morning too."

"And what if I did?" He was suddenly angry. "We've waited thirty years. I'm hardly acting impulsively."

"I'm married. You're married!"

"Only technically." He shoved the ring closer to her, as if that might help her make up her mind. "You've been my true wife from the beginning."

His words cut a string in Nan's face, and her muscles went slack. In the extreme chill, her skin was flushed. She took the ring box from his hand. A tear bubbled out of each eye.

"Michelle is dying," she said.

The turn was so sudden that he thought he'd misheard her.

"She's fine," he said. "She's with her new boyfriend. Love cures all."

"No." Nan's throat moved up and down. "I went to visit her last night. I'm so sorry I didn't tell you, but I wanted to get her blessing."

Ah-Jack started to shake from the cold. His nose ached when he breathed in.

"How do you know she's dying? She didn't tell you."

"Of course she wouldn't," Nan said. "But I have eyes! She's so thin. She never leaves her bed. She has to be carried out of it. She's never looked this bad. You have to see her."

Nan caught her breath and waited for him to react. But it was his turn to disappoint. He couldn't come up with a single thing to say. His mind was completely blank. Why were they in this fridge? Why was he in this awful restaurant with this woman who was not his wife? A roaring sound filled his ears. He pushed his way out of the fridge. The heat of the kitchen nearly knocked him over. The cooks looked up from their family meal.

"I'm so sorry," Nan called out after him.

He was already in the dining room, tearing at his bow tie. Jimmy asked him where he was going, but Ah-Jack shook off the little boss's fingers. He croaked out, "The hospital," before continuing to stagger away.

The outside of the restaurant brought no relief. Minutes ago he'd been freezing in a walk-in fridge, imagining himself on the precipice of happiness. Now he was burning his hand against the hot handle of his car door. He climbed into his car, the inside even hotter from soaking in the sunlight. He let the sweat drip down his face, heavier and fatter than tears. He didn't know if Michelle was in the hospital, but that was the route he took. His luck had always been good, his guesses often right. At four the Washington traffic had yet to build to critical mass on its exodus out of D.C. He slipped right down the parkway and joined the current of the crowd.

22

Nan intercepted Jimmy before he could follow Ah-Jack to the door and pulled the little boss aside. She explained Ah-Jack's situation, ready to argue herself into a one-week vacation, but Jimmy seemed to wilt at the sight of her.

"I hope his wife's okay," he said, avoiding her eyes. "If *you* ever need to take time off in the next few weeks . . ."

"You firing me?" Nan asked. She couldn't handle any more bad news.

"No, of course not!" Jimmy swiped his hands in front of him, as if trying to erase the possibility. "I just thought you'd want to be there for Jack."

Nan wasn't surprised that Jimmy knew about their new relationship. Even in a restaurant filled with young Americans, word traveled fast. But she couldn't believe what he was suggesting.

"I am fine," she said firmly. "I can work. No worry, boss."

Jimmy rubbed his hands as if they were cold. He kept looking over at Johnny, who was working the room like a restored king. Nan put two and two together. Who would have thought that the little boss, tough as he was, could be struck down by a case of the nerves? Jimmy was almost cute, worrying about his first Friday-night service.

"Tonight will be a success," she said. She hadn't touched him since he was in his twenties and the worst waiter the Duck House had ever seen, but she reached out to calm his hands. "Make the Duck House's first night look empty."

He grabbed her hands and gave them a short squeeze.

"Will tonight be as big as when John Travolta came?" he tried to joke.

"Let's not getting crazy," she said.

Jimmy rolled back his shoulders. "You'll tell Jack what I said?"

"I will." Nan turned toward the kitchen. She scraped a straw wrapper off her shoe and felt the ring box shift in her pocket. Would she ever talk to Ah-Jack again? Not literally *talk* but talk in the same spirit? He had an open voice with everyone, including strangers, but with her, she'd always detected a slight lilt, an extra pinch of joy. She was wiping a tear away when Pat suddenly jumped into her path.

"Did Uncle Jack talk to you?" he asked. He put his hands on her back and rushed her into the closest waiter station. It was empty except for a busboy's tray of water.

"He did." Nan looked her son over. She couldn't remember the last time Pat had initiated a conversation with her.

He grabbed her hands and lifted them up, as if to kiss her knuckles, but she saw that he was inspecting her fingers. He was looking for a ring. She gently took her hands away and hid them behind her back.

"What did you two talk about?" Pat asked.

Nan studied her son's face. Perhaps if Ah-Jack hadn't used Pat as an excuse to get her alone, she would've said yes. But he had put her son in her mind, and not just her son but her son in distress.

"Your uncle Jack asked me to marry him," she said plainly. "And I told him that his wife, your aunt Michelle, needed him more than I did."

Pat rubbed the back of his head. "I'm not sure that was the answer he wanted."

"I think I've been in a strange fog lately." Nan felt her head too, as if looking for a bump. "Maybe with the restaurant burning down, seeing all those years go up in flames, it made me a little crazy. But I'm awake now."

"Everyone's been acting weird," Pat said.

"I guess it took something big, like a proposal, to make me see that I'm your mother first. I'm sorry, Po-po," she said, using his pet name. The endearment felt good in her mouth. "I shouldn't have tried to send you away. That wasn't what I was trying to do, but it does seem that way. I was only scared that I couldn't be good to you."

"You're okay," he said. He reached out and put his hand on her arm. The pressure felt good, but then his grip tightened until it started to hurt. A terrible look crossed his face.

"What's wrong?" She tried to move closer, but his grip held her back.

"I have to tell you." He was starting to shiver, and, decked out in his waiter's uniform, he looked like a strung-out businessman, ready to crash.

"You can tell Ma anything." She was trying to reassure him, but she was only making him more upset. She tried to hand him a glass of water from the tray.

"I met this guy, Jimmy's friend, this old dude who was at the restaurant, and—"

Before he could keep going, Jimmy stepped in. Any trace of softness from earlier had vanished. He was red in the face.

"What're you two standing around for? Dinner's started, can't you see? For fuck's sake, don't mess this night up." He separated the two of them and grabbed Pat by the shoulders.

"Stop pushing," Pat snapped. He reached into his pocket and pulled out his cell phone. He handed it to Nan, closing her fingers around the gray shell. "This will explain," he said, blinking fast. "I'm sorry, I really am."

"Apologize later," Jimmy said, leading Pat out into the dining room. "Nan, there are tons of ducks waiting."

Nan tucked the phone into her apron and headed back into the kitchen. Her steps were blocky, as if her joints had been taken out and put in backward. She wanted a moment to breathe before she was forced back into the day's current, bouncing against decision after decision. But as Jimmy had predicted, a duck was waiting for her at her station in the kitchen, and she was in a revolving door for the next few hours. She became so focused on carving, on smiling for photos, on reassuring patrons that twenty-eight slices of duck was the standard amount, that she could forget the cell phone in her pocket. When she glimpsed her son, balancing his heavy tray, he looked so professional that she convinced herself his panic was a momentary spell, a nip of nausea after too many nights of partying. His confession was that of a tired little boy exhausted by his own freedom, who wished to climb back into bed. She wouldn't let herself consider other possibilities. Better to trust in his goodness, as she had done before the trouble at school. Her son was a good man. He had raised himself to be a good man.

Even so, when she saw the pair of policemen enter the Glory, she lingered back in the dining room. She tailed them when they started to thread their way over to Jimmy.

"You weren't supposed to come tonight," she overheard him say.

Jimmy called to his brother, who had just noticed the policemen. His rusty Chinese was strained as he tried to hide his anger from the officers. "What the hell are they doing here?"

"Hello, Officers." Johnny shook their hands. "I think there's been a misunderstanding."

"You're saying you know our orders?" the more senior officer said. His skunk-striped hair was gelled into an imposing block on top of his head.

Johnny's hands jumped up in front of his chest, palms out. "Not at all," he said.

A small commotion interrupted Nan's eavesdropping, and she turned to see Annie sobbing into her fists. Nan went over to the girl and asked her what was wrong. A strong whiff of body odor hit her when she hugged Annie close.

"They've caught me." Annie managed to say in between sharp intakes of breath.

"Let me get Johnny." Nan peered over Annie's head. "You need your dad."

"No!" Annie tore out of Nan's arms and ran for the door. She tripped, nearly pulling the hostess stand down with her, and when she got up, the slit in her dress had ripped. The strip of loose fabric flapped open. A customer tried to help, but she pushed him away. Then she was out the door. Nan turned back. The men were huddled together.

She went toward them, toward Johnny. "Where is he?" the younger officer said. Gray in the face, Jimmy pointed, and following the direction of his shaking finger, Nan choked on a shriek. The police, and Johnny with them, converged on her son.

"Stop!" she cried. "Wrong person!" She sprang after them, throwing half her apron off in her animal panic, but Jimmy grabbed her around the middle and held on tight.

She threw her arms around, trying to batter Jimmy's pale face, trying to alert her son. Her hands caught her carver's hat, tearing it out of her hair. Pat saw the police when they were halfway across the room. He looked around wildly, spotting the exits. She wanted him to run, nearly screamed at him to go, but he gently set his tray down on the bar and waited. Nan struggled against Jimmy's arms, but they only squeezed harder. When the first policeman grabbed Pat by the wrist and wrenched it around his back, she lunged and tripped, pulling Jimmy down with her. The dark carpet was full of unseen debris.

She could hear Jimmy now. He'd been speaking the entire time. He was saying, "I'm sorry," over and over again. She pulled them both to standing, wheeled around, and slapped him across the face, just to get him to stop. Pat was in handcuffs. The officer who'd arrested him was reading him his rights. The entire restaurant had turned around in their seats, mouths agape and phones out. A terrible quiet descended. Even the kitchen ceased its clattering.

Johnny murmured something into the senior officer's ear. The man nodded and jerked his head at his partner. They pulled Pat toward the back exit, away from the crowd. Somewhere, a fire whooshed around a wok. Without meaning to, Pat kicked over a chair, and the policeman holding on to his wrists shoved him hard.

"Don't touch him!" Nan said. The officer's hand went to his hip holster.

"Ma'am," the officer started to say, but Pat interrupted, speaking in Chinese so ragged that Nan had to listen with all her concentration.

"Please forgive me," he said. "Look in my phone. I'm sorry."

A sob seized Nan by the throat and bent her in two. She pressed her hands against her thighs. When they disappeared into the kitchen, the sound of their departing footsteps too quiet for her to hear, the crowd released a communal breath and chatter filled the vacuum.

"I'll take you home," Jimmy was saying into her ear.

"What did he do?" she asked. Jimmy's left cheek was red and she remembered that she'd hit him only moments before, but she glimpsed no anger in his face, only a muddy blend of shame and unease.

"He burned down the Duck House," he said. Nan pulled off her apron and Jimmy waved his hand in front of his face, as if to deter another slap. "Please, let me take you home."

"Not home!" Nan went to the employees' closet to grab her purse. She saw her shopping bag from earlier. How could she have let her son be taken away with holes in his shoes? She grabbed the bag, hooking her wrist through the thin plastic handles. Remembering the cell phone in her apron, she dove back to wrestle the phone from the folds of fabric.

"Where are you going?" Jimmy shouted after her.

"They took my son." She struggled to keep her purse on her shoulder. Giving up, she let it swing freely, dangerously, while she whipped around, looking for some sign of where to go. Which police station did they take him to? How would she find her way there? The heat of everyone's eyes hovered over her while they pretended to look somewhere else. She wanted to tell them that her son was innocent, but there was no strength in such an obvious lie. So she fell on the phrase she'd heard in the crime movies she used to watch with Pat.

"My son was set up!" she called out from the front door. Then she was outside, where no one knew who she was or why she was having trouble standing upright.

Annie did not know how long she'd been in this alley. She'd gotten only a few yards from the restaurant before her legs had started shaking so badly that she'd had to lean against the closest wall. Squatting in her ripped hostess uniform, she burrowed her face deeper into her arms, breathing in the musky odor of her knees. How much longer until she should try to stand?

Suddenly, gravel crunched in front of her. Something touched her shoulder. Annie jumped back and her face shot up. Pat's mother! Annie palmed the ground with her right hand. Without knowing why, she'd wanted to grab the first thing in her way and throw it at Nan's head.

"What do you want?" Annie spat. There was snot in her mouth; she wiped it away with the back of her arm. "It's all your son's fault."

Nan squatted beside her, grunting slightly from the effort. They were not quite looking at each other. "Did he do something to you?"

"I'm going to jail." Annie started crying again. "He ruined my life." She wanted to push herself into Nan's body, to burrow through her soft chest and hide there.

Nan rubbed Annie's back until her hiccups subsided. Nan's hand was almost as big as a man's. Her strokes were strong but gentle. Annie's father used to rub her back like this, to get her to fall asleep at night. Annie wished she could fall asleep right here and wake up in her own bed.

"Let me take you home." Nan lifted Annie up by the crook of her elbow. Her Chinese was sweet, almost dreamy, like the way Annie's mother spoke. "You'll feel better after a hot shower. You'll get in pajamas, eat some food, and you'll see, the world will get brighter."

"You can't take me home," Annie said. She wiped away the crud beneath her eyes. "I can't be around my parents right now."

"Come back to my place," Nan said. "We can have wine. Try to settle down."

Annie stopped inspecting the grime on her thumbs. "How are you so okay?"

"I'm going to be having a little wine too," Nan said, and then, softly, "I don't want to be alone right now, do you?"

Annie reached out her hand and Nan pulled her up. Annie struggled to stand, stumbling when the blood rushed back into her dead feet. But Nan kept tugging her forward, like a child with a kite string.

"Don't tell my parents," Annie said.

"Let's go," Nan said. "Who knows what traffic is like?"

23

After Nan shouted at his customers, a sly part of Jimmy reared up in anger. The night would never return to normal. But a different, larger force inside him squeezed the life out of his pettiness. He'd witnessed a tremendous kind of violence, and he couldn't convince himself that what had happened was okay. Would he feel this sick if he'd called the police himself?

Johnny had already left to make sure Pat was treated right at the station. At least that was what he'd announced to Jimmy and the rest of the restaurant staff.

Jimmy went behind the bar and poured himself a tall glass of bourbon. He'd been drinking, steadily, secretly, since the morning. These constant nips—more like full drinks if he was being honest—had padded his head, made him pleasantly fuzzy, but they were no longer enough to block the rising panic. Like weak deodorant, his buzz masked nothing; it only amplified the stench of his actions. What if he drank more? The sweet heat of the liquor made the glassful go down easy. He choked once, then the drink was gone. His body hummed pleasantly. But the pit of his stomach remained ice cold. He poured another. He estimated fifteen or twenty minutes before all the alcohol converged in his system. He should try to drive home now.

"Tom, take over," he said to the nearest waiter.

"After that?" the kid had the guts to say.

"Yes." Jimmy finished his drink, the ice wetting his nose. Through the glass, he saw the kid widen his eyes at another waiter. Jimmy would get rid of them all soon.

He tucked the bottle of bourbon inside his jacket, though the boxy bulge fooled no one. He secured a nice long straw.

"Enjoy your meal," he said to the table nearest the front door, bending slightly toward the nervous couple. He almost stumbled; the liquor was moving fast. "This lovely table needs some complimentary desserts," he shouted.

The woman whispered a thank-you. The man stared steely-eyed at his plate.

"You have a great night." Jimmy tipped an invisible hat. They would not be back. Would any of them? He took a contemplative sip from his straw and sneezed. When he got to his car, he remembered the tranquilizers his doctor had prescribed him after the fire. He scarfed down a handful with the help of some bourbon. He was getting tired of the taste, and on a whim, he smashed the bottle down on the pavement, kicking up a small geyser of liquid and glass and catching every eye on the street. Someone, maybe an officer, turned around and strode toward him. He hurried into his car and peeled out of the tight parallel space. He hit both cars, but what were bumpers for? He was tired of apologizing for what was clearly his fault.

He didn't usually drink and drive while the sun was out, though the glowing orb was on its way down, floating mistily above the trees that lined Rock Creek Parkway. He rounded the tight corners with little whoops escaping his mouth. It was like controlling his own roller coaster, feeling safe because he kept forgetting the presence of danger. He didn't know where he was headed. The night was rife with people he could visit. He bent his head down toward his jacket, only to remember he'd chucked the bourbon. Feeling around in his glove compartment, he let out a crow when he palmed the container of scotch Uncle Pang had gifted him earlier that summer. True wonder that he'd forgotten the half-drunk bottle. He clenched it between his thighs and flicked the cap into the backseat. The car swerved, upsetting the rumble tracks that lined the highway lane. Jimmy spilled a glug of scotch on his jacket. He sucked at his shirtsleeve. A voice came into his head, unbidden.

"A glass of scotch is the perfect male accessory."

Had Janine actually said those words? Or was he so well versed in the cadence of her voice, the pitch and degree of her teasing humor, that he had become a generator of Janine-isms? Only a day and he'd missed her enough to turn her into a ghost. But this wouldn't stop him from drinking the scotch. Not when he was this thirsty.

He kept his eyes on the road and lifted the bottle to his lips, and again she spoke: "All great men drink scotch, and so do all other men." If he weren't on the highway, he would have thrown the bottle out the window. She was a poisonous woman, with long-lasting venom. He fooled around with the GPS on his phone.

Finally, a new voice in his head—the gentle, dulcet tones of his GPS navigator leading him toward a cramped neighborhood in Takoma Park. He eased his seat forward, cramming the steering wheel into his chest. The vibrations of the car calmed him, scattering his vicious thoughts. Whenever he thought he might doze off, he took another sip. At some point, it all went black.

Jimmy woke up to the sounds of buzzing, clanking, and distant conversation. A terrible smell hit his nose: a musty combination of sweaty feet, piss, spilled beer, and unwashed human bodies. His eyes felt glued together. A terrible pulsing headache scrambled his brains. He could smell his own breath, even with his mouth closed, and his teeth were somehow looser in their gums.

He couldn't figure out where he was or how he'd gotten there. The last thing he remembered, he was headed toward Janine's. Had he crashed? He wiggled his fingers and toes and ruled out a car accident.

He kept guessing because he couldn't handle knowing for sure yet. Maybe he was at the bottom of a bar, forgotten by the cleanup crew sweeping up around him. That would explain the noise and the smell, as well as what he was lying on. He felt drunk, despite the headache. What time was it?

Curiosity and the growing pressure in his bladder finally forced his eyes open. He was in a jail cell, lying on the cement floor. He had no idea what he'd done to end up here. They'd taken his watch. The clock on the wall told him it was barely nine p.m.; his mouth told him he'd definitely vomited once already that night. A tarnished, seat-less toilet was available in the cell, but Jimmy's bladder would get no relief. He struggled to sit up, leaning his back against the metal bars of the cell. The pads of his fingers were dark, but he couldn't remember getting his prints taken, or his mug shot, or even a ghostly sense memory of the back of a police car.

He was not alone, though it took him a moment to realize this. A skinny white man was curled up beneath the metal bench, nearly hidden inside a large gray T-shirt. Only from the way the shirt lifted and fell could Jimmy tell the man was alive. He had a terrible feeling that, this being Friday night, the tiny cell would be crammed within the next two hours. Few of these gentlemen would be the docile type. He'd been in a cell almost identical to this one years ago, when he'd been picked up for possession, but within the first five minutes he'd gotten into a fight with an Englishman who wouldn't stop screaming. The other men in the cell—there'd been so many people that they had to take turns sitting down—had ignored the wild-eyed man. Only Jimmy, wounded from his father's decision to hire Johnny as a manager, had screamed back. They had both been impossible to cow. The fight ended with Jimmy kicking the screamer in the gut after the man spat in his face. They'd placed him in a single cell after that.

He no longer recognized the man he'd been before, a human animal who changed the chemistry of the room just by walking in. He'd started pacing the small confines of the holding cell right after he was placed inside, not to intimidate the others but because he had to move to displace the energy coming off him. It had been almost a decade since that incident, but being back in a holding cell made him wonder if he had retained some trace of that animal. Why else had he shaken Uncle Pang's hand a year ago? He must have known, like everyone claimed he did, what that hateful man's plan would be—and so he must have wanted to see the Duck House destroyed. Jimmy never saw himself as holding a grudge, but he could admit, in this woozy, translucent state, that his pride still smarted at the thought that his father had not trusted him with the restaurant.

Perhaps his father had been right.

His pattern of behavior had not traveled far. Rather than being hopped up on an army of uppers, he was swimming in tranquilizers, which were barely cottoning his head from his hangover. His body was leaden, and the effort to move his arm was like asking a stranger to do it. He shivered at the thought of having to defend himself when he couldn't even rise to his feet. He shot another look at the man in the T-shirt, furious that the other man had taken the best hiding spot. His hands on the bars, Jimmy finally managed to pull himself up, and though he was unsteady and panting from the effort, he felt stronger. An officer passed; Jimmy flagged him down with slow, frantic gestures.

"You can use the phone," he told Jimmy. He turned out to be one of the arresting officers, and he spoke down to Jimmy as if he were a spoiled child who'd finished his tantrum. "You're in the Takoma Park police station. We picked you up for drunk and disorderly. Also trespassing. Your lady friend says she won't be pressing charges."

"Why not?"

"She says you've had a tough couple of weeks and she doesn't blame you. I wouldn't have been so nice. Especially if you'd busted up *my* windows and scared *my* son like that. You've got a lot of thinking to do."

"Can I call her to apologize?" Jimmy expected at any moment to be plunged back into his waterlogged memories. But his mind stayed blank. Blessedly.

"You leave her alone. She didn't seem *that* forgiving."

Jimmy called his brother instead. While he waited for Johnny to pick up, he allowed himself to grow hopeful. Janine could have pressed charges. Or had the officers rough him up a bit. He picked at an old piece of gum stuck to the painted cement wall. She'd been good to him, and for no reason he could think of. Did that mean he had a chance? Would she take him back? The phone kept ringing, and he realized he'd been stewing over Janine for too long. His brother never waited more than three rings to answer his phone, not even when he was sleeping.

The phone line finally clicked open, but Jimmy's heart sank when a female automaton informed him that John Han was unavailable. Why wasn't he back at the restaurant? He couldn't still be with Pat. Hours had passed since the arrest. Even Johnny had his limits. The woman suggested that he leave a message after the beep, and Jimmy's stomach cinched itself one notch tighter. He wished the robotic voice would continue forever, but with the beep came the dreaded silence. His frightened voice echoed off the walls.

"Hey, Johnny, I'm at the Takoma Park police station. Come get me. Don't tell Mom."

He stayed breathing on the line for a few seconds longer. He had nothing else to say, but he wasn't ready to be alone. He couldn't call his mother. He couldn't call Janine. Who else did he have in his life? He'd felt such gratitude when the officer told him that the one-phone-call rule only happened in the movies, but he wished now that he could just hang up the phone and go back to his cell. Instead, he held on to the plastic receiver, which was growing wet from the sweat of his hand. He stared at the number pad, as if that might make a ten-digit sequence appear.

An impulse from childhood crept in; Jimmy began to slip into character. He was a secret agent, faced with breaking the code that would connect him to a real voice. A heavy calm went through his body. He was in the police station but not in the police station, because he was now a code breaker, nameless and faceless, a man defined solely by his task at hand. His finger almost went back to the number pad, he was so transported by the dreamy feeling. A loud buzz in the next room pulled him back out.

He'd existed in this fugue state for most of his early years in America, when he'd had to make his own kind of sense. But the world was no longer that breed of unfamiliar, and the only thing that was unintelligible was how he'd gotten himself here. Even this, in the end, was translatable. He only had to follow his own tracks.

What a mess he'd made, all by himself.

24

Johnny had no idea why his daughter was at Nan's house, but he was grateful all the same. He'd been apprehensive when he'd stepped out of the police station and seen Nan waiting by his car. Neither of them had been able to get to Pat. He'd expected tears, remonstrations, all deserved. Instead, she calmly informed him that, in case he was looking for his daughter, she was found.

He hadn't been looking for his daughter. She was nineteen. She had her own life. But on his drive over to Nan's, he had to admit that Annie had been acting strangely since he'd gotten back from Hong Kong. She'd been sleeping a lot lately, even more than she usually did. He hadn't been hard enough on her when she was a child, her sleeping face too beautiful to disturb. It was a rare day if Annie didn't sleep past noon. Though she'd never gone past three or into the evening. He hadn't thought much of the hours she was keeping, but that was because he'd been busy. He rubbed his eyes, partly from the sun, sinking down the sky, and partly because this refrain—busy, busy—was too familiar. He caught the patterns of an excuse in its repetition. So she'd been sleeping irregularly, that was one piece. And there had been, coming back from the airport, her puffy eyes. He'd assumed a recent heartbreak, and she had quickly corrected him. Only later had he figured out the boyfriend was Nan's son.

The puzzle piece snapped loudly into place, shocking him with the obvious picture it made. Of course she would be upset. Her boyfriend had set fire to the family restaurant! And if they were still dating, then he must have told her, which meant that his daughter had kept this terrible secret for weeks. Johnny slapped the sun visor down, blocking the rays from his tired eyes.

He knew what Annie had seen from her hostess stand: A garish Chinese restaurant. Uppity, gloating, and hopelessly Oriental. But if she'd look a little harder, she would see what a magical establishment her grandfather had built. She might understand the limitations and expectations her father and uncle had managed to surpass and the lives they had affected. Almost every waiter had a house in a nice neighborhood because of the Duck House. Waiters who had never finished high school, who came to America with nothing, now had savings, healthcare, SAT tutors for their children. Yes, a handful of these waiters were past the age of retirement and still working, but they told him they liked the job. It kept them young.

Without the Duck House, Johnny himself would still be toiling in a research lab, getting passed over for promotions year after year while his better-connected colleagues were bumped up. The day the biggest idiot in Johnny's lab, Chris Anderson, got his own office was the day Johnny finally accepted his father's job offer. So he was *damn* proud of his father's restaurant, no matter what his daughter thought. He could understand embarrassment or frustration—these were things he also knew—but never would he have expected her to protect the boy who'd destroyed her family's legacy, especially when she could see, right under the same roof where she did all that sleeping, the chaos the fire had caused.

Johnny made himself take deep breaths through his nose while he drove. He recognized, in his frenetic thoughts, the guilt he was trying to extinguish, or at least smother, with his anger. He hoped Nan understood why he'd had to have Pat arrested. His list of reasons lined up in his head, like a row of soldiers. Pat would certainly have set another fire. Their family needed the money to continue. Pat was young enough to receive a lenient sentence. Most important—a reason he would not share but that gave him the greatest strength of all—the system would break down the black pillar of anger that had grown inside the boy. With force but a necessary force, which Nan had never been able to use against her son. Her gentle, nervous love couldn't begin to scrub Pat clean. Only punishment could fix him. Just as Jimmy had been fixed, for a time, by his rehab stint. Some people needed to have control thrust upon them. It was a good sign that Nan had invited him over, an even better one that she had been kind enough to take his errant daughter in. But was it wise to take in another person's child when her own child was so clearly in need? Wasn't Nan's distracted kindness in some way the reason Pat was in jail in the first place? He hated to say it, it went against the grain of his own core beliefs, but after a certain point compassion hurt more than it helped. He felt stronger as he found Nan's street and took the turn. He was doing the right thing.

Nan had gotten home before him. Before he could ring the doorbell, the handle twisted open.

"I'm sorry for this trouble," Johnny said, when she appeared at the door. He immediately turned red. He'd only meant to refer to his daughter. "Annie is a dramatic girl," he tried to clarify. "I'll get her out of your hair."

"When I can see Pat?" Nan asked, once Johnny had stepped inside. "You know police well?"

"I'll talk to the sergeant," Johnny said, which he told himself was not a lie. Just because the police had barred him from seeing

Pat at the station did not mean Johnny had no clout at all. "I'm sure he'll be fine. They'll probably put him in his own cell."

"He is not alone?" Nan wrung her hands, which looked like they'd been recently dunked in ice water. "He be with killers?" Her voice was hitting a volume that Johnny had never heard her reach. He felt a tingle of irritation in his jaw and he was ashamed to wish that the woman in front of him would just calm down.

"You can speak Chinese," Johnny said. "If that's easier."

But the switch in language did nothing to mute Nan's alarm.

"I need to call the police chief," she said. "How could they put him with dangerous people? He's a kid!"

"He's protected," Johnny said. "I know you have to worry, but he's a seventeen-year-old Chinese boy. No one will hurt him."

Nan looked at him with dark eyes. She seemed to have rooted out from his placid words his desire to shut her up. With deliberate slowness, she ran her tongue along the front of her teeth.

"Annie's sleeping upstairs," she said. "Come with me. There's something you should know." He followed her into the living room. A TV sat in the corner. A pile of what looked like bedsheets lay next to it. Her hand went into her pocket and came back gripping an old cell phone.

Johnny took a seat on the couch. But Nan began to pace in front of him, switching the phone from hand to hand.

"I'm sorry about Annie," he said, scrabbling for an appropriate foothold. "We tried to teach her how to be considerate of other people's time—"

"Look at this." Nan shoved the cell phone under his nose.

His eyes blurred, then refocused on a picture—Pat, pixelated and grainy, holding two bottles stuffed with cloth. The fire investigator had used a term: "Molotov cocktail."

"I appreciate you showing me this," he said, confused. "I suppose now we know for certain—"

"Look at the next picture," Nan said. Her impatient finger shot out and pressed the button for him. Again his eyes blurred and he had to hold the phone away from his face. His irritation with his farsightedness quickly died away.

"What's Annie doing here?" His daughter looked drunk, a lewd sneer on her face. Her small hands barely fit around the bottles. His finger moved to delete the photo, but Nan was faster. She snatched the phone away and tucked it into her back pocket.

"Now you know a fraction of how I feel." She was pacing again. "You took my son away in handcuffs. You made me watch. I can do the same thing to you."

Waves of heat then ice crashed over Johnny's body. His knees would not stop shaking. He put his hands over them, but he'd lost the strength to keep his body still. He couldn't have imagined this; it had not even entered his mind. The picture of his baby girl pulsed in his eyes, her soft shirt ripped in two, her little belly exposed for the camera. She was only nineteen. She hadn't even declared a major. Anger licked at his sides, threatening to consume everything, but he breathed through the impulse to rage.

"My daughter—" He was too winded to talk. "She—" He faltered; he fell out of his seat and without thinking he clambered over to Nan's feet on his knees. "She's only a—" He dug his fingers into the carpet's heavy piling. He pressed his forehead to her feet. Staring at her slippers, he came back to his senses. He felt like an animal and a fool, and in his shame, he was able to force this vibrant, terrifying part of himself to lie back down.

Breathing heavy, he propped himself up on the arm of the sofa and wiped his forehead. It was soaking wet. "You do what you think is right," he managed to say.

"If I do what is right, your daughter goes away." Nan pushed the phone in front of his face again. "She's not like my son. She's an adult. She has a record. You want to send your baby girl to prison? You think that's what you should do?"

"Yes," he gasped. His head throbbed from the tears he wouldn't let fall. "That's the correct thing to do." His wife would kill him. His mother would tear him to pieces. "I would be a hypocrite to make Annie the exception."

Nan made a strange growling noise, rising in pitch until it became a screech.

"What are you?" She seized his head between her cold hands. The hard plastic of the cell phone pressed against his temple. "You call yourself a good man! Yet you would do nothing for your child. You coward. You snake." Her face was fierce from crying.

"Your tears are so big." He couldn't think of anything else to say. He wished the phone would crack his head open.

"Everyone, they called you cold, or difficult, or prideful, but you've always tried to be a good boy. I see that. You have your own ways. But if you send your daughter to prison, you will never forgive yourself." She released her hold on his head and touched the side of his cheek gently. "There *is* a bigger picture. Believe me."

Johnny had forgotten to breathe. The shock of Nan's soft touch forced his lungs to expand and suck in, and the sweet relief of air in his chest, the release of the chokehold he'd had on himself, in its small way convinced him to listen.

He folded his body into the deep cushion. He closed his eyes and tried to find peace in his choice. "What should I do?"

"You have to save Pat too," Nan warned.

"Your son burned down my family's restaurant," he said. "I had to turn him in."

"It wasn't just him," Nan said. "Mr. Pang was around that night, He had a huge fight with Jimmy. He must have been the one to give Pat the orders, for revenge."

Johnny realized how white his face must have gone only when Nan reached toward him. She looked as if she thought he might faint.

"Pang," he whispered. "Oh God."

"So Pat is innocent." Nan looked down at the picture on her phone.

"He isn't totally guilty," Johnny said. He was, miraculously, starting to feel awkward. Was this how his brother had felt the other night?

Nan pressed her hands into her chest. "We can turn Pang in," she breathed.

"We can't." Johnny rubbed at his knees, which still felt the impact of the carpet. "He's untouchable. He's like the moon. He might shrink, but he never goes away. Otherwise my mother would have gotten rid of him decades ago."

"Feng Fei knows him." Nan chewed on the cell phone antenna, her teeth leaving soft marks on the plastic. Johnny wished he had something to chew on too.

"He controls your family, but he controls more than the Duck House, is this true?"

"He has connections, yes." Johnny massaged his jaw. "He got Jimmy out of trouble. He could have helped Annie with the shoplifting."

"Can he help my son?" Nan was beyond embarrassment. Johnny's vanity should have been struck dead too. But his flesh continued to prickle, mortified.

"Maybe."

"Call him now and ask."

"Not me," Johnny said. "But . . ."

"Your mother." Nan went through the jacket Johnny had folded across the back of the couch. She grabbed his phone and shoved it under his nose.

He didn't feel the need to catch Nan up on how his family worked. Forgiveness was harder to come by when family wronged family than if a stranger had done the hurt. But whereas he did not have a thing to offer Uncle Pang, he knew what his mother wanted. He rose unsteadily from his seat.

"Give me a little privacy, please."

*

The first thing out of his mother's mouth was, "Are you in trouble?"

"I might be," he said. "I need you to call Uncle Pang."

"After everything you put me through." His mother laughed on the other line, no performance behind her glee. "You need help?"

Johnny could have thrown Annie's predicament in his mother's face. That would shut her up. But he would never forgive himself if he dragged Annie into this grave inheritance. He leaned the hot phone against his cheek.

"We made a mistake with Pat," he said. "You need to ask Uncle Pang to get him out. He's just a boy, and we don't even know for sure if he did what we say he did."

"You keep talking nonsense," his mother said.

"I'll give you back financial power." He knew this wasn't enough. "And I'll give you the Duck House. I'll make sure Jimmy signs it over to you."

"Why would I want the Duck House?" His mother could barely hide the yearning in her voice. "Throwing money down a hole."

"That place was your vision." His sweat made the phone slick against his temple.

"Uncle Pang won't listen to me."

"Don't play dumb, Ma," Johnny said; he couldn't help himself. "He calls you Little Feng, for God's sake. Just tell him you'll owe him a favor. That's all he cares about."

"I don't like this rudeness," his mother grumbled, but then she spoke slowly, thinking her words through. "He can't move mountains. Pat set the fire, and that's what we're telling the insurance company. We'll see about the sentencing."

Johnny expected his mother to hang up. All the cards had fallen in her favor. But she stayed on the line. A silence like taffy stretched between them.

"This change in you," she said. "It's not terrible."

"Thank you," he said. The line went dead.

*

He found Nan sitting on the stairs. She hadn't gone more than halfway up. Her free hand gripped the railing and she didn't let go, even after he'd walked up to join her.

"She'll call him," Johnny said. He stopped a few steps below Nan so that their eyes were even. "He'll fix everything, as best he can."

"Thank you." She finally released the railing. She held out her hand to him. "I'm sorry for Pat." They pressed their palms together, a strange bridging that lasted for seconds, neither of them speaking, neither of them turning away.

Nan let go first. She pulled her work uniform straight and hefted herself up.

"Should I go to my daughter?" The doubt sat strange in Johnny's throat. He did not talk in uncertain terms. He started to move up the stairs.

For a moment, Nan seemed torn. She looked over her shoulder, staring up at the second story. Then she stretched her arms across the staircase, blocking his path.

"I need you to take me back to the police station," Nan said.

"I don't have the power," he said. "I'm sorry."

Nan pressed her palms to her eyes and rubbed them hard. "I locked the door from the inside. She's fast asleep. I gave her too much wine."

After all they'd been through, Johnny wished he weren't angry. He wished his first impulse wasn't to throw Nan aside to get to Annie.

"They have to let a mother see her child." Nan chewed at the dry skin on her bottom lip. "I need you to speak for me."

Johnny's anger was no smaller, but he found himself relenting. He had always considered Nan to be like a sweet aunt. A woman without temper, blanched of desire. How totally wrong he was. He saw her for the first and last time not as a waitress or a manager, not as a struggling single mother, but as a person in his life, who had taken up more space than he'd understood. He wanted to give her a parting gift. It was rare to find a person who'd seen an entire arc of his life play out.

"Okay," he said, and then, the first thing that came to mind: "You win."

Nan patted his arm. The way she breathed in and out sounded almost like laughter.

"What have I won?" she said. She was gentle, but Johnny still felt reprimanded.

"Yes, of course." He patted his pockets for his keys and wallet. "I'll drive."

"That would be good." Her eyes shook loose a few forgotten tears, which streaked down her face almost too quickly for him to see.

Johnny wanted to close the space between them, to stride up the stairs and hold her. The woman in front of him had always embodied the qualities he most valued: generosity, evenness, good humor, a backbone. But she was a vessel for so much else, which he had never thought to consider. He felt, in her mystery, that he no longer knew himself. He wanted, in this moment, to take her away to somewhere exotic, with sights that might distract from her life's tragedy. But while the thought of helping another soul usually lifted his, for once, Johnny stayed flat on his feet. He stuck himself in this difficult moment, with no escape, and no distraction.

25

Few moments in Ah-Jack's life had compelled him to move too quickly for memories to form. Hours had passed and he could not remember how he had gotten to the edge of Michelle's hospital bed. His wife was dozing. Her monitor beeped gently. Black and metal equipment hung overhead.

Just as the sensations in his body finally arrived—how his hips and knees ached from rushing around—so too did the questions. What would happen with his job? Had he lost it, or had Nan done her magic? Did she have the ring box? Where was Gary? When would the lunkhead be back to check on Michelle? And could asking these questions keep him from thinking about the one question that pressed against him with the silky insistence of a cat: *What was wrong with Michelle?*

Nan, always right, was right again. His own queer intuition had also paid off: Michelle had checked in to the hospital that morning after a sudden, terrible pain in her hip made her faint in the bathroom. They hadn't talked about what had happened outside the most pertinent details.

Instead, they talked about Nan. Ah-Jack started out apologizing, but Michelle interrupted to tease him about his bad household habits. She asked if he was also leaving Nan's sponges soaking wet and shedding his little gray hairs all over her bathroom.

"Gary looks like the gassy type," he shot back. "He says hello with a burp and leaves with a fart, doesn't he?"

"You're one to talk," she said, catching her breath from laughing. "Before I switched you to soy milk, you were passing gas more often than you were talking."

"I am the man with two mouths," he agreed.

Then she had winced and pressed her hands against her back: twin twinges from her kidneys. He'd gone to find a hot-water bottle, and when he came back, she was fighting to stay awake. The sight of her fluttering eyelids nearly choked him. There was his sweet, steady wife.

"Take a nap," he told her, one hand cupping her right cheek. He smoothed a sunspot that had formed when she was fifty. "I'll be here when you wake up."

"There's a TV." She pointed to the corner of the room. "You can watch the races. But no betting."

"I wouldn't waste my luck," he said, stroking that soft little spot.

When perching at the end of the bed started to hurt his back, Ah-Jack dragged a plastic chair over. He was glad that Michelle had a private room. She was so shy around strangers. What a fluke that she'd managed to find herself a lover. Ah-Jack pinched his wrist for the nasty thought. Now that he had time to think, he was surprised he could be in the same room with his wife. Everything had changed between them. She was in love with Gary; he had betrayed her with Nan. But when they were together, all he wanted to do was make her laugh. Perhaps they were too old to discount all the years they'd passed together. Why throw away decades because of a few months of hurt? But the pain . . . He'd really expected to be beyond the age of such sensation.

When he wasn't with Nan, his chest sank and caved into its new hollow, which only grew with every passing day, scraped larger by invisible, impassive fingers. He was frightened of this pain, how it moved, how it hid, how it cast a long shadow. Even when Nan was there, those fingers were waiting to creep back from the horizon. Mornings were the most difficult. Waking up, he would grow aware of Nan's warm body beside him. So comforting and neutral the night before, her body curdled in sleep, and while she didn't smell bad or even that strongly, her scent was so different from Michelle's that it startled him. Worse was waking up to an empty bed. His pain was banal, the stuff of pop songs, but it was blindingly new to him. Nearly seventy years of emotional placidity were a blessing, but he had no stores to draw upon, no old fortresses built in his twenties and thirties inside which to recover. The only person who might understand was the one who'd broken him in the first place.

He looked back at his wife, jumping when he saw her open eyes. She'd developed a slight flush in her cheeks, a few shades from being feverish.

"Go back to sleep," he scolded, but he got up and fit his body next to hers.

"Sometimes this happens." She tried to untuck the sheets to throw over him. "I get a big burst of energy and I can't sleep a wink."

"I'm glad you're awake." He stilled her busy hands. "I was getting lonely watching you snore."

"I don't snore; you snore."

"I snort," he corrected her. "And just once. You snore, continuously."

She took a drink of water. "Well, you sound like an old goose with a sore throat."

"Cancer makes you mean." He played with the plastic on her left wrist. "I sound like a young goose in good health."

They settled back into comfortable silence. Sometimes Ah-Jack thought that he only teased his wife to get to this quality of silence, which was never as rich or layered with anyone else. As his friends and colleagues would attest, quiet was not a flavor he came in. Without Michelle at home, his jokes and pranks could take on a yapping frenzy, like a small dog in the company of strangers. He would keep going, spinning stories, eager to delight and charm, until his own energy overtook him. After all, he'd proposed to Nan just this afternoon, and while he wasn't ready to admit that he'd been out of control when he'd barreled into that pawnshop, he could admit that the walk-in fridge was the least romantic and least practical place he could have popped the question.

He admitted this ridiculous chain of events to Michelle. When he got to the part where he crashed down on one knee, she laughed so hard she started coughing.

"Poor Nan," she said when she managed to calm down. "How could you put her through that!"

Ah-Jack laughed with her, always pleased to be the butt of the joke he was telling. But then, without warning, Michelle started to rub her face, massaging her cheeks in elastic circles. At first he thought she was showing how her face had been strained from laughing. But the rubbing continued. He waited, unease slowly eating away his own smile.

"A proposal?" she finally gasped out through her hands. "You bought her a ring?"

Ah-Jack was at a loss. He'd assumed his wife was too clean-hearted for jealousy. And even if she wasn't a saint, he didn't expect her to care. She was the one who'd left. But her skin was growing redder under her fingers. She wouldn't look at him.

"She was thinking of moving to California." He wasn't sure if he should try to touch Michelle. "I didn't want her to leave me." He swallowed the "too," but they both heard the absence of that pairing word.

314 · LILLIAN LI

"So you were going to marry her?" She tried to laugh again, but the noise came out strident and off.

"What about you?" he said. "Aren't you going to marry Gary? He's basically your husband now."

"You are my husband!" Michelle's volume made Ah-Jack lean back. He balanced on the edge of the hospital bed. "How dare you say those things to me."

"But you don't tell me you're this sick." Ah-Jack scrambled for his defenses. "You don't want me in your life, or even to know about your life, but you don't want me to move on either? Wifey, you used to make sense."

"I wanted you to have a chance at happiness," she said. "If you knew about my health, you would have dropped everything. But it's not the same as what you and Nan have. You must have saved her in your past life. I wanted you two to have your opening. But that doesn't mean I don't hate that she has you now. I'm not perfect."

"Of course you're not perfect," he said. "You betrayed me. You left."

"You left *me*," she said. She threw the hospital covers off, yanking the neatly tucked corners out from under the mattress. "You left first."

Ah-Jack was stunned. He had never done what she had done, and certainly not first.

"I never, *never* cheated on you. Not with Nan, not with anyone, I swear. Is this why you left? Because of this thing you made up in your head?"

His wife ran a finger down her IV. Her eyes held the same intelligent light that had first caught his attention in school. She started twisting the frayed hem of her hospital blanket.

"I don't mean to accuse you of something you didn't do," she said slowly. "I left you because Gary made me happy. It wasn't your fault."

In her stilted delivery, Ah-Jack heard a great weight of words unsaid. He hated that she had so much that could hurt him locked up inside her. He didn't want to know the ways that Gary made her happy; he didn't want to see the inverse image of all the ways he had failed.

"I'm glad you're finally happy." He stood up. "I'm sorry I made things so hard to bear. I guess you have nothing to be sorry for."

Michelle made a rude noise with her mouth, her eyes rolling up to the ceiling while her head slumped into her pillow.

"I *am* sorry. You have to know that," she said. "And I care for you more than you could fathom. But I'm not going to die alone and afraid of everything. Not even for you."

Michelle didn't bring up her illness or its implications—not lightly, not ever. He understood why now. The argument was over. Michelle had won. Her infidelity, the ways she had contributed to her own unhappiness, the times she might have spoken up—these wrongs, in no way inconsequential, were impossible to scale against the great wrong her body had dealt her. The end to their fight was abrupt, unnatural, but he couldn't blame her. He deserved this small unfairness. He didn't know why, but he was certain he did.

"I should leave," he said. "Gary will probably be here any moment."

"He will," she said. "But I don't want you to go. Not after everything we said."

"I wish I had known how to make you happy," he said.

"You know that you did," she said. "I'm the one who didn't make you happy. That was Nan. That was her job."

"Nan is a great friend," he admitted, and his heart filled up and collapsed with its own heaved sigh. "But she's not my wife. You are. It was you in the past life, and it's you in this life." He didn't know where he was lying and where he was telling the truth and where he was simply confused. He only knew that this reality was the safest one to believe in. He was learning how to protect himself.

"Thank you for saying that." Michelle sniffed, and the cords in her neck stood out sharply. Her eyes brightened with tears. "But whatever you end up doing with Nan, just treat her well. She likes to look after other people and ignore herself."

"I've been taking advantage of that." He bowed his head and studied his callused hands. "I make other people's lives heavier, lightening my own load."

"No, Jack." She turned his hands over and patted them with surprising vitality. "You are lightness itself."

She pulled him back onto the bed. He cradled her head against the crook of his neck and wrapped his arms around her shoulders. He rocked her slowly and sang an old song that had been popular when they were classmates. The words and the melody evoked the right time, back when she was his shadow and he was her guide. Her fists clenched his work shirt, until eventually they loosened, and small, gurgling snores escaped from her nose. He gave her cheeks a small squeeze—he could pick them out of any lineup—and gathered his blazer. He took the usual roads home, not to Nan's place, but to his old house. Without embarrassment, he climbed the stairs hunched on all fours, like a child, and after washing his face in their bathroom, he shed his clothes in the guest room. She'd kept the room clean, but she hadn't stripped the sheets, so the room still smelled like him. She'd left his pajamas, neatly folded, at the foot of the bed.

Sliding under the sheets, lying flat on his back, he allowed himself to cry his old-man tears. His open-throated moans, unmuffled by any pillow, shot out toward the dimpled ceiling. The tears slid hot around his ears and down his neck. When he finally quieted down, hiccups dancing away with his breath, he fell asleep unaware of the time, of the position of the sun in the sky. All he knew was that his wife was secure in a place he could visit, and his home was his own again.

26

Some people could split their voice and sing out entire chords on their own; Jimmy's mother had this power in her face, which could turn out the most colorful combinations of feeling. Rising from the waiting-room seats, she appeared most pleased by her utter disappointment in her son, as if she'd been told she'd broken a world record in despair. Johnny, on the other hand, held his face as still as a mirrored lake. His entire face might as well be wearing reflective glass. Jimmy wanted to punch his brother in the nose. He shook his hand instead.

"Thanks for picking me up," he said. "And putting down for bail."

"Only you would go crazy and harass a woman." His mother dove in. "I must have angered someone powerful to be stuck with a son like you. Your birth alone, that melon head of yours."

"Not here, Ma." Johnny herded them out of the police station. He nodded to an officer behind the bulletproof glass. "We don't want to get you both locked up."

"Who is going to lock up an old lady!" She shouted the question as a challenge.

"No one, no one. Let's just get Jimmy home."

318 • LILLIAN LI

"Have you no shame?" She got her face close to Jimmy's. "Throwing a tantrum in front of that country girl. You won't be happy until you've destroyed our family name."

"I can still get rid of *your* house," Jimmy said. His drunken haze had lifted about an hour ago, and his tranquilizers were fading.

"No one is getting rid of any restaurants or houses," Johnny said.

"So shut your big mouth, little boss." His mother settled into her seat.

Though the question had been on his mind since he'd woken up in jail, Jimmy waited until they were on the highway to ask Johnny how Pat was doing.

"He seemed a little scared, but he was acting brave for Nan." Johnny watched his speedometer. "He was the youngest kid in holding. They really should have put him in a juvenile detention center. I guess there was a mix-up. A night of mix-ups." He sounded, for the first time, angry; then, just as quickly, his voice dropped back down to its baseline.

"You're the hero once again." Jimmy flicked his nails at the passenger window, making a sharp, thudding sound. His mother, from the backseat, reached forward and batted his fingers away from the glass.

"If you hadn't forced me to act so hastily, there would be no need to save anybody," Johnny shot back.

Jimmy's own antsy-ness was irritating him. His problems were solved. The insurance would soon be paid, the Glory financed, the Duck House rebuilt. His mother would eventually die in the recesses of their giant house. He would meet a nice girl, get remarried, finally have kids. And no one would remember the fiery summer that threatened to topple their little Han dynasty, just as no one spoke about the years his father had entertained equally distasteful men while planning to build his restaurant. Jimmy twisted his piercing until his ear sang.

"Drop me off at the Glory," he said to Johnny, who was about to merge onto the interstate. "I want to close up."

"Your car is impounded," Johnny said.

"I'll take a cab home, no biggie."

"Can't stand to be in the same car as his family," his mother grumbled from the back.

"I need to check in on Annie anyways," Johnny said. "Ma, I'll drop you off after Jimmy."

"Fine, get rid of your mother," she continued in the same tone. "I didn't need to get up in the middle of the evening to make sure my delinquent sons were behaving, that Jimmy wasn't being abused by the police, and that you weren't going to abandon your brother to go fix your employee's problems." She grouched herself into a daze and then summarily dropped off into a droning sleep.

"Crazy how we never figured that out." Johnny adjusted his rearview mirror to look at their dozing mother. "She'll just talk herself to sleep."

"Dad figured it out," Jimmy said. "That's why he always ignored her."

"Smart man," Johnny said. He input the Glory's address into his GPS and signaled to get off the Beltway. A sunny yellow sign beseeched them to KEEP MARYLAND BEAUTIFUL. "You can have the insurance money." He blurted the words out, tongue tripping from haste. Jimmy hadn't heard him speak like that since they were children. "Pay me my year's salary, and use the rest for the Glory. Call it an investment."

"No Duck House?"

"All this mess, this craziness." He signaled for the exit. "It reminded me of what I was signing myself up for. Besides, I have a buddy who needs a partner on his farm. He caters to high-class restaurants. Maybe the Glory will be a client."

"We're a Chinese restaurant," Jimmy said. "We buy what's cheapest."

"American soil isn't too bad for Chinese broccoli," Johnny continued, as he always did when Jimmy acted out. "You could get that sweet spot between local and authentic."

"Not right now." Jimmy waved him off.

"I'll come back to you when you're ready to listen." Johnny merged into the slow lane.

"You're the fucking worst," Jimmy said, but he knew he hadn't sounded convincing. He would have to try again, when he got his strength back.

His phone told him it was half past ten when he walked into the Glory, but the gaping emptiness of the restaurant made him second-guess the time. The dinner service had not recovered from the earlier outburst.

Most of the waiters had escaped somewhere; either that or they were all on their cigarette break. Tom, whom he'd put in charge, was nowhere to be seen. In the kitchen, the cooks leaned against their stations, in clear view, picking at their teeth. The busboys were roughhousing in the hallway outside the restrooms. In his exasperation, Jimmy almost didn't see the lone person sitting at the bar. He shaped his face into a friendly expression and swung around the back to say hello.

"Quiet night?" Uncle Pang swirled the liquid in his drink.

"We had an incident earlier." Jimmy wiped down the bar for lack of anything better to do with his hands.

"So I saw," Uncle Pang said, though he didn't elaborate on how.

Jimmy realized—how obvious—that the police arriving tonight had been Uncle Pang's doing.

"Well, looks like everything has settled down," Uncle Pang said, for once cracking a smile. His teeth were a spectrum of shades, some crooked, and others the meticulous square of veneers. "Someone's looking out for you."

Jimmy sucked at his own teeth. Someone indeed.

"I'm sorry no one's helping you." Jimmy gestured at Uncle Pang's glass. "Can I get you another?"

"Why not." Pang relinquished his empty drink. "Something on the rocks. Dealer's choice."

Jimmy looked at the bar shelf, his eyes scanning from the lowest well liquors to the highest. It was just as well that Uncle Pang was the only one here. How long would this restaurant hold its head above water without him as a flotation device? Where would Jimmy work when his money ran out? In all their plans to sabotage his success, his mother and Uncle Pang had never once told him he was hopeless without them. It was a double-edged kindness to let him believe he wasn't, even for a short while. He put his hand on the top-shelf vodka. He sincerely hoped it was up to Uncle Pang's standards.

"Gan bei," he said, filling the glass.

Nan and Ah-Jack's favorite hotpot restaurant was so packed that the windows had steamed over, but Ah-Jack was sitting pretty across from Nan, his bad foot propped regally on an old cushion.

"Don't you have customers to serve?" She playfully batted his foot. "I bet they regret hiring this old racehorse now."

"I'm on my lunch break. Besides, I'm top of the tips charts," he bragged. He gestured at their finished meal. "I don't see you complaining about the VIP treatment. Look at the size of these deluxe fish balls. We didn't know these existed!"

"Can't say I taste the difference." She dipped the ends of her chopsticks into the shacha sauce and savored the salty flavor. "What time is it?"

He glanced back at the register's clock. "Almost one."

"I have to go." She heaved herself up and brushed imaginary crumbs off her civilian clothing. She hadn't gotten used to thinking of these clothes as her ordinary outfit, though once she touched down in San Francisco, she'd go right back to wearing an apron or whatever the uniform was at Ray's dim sum place. He promised the joint was relaxed, no tips, and no "crazy owner." She told herself she wouldn't be disappointed if she ended up in the same situation as before. Just like she told herself that she was making the right choice in moving in with Ray, if not for her, then for her son. Hope teased her insides— she and Pat were going to get their second chance.

The first months after the arrest and the treatment program, Pat's progress had seemed unbearably slow, and no matter how Nan pestered his therapist, she heard only that her son's haziness was normal. He just needed more time. Nan promised herself she would be patient, but she couldn't help worrying that she'd lost her son in the fire after all. Then, two weeks ago, after his mandated counseling capped off its final hour, Pat took his first faltering steps toward his new life. One morning, she came downstairs to find him waiting at the kitchen table, two pieces of paper in front of him. He'd printed out their airplane tickets.

"You can have the window." He'd held the papers delicately in his hand.

"No, not for me," she said. "I don't like to be so close to the outside of the plane."

"It's a long flight. Seven hours. Maybe we can buy a neck pillow at the airport."

He hadn't spoken so many words at once since his arrest. The proximity of a new start, with both his parents, had shaken the impassive mud off his face. Nan could accept, finally, that the program had not damaged Pat beyond repair and that she, who had put him there in so many ways, was not an accomplice to any more crimes. The day she'd dropped him off at the treatment center in Pennsylvania, she had been sure she was putting him in more danger. The center treated both juvenile fire setters and sex offenders, and if the alternative had not been prison, she would have driven him straight back to Maryland. During visits the first few weeks, she saw that her son had developed a series of nervous tics: chewing on his mouth and nails, scratching at the back of his hand. He was afraid of the other boys in his program, though he refused to admit it. But, as his counselor reassured her during their weekly phone calls, "Teenagers are resilient."

The day she picked her son up, he let her hug him for as long as she dared. She felt his ribs through his shirt. When they walked to the car, his eyes never left the ground. On the highway, he'd shuddered at a cigarette dropped out of a truck window.

Though Pat held on, almost stubbornly, to his tics, once Nan could see that he was excited about his future, she felt strong enough to push back her own feelings about the move. She had yet to find anything more invigorating than her own child's excitement.

"You've never tried cocaine," had been Ah-Jack's little quip. But he was trying not to let his glumness taint their meetings, which had taken on the gloom of a countdown.

She reached out for his hand now and hooked her fingers around his. He patted them with his free hand, then shifted in his seat, embarrassed by the quiver in his chin.

"It'll take some time to save the money for the ticket." He clapped his hands and rubbed them quickly. "But I'll come visit you."

"I don't doubt that for a second," Nan said.

She shrank back into her chair. How small Ah-Jack's life looked without her in it. His new job let him sit down but required no more skill than walking a plate from the kitchen to the table. His customers enjoyed his presence, but they were mostly Chinese. They didn't respond to his clowning ways the same as Americans had. Or, perhaps, they were merely reacting to the new strangeness in his antics, which had grown weary, like a forced smile.

Michelle had not survived. Cells from the original cancer had been hiding in her bone marrow, dormant for years. Her decline had been aggressive, so shocking that even now Ah-Jack refused to talk about the weeks he'd spent at her bedside, rubbing elbows with Gary while she slept. He had never come back to the Glory, forfeiting his job without fanfare. Equally soundless, Nan's relationship with him had ended.

Nan understood that Ah-Jack's guilt had swallowed him up. He'd spent some of the last moments of Michelle's life in bed with another woman. It didn't matter that she and Nan had worked in tandem to keep him in the dark. It didn't matter that in the terrifying days after Pat moved to Pennsylvania, Nan needed her friend more than ever. She knew that for a while her presence would only wound him. Whenever she felt the urge to call him, she called Ray instead. Listening to her husband complain about his employees soothed her. It was, at least, a voice in her ear.

Ah-Jack broke his silence on the day Michelle died, weeping but intelligible while he passed on the news. Slowly, they had started meeting for lunch, and while so much had changed in the landscapes of both their lives, the core of their individual selves, and therefore the core of their love, remained. As long as Ah-Jack was himself, Nan would always be devoted. As long as Nan was herself, Ah-Jack would always have someone devoted to him.

If she was so devoted, then why wasn't she staying with him? She swallowed the question, a burning lump in her throat. Devotion, she could only say weakly to herself, was a case of mind over matter. Ah-Jack would always be in her thoughts; he would never go a single day without knowing that someone across the country was thinking of him. This was all she could offer: a domain inside her head, where he was as good as king.

Her own domain was about to grow beyond her control. She had fought against such expansion since she'd left Macau. She knew the growing pains. Ambition had numbed the ache when she was younger. No such solution could be brewed up now. Here, she was happy in spite of her hardships; in California, would she be able to see beyond the spite? Would the smell of grease and the pain in her fingers and feet ever be secondary in a sentence? But that kind of happiness wasn't the point. She had let her son go hungry for too long. She was determined to starve for the rest of her life so that he might be able to eat.

The day she'd told Ah-Jack about the move, she was surprised by how ready he was to receive it. She had talked on and on, too nervous for his reaction, until he'd stopped her to reveal that Pat had broken the news to him weeks earlier.

"Your husband is there, and your son," he said, showing an empathy that almost shocked her eyes dry. Ah-Jack had seen beneath her chipper optimism, her talk of travel guides and new suitcases, to the quiet devastation that moved between her bones. He didn't require her false smiles or her real tears. He had held his finger up to her nose, a return to his old sense of humor. "You promise you'll fly back when I'm about to meet my maker."

She'd grabbed his finger. "I promise."

At the hotpot table, they both stood up and he slapped her shoulders as if she were a young man going off to war.

"If I had my way, you would never leave my sight," he said. "Or you would at least be within hearing distance. In case I fell down the stairs." They both laughed, and Nan took the opportunity to blow her nose.

Then he turned her around to face the door. A chill shot straight up her spine. Everything around her looked too beautiful to leave. He gave her a little push, and she finally walked away.

Nan had the unsavory last task of returning her carver's uniform to the Glory and picking up her final check. To pay off Pat's legal and program fees, she'd had to return to her job. With the pregnant, ruddy moon extended over the sky, she had carved duck after duck on the outdoor patio. Her picture had gotten into a newspaper review of the new restaurant, which had its official grand opening during the Harvest Moon Festival.

She never grew as close to the Beijing Glory carvers and waiters as she had with the Duck House staff, and, of course, she didn't see Ah-Bing, Ah-May, and the rest of them either, except for accidental run-ins at the H-Mart and Costco. She hadn't expected to learn such an unkind lesson this late in life, of the fleeting nature of friendship built on context and proximity. She didn't see much of Jimmy either, in the back of the house, and when she dropped into the Georgetown restaurant at the end of lunch service, she wasn't surprised to see him crouched by a table, entertaining a potential VIP. She'd never seen anyone adapt so quickly and fluidly to so much adversity. A fire; an arson investigation; a new, at first faltering restaurant; potential bankruptcy. Yet here he was, not a pound heavier or lighter, not a single hair missing from his head.

She gave him a small wave after she'd exchanged her hat and tools for her month's pay. He surprised her by standing up to wave goodbye to her. The man he was speaking with also turned around in his seat. The oily way he waved his hand—she nearly mistook him for Mr. Pang. Then saw that he had all five of his fingers.

She left quickly through the swinging glass doors. The goosebumps on her skin had nothing to do with the whipping wind outside. She turned the heat all the way up in her car before she drove away. Her son was waiting at home.

"You should go see Dad's restaurant," Johnny had said over the phone that morning, and for once Jimmy had listened. Now, when he should have been resting, he was here instead. He looked up at the Duck House, its new-old brick façade. What color had his father's bricks been, before the fire?

The construction of the building's exterior had finished a few days ago. His mother, true to her word, had rebuilt the entire restaurant. It was slated to open in a few months. He'd driven over right after he'd sent the last customer away with a carryout bag of duck.

From the outside, the Hans had come out on top, and, according to his mother, the outside was all that mattered.

"You are the stories people tell of you," she always said. Jimmy had never agreed.

He lit a cigarette and took his time dragging on it while he circled the restaurant. What did he know, in the end? The Glory was doing better, but his customers had yet to repeat, no matter how many tables he'd chatted up, how many bills he'd comped. Had he hoped that a sight of the small cage that once held him would make the Glory look downright palatial? He was a true idiot. All the Duck House did, surrounded by the same dirty establishments and rushing traffic, was to remind him that the Glory was only another cage, slightly larger, slightly fancier, but not so different, after all, from his father's glory.

Back at the entrance, Jimmy ripped the plastic covering off the front doors. Sure enough, golden ducks perched where the handles should have been. He passed his hand over one of the gleaming heads before stubbing his cigarette out, leaving an ugly gray streak on the mallard's bowed head. He might never crawl out from under the shadow of the Duck House. But he would not be Jimmy if he did not keep trying, setting aflame what could not be burned down. This was the story he would tell.

He rubbed again the gray streak on the duck's head, until the color dulled, and the raised ash fell away. He convinced himself the mark was permanent. That this bit of gray and gold would outlast them all.

ACKNOWLEDGMENTS

I am nothing without the people in my life. Thank you to the following, who have rendered me speechless with my own good fortune:

The faculty at the Helen Zell Writers Program, who taught me all that is tangible and intangible about writing: Michael Byers, Sugi Ganeshananthan, Peter Ho Davies, and Eileen Pollack.

My beautiful cohort and the entire Michigan MFA community.

My Princeton teachers—Susan Choi, Jeffrey Eugenides, Chang-Rae Lee, John McPhee, Lorrie Moore, and Evan Thomas. With special thanks to Ed White.

All my early, middle, and late readers: Rach Crawford, Maya West, Emily Tseng, and Sam Krowchenko.

Mike and Hilary Gustafson, and all the Literati staff, for loving books as much as you do. And Kundiman, for giving me hope.

Adam Eaglin, my agent with a poet's soul, who rescues me again and again with his unflappability, his intelligence, and his beautiful phone voice.

Barbara Jones, who has done more than any editor should, who has approached my book like a surgeon, a personal trainer, a therapist, and a magician; and her intrepid assistant Ruby Rose Lee. A blessing also for Kanyin Ajayi, my fairy godmother, who plucked my book from the pile.

Finally, my parents, Yin Li and Hongying Wang, and my didi, Christopher. I would not understand the world without your eyes. Your love has been my earth and sky.

AN IMPRINT OF PUSHKIN PRESS

ONE – an imprint of Pushkin Press – is the home of our contemporary, original English language publishing. The list is as varied as it is distinct, encompassing new voices and established names, fiction and non-fiction. Our stories range from dystopian tales to comic ones, prizewinning novels to memoirs. We select only a small handful of titles each year, and publish them with particular care and attention, which means that every book is a gem. And what makes them ONE? Compelling writing, unique voices, great stories.

THE EXTRA MAN
Jonathan Ames

THE BEAUTIFUL BUREAUCRAT
Helen Phillips

ONLY KILLERS AND THIEVES
Paul Howarth

AMONG THE LIVING AND THE DEAD
Inara Verzemnieks

SYMPATHY
Olivia Sudjic

SCHOOL OF VELOCITY
Eric Beck Rubin

DON'T LET MY BABY DO RODEO
Boris Fishman

DAREDEVILS
Shawn Vestal

LAYOVER
Lisa Zeidner